EVASIVE ACTION

Evasive Action

The Hunt for Gregor Meinhoff

John Reisinger

Writers Club Press
San Jose New York Lincoln Shanghai

Evasive Action
The Hunt for Gregor Meinhoff

Writers Club Press
an imprint of iUniverse.com, Inc.

For information address:
iUniverse.com, Inc.
5220 S 16th, Ste. 200
Lincoln, NE 68512
www.iuniverse.com

ISBN: 0-595-18483-9

Printed in the United States of America

To Karen, H.P., Allie, and Kristin

Acknowledgments

Many people contributed to this book and helped to make it as authentic as a work of fiction can be. I especially wish to thank the following organizations and people for their generous assistance:

The National Archives of Canada, especially Paul Lemieux, who provided official microfilmed records of escapes and captures.

The Royal Canadian Mounted Police, especially Cpl Bill Crich, Bowmanville, Ont, and Robert Henderson, RCMP historian, who provided valuable information on POW camps and the RCMP.

Ulrich Steinhilper, Stuttgart, Germany: former Luftwaffe pilot and POW in Canada, with five escapes to his credit, who provided a view from the other side.

The National Aviation Museum, Ottawa, Ontario.

Lorne Fleece, North Bay, Ontario, who provided details of Camp Q and Canadian life in general.

JoAnne Morin, Monteith, Ontario

Karen Barber, The Thelma Miles Museum, Matheson, Ontario

Josee Vallerand, The Canadian Railroad Historical Association

Nancy Renwick, The Iroquois Falls Pioneer Museum, Iroquois Falls, Ontario

The Nanton Lancaster Museum, Nanton, Alberta

Max Charson and Lillian Silver, who shared their recollections of Canada during the war.

Historical Background

In the spring of 1941, England stood virtually alone against the Nazi war machine. Hitler had overrun France the year before and was the master of almost all of Europe. London was being bombed and German armies were gathering to invade. The United States and the Soviet Union were not yet in the war.

Much of the food, medicine, munitions, and supplies needed to fend off disaster had to be brought to England from Canada across 3,000 miles of submarine infested ocean in convoys of cargo ships. German U-boats took such a heavy toll of this shipping that England seemed likely to be starved into submission.

So with the war in the balance, brave men on both sides fought a bloody running battle above and below the Atlantic. And with defeat a real possibility, England and Canada desperately searched for a way to gain the advantage and defeat the U-boats. One important step towards turning that advantage away from the Germans came on May 9 and is the basis for this story.

-1-

Friday, May 9—Saturday, July 12, 1941

Gregor Meinhoff scrambled from the hatch on the conning tower, blinked in the daylight, and inhaled cool sea air heavy with the smell of salt and diesel fumes. Below him, his stricken submarine wallowed helplessly in the greenish-gray swells of the North Atlantic and dazed crewmen were emerging from every hatch. As he struggled to keep his footing on the swaying deck, Meinhoff shook his head to try to clear away the aching and confusion remaining from the depth charge attack that had crippled the U-110 and forced it to the surface.

"Oberleutnant Strauss, you and Kolza report as soon as everyone is on deck," shouted the captain, Fritz-Julius Lemp standing next to him. The other officers, Heinrich Strauss and Hans Kolza, were below on the main deck making sure the crewmen got out safely.

Lemp turned to Meinhoff, "Gregor, the U-110 must be sent to the bottom or it will be captured by the enemy. When everyone is out, I want you to go below, set the scuttling charges and open the vents.

Bring along the log when you return." Lemp glanced at his watch. "You may report that the scuttling order was given at 1242 on 9 May, 1941."

"*Jawohl,* Kapitan," Meinhoff replied flatly. His head still throbbed and he was sure he could hear his own heart beating in time with the aches. "Are you going to give the order to abandon ship?"

"When the British get a bit closer," Lemp replied, pushing his white captain's cap back slightly. "There's no sense driving the crew into that cold water any sooner than necessary. Set the charges for 15 minutes."

Meinhoff hesitated, reluctant to be the executioner of his own boat, then turned towards the hatch.

As he prepared to go below, Meinhoff took a quick look around. On the horizon, he noted with satisfaction, was the rapidly sinking merchant ship the U-110 had torpedoed, burning furiously with billowing clouds of oily black smoke drifting across the slate gray sky. As he shifted his gaze to the south, he stiffened.

"English destroyer, Kapitan, off the starboard quarter and headed this way."

Lemp swung his large gray Zeiss binoculars to his eyes and looked in that direction. The destroyer was a wedge of gray except for a boiling white bow wave.

"What the hell's the matter with them?" he gasped. "They are coming at us full speed. *Mein Gott,* she's coming on as if she's going to ram! Gregor; belay the scuttling and get over the side." Lemp leaned over the combing of the conning tower and shouted to the crewmen below. "Abandon ship! Everyone over the side and swim clear! *Macht schnell!*"

Meinhoff stumbled to the rail. Crewmen still shaken from the depth charges flopped over the side into the cold churning water and began swimming away desperately. The British destroyer came on relentlessly, growing ever larger. Now the U-110's deck and the water around it was a rising chaos of excited, shouting men and confusion as the crew saw the destroyer bearing down on them.

"Come on, Gregor," said Lemp, pushing Meinhoff towards the ladder. "Over we go. The U-110 is going to the bottom, but this time, we are not going with her."

Meinhoff shook his head again. The throbbing eased off slightly. "Let me fire the deck gun at the English destroyer, Kapitan," he pleaded. "I could put a shell in her bridge. Then we'd see how anxious they are to ram."

"No," Lemp said sternly. "You'd only get a lot of good shipmates killed. The U-110's fighting days are over. We have done our duty. Now get over the side."

Reluctantly, Meinhoff made his way towards the water, fighting to keep his balance against the drunken rolling of the boat as he ducked under the railing and climbed down the ladder from the conning tower. When he reached the main deck, waves were lazily sloshing over it, leaving swirls of white foam against the base of the gun mount. As he was about to fall into the embrace of the Atlantic, he looked up. There, cutting angrily through the swells, the knifelike bow of the destroyer towered over him, its cold steel edge about to cut the U-110 in two and send it to its grave. There was no time to escape. Meinhoff opened his mouth to scream, but no sound came out. With a rumble and the grating sound of metal dragging across metal, the submarine lurched and vibrated with the impact. A hand came from nowhere and grabbed at Meinhoff's shoulder, shaking him. Now everyone around him seemed to be screaming in a hellish din of shrill noise he thought would never end ....

"Wake up Gregor," a muffled voice called from the darkness. "Come on, I think we are stopping."

Meinhoff sat up in his seat with a jolt as he was jerked from his dream by the sounds of the train coming to a halt. With a long sigh of escaping steam and a chorus of squeals and rattles, the train shuddered to a stop. In the unaccustomed silence that followed, Gregor Meinhoff rubbed the remnants of his nightmare from his eyes.

"I was dreaming about the British destroyer again," he said.

"Ah, the HMS BULLDOG," his companion, Hans Kolza replied. "That is one dream I have no wish to repeat. But cheer up, Gregor. The BULL-DOG is gone and we have survived, although I have to admit I was ready to make out my will when that destroyer bore down on us. Fortunately, the English captain turned away at the last moment. Perhaps he just wanted to frighten us. He certainly succeeded in my case."

Meinhoff grunted a reply, pulled the window curtain back. The view of the world outside was somewhat obstructed by heavy Plexiglas and metal bars over the window, all held in place by large brass screws . The Canadians were obviously concerned about escapes. He looked through the window intensely.

"So tell me, Gregor. What does it look like out there?" Kolza said, squinting through his spectacles.

"We have stopped at a small station," Meinhoff replied, rubbing the last remnant of sleep from his eyes. "I can see a wooden platform and a station building. Otherwise, it looks like any other place we've passed through in Canada; lots of rocks and pine trees and not much else. What time is it?"

Kolza looked at his watch and yawned. "Almost 0300. Really, these Canadians seem to have no appreciation of the importance of a good night's sleep. Between that and the bacon they eat, I'm surprised they haven't all had heart attacks."

Meinhoff looked around the train. In the dim lighting, he could barely see the passenger seats filled with the 32 crewmen of the U-110, former wolves of the sea, now prisoners of war. They sat in the railway car in the various postures of boredom and squirming discomfort typical of passengers who have been on the same train for too long. At each end of the car stood a brown-uniformed Canadian guard.

"I wonder if we are still heading west?" Kolza thought aloud, slowly scratching his neck. "We were earlier; I could tell by the sun. Imagine, Gregor, a country so big you have to ride for three days in the same direction merely to get to the middle of it. Of course we could have turned north after dark. You don't see any Eskimos out there do you?"

Meinhoff grunted, let the curtain fall closed, sat back in his seat, and rubbed his eyes. "I still can't believe it happened. The U-110 forced to the surface by depth charges, the captain lost, and the crew captured. We abandoned the U-110, Hans. We surrendered to the enemy. We have failed the fatherland."

Kolza snorted. "Nonsense. The U-110 was spewing smoke and acid fumes. She didn't respond to her helm and was leaking like an old boot. We were damned near fish food. It was a miracle we were able to surface at all. We did our duty; let someone else have a chance to win the Iron Cross posthumously."

Oberleutnant Heinrich Strauss, seated directly behind them, leaned forward. "I can see two vehicles approaching. This may be where we get off. If it is, you and Chief Muller keep the men in order."

Ghostly gray light washed against the side of the train and cast liquid shadows in the darkened car. First one tired face, then another was briefly illuminated as the light drifted across them.

After a few moments of silence, voices and shuffling feet could be heard outside in the darkness. Suddenly, the door at the end of the compartment flew open and the lights were switched on. Temporarily blinded, the prisoners rubbed their eyes and squinted while a Canadian army sergeant strode down the aisle and bellowed orders in badly accented German.

"All right, you lot; *raus*! We are now at your home away from home. Line up and prepare to disembark."

"Come on, Gregor," said Kolza, standing up and stretching to his full 5 ft 6 inch height "this is one ship I will be quite glad to abandon."

In the cool darkness of the Canadian night, the prisoners were herded out of the railroad car, lined up in two rows on the wooden platform, and carefully counted. Harsh light from the headlights of several Canadian army trucks made the sleepy men look gray and ragged, and cast long distorted shadows across the platform and onto the side of the train. The only sound was the quiet counting of heads and the low hiss of vented steam from the train engine. Meinhoff stretched and felt refreshed after sitting in the train for so long. Strauss stood stoically and Kolza looked around with little jerks of his head, as if determined not to miss anything of interest.

A captain who had been in charge of the train called the roll, checked off the names, then handed some papers to a tall thin man.

"All present, Sergeant Henderson," the Captain said. "The Provost Corps hereby turns the prisoners over to Prisoner of War Service. Here is the nominal roll of the prisoners, and the train diary."

Sergeant Henderson thumbed through the papers and nodded. "Thank you sir. And here is your receipt from the Camp Commandant for 34 live bodies. We'll take them from here."

The prisoners were put in two files between ten armed guards and marched off into the night. The air was damp from a recent rain, and thick with the smell of freshly turned soil. About a mile or so distant, a soft halo of light hung in the blackness. As they got closer to the lighted area, The Germans could see that the light came from a series of searchlights on guard towers. Their destination was a prison camp.

The column came to a tall gate in a newly built barbed wire enclosure. There was a freshly painted sign on the gate, barely legible in the dim light.

INTERNMENT CAMP Q
Commonwealth of Canada
Department of National Defense,
Director of Organization and Administration,
Prisoner of War Service

The Germans entered the compound and the gate swung shut behind them, shutting them off from their former life.

The column finally was halted in a small floodlit courtyard with three barracks buildings on one side and two other nondescript buildings across from them. A dozen brown uniformed Canadian soldiers stood with guns at the ready. Behind the guards was a large two story building that looked as if it had once been a school. There were a few seconds of silence as the crew of the U-110 looked around anxiously. The smell of cooking mingled with the smell of tarpaper, and shadows cast by search-lights around the yard radiated in all directions. Meinhoff, Strauss, and Kolza looked at each other with expectation, but none spoke.

"Everyone fall out and line up in single file!" shouted a raspy voice. The Germans rearranged themselves, blinking and squinting in the floodlights. A tall thin Canadian stepped into the light and looked around, like an actor in a badly lit play. After a few more moments of awkward silence, the raspy voice broke the stillness again in the same barely understandable German.

"On behalf of His Majesty King George, I wish to welcome you to Internment Camp Q. I am Sergeant Henderson, in charge of camp security. If you behave, you will find this a pleasant enough place, and a damned sight more comfortable than a U-boat."

The prisoners stirred somewhat, but remained silent. Gregor Meinhoff looked critically at Sergeant Henderson. The Canadian was a tall, thin man of about middle age. Probably a home guard type, he thought, unfit for combat but satisfactory for guarding unarmed prisoners. Meinhoff looked around at the rest of the camp guards and confirmed his opinion. Several of the other prisoners also frowned in derision. Most of the guards wouldn't last a week on a U-boat, they thought.

Sergeant Henderson squinted at a paper. "Oberleutnant Heinrich Strauss?"

"*Ja?*" said Strauss, stepping forward.

"You and your second in command," Henderson consulted his list once again, "Leutnant Gregor Meinhoff, will report to Major Reynolds' office. The rest of you will go to your assigned barracks after roll call, photographing and fingerprinting."

"*Jawohl*," said Meinhoff, raising his hand in the Nazi salute.

"And we'll have none of that!" snapped Henderson. "You will salute in the traditional manner. Now Oberleutnant Strauss and Leutnant Meinhoff, please go with the corporal here. Major Reynolds is waiting."

As Henderson read the rest of the names and gave out barracks assignments, Strauss and Meinhoff followed a short, dumpy looking corporal to a building on the other side of the compound and through another barbed wire inner fence. Even in the floodlights, it was clear the barracks buildings were new and hastily constructed. They looked like small barns covered with black tarpaper, even on the roofs. The buildings were constructed off the ground a few feet on concrete block supports to discourage tunneling.

As the three men walked, their feet crunched in the gravel and the floodlights threw long shadows that flowed over the ground. Had Kolza been with them, he probably would have made some remark about the commandant being an insomniac, but Strauss and Meinhoff walked in silence. In a few moments they were shown into a small office in the old school building which now served as administrative offices.

The room was plain but neat. On one side was a bookshelf and on the other was a large wall map of Camp Q along with a picture of King George and a duty roster for the guards. In the center of the room was a battered metal desk. A stocky, ginger haired man of about 45 was sitting behind it and wearing a brown Canadian army Major's uniform, his rank indicated by a single crown insignia on each shoulder strap. Behind him stood a younger, dark haired man in a Lieutenant's uniform.

Both men looked at the Germans without expression, sizing them up. Strauss was of medium height and black haired, with a scraggly beard. Meinhoff was taller, a little over six feet, and had a thicker, more neatly trimmed beard with light brown hair. His eyes were blue and had a curiously cold look. The Germans had a slightly condescending air about them, as if they were bemused by the situation.

"Good evening, gentlemen," said the man at the desk in a quiet, reasonable voice. "I am Major Reynolds, Commandant of Internment Camp Q. This is Lieutenant Willoughby, our morale officer. You are now prisoners of war. You will be here for the remainder of the hostilities, unless there should be a transfer or prisoner exchange. I can't tell you our exact location, but I can assure you it is a very long way from Germany."

He waited for a reaction; there was none.

"For this reason, escaping is a dangerous exercise in futility. We have arctic weather in the winter, ferocious flies and mosquitos in the summer, and isolation year round. In short, there is simply nowhere to go; no place for shelter, and no one who will give you the slightest sympathy or support. You won't be able to live off the population, and unless you're an Indian, you won't be able to live off the land. So I will expect you not to waste your time or mine."

Still no reaction. The Germans were looking at him with bored indulgence, the way a parent would look at a child throwing a tantrum.

"As senior POW officers, you will be held responsible for the behavior of your men. You will chose a prisoner spokesman and he will coordinate any requests, complaints, etc., with Sergeant Henderson. You will find we treat POWs very well. We adhere to the Geneva Convention and provide good facilities and good food. In fact, you will probably eat better here than you did on the submarine. During the next few weeks, Lieutenant Willoughby will be talking with each of you individually to see to it your concerns are addressed and you are treated fairly. So make the best of your stay here, gentlemen."

"We have noted the good treatment, gentlemen," said Meinhoff, finally. "It will be a point in your favor when we have defeated you."

Lieutenant Willoughby became red in the face, but Major Reynolds looked at Meinhoff without expression. There was a smirk at the corner of Meinhoff's mouth. After a moment, he responded. "Arrogance is not an attractive trait under the best of circumstances, Leutnant Meinhoff; but when it is displayed by a prisoner of war, the effect is merely laughable. You are dismissed."

Meinhoff, he noticed, clicked his heels before leaving.

When the Germans had gone, Major Reynolds turned to Lieutenant Willoughby. "Well, George, what do you think?"

"I think," said Lieutenant Willoughby, "that Herr Leutnant Bloody Perishing Meinhoff is going to be the one we will have to watch. In England, we classify prisoners as black, gray, or white, depending on how Nazi they are, and how likely they are to cause trouble. I suspect Meinhoff would be solidly in the black column. Cheeky bastard."

Reynolds nodded. "And Strauss?"

Willoughby shrugged. "He seemed civil, at least, but it's too soon to tell. Frankly, i wouldn't trust any of that lot."

"Do not irritate the Commandant unnecessarily, Gregor," said Strauss as they arrived at their barracks. "It will merely make the Canadians more alert."

Meinhoff smiled. "Don't worry, Heinrich. I will remain as charming as ever."

Strauss raised an eyebrow. "Yes, that's what I'm concerned about."

They entered the barracks building, a large barnlike affair with steel bunks lining each wall. What caught their eye, however, was the presence of no less than four pot bellied stoves. Strauss raised his eyebrows.

"*Gott in Himmel*," he muttered. "The winters must be brutal here, *nicht wahr*?"

The three officers had a separate room at the rear of the barracks, and Kolza greeted them when they opened the door.

"*Guten abend.* Welcome to the Hotel U-Boatlager. I trust you had a nice chat with the chief jailor. Did he tell you who to call for room service?"

Strauss smiled. "No room service, Hans, and I'm afraid they have also neglected to employ a maid."

Kolza shook his head in mock amazement. "And they call themselves civilized."

"Did you see this?" asked Kolza, indicating some shelves behind the bunks. "We have towels, soap, shaving gear, extra blankets…even toothbrushes. I have been in hotels that didn't have such things."

Strauss was looking at a handout that had been left on his bunk. "And they have a camp store, recreation hall, wood shop, infirmary, and facilities for classroom instruction. Very impressive, I must admit."

Meinhoff, who had been reading a similar handout crumpled it up and sneered. "Capitalist tricks. They wish to make us as soft as they are. Well, I say we may be prisoners, but we are still officers in the Kreigsmarine. We must find a way to carry on the fight."

Strauss nodded without enthusiasm and looked out the small window. The searchlights, he noticed, were still on.

By daylight, the camp looked much bigger than it had appeared the night before. Camp Q held well over 1,000 men already. Although there were several rows of barracks, only two buildings were used for the men of the U-110. One building was used as a dining and recreation hall, another as a hospital. There was also a commissary where men could exchange coupons for tobacco, soap, and personal items.

In the open "parade ground" between the barracks and the administration building, the crew of the U-110 marked out a soccer field and a number of garden plots along the edges. The camp sat next to a town with a seemingly endless expanse of farms and deep green woods of pine and birch on one side, and a few civilian houses near the other. A river ran a few hundred yards behind the camp and was crossed by a north-south railroad line and a steel truss bridge. The guard towers were built along a road that ran around the entire perimeter of the camp, and a paved road ran north and south from in front of the camp.

Internment Camp Q held several hundred internees, and about 1,000 German and Italian merchant seamen, most of whom had been captured in British or Canadian ports when war was declared. The internees were native Canadians or British who by reason of ancestry or suspicion of German sympathy, were being held for security reasons. For the most part, they had no contact with the German or Italian prisoners. None of them had much contact with the U-110 prisoners.

In the first week, Strauss, Meinhoff, and Kolza got to work organizing classrooms, religious services, and recreational activities. They also dealt with the Canadians, but acted as if they alone were in charge. They set up an *Ausbrecherkomitee* (escape committee), although they realized how hopeless it really was. The prisoners noticed that, in addition to the guards on the towers, the Canadians had men assigned to patrol inside the wire. These guards, who were obviously looking for evidence of escape attempts, were soon called *Frettchen*, or ferrets by the Germans. Meanwhile, the men organized English language classes, chess tournaments, and various study groups. In spite of Meinhoff's desire to contribute to the German war effort, life soon began to take on a satisfied routine for most of the men of the U-110. They knew they would probably be in camp a long time and decided to make the best of it. Various escape schemes were always in the air, but always came up against the same problem; the vast distances and the climate.

Two weeks after the crew of the U-110 had arrived at Camp Q, Major Reynolds sat with Lieutenant Willoughby over steaming mugs of tea in Reynolds' office. The day was overcast and the room was illuminated by a bare light bulb.

"So, have you had a chance to talk with the prisoners?" Reynolds asked.

Willoughby put down his tea and frowned. "Oh, I've talked with them right enough. I might as well talk to that bleeding wall over there.

But I know enough to confirm that Meinhoff is the one we've got to look out for. He's smart and a Nazi to boot. Strauss is a loyal sailor, but an indifferent National Socialist, in my opinion. Kolza is certainly not a Nazi. He's really a civilian at heart, but he's smart and likes an intellectual challenge, so under the right circumstances, he could be dangerous as well. He would never start trouble for its own sake, though."

Reynolds nodded. "Well, you did learn something after all. Have they figured out that you're with British Intelligence?"

"I think they suspect it. At any rate, they certainly didn't swallow the bit about me being the 'morale officer'. Still, I don't think it would make any difference. That lot isn't about to chat freely with the enemy. All they say is a lot of blather about their final victory; nothing we can use. Still, they might let their guard down if we give them enough time."

Reynolds shook his head. "I doubt it; not the U-boat crews. You find this sort of thing with the elite units. The Luftwaffe pilots are the same way; not Nazis necessarily, but loyal team players for their side. Give me army draftees any day. But what about the sinking of the U-110? Are any of them suspicious?"

"Oh, a few of them asked how the sub sank, since none of them saw it. They were all hustled belowdecks on the BULLDOG as soon as they were fished from the water. I've been telling them that the U-110 was taking on water so fast it sunk within a few minutes of their capture."

"Do they believe it?"

"They don't have any reason not to. They know the sub took a good thrashing before it surfaced. No one is surprised to hear that it sank almost immediately."

Reynolds finished the last of his tea and placed his mug back on the tray. "George, if you get any useful information from them, it will be welcomed, but your most important task is to keep them convinced that the U-110 sank as soon as they were captured. Remember that."

Willoughby smiled. "Too right, I will. And they'll believe it, because they want to believe it."

Two weeks later, over dinner one evening, the U-boat officers sat at their mess table and idly discussed the possibilities of escape. Kolza, as usual, was enjoying the food immensely, and was sopping up the various juices on his plate with a chunk of bread.

"Ah, this is *wunderbar*," he said. Although his mouth was still full, the contentment in his voice was unmistakable. "On the U-110 the bread would turn black on the outside from mold and we would have to dig to the white part in the middle. A man couldn't eat any crust after the second day at sea."

"How well I remember. And don't forget the hams and sausages hanging from the overheads like bats in a cave," said Strauss.

"How could I forget? I was the only one in the crew who was short enough not to risk hitting his head on a future dinner."

"All of this is true," said Meinhoff grudgingly, "but we must not be seduced by comfort, or by the decadent pleasures of the west. We have a duty as German officers to escape."

"Well of course; but just where would someone escape to?" asked Kolza, gesturing towards a window. "We're in the trackless, howling wilderness. A man wouldn't get far. If the local farmers didn't get him, he'd probably get eaten by a moose or something." Kolza's spectacles reflected in a ray of sunlight slanting through a window, making him look like a misplaced university professor more than ever.

"Has anyone figured out where we are?" said Strauss, brushing a few crumbs out of his black beard.

"I noticed the railroad car we came in was labeled 'Temiskaming and Northern Ontario Railroad'," said Kolza. "So I would suppose we are in Ontario somewhere."

"I believe we are near the border between Ontario and Quebec, perhaps several hundred miles north of Ottawa and Montreal," said Meinhoff.

"*Wunderbar*," said Kolza. "I can hardly wait for winter. Perhaps they will serve walrus steaks."

"The guards seem to be lax in security," Meinhoff continued, ignoring Kolza. "I have learned that, as we suspected, they are not regular Canadian Army troops; but are units of the Veteran's Guard of Canada, older men who fought in the last war and are less fit for front line duty. Eluding such men should be easy, even the *Frettchen* inside the wire, but we'll need better information before an attempt is made.

Strauss frowned and rubbed his chin. He was not enthusiastic about escape attempts, but he couldn't resist a challenging problem. "On the contrary. Rather than needing information to make an escape attempt, perhaps we need an escape attempt to get information."

Meinhoff smiled. "Of course. If we can get someone outside the wire, we can find out about the countryside and plan a real escape next time." He pushed aside his plate and drew a sketch on a piece of paper.

"Here is the camp. The buildings are arranged like so, and the guard towers are placed along this road that runs around the outside of the fence. I've heard the guards refer to it as the Burma Road. Now we only have access to part of it, but there are still several places along the wire that are partially obscured from the guard towers by buildings or trees, not to mention the gate where construction vehicles go in and out. We should be able to find some way to get a man out."

"Why only one?" asked Kolza, his fork stopped in mid air.

They looked at each other.

"Well, I mean to say," Kolza continued, "wouldn't it be just as easy to get two men out?"

-2-

Tuesday, July 15—Wednesday, August 13

"An escape?" shouted Reynolds jumping up from behind his desk and knocking a tea cup onto the floor. "Already? Goddammit, the internees and merchant seamen never give us this trouble. I want them caught! How did this happen?"

Sergeant Henderson stood red faced at attention in Reynolds' office. "We're not sure, but we were two men short at noon roll call. We had a work crew finishing up the drain lines for barracks three, and…"

"Yes? and what?"

"Well, there was a lorry filled with dirt and a stack of brush they had cut down just before the prisoners arrived, and they had to haul it away. We think the prisoners were probably hiding in the back."

"And no one checked the bloody truck before it left?"

"The guards did probe the stuff, of course, but the brush was thick and there was a fair amount of dirt as well, so they must have missed the prisoners."

"All right, all right." Reynolds waived his hand in an exasperated gesture of dismissal. "Who escaped?"

"Two enlisted men; Fleisher and Theimann."

"How long have they been gone?"

"About six hours at the most, probably less. They were both present at the roll call six hours ago, and the truck logged out about five hours ago."

"Right. Activate the recapture plan immediately. Have scout units inspect the wire inside and out, in case they went that way. Notify the Commissioner of Prisoner of War Services at the Department of National Defense in Ottawa, District Military Headquarters 13 at Kingston, and the Ontario Provincial Police. I want roadblocks and search parties along the main road. If they're on foot, they should be within 20 miles. I want them back in a hurry. I needn't remind you, sergeant, that these men are high security risks. Let's get cracking."

Meinhoff, Strauss, and Kolza sat under the shade of a tree in the yard, watching the growing commotion with satisfaction. Guards were running to and fro and roaring away in vehicles with the gears grinding. More guards were coming out and going into Major Reynolds' office looking worried.

"Well," said Kolza, leisurely polishing his spectacles, "I don't know how far they'll get, but they've certainly gotten everyone's attention. Confusion seems the order of the day."

Meinhoff nodded with satisfaction. "And just think how confused the Canadians will be when they discover that Fleisher and Theimann have gone in two different directions!"

⋆   ⋆   ⋆

Fifteen miles to the south, Torpedoman Werner Theimann was sweating profusely as he pushed through the undergrowth by the side of the road. There wasn't much traffic, but every time he heard motor noise, he ducked into the underbrush for concealment.

With a rumble, another truck passed by, then the sound faded into the distance. When all was quiet, Theimann stepped out on to the road and began walking once again. In the stillness, his footsteps made soft thumping noises on the pavement. He looked ahead and thought he saw some buildings through the trees where the road curved. Then a small sign appeared ahead, partly obscured by trees. Theimann quickened his pace until he reached the sign. He pushed some leaves out of the way and read.

Val Gagne—2 km

So there was a town ahead. He had to get a good look at it, then decide how to get around it. Theimann wiped his forehead, looked at the sun to try to judge his direction, then set out once again. A few minutes later, he saw a brown car parked by the side of the road under a shade tree and noticed the tree effectively hid the car from the nearby house to which it apparently belonged. Theimann looked around and, satisfied no one was about, quietly opened the door of the car and slid into the front seat. To his disappointment he saw there were no keys in the ignition and looked through the glove box for a spare set. There were still no keys, but he found something almost as good; a road map of Ontario. After looking at it, he quickly slid it into his pocket and got back out of the car. He still would have to walk, but now he had a much better way of finding out where he was going.

*   *   *

Just a few miles away, Corporal Nelson Ogleby of the Ontario Provincial Police sat in his patrol car grumbling to himself. His brother in law had come to visit two weeks ago and showed no inclination to leave. The lout seemed to have only two phrases in his vocabulary: "What time's dinner?" and "Give me another Molson's."

"I should throw him out on his arse, that's what I should do, eh?" Ogleby muttered. "But then there'd be hell to pay with Mabel. She thinks Floyd's just 'between jobs'. What a laugh. The last time that sod worked was almost five years ago. Anybody who can't find work in the middle of a war doesn't really want to. Even women are working now, filing the factories, farming and generally taking over for the absent men. I ought to take my baton and…"

Mercifully, his thoughts were interrupted by the crackle of his radio. "All units in the Shillington, Roberts, and Val Gagne areas be on the lookout for two escaped POWs. One is of medium height with blonde hair and a beard; the other is short with brown hair and a moustache. Suspected to be in the vicinity of Val Gagne or Shillington proceeding south on foot. That is all."

Ogleby snorted. That was all he needed, chasing some escaped Jerries around in the woods. And just where did the damned fools think they were going to escape to, anyway? They probably just wanted to cause trouble. Oh well, he wasn't far from Val Gagne. It wouldn't hurt to take a look.

"Fritz'll probably try the Old Mill Road around town," he said out loud. "It's overgrown and would provide concealment." He picked up the microphone. "This is OPP unit 12 calling unit 16. You there, Charlie?"

"Unit 16 here," came a crackling voice over the radio. "What's up, Nelson?"

"How about meeting me at the Old Mill Road over to Val Gagne, eh? We might need to give a couple of foreign visitors a ride back to their hotel."

∗   ∗   ∗

Fifteen miles to the west, in a white clapboard farm house near Shillington, Joe Fergusen was preparing to do some grouse hunting to supplement his meager meat ration. Standing at the kitchen table, he loaded his old Winchester shotgun, snapped it shut, then put a handful of shells in his pocket for good measure.

"I guess that does it," he said to himself, and started to step out the back door. As always, he paused to look at the faded photo of his wife, Beth. She'd been gone almost five years now, but he still wished her picture goodbye whenever he left the house.

He stepped out the back door and looked around the yard. The air was misty with humidity and insects; a good day for a stroll in the woods. Suddenly, he noticed a rustling in the bushes and a young man of about twenty stumbled through the tangle of vines and into the yard. He also noticed that the stranger was wearing his shirt inside out. The stranger looked around to get his bearings and started when he saw Fergusen standing there with his shotgun. For a moment, neither of them spoke. Finally, Fergusen addressed him suspiciously.

"Good afternoon, young fellow. And who might you be, eh?"

Seaman Gunther Fleisher was visibly sweating, and not just from the heat. He tried a smile and a friendly greeting. Maybe he could bluff his way out.

"Goot aufternoon. How ah you zis fine day?"

Joe Fergusen cocked the shotgun with a click that echoed in the stillness.

"I guess you ain't from around here, eh?"

"I vas chust valking und got lost."

"Well, you get in the house and I'll call someone who can show you the way. Then you can 'valk' back to that there prison camp you come from."

"Oh, no thank you…" He started to turn to walk away, and Fergusen could now see why the man's shirt was inside out. The wetness of the man's sweat had revealed a formerly hidden large red circle on the back of the shirt; the mark of a POW.

"You know," said Joe Ferguson loudly, "I ain't shot a Hun since the last war, but I think I still know how. Now you get in the house or you're going to find out the hard way."

*   *   *

"Well, that's both of them," remarked Strauss as he stood by the barracks window with Meinhoff and Kolza watching the OPP cars drop off Theimann and Fleisher an hour later. The two would-be escapees looked somewhat embarrassed and tired, but otherwise no worse for the experience as the camp guards marched them off to the standard punishment for first-time escape attempts: 14 days of solitary confinement.

Meinhoff turned from the window. "When they get out, Fleisher and Theimann can fill us in on the surrounding countryside. Maybe we can start planning real escapes. We'll have to start thinking of things like forged documents, escape routes, diversions, and making uniforms look like civilian clothes. Certain foods can be used to dye cloth; beets for example."

Kolza smiled. "Wouldn't an escapee look a bit conspicuous in a beet colored suit?" he asked.

"That's just an example," said Meinhoff impatiently. "If we get some bowls or containers from the mess hall, we can mix different foods for proper colors."

"Fine," said Strauss, "but it will take more than food color to prepare for a better escape. Theimann and Fleisher were caught in only seven hours."

"Yes," said Kolza. "And the Canadians didn't even start looking until they'd been gone five. That means two hours from discovery to capture. Not a very impressive breakout."

The three officers casually emerged from the barracks and strolled out into the yard. In the late afternoon sunshine, the other prisoners had gathered in the parade ground and watched the returning escapees, but had since returned to digging gardens, washing clothes, and playing an impromptu soccer game. The usually ashen faced men were getting some color in their skin and looked healthier than they ever had on the U-110.

"*Guten tag,*" came the voice of Chief Muller. He was a muscular bald man with a neatly trimmed goatee of red. "What do you think will happen to Fleisher and Theimann?"

"Two weeks of solitary confinement, then they will return to us," said Strauss. "Do not concern yourself, Chief. They have performed a service and have had an adventure to boast of as well."

The chief considered this, then began walking with them. "I heard one of the guards talking today. My English is not so good, but I think he was making a bet with another about who would apprehend Fleisher and Theimann. One of them said his money was on the provincials, because the escapees had gotten too much head start for the camp guards to get them, but they hadn't been gone long enough to call in the RCNPA."

The officers looked at each other. "The RCNPA did you say? What is the RCNPA?" said Strauss. "I've never heard of it."

Kolza laughed. "Yes you have. You just need a better ear for language."

Strauss looked at him. "Language? What do you mean, Hans?"

"Well, perhaps not language so much as recognizing certain pronunciation and speech patterns."

"Yes, yes; get to the point," said Meinhoff, who was becoming annoyed.

"The point," said Kolza, "is that you have perhaps noticed the tendency of the local inhabitants to end sentences with 'eh?.'"

"Yes, well what of it?"

"This peculiarity," said Kolza, obviously enjoying the moment, "coupled with Chief Muller's lack of familiarity with English pronunciation are the keys to this little mystery. The chief did not hear 'RCNPA', he heard 'RCMP, eh?.'"

"RCMP?" said Strauss. "Isn't that…"

"The Royal Canadian Mounted Police," said Meinhoff. "Of course. If an escapee gets far enough, the Mounties take over."

Strauss nodded. "So that is their system. First we must get past the guards, then the Ontario Provincial Police, then the Royal Canadian Mounted Police. And even if by some miracle we can do all that, we will still be 4,000 miles from home."

*   *   *

"That's right, Major," Corporal Ogleby was saying, "one was apprehended just outside of Val Gagne, and the other was caught by a farmer near Shillington."

Major Reynolds and Sergeant Henderson were studying a map of the area. "Why were they over fifteen miles apart when they were caught?" said Henderson. "Why didn't they stick together? How the devil did they expect to escape that way?"

"I don't think they were really trying to escape," said Reynolds.

"Not trying?" said Corporal Ogleby. "Then what in the world were they doing, eh?"

"Gathering information. It wasn't an escape, it was a reconnaissance mission. The Germans are gathering information about the countryside so they will better be able to plan a real escape, or at least cause maximum disruption. That is why the two men were not together. One scouted the southeast, the other the southwest. No doubt they will sketch the roads and towns from memory when they get out of isolation."

"Sneaky bastards," said Henderson, shaking his head.

Reynolds sighed. "A prisoner of war is supposed to try to escape. They're simply doing their duty, sergeant. So let's make certain we do ours. I want every guard to be on his toes from now on. These prisoners are to remain here."

As Sergeant Henderson left, Lieutenant Willoughby entered the room.

"Good show," he said with satisfaction. "Caught the blighters in a few hours."

Reynolds glared at him. "Good show? We've allowed two men to go tromping about the countryside and you say it's a good show? Didn't you have any wind of this?"

Willoughby reddened. "I say, you can hardly expect them to confide in me about a bloody escape attempt."

Reynold muttered to himself for a few seconds, then seemed calmer. "All right, I suppose an intelligence officer isn't the same thing as a palm reader, but we've got to stop this sort of thing before it gets out of hand."

*   *   *

July in northern Ontario proved to be surprisingly hot during the day, and the prisoners soon learned to look for shade and became familiar with the smell of hot tar given off by the barracks baking in the sun. The tarpaper that gave off the smell absorbed the sun's heat so that the barracks were unlivable much of the day, so many of the prisoners sat around listlessly during the noon hours. The younger and more energetic played soccer. Instructional classes in English, history and science were held in the mess hall or in the shade of a tree. For most Germans, the enemies were now boredom and homesickness. Occasional work details were welcomed as a diversion and as a chance to get outside the wire, if only for a little while.

During this time, Meinhoff could usually be seen pacing the grounds in a determined manner, like a lion in a cage. Strauss and Kolza often sat under one of the few trees and observed this performance.

"Do you think Gregor is restless?" said Kolza.

Strauss looked at the figure approaching and shrugged. "Probably. If I know Gregor, he's still itching to get back in the action. Here he comes. Why don't you ask him?"

"*Guten Tag*," said Kolza, when Meinhoff approached. "Come have a seat in the shade."

Meinhoff sat down and wiped his brow. "It is warm around here. I think, Hans, that you will not be seeing your Eskimos just yet."

"Maybe not, Gregor, but winter is coming."

"Don't remind me of the passage of time," said Meinhoff resentfully. "The great struggle for the future of the world is raging and we sit here under a tree watching good fighting men kicking a soccer ball. Great battles are going on in Russia. The Bolsheviks are being crushed and we are making no contribution to the remaking of the world."

"Such things happen," Strauss suggested, shrugging his shoulders. "The fortunes of war. My father was in the last war. He spent the time repairing trucks while my uncle was with Ludendorff in Belgium when the Liege forts were captured in 1914. My father used to say that his brother got the Iron Cross and all he got was iron scrap."

Meinhoff leaned back against the tree and looked at the ground. He frowned as if undecided on what to say. Finally he spoke. "My father did not survive the war. He was killed in the 1918 offensive that almost won the war for us. A mortar shell fell and that was that. He never even knew that my mother was pregnant with me from his last leave."

Kolza and Strauss looked at each other. They had never heard Meinhoff speak about anything personal before.

"That is why I know Hitler is the salvation of Germany," he continued. "He will lead us to our rightful place in the world order, and men like my father will have died for a great purpose. But thanks to this 'fortune of war', I can not be a part of it." He threw a rock in frustration. It went skittering across the parade ground, raising small puffs of dust as it went.

"Gregor," said Strauss, "we have all done our duty and played our part. Surely you would not have preferred to die on the U-110?"

He gave them an odd, far-away look. "Sometimes I am not so certain, Heinrich."

Meinhoff suddenly stood up and resumed his walking, and his think-ing. Kolza watched him go and shook his head.

*   *   *

On August 2, just a few days after Thiemann and Fleisher had been released from solitary confinement, Strauss, Meinhoff, and Kolza were lingering over dinner. Most of the others had left and they were alone at the table. Meinhoff was unusually agitated.

"I'm telling you," he said, "there is something wrong with this camp, something they are keeping secret."

Strauss looked at Meinhoff over his dinner of sausages, potatoes and peas. He took a drink from a steaming metal mug of coffee and settled back in his chair and sighed.

"All right, Gregor. What do you think is wrong?"

"First of all, there are no other U-boat prisoners here, just the 34 sur-vivors of the U-110. The others are mostly merchant seamen and some civilian internees. And why build a camp so far away from everything. And why do we not get mail?"

"Lieutenant Willoughby says the mail service has been disrupted by the U-boats…"

"That is nonsense," said Meinhoff, shaking his head. "And that Lieutenant Willoughby is obviously an intelligence officer. He might as well wear a sign. He has as much interest in our welfare as the captain of the HMS BULLDOG. We are also not allowed to have any contact with any local people except for the occasional well supervised work detail."We can't even have newspapers. These scraps one of the men found near the guard hut are the only papers we have seen."

Meinhoff had been looking through a torn newspaper page, but threw it away in disgust. "Weather reports and farming news. Here's another piece. There's an article of war news claiming the convoys are mostly getting through. What lies! They even claim to have sunk several U-boats."

Meinhoff stopped, staring at the end of the article. There, almost illegible from a grease stain was a small paragraph about a U boat sinking. The headline said "**U-BOAT SUNK WITH ALL HANDS**". The number of the U boat was not known, but the sinking had occurred on May 9, the same day the U-110 was sunk. He read further and saw the HMS BULLDOG, along with HMS BROADWAY and HMS AUBRETIA had sunk the submarine. There was no doubt about it, they were referring to the U-110.

According to the article, the entire crew had gone down with the U-boat. Meinhoff stared at the paper. Why would they say the U-110 was lost with all hands, when most of the crew had been taken prisoner? What purpose would such a lie serve? Could it have been some kind of a mix up, or was there a purpose behind it?

Suddenly Meinhoff's eyes went wide.

"Of course," he whispered.

"What is it, Gregor?"

Meinhoff didn't answer right away. He sat staring at the paper as if in a trance. Strauss and Kolza looked at each other. They were used to strange behavior from Meinhoff, but this was extreme even for him.

"I have to go. I must," Meinhoff said finally.

"Go? Go where?" said Strauss.

"To Germany. The fate of the fatherland depends on it."

"We all want to go to Germany, Gregor…" said Kolza cautiously.

"I MUST go!" Meinhoff shouted. "Or the war will be lost!"

As Strauss and Kolza sat dumbfounded, Meinhoff explained what had become so suddenly clear to him. For he had put the pieces together and found out why they were being held in isolation. As incredible as it sounded, they were sitting on one of the biggest secrets of the war, a secret that could make the difference between victory and defeat. If only they could get word back to Germany.

"All right, Gregor," said Strauss, when he had recovered somewhat. "You must return to Germany. Now we must find out how it can be done."

An hour later, they had worked out a basic escape plan; one that would take Meinhoff all the way back to Germany. The plan was clever, but prospects still did not look good.

"All right, Gregor," said Strauss. "Let's see that map again."

Theimann had found a road map during his escape and had carefully memorized the main towns, roads, and distances before he was recaptured. While in solitary confinement, he had reconstructed the map to scale in the dirt on the floor. He had noted that the length of his little finger was almost exactly 50 miles, so he was able to keep everything more or less to scale. When he returned to the barracks, he was able to reconstruct the map with the aid of another prisoner who had been a student of geography.

"Here it is," said Meinhoff, spreading a map out on the table. "We are here, near Cochrane and Timmins, in the northern part of Ontario not far from the Quebec border. South of us, going from east to west is Montreal, Ottawa, Toronto, and Sault St Marie, the closest access point to the United States. For the plan to succeed, it is critical that I reach the United States. Although they sympathize with the English, the Americans are officially neutral, so getting to Germany would be easier from the United States than from Canada."

Strauss nodded. "All right. But it appears you will need someone to go with you."

"Theimann and Fleisher will do nicely. They have experience for what we have in mind."

"When can you be ready?" Kolza asked.

"I should have at least several weeks to accumulate supplies and gather more information, but every day that passes puts the Reich in more danger. I propose we aim for two weeks. That would be August 13."

"Done," said Strauss. "Fleisher was a tailor in civilian life. We'll get him to put together some approximations of civilian clothes. Does anyone know what kind of I.D. cards will be needed? No? Well, we'll have to find out in the next week. Kolza, you are a bit of an artist and draftsman are you not? Perhaps you could forge the necessary documents."

"I suppose I could try," Kolza said uncertainly, "but I don't know what documents are needed and what they look like. I'll need a model."

"We'll get you one," said Meinhoff. "The escape will be difficult, but we must not fail. The war may depend on it."

"All right," said Strauss. "Now we know who will go and when; we will have plain clothes; we will have forged documents; but we still have the problem of how to avoid capture."

"The fastest way would be to board the train," said Meinhoff. "After all, it is only a mile or so from camp and comes by several times a day."

"No," said Strauss shaking his head. "That is too obvious. There will no doubt be guards and searches of every meter of that train. They would have you before you crossed the bridge. No, to have any chance of success, you must do the unexpected."

Kolza frowned in thought, then polished his spectacles for the third time. "Getting out of the camp can probably be managed easily enough. The Canadians are somewhat lax since they know we have no place to escape to. The problem is how to cover the necessary distances by road without being captured. I think it is safe to assume roadblocks or check points will be set up."

"Undoubtedly," said Meinhoff, who was pacing the floor as if already on his journey. "And the more time that elapses from when we escape, the further along the roads the roadblocks will be placed." Meinhoff's cold blue eyes seemed to flash as he spoke.

"So avoiding the roadblocks is essential," said Strauss. "Going after lights out will give you cover and elude the *Frettchen* as well. The roll calls and bedchecks are six hours apart, so the maximum head start we can achieve will be that long. That will get you perhaps 12 to 15 miles away. Unless you can obtain a vehicle or some form of motor transportation, you will be within easy reach of search parties. Even with a vehicle, the Canadians will probably set roadblocks 50 to 100 miles away and you will be picked up at one of them."

"If only we could get beyond those roadblocks," muttered Meinhoff. "That is the key."

"Of course," said Kolza. "But how?"

"Well, we will have to proceed with the rest of the preparations and figure out what to do about the roadblock problem later," said Strauss.

"All right," said Meinhoff. "As long as its not too much later. We don't have much time."

The next day, a near riot broke out at the soccer match, and the Canadians took some time getting it under control.

Finally, the prisoners dusted themselves off and slowly made their way off the field. With them, they carried the ball, some torn clothing, several loose shoes, and a Canadian corporal's billfold. Two days later, the corporal found the billfold near the wire. It seemed like a miracle. He couldn't remember dropping it there and didn't know how he could have missed seeing it before. He was greatly relieved; especially since he had been afraid to report it missing.

*   *   *

"I don't like it," said Major Reynolds, looking out of his office window towards the parade ground. "I don't like it one little bit. The Germans work like a well oiled machine, then one day they suddenly break out in a donnybrook."

"It could be a bit of restlessness and boredom," said Henderson uncertainly.

"Or it could well have been a diversion for another escape attempt," said Reynolds. "Don't ever underestimate the deviousness of these people, sergeant."

"Well, we finally stopped it, sir," said Sergeant Henderson. "and no one is missing."

"Not at the moment. But the Germans are going to get the idea they can pull our strings any time they choose. Well I won't have it, sergeant; I won't have any part of it. We are in charge here and must remain so. I want the guards increased until further notice, and I want the inside men to make extra sweeps for tunnels, contraband, or anything that might be used in an escape attempt. And I want patrols along the Burma Road around the enclosure."

"Yes, sir."

"We'll show them who's the bloody boss around here. I'll not be responsible for another Von Werra."

Henderson nodded glumly. Earlier that year, a captured Luftwaffe fighter pilot named Franz Von Werra had escaped from a POW. train en route to a camp in northern Ontario, made his way through the Canadian winter all the way to the St. Lawrence and crossed into the neutral United States with a stolen boat he dragged across the ice floes. With the help of the German embassy, he was able to flee to Mexico and eventually, home. The Canadians were determined not to let that happen again, especially with these particular prisoners.

*   *   *

"We'll go at night, right after roll call," Meinhoff said after supper that night. "I must have at least four hours head start."

Rain had halted all activity in the yard and was pounding a steady drumbeat on the roof. Streams of silver water were running from the eaves like shimmering icicles. Puddles rippled by the drops were forming around the yard.

"You would do better with five hours," said Strauss, looking out the window.

Just then, the door swung open and Kolza stepped into the room, stomping his feet on the wood plank floor to shake the mud off his boots. He smelled strongly of wet wool.

"Bad news, I'm afraid. I was just talking to Sergeant Henderson. Captain Reynolds is nervous because of our little drama at the soccer match. He's increased the guards and what's worse, has ordered random bedchecks until further notice."

"Random bedchecks?" said Meinhoff, "That could ruin everything. We were counting on six hours between roll calls or bed checks. Now we can't properly time the break. If they check soon after we make the break and find us missing, they could catch us before we make the tree line. And even if we get away clean, they could discover we're gone within an hour or so."

"Yes," said Strauss. "We've got to find a way to gain more head start. Simply going after a bedcheck or roll call won't be enough. If we guess wrong, the escape will be over almost before it begins."

Kolza wiped his glasses and smiled slyly, even though he was still dripping water on the floor. "I have been thinking about the bedcheck situation, and the problem of getting beyond the roadblocks. I believe I have an idea to deal with both problems."

Kolza walked to the table in the center of the barracks where the chess board was set up. He picked up a knight and held the carved wooden horse head up to the light.

"Did you know that Toller was once an art student in Munich? He has quite a talent for woodworking as well. He carved these chess pieces, in fact. It's quite good, don't you think?"

"I am aware of that, Hans," said Strauss. "What do you propose?"

Kolza put the knight back on the board. "I've always been partial to the knight. It's the only piece on the board that can not be blocked by any other piece; a valuable attribute when trying to escape a trap. That is what we seek. I propose that we put Toller's talents to work. I believe there is a way he can make a knight out of Gregor."

*   *   *

The Canadians were convinced that keeping the prisoners busy was vital to keeping them out of trouble. So they encouraged the various classes, sports, and handicraft activities of the Germans. For this reason, they had set up a wood shop behind the mess hall. The wood was mostly lumber scraps from camp building projects, but the work area and the tools were adequate for making bookshelves or most of the handicraft items confined men might work on. The workshop was used almost from the first day. The guards were gratified to see the interest the Germans were taking and the enthusiasm with which they worked in this shop. For all their reputation for efficiency, however, the Germans seemed to produce very little, considering the amount of wood they used.

*   *   *

"Who in the devil keeps doing that?" demanded Sergeant Henderson one afternoon as he looked at the camp bulletin board. For days now, several important notices had disappeared from the board within hours of their being posted. At first, Henderson thought the wind had blown them off, but then he observed that the notices on heavier paper seemed to disappear the fastest, so someone was intentionally removing them. The bloody Germans ought to be above petty vandalism, Henderson thought angrily. What could they be thinking? Just a bunch of foolishness designed to aggravate the guards, no doubt. He posted another notice and instructed the guards to keep a close watch on the board.

In the mess hall, there was a rash a pilfering as well. The cook noticed several bowls and glasses missing, although what anyone could want them for, he couldn't guess at first. After giving the matter some thought, he decided the Germans were probably smuggling food back to the barracks, and he felt strangely flattered. A man didn't get many compliments cooking for prisoners, even indirect ones. Still, he would have to replace the missing items. He considered reporting the loss, but didn't want the Commandant thinking he'd been careless, so he kept silent about it when he made his daily report to Captain Reynolds.

*   *   *

"Is anything happening, sergeant?" asked Reynolds. It had been almost two weeks since the incident at the soccer match. With the middle of August, the warm weather had returned and the sun cast harsh shadows from the fences.

"Everything has been quiet, sir," he replied. "After that row at the soccer game, everyone settled down nicely."

Reynolds looked out the window at the prisoners moving about the parade ground. "Maybe. But one thing I'm sure of; The U-boat prisoners are not to be trusted."

Henderson knitted his brows in thought. "I think that Kolza isn't too determined to escape. He seems like he's too smart and too contented with the food. And Strauss strikes me as very level headed. Surely he wouldn't try anything foolish."

Reynolds looked around from the window and regarded Henderson curiously. "I notice you didn't include Herr Meinhoff in your list of sensible Germans, sergeant."

Henderson cleared his throat. "Well, no. In fact, I think he's the one who's most likely to give us trouble, if you want my opinion, sir. He's the worst Nazi in the bunch. I've seen him several times just sitting and staring at the eagle and swastika insignia on his hat, and tracing its outline slowly with his finger. And if you want to make him mad, just make a crack about Hitler."

Reynolds nodded. "I agree with you on that score. He's a fanatic, and what's worse, a smart one. He could very well egg the others on to god knows what kind of scheme. The reports I've gotten from Lieutenant Willoughby say the same thing."

The room was quiet for a moment, then Reynolds spoke again. "Well, you'd better get back to your rounds. Just keep your eyes and ears open."

"Yes, sir," said Henderson as he turned on his heel and left. Reynolds looked out the window once again and cursed his luck at being stationed in this god forsaken corner of Canada playing nanny to a bunch of Nazis. It was better than getting shot at, he thought, but at least at the front he could shoot back.

*   *   *

Early in the morning three days later, Sergeant Henderson stood near the door to barracks one and yawned. The sun was finally coming up behind the rows of pine and birch trees surrounding the camp. He was due to go off duty in another hour. Ever since Captain Reynolds had increased the guards and started random bed checks, most of the guards had worked double shifts, and Henderson was weary of it. He had made bed checks four times last night, no more than three hours apart. Everyone was still here.

He decided to take one more turn around the wire before going off duty, so he strolled along the inside of the fence looking for nothing in particular. Maybe he could get some fishing in when they went back to normal shifts, They certainly couldn't keep this up indefinitely. The northern Ontario winter would be along before you knew it, so a man had to fish while the air was warm and the days were long. He thought fondly of the trout he had caught just a few weeks before. He could almost still taste it. He had always loved the woods. Sometimes, patrolling behind the wire and seeing the forest just out of reach, he felt he was a prisoner as well.

In the barracks, it was time for the prisoners to rise and start to straggle out to the wash building, but no one stirred yet. Henderson looked in at the men still in their bunks and felt a strange resentment that they had slept while he had had to stay awake. He walked in the door to go from bunk to bunk shaking the sleeping occupants.

"Come on you sleeping beauties, it's morning in Ontario. Rise and shine. You don't want to be late for morning roll…"

He stopped in his tracks. With a sickening feeling he realized two of the bunks in the enlisted area were empty. With rising panic, he opened the door to the officers' room. One more bunk was empty; Meinhoff's. Henderson stood with his mouth open trying to speak, but only two hoarse words came out;

"Oh, shit."

-3-

Wednesday, August 13

American FBI agent Tom Van Marter sat in a cluttered office in the Royal Canadian Mounted Police Headquarters in Ottawa, stifled a yawn, and wondered, once again, what he was doing there. On the grayish-green wall across from him was the coat of arms of the RCMP; a buffalo head surrounded by a wreath of maple leaves and surmounted by a crown. The motto circling the buffalo head said "MAINTIEN LE DROIT". Maintain the right.

Below the coat of arms and behind a littered desk sat Van Marter's Canadian counterpart and nemesis, Inspector Andre MacKensie, RCMP.

No one would have mistaken the two men for brothers; Van Marter was in his early twenties, thin, and with neatly groomed dark brown hair cut so close around the sides that the whiteness of his skin showed through. He wore the standard three piece dark blue suit that all FBI agents wore, complete with a folded white handkerchief showing above the breast pocket and a fedora to wear outdoors. The suit included a vest that Inspector MacKensie insisted on calling a waistcoat. All in all, Tom Van Marter looked as much like an accountant as a law enforcement officer.

Inspector Andre MacKensie of the Royal Canadian Mounted Police, on the other hand, could best be described as comfortable looking. In addition to being almost 15 years older, he was several inches shorter than Van Marter, and an equal amount wider. He too was wearing a suit, but it was a muddy brown color and needed ironing. He had no vest, and the beginning of a comfortable middle aged stomach pressed against a belt that his wide, hand painted tie failed to reach. What hair he had left always seemed to be flying in several directions as if trying to escape his head. In spite of his stockiness, MacKensie had a chiseled sort of a face that had a tendency to redden when he was irritated. His face had been red quite a bit during Van Marter's visit.

They had spent the last two weeks comparing notes on techniques of detection and fugitive apprehension, an outgrowth of the their governments' developing cooperation in matters of espionage and POW escapes. In spite of their common purpose, the men often seemed to end up arguing about which agency did it better; the FBI or the RCMP. It was an argument that was both unprovable and ultimately pointless. Van Marter had argued the rational approach, in which the hunt, especially in its early stages, was a matter of time, distance and mathematics. MacKensie seemed to lean heavily on local knowledge, informers, and what he called his nose.

"Tracking is a science," Van Marter would insist. "They can only cover so much distance and they leave tracks no matter what they do."

"A science?" MacKensie would snort, "How can outguessing a fugitive be a science when even he doesn't know what he's going to do next most of the time, eh? No, just give me a couple of dogs and few phone calls to local people, and I'll have our man in custody while you're still playing with your slide rule."

But now, two weeks later, both men were getting tired of the routine and were grateful the ordeal was coming to an end. Van Marter idly looked out the window and was vaguely aware of the a sound in the background; the sound of Andre MacKensie's voice.

"Hey, I'm talking to you," MacKensie said with annoyance. "Keep your stick on the ice; you might learn something."

Van Marter looked back at MacKensie. "Like what wine to serve with moose?"

MacKensie ignored the comment. "Tomorrow you head back to the states. I guess the Can will just have to get along without you."

"Hey, coming up here wasn't my idea," Van Marter replied. "I was perfectly happy tracking Axis spies in New York."

In fact, just a few weeks before being sent on this hare-brained information exchange mission to Canada, he had tracked and arrested the notorious Bruno Krause. Using taxi records and train schedules, Van Marter had cleverly succeeded in running Krause to ground just when he was about to board a ship in Baltimore. But now, he thought, he was stuck in the frozen north with a Canadian Neanderthal whose idea of tracking seemed to involve sniffing the air.

"Well," MacKensie continued, "Mr. Hoover saw fit to send you up here to exchange information on man hunting techniques. Now maybe you can go back and help the FBI to get its man the way we do."

"The way you do? You mean by hanging around the general store and asking old Pierre by the cracker barrel if he's seen any strangers around? No thanks."

MacKensie started to redden again and Van Marter thought it might be wise to let up a bit.

"Look," he said soothingly, "I suppose your methods work well enough up here. I just don't think they're for us. Maybe you'll get to D.C. one of these days and see how we do it."

"Washington is too hot, crowded and unhealthy for me," MacKensie grumbled. "I was there in July once. You could grow bloody bananas through the cracks in the sidewalk, eh?"

Van Marter winced. Why did everyone up here insist on ending sentences with "eh?"? It made people sound as if they were hard of hearing.

"As far as you're concerned, anything below Buffalo might as well have palm trees. You don't have any use for anything that's American."

MacKensie looked shocked. "Why that's not true at all. Just yesterday, someone asked what I thought of you and I quoted that famous American, Mark Twain, eh?"

"Mark Twain? And just what did you say?"

"Agent Van Marter, I told the man, has all the virtues I dislike, and none of the vices I admire."

Van Marter suppressed a smile. "I'm glad to hear you read good literature during those long winter nights. Well, stay here in your igloo with Mr Clemens if you want. Just show me the way back home."

MacKensie growled as if to second the motion then, pulled out a report and studied it. "Well, I suppose we've covered the basic areas we were told to: search coordination, finding evidence, tracking, fugitive interception, public relations."

"Better make sure," said Van Marter. "I wouldn't want to have to come back."

MacKensie threw the report on his desk to take its place among the rest of the debris. "Well, I hope you've learned something. The FBI may brag about apprehending fugitives, but you can't beat the RCMP for dogged determination and a high success rate, eh? After all, we always get our man."

"Oh, banana oil," said Van Marter, "when we caught…."

"And don't bring up Dillinger again," interrupted MacKensie. "The man was caught at a movie theater, eh? And even then you had an informer."

"Actually, I was about to point out the FBI's record of fugitives apprehended."

"Hah! Those figures don't mean a thing," said MacKensie. "Most of the apprehended fugitives are actually men AWL from the military, and they are apprehended when they return home. Not exactly a serious test of detection and tracking."

Van Marter leapt to his feet to defend the honor of the FBI.

"Oh, and I suppose the RCMP doesn't pad its figures just a little? You have to ask for budget appropriations the same as we do. And it's AWOL, not AWL. At least get that right."

MacKensie's face was reddening again. "Pad? For your information, the RCMP…."

The jangling of the telephone interrupted the argument. The two men glared at each other while the phone rang a third time.

"You'd better get that," said Van Marter, nodding towards the phone. "It might be the Prime Minister wanting your help in finding his house key."

"That's latch key," MacKensie muttered as he picked up the phone. "Hello, Inspector MacKensie here. Yes? Yes, I see. I'll be right there." MacKensie stood up. "I have to see the superintendent."

Van Marter watched him go and shook his head. Holy cow, he thought, talk about provincial…

For another 15 minutes or so, he arranged and finalized his report. He thought it best to downplay some of the disagreements they had had and talk about some of the comparative methods. Van Marter worked at his desk, a temporary table set up opposite MacKensie. In contrast to MacKensie's desk, Van Marter's table was so neat it was almost bare, with only three folders arranged alphabetically from left to right. When he had finished the report, and MacKensie failed to reappear, Van Marter put it away, then stood up and stretched. He wandered around the office for a few minutes, then sat in MacKensie's chair and put his feet up on the desk. This was more comfortable, and had the additional advantage of being sure to annoy MacKensie when he returned. Van Marter sat in the chair a few moments, then frowned, stood up, and turned the chair over to inspect the swivel mechanism. He was interested to see the Canadian manufacturer's design was somewhat different than the American ones. He made an adjustment to the spring tension, sat back down, and smiled contentedly.

In one corner of the desk he noticed a picture of Andre MacKensie and his wife, along with a girl who looked to be about 5 or 6, apparently taken on a vacation in some area of woods and mountains. MacKensie was thinner in the picture, and his hair was thicker and darker. Probably at least ten years ago, Van Marter thought. Next to the picture was a newer looking graduation picture of a teen aged girl. Van Marter guessed it must be the same daughter, now almost grown. Maybe MacKensie had a softer side after all.

On the other side of the desk, he saw MacKensie's pipe rack with three gnarled briar pipes in it. Next to the rack was a wrinkled pouch of pipe tobacco. The pipes were obviously well used, but in the two weeks he had been with MacKensie, Van Marter couldn't recall ever seeing him smoke one. Strange. Then he noticed a round brass paperweight almost buried in another corner. He picked it up and saw it was inscribed with an anchor underneath a crown. Beneath that, script lettering read:

To Lt Andre M. MacKensie, RCNR
From the Officers and Men of HMCS Oshawa
November 15, 1940.

"So he was in the Canadian Navy until last year," Van Marter said to himself. "I wonder why he was discharged? Probably something to do with that limp I noticed. Well, to hell with this; if I look around much more, I'll be able to recite his biography." Van Marter decided to direct his attentions elsewhere.

He looked around him in the office and watched the bustling activity. He had been surprised to notice that the RCMP did a lot of domestic surveillance and security. They seemed to think everybody was a Nazi spy. Of course there was a lot of spy activity in the states and America wasn't even at war.

He looked at the tall windows set in the stone walls and wondered how they managed to heat the place in the brutal Canadian winters. He shivered involuntarily, grateful he wouldn't be around to find out.

"Oh, well," he mumbled aloud. "I'll soon be back home. Maybe I'll call Mary Ellen up and ask her out. I'm sure she didn't mean it when she told me she hoped my plane crashed. She always was a great kidder."

Mary Ellen Heaver worked at the New York office and had gone out with Van Marter several times. The last time they had been together had not gone well. They had argued about President Roosevelt, who Mary Ellen admired. Van Marter scoffed and said that what the country really needed was a good engineer or scientist as president. After this discussion escalated somewhat, she had told him that arrogance and pig headedness were obviously his *Sine qua non* and that she didn't care to see him again in this world or the next. (He really wished she would stop reading those P.G. Wodehouse novels.) Still, Van Marter was convinced she was joking. He sat up and reached for the address book he kept in an inside pocket so it didn't affect the line of his suit. Mr Hoover was very big on his agents looking sharp. He flipped through the pages until he found the number he was looking for.

"Ah, here it is; Mary Ellen Heaver; Forest 3094. Maybe I'll give her a call. I'll just turn on the old charm and all will be forgotten."

He looked around and saw no sign of MacKensie returning, so he shrugged and reached for the phone on the desk. Before Van Marter could pick it up, however, the phone rang loudly, shaking him out of his daydream. Reluctantly, he answered.

"Hello; Inspector MacKensie's desk."

"Tom, is that you?" said the gruff and familiar voice of Ted Winters, Van Marter's boss at the FBI.

"Ted? Holy cow, it's good to talk to somebody who doesn't end every sentence with 'eh?'. I can't wait to get back. How did you know I was at this phone?"

"We're the FBI; remember?" Winters replied. "If we can't find our own agents, we're in trouble. But I have a reason for tracking you down. I've got a new assignment for you."

"Great; it's about time," Van Marter replied enthusiastically. "This MacKensie guy is driving me nuts. You can't teach someone like him anything. Would you believe that just yesterday…"

"These orders come from the top," Winters interrupted. "and that's all I can say about it, so listen carefully. You're not coming back just yet. You are to stay in Ottawa and assist the Canadian government with an important investigation."

Van Marter's heart sank. "Stay in Canada? Aw, wait a minute, Ted. Show some compassion for a poor traveler. If I don't get away from here soon…."

"This is big, Tom, really big," Winters continued. "I can't say any more. You are to be temporarily attached to the Royal Canadian Mounted Police on a special assignment.

Van Marter groaned. "Oh no. Anything but that. Look Ted, if I spend any more time with these guys I'll wind up wearing a red coat and drinking Molson's."

"Do you know where Commissioner Wood's Office is?"

"Uh…sure, I know where it is, I think. But…."

"Good," said Winters. "Go there now; they're waiting for you. Call me when you can. I expect you to do us proud on this assignment, Tom. I doubt that you'll ever get a more important one. Good luck."

Van Marter heard a click and the line went dead.

What was going on?

Van Marter had been past the Commissioner's office several times, but had never been inside. As he approached, a crisp looking secretary smiled and motioned him inside. She had obviously been expecting him.

He stepped into a large, high ceilinged room with rich dark oak paneling, leaded windows, and long green velvet draperies. On the far wall was a large carved wooden coat of arms of the Royal Canadian Mounted Police, complete with crown, buffalo head, and maple leaf wreath. Most of the room was taken up by a long polished oak conference table around which sat RCMP Commissioner Stuart Wood, Andre MacKensie, several other RCMP officers, and several civilians, including a very attractive young woman with ash blond hair. Their faces all had the grim look of an assembly of the bereaved. Whatever they were meeting about, Van Marter thought, it wasn't to throw a party. Something unpleasant had happened, or was about to.

The Commissioner looked up at him, and introduced everyone. Van Marter was still too confused to remember any of the names, but he heard the words 'Prisoner of War Service' when one man was introduced and 'Veteran's Guard of Canada' with another.

"Now then, Agent Van Marter," the superintendent was saying, "I'm glad Mr Hoover has acted so quickly to my request for your help. We have a bit of a situation here that requires all the apprehension expertise we can muster. Your being here among us at this time is fortuitous, and we may as well take advantage of it."

"I'll be glad to do anything I can, of course," Van Marter replied. He looked at MacKensie, but MacKensie was looking at some papers. The superintendent looked intently at Van Marter as if sizing him up, then began.

"It seems we have three fugitives we badly need to apprehend. We need to do it discretely and we need to do it quickly. The men are from one of our prisoner of war camps at Monteith, near Cochrane, in the northeastern part of Ontario." He indicated a point on a map that was spread out on the table.

"The three men who broke out are captured German U-boat sailors; one officer and two seamen. Now, ordinarily this would be a local matter; escapes are usually impromptu affairs. Escapees are generally caught within a few hours when they stumble into local police or are seen trying to hitch hike or sneak onto a train. We have reason to believe, however, that this escape is well planned and serious. You see, these men have information that must not get back to Germany; information that could have a profound effect on the outcome of the war, so their swift and quiet recapture is vital. Inspector MacKensie will be in charge of the search for these men and you will assist him."

Van Marter started and looked at MacKensie again. MacKensie was still silent but was looking at him for his reaction. The others at the table were looking on with interest.

"Now, if they're really serious about returning to Germany," the Commissioner continued, "they will most likely try to get to the United States. As an officially neutral nation, your country has fewer security measures and restrictions on travel. The closest crossing point by land is here." He indicated a point to the left of the camp.

"This is Sault Ste Marie, or the Soo as we call it. It's about 300 miles to the southwest from the camp. The next closest is south through Toronto and on to Buffalo, New York, or possibly Detroit. That's about 360 miles. We've alerted border crossing personnel at those locations and are setting up check points along the roads leading away from the camp, but at the moment, we have no idea where our escapees are or how they are traveling."

Van Marter looked at the map and did some quick calculation in his head. It was a little past 9:00. If the prisoners escaped just after 4:30, they had been running for over four hours. If they had somehow obtained a vehicle, they could possibly have covered maybe 100-150 miles, halfway to the United States.

"Miss Hastings here will be your contact at RCMP Headquarters," the Commissioner continued. He indicated the attractive woman Van Marter had noticed earlier. She nodded slightly and Van Marter noticed she had a marked resemblance to a movie actress whose name he couldn't quite remember..

"She can help you coordinate searches, obtain information, make transportation arrangements or anything else you may need."

Van Marter was still looking at Miss Hastings and wondering if she was as efficient as she was attractive. She returned his glance but her eyes revealed nothing.

"Well, that is all, I think. Inspector MacKensie has been briefed and he'll fill you in on the details." The Commissioner leaned slightly foreword in his cushioned seat. His gray moustache seemed to bristle.

"I cannot overemphasize the vital importance of apprehending these men before any damage is done. They must not be allowed to escape, and they must not be allowed to contact anyone who would relay their information to Germany. To further assure secrecy, the situation must be kept from the public, so you will have to move in a quiet fashion. Your presence, Agent Van Marter, will not only be helpful in its own right, but will enable you and Inspector MacKensie to claim you are on a training exercise if any outsider gets too curious. You will be provided with coded clearance authorizations that will enable you to use any transport, personnel, or facilities that you may need. Miss Hastings can make the necessary arrangements very quickly. Good luck."

A few minutes later, Van Marter and MacKensie were back in MacKensie's office. Van Marter was still overwhelmed and confused, but had recovered enough to begin asking questions as MacKensie unfolded several maps of Ontario and Quebec.

"Andre, will you tell me what is going on? This is the most…" Just then, Donna Hastings walked in with a clipboard. Van Marter noticed how tall she was. She had a finely featured face and blue eyes under her thick ash blond hair. Van Marter had once walked into a telephone pole while looking at a passing woman in Washington who looked very similar. Under any other circumstances he would have tried to ingratiate himself with her, but he was still trying to organize his thoughts.

"I expect you'll be wanting to go to the camp and interview the other prisoners," she said. It was less a question than a statement.

"Oh, yes Donna," said MacKensie without looking up. "And I'll need to talk to the local RCMP and OPP as well."

She nodded. "I have their names here. I've arranged for a pilot and plane on loan from the Service Flying Training School. The plane will be ready at the RCAF Station, Rockliffe to take you to Cochrane in fifteen minutes. The pilot and plane will be for your exclusive use and will remain at your disposal as long as necessary. The pilot's name is McLaughlin, one of the instructors. Also, I've contacted the Department of National Defense for any information or dossiers they have on the escapees. I should have it by the time you get to Cochrane. Oh, and I've made a sketch of where check points and roadblocks have been set up."

Van Marter finally recovered somewhat, reassured by this efficiency.

"Uh, Miss Hastings," he began.

"Donna," she corrected him. "We will be depending on each other too much for formalities."

"Yes, of course. I don't think we've met before. I seem to remember Andre mentioning you this last week, but this is the first I've seen you." He extended his hand and smiled.

She shifted the clipboard to her other hand and he noticed there was no wedding ring, a good sign. He thought he had heard the commissioner call her Miss.

"Actually we just met in the commissioner's office," she said with a slight smile. "I've been on leave; this is my first day back." Then, just as abruptly, she was back to the matter at hand.

"I'm having them bring a car around, Andre," she said. "The border patrols and customs posts at Sault Ste Marie and Niagara Falls have been alerted and told to inform this office of any developments. Oh, and I'll call your wife and tell her you're going out of town for a few days."

"Donna, how about calling my wife and telling her what's going on?" MacKensie had been pouring over the maps and wasn't fully paying attention. "Dinner will have to wait."

"Why didn't I think of that?" she said dryly. Then turned to Van Marter. "You've got to get going. You've got a plane to catch."

Van Marter nodded. "Among other things."

She looked at him with pale blue eyes that seemed to sparkle and placed her hand lightly on his forearm.

"Tom, this is important. You have to capture these men. You simply have to. A great deal depends on it. Do you understand?"

"Well, to tell you the truth….no. I can't figure out how a couple of minor league fugitives can possibly be so important."

"At this point, you'll simply have to take our word for it. Just remember one thing; they have to be recaptured. The consequences if they aren't could be catastrophic. Now get going."

Van Marter looked around uncertainly, "Uh…Donna. May I ask you something in private?"

"As long as it's short."

He took her to the other side of a partition while MacKensie continued to pour over the maps.

"Look," he said. "If this job is so important, isn't there someone else besides Andre you could put in charge? I mean, maybe someone younger and more open to new ideas would be better. Do you really think he's up to it?"

She looked at him coldly. "An FBI agent shouldn't be taken in by appearances, Tom. Don't let Andre fool you; he's the best we've got. He once found an escaped convict who had had reconstructive surgery and was hiding out on an island in Hudson Bay. If we asked him to, he could probably find the Holy Grail. I can assure you that the biggest problem you're likely to have with Inspector MacKensie is keeping up with him. Any more questions?"

"I guess not," Van Marter replied, embarrassed. "Sorry."

After some effort, Van Marter got MacKensie to bundle up his maps and got him into a grey car that headed off to the Rockcliffe Field with MacKensie driving.

"All right, Andre, now will you tell me what's going on?"

MacKensie grinned. "Geez, Tom, if you target those escaped Jerries as fast as you targeted Donna Hastings we've got nothing to worry about, eh? What, are you in heat or something?"

"If I am, you should be grateful. This country can use all the heat it can get. Isn't she the one you've been bragging about?"

"That's right. Two years ago she was a secretary, and now she's the best search coordinator I've ever seen, male or female. She could even keep the FBI straight."

"How encouraging. But what about this assignment?"

"What about it?"

"Look, I'm dragooned into a hunt for three miserable prisoners who are probably lost in the woods somewhere at this very moment, and haven't a hope of even getting to a town, let alone Germany. I'm apparently under direct orders from Mr Hoover or possibly Mr Roosevelt himself. These people we're looking for must be incredibly important to warrant that kind of attention."

"Well, you heard the commissioner say they had vital information," MacKensie said in a noncommital way.

Van Marter frowned. "One U-boat officer and two sailors have somehow obtained vital information about a war in Europe while in a prison camp in the frozen north of Canada? Come on, Andre; I didn't just fall off of the cabbage truck."

"The what?"

"But even if by some miracle that's true, why isn't there a nationwide manhunt going on? If these guys are that important, there should be roadblocks everywhere, wanted posters, and a nationwide alert. There should be notices on every street corner and radio announcements. Yet the commissioner says we have to work 'quietly' and the public isn't to know. Now what gives? Do you want these birds or not?"

MacKensie smiled and nodded. "I told them you'd never buy the story, but they said you weren't to know unless absolutely necessary."

"Andre, it IS absolutely necessary. If you think I'm going to be a big help when I know important information is being withheld, you know very little about human nature and even less about Tom Van Marter. As far as I'm concerned. the only thing worse than my being here is being here and being kept in the dark. Now spill it; what gives?"

"All right; all right. Don't get your knickers in a twist."

"My what?"

MacKensie passed the gothic stone towers of the houses of parliament with their green copper roofs gleaming somewhat dully in the sun and crossed the Rideau Canal by the Chateau Laurier Hotel. The day was warm without a cloud in the sky.

"Actually," he began, "what you were told was quite true as far as it went, but as you noticed, it didn't explain the curious combination of urgency and secrecy this job entails, eh? Or the real reason these guys broke out." MacKensie pronounced "out " as "oat".

They were almost to the airport now. Wartime traffic was thin, mostly consisting of official vehicles, army trucks, civilians on bicycle, and several horse drawn carts, a result of gasoline rationing.

MacKensie spoke matter-of-factly. "The problem is, these men are not supposed to exist."

"What?"

"The military men in this particular prison camp are from the same German U-boat, the U-110. It was captured back in May; only the Germans don't know it was captured; they think it was sunk with all hands, and that's just what we want them to think."

"But why?"

"I'm sure you're aware of the shipping convoys carrying war supplies to England and the U-boats that try to sink them."

"Yes, and the U-boats are winning."

"So far. Anyway, the U-110 had attacked a convoy and sunk two ships, but the captain, a man named Fritz-Julius Lemp, kept his periscope up a little too long and was spotted. The bastard probably wanted to admire his handiwork. Anyway, three British destroyers spotted him and depth charged the living hell out of him until the U-110 was forced to the surface. The captain of one British ship, the HMS BULLDOG, was so mad he attempted to ram the sub as it sat on the surface. Well, this apparently spooked the Krauts so much they jumped overboard before anyone could set the scuttling charges to sink the sub, which is their standard procedure in such situations. The BULLDOG veered off at the last second and the sub was captured, along with the surviving crewmen. But here we are at Rockliffe, and we've got to find our ride. I'll tell you the rest later."

-4-

They had arrived at the Royal Canadian Air Force Station, Rockliffe, which turned out to be a medium sized airport just a few miles out of Ottawa. Rockliffe had a modest control tower, a scattering of hangers, and several rows of olive colored military airplanes. MacKensie pulled up onto a side area of the tarmac in front of a hanger. A small wooden sign in the shape of a wing announced it was the home of the 12th Communications Unit, RCAF. Several assorted military airplanes marked with the distinctive circular insignia of the Royal Canadian Air Force were parked nearby.

"I always wondered why the Canadians and the Brits use that insignia on their airplanes," said Van Marter, "it looks like a target. Hey, is that a Spitfire? I've heard about them."

"No, that's a Hurricane," said MacKensie. "The Spitfire gets all the publicity, but the Hurricane is the fighter that does most of the work over England these days. The bomber next to it's a Bollingbroke, made right here in Canada, and the even bigger bomber next to that is a new type called a Lancaster."

"A Lancaster," Van Marter said with awe. "I read about them in Popular Mechanics. I've got a subscription. The Lancaster's got the highest altitude and highest bomb load of any bomber built."

"I'm not surprised," said MacKensie.

"About the bomb load?"

"No. I'm not surprised you have a subscription to Popular Mechanics."

"Well, maybe up here I should read the Moose Antler Monthly. So which one of these planes is ours?"

"That one, I expect," said MacKensie, pointing to a small two engine plane that had been hidden behind the Lancaster. "The yellow one."

"Yellow?" Van Marter said, amazed. "I thought we were supposed to be inconspicuous."

"It's a trainer," MacKensie replied. "Under the British Commonwealth Air Training Plan, allied aircrew are trained all over Canada. Yellow is the standard color for the airplanes. No one will give it a second look, believe me."

They got out of the car walked towards the plane. It wasn't a very big airplane, and Van Marter had never been partial to flying. He regarded the plane warily, and was about to ask if there wasn't a train they could take instead when the pilot appeared. He was a thin, weathered looking, middle aged man in a battered flying jacket, and he was walking out from behind a wing wiping his hands on an oily rag. Van Marter wondered what he had been working on and if he had fixed it, but wasn't sure he really wanted to know.

"Howdy do. Name's Rags McLaughlin. They said I was to take you boys to Cochrane and to be at your disposal as long as you wanted." Rags had a shaggy red moustache and a prominent nose.

"Glad to meet you," said MacKensie, extending his hand. "You sound like a bayman from the rock."

Rags nodded. "That's right; from the outport of Argentia Bay, Newfoundland. I guess you could tell by the fact that I don't have an accent."

"I know," said MacKensie. "People from Newfoundland don't have accents; it's just that everyone else does, eh?" MacKensie pronounced Newfoundland with the accent on the last syllable.

"Speaking of strange accents," MacKensie continued, "this confused looking gentleman is Agent Tom Van Marter from the American FBI."

Rags nodded. "I met someone from the states once. He said 'yawl' all the time."

"Yawl?"

"Yeah. He'd say something like 'how are yawl?'"

"Oh," said Van Marter. "He was from the south."

"Well sure he was. Didn't I say he was from the states?"

"Uh…"

Rags looked up and squinted at the sky. "Well, it looks like we got some severe clear up there, so let's see if we can get this old girl up off the tarmac and start boring some holes in the sky."

"Uh…Just what kind of an airplane is this?" asked Van Marter nervously. The plane seemed small and fragile to him.

"It's an Annie," Rags replied. "An Avro Anson Mark II. It's made by the same folks who make the big Lancaster bomber."

"Out of the leftovers, no doubt," muttered Van Marter.

After stowing some gear, they climbed in the tiny plane and made themselves as comfortable as possible. The seats were small and cramped and the seatbelts had to be dug out from beneath the seat cushions.

"So," said Van Marter, "I suppose Rags is short for Raglan or something?"

"Well, no," said the pilot, checking out the controls and preparing to start the engines. "My proper name is Reginald. I learned to fly in the Great War in 1918, but the war ended before I got in it. Afterwards, I was a barnstormer, then I joined the RCAF in '39. Anyway, back in my barnstorming days we flew biplanes with fabric covering as the skin. I flew an old Curtis Jenny and I flew it so hard I usually came back with patches of fabric missing or ripped and trailing behind. They used to say 'Here comes Rags McLaughlin.' and the name stuck."

"Oh, great," mumbled Van Marter. "Just great."

"So now I teach new pilots. Of course, it's just temporary until they come to their senses and send me over to a combat squadron. Then I can teach the Jerries a thing or two."

"All right," said MacKensie. "Let's shove off, eh?"

"Roger that," said Rags, reaching for a control, now let's see if we can fire up them 'Shakin' Jakes'".

"My God, is he referring to the engines?" asked Van Marter.

As if in answer to Van Marter's question, the twin Jacobs engines came to life with a series of explosions and a teeth rattling tremor that threatened to shake the airplane to pieces. From his cramped seat, Van Marter had a better view than he wanted of the smoke and flame belching from the exhaust.

Rags revved up the engines with a roar that was deafening. A ground crewman pulled out the chocks and the plane taxied the short distance to the end of the runway. After a quick take off, the yellow Anson climbed steeply and banked towards the northwest.

"We should be there in about an hour and a half and I'll tell you the rest," MacKensie shouted above the drone of the engines. "Meanwhile, got any ideas?"

Van Marter was anxious to hear the rest of the story of this unusual mission, and to take his mind off the flying, so he forced himself to look at a map that was only partly unfolded in the claustrophobic interior of the plane. He saw Cochrane and the surrounding country and made some mental calculations.

"The Commissioner said the escape was between 4:30 and 6:00 this morning," Van Marter said. "How do we know that?"

"The camp guards did an unscheduled bedcheck at 4:30 and everyone was present and accounted for, but at wake up time at 6:00, three men were gone," was the reply. MacKensie looked at his watch. "It's about 9:35 now."

Van Marter nodded. "About four hours head start. Are the three traveling together or did they split up?"

"We don't know yet. There have been no sightings."

"Are they on foot?"

"We think they left on foot, but they could have stolen a car or hitch-hiked since then."

"So we have no idea which direction they went or how they're traveling?"

"Not at the moment."

"Great," said Van Marter sarcastically. "Four hours head start; possibly in a vehicle; no clue which direction they went or even if they're together. Why don't we just ask Hitler to tell us when they arrive in Germany? It'll save a lot of time."

"I thought you G-Men thrived on challenges."

Van Marter groaned and shook his head. He couldn't believe his bad luck; flying to some god-forsaken chunk of Canadian tundra in a rattling airborne death trap with a half crazy Canuck whose only consistent talent seemed to be aggravation. And for what? Some escaped prisoners of war who were probably just lost in the woods somewhere. Well, he'd give it his best; maybe show MacKensie and his red coated cohorts what a little FBI logical thinking could do.

"Well, ordinarily, I'd recommend cordoning off the area to contain them, setting up roadblocks at key places, alerting the local police, and alerting the public as well. Then I'd do a saturation search of the cordoned area with search teams and bloodhounds."

MacKensie nodded. "I'd do the same, but the trouble is they've got too much of a head start for a saturation search with bloodhounds; the area's gotten too big. And we can't alert the public because of the need for secrecy, eh? We've got to out think them."

Van Marter looked grim. "All right, let's see, has it rained in the area recently?"

"No. It's been a dry summer. Fritz won't leave many tracks if that's what you're thinking."

Van Marter looked at the map again. "I assume Donna alerted the police in these two nearby towns?"

"You can bet on it. So did the camp."

"What's the terrain like?"

"Mostly farms with a few patches of woods. The ground is rolling and hilly in some places with a number of streams and the Abitibi River to the east and the Mattagami River to the west, but nothing that would be a serious barrier this time of year."

Van Marter looked up from the map and let out a long breath.

"All right, here's how I see it. The escapees have four hours head start, maybe three hours were in darkness. If they were on foot, they could have made, oh, ten miles."

"Ten miles?" said MacKensie.

"Don't forget, they were in the dark in a rural area. If they stuck to the road, they'd be unlikely to either get lost or run into prying eyes so they could concentrate on covering distance. And if a vehicle did come along, they would have plenty of warning from the approaching headlights."

"Yes," MacKensie nodded. "Plus they'd be fresh and have the adrenalin pumping."

"Right, but once the sun comes up, they'll slow down considerably. They'll be tired and they'll have to avoid being seen. That means travel through the woods. I'd estimate they haven't gone more than maybe two miles more since sunup. So we've got a circle with a 10 mile radius to search. That's over 300 square miles."

"Wait a minute, it's not a circle because the road only goes north and south from the camp. They wouldn't go north."

"Why not? Do they know where they are?"

"We try not to tell them, but between natural signs, loose conversation from the guards and the like, we have to assume they at least know that they have to go south."

"Yes, I suppose that's true," Van Marter admitted. "But if they got hold of a vehicle, they could be over 100 miles away by now."

"Well, according to this sketch Donna made, roadblocks were set up at 0630 at a distance of 20 and 50 miles in each direction, so even if they got a vehicle, they should get nabbed."

Van Marter looked at his watch and did some quick calculation. "Based on what we know, they should have been intercepted an hour ago, but they haven't been. The question is why not?"

MacKensie and Van Marter fell silent as they looked down on the countryside below. They both were suddenly aware of just how big and empty it really was.

*   *   *

The landing strip at Cochrane was rough and Rags brought the Annie down in a series of bone jarring bounces that had Van Marter digging holes in the armrests with his fingernails. Rags was only concerned with his lack of form.

"I don't usually do those crow hopper landings," Rags said with distaste as the plane finally set down. "I guess I've been spoiled landing on tarmac so much. I got to remember to come in slower on these unpaved strips."

The plane finally came to a halt in a cloud of swirling dust near a small terminal building. Two Hurricane fighters were parked nearby, part of a small air wing stationed there. As they unfolded themselves from the plane and felt feeling return to their legs once again, Van Marter and MacKensie saw two Canadian army men standing by a waiting automobile.

"Good morning," said the shorter of the two. "Major Ian Reynolds of Camp Q. This is Sergeant Henderson."

"Pleased to meet you. I'm Inspector MacKensie of the RCMP and this is Agent Van Marter of the American FBI."

"A Yank?" the Sergeant said aloud, then blushed. "Oh, sorry. It's just that I didn't know the Americans were involved in this war; not formerly at least."

"That's all right, sergeant," Van Marter laughed. "I didn't think so either. I guess we both got a rude awakening."

"Yes, well…Your Miss Hastings asked us to meet you," said Reynolds. "She said it would save time."

"Just so," said MacKensie. "And time is in rather short supply at the moment, eh? Let's go." He turned towards the airplane as he got in the car. Rags was busy poking at something under the cowling of the port engine.

"There's a restaurant next door," MacKensie shouted at him. "We'll contact you there when we need to go somewhere else."

Rags waved and nodded, but didn't turn around as the car started down the road.

"The three men who escaped were all members of the same crew," Reynolds was saying, settling back in his seat.

"We have the three names, Major," said MacKensie abruptly, "the question is, are you certain they're the ones who really escaped? Sometimes they'll have someone else substitute for the escapees at roll calls so the camp guards will get the identities of the escapees wrong and circulate inaccurate descriptions."

"I'm aware of that trick, Inspector," said Reynolds, "but these three are well known to us. There was no substitution. Leutnant Gregor Meinhoff is the obvious leader. We've been keeping an eye on that one, I can tell you. Anyway, Sergeant Henderson noted the men missing at morning bed check at 0600. The men were all present at the previous bed check at 0430, so they made their break some time after that. They apparently escaped through a cut wire on the north side of the fence. No one has reported seeing them yet, but roadblocks have been set up."

Van Marter frowned. "Did you say the north side?"

Reynolds nodded.

"I suppose we would have to assume that this Meinhoff is in charge," said MacKensie, shifting the subject. "He's the only officer in the group. You said you've had an eye on him for a while; why is that?"

"He's a Nazi for one thing."

"I thought they were all Nazis," said Van Marter.

"Not really. A lot of them are practically kids. They're patriotic and loyal to their comrades. That means loyalty to Hitler as well since he's the boss, but they're not party members. But others are more dedicated to the Nazi ideology and they keep the rest in line."

"Keep them in line?" asked Van Marter. "You mean they're superior in rank?"

"Not necessarily. The more fanatic ones sometimes form an enforcement organization. They call it the *Lagergestapo*. Ostensibly, its purpose is to prevent collaboration, but in fact, it serves as a Nazi secret police. Several prisoners have been murdered in other camps for some party infraction or other. The British try to segregate prisoners by how Nazi they are to prevent such things."

MacKensie nodded. "The Heinies think they're winning the war so they have arrogance to spare. And I'll tell you something else; the U-boat Krauts are the worst of the lot."

There seemed to be no appropriate reply to this, so Van Marter addressed Reynolds. "Have you questioned the other prisoners?"

"We talked to the two remaining officers, Oberleutnant Strauss and Fahnrich Kolza," said Reynolds. "They admit to knowing the attempt would be made, soldier's duty and all of that, but both of them claim they didn't know the plans for security reasons. They're lying through their teeth, of course."

"Probably," said MacKensie, "but by now I imagine the plans have changed considerably anyway. Have you or any of your men said anything that would have helped them?"

Reynolds looked insulted. "Absolutely not. If anything, we've discouraged them by pointing out how far they were from home."

"How about documents?" asked Van Marter. "Would they need a driver's license, I.D. card or anything like that?"

"There's a national I.D. card the government started using last year," said MacKensie, "but it's fairly easy to forge and I expect they've got them already."

"But they've never seen one," the sergeant protested. "How on earth…"

"Yes, how would they forge something they haven't seen?" said Van Marter.

"Oh, it's really quite simple," MacKensie said matter-of-factly. "They create a scuffle with a few guards and steal someone's billfold, eh? Then they can copy whatever cards he carries."

"Impossible," Reynolds shook his head emphatically. "No one has reported a billfold missing."

"I'm not surprised," said MacKensie calmly. "Any guard would be reluctant to report such carelessness, especially when he isn't certain if the prisoners took it or it was simply mislaid, eh? After a day or two, when the copies have been made, the prisoners plant the billfold in some corner of the yard. The guard finds it and is relieved it wasn't stolen after all. So the prisoners get the documents they need and the camp guards are none the wiser. Simple, eh?"

Major Reynolds and Sergeant Henderson looked at each other uncertainly, remembering the fight at the soccer match. Van Marter shook his head in grudging admiration. Maybe Andre MacKensie knew a thing or two after all.

Van Marter suddenly snapped his fingers. "How about rationing? Do you have to use ration books?"

"Do we ever," said Henderson. "I know men what would sell their soul for some sugar."

MacKensie nodded. "Good point. Ration stamps aren't usually kept with the billfold. The Germans are going to have a time trying to buy anything."

"Of course, they could just steal what they need." said Van Marter. "After all, that's how they would get money in the first place."

"Yes, well, here we are at the camp," said Reynolds, indicating the barbed wire enclosure a hundred yards ahead. Behind the gate stretched three long lines of tarpaper covered barracks, like large black bricks lined up in the sun. On the north side of the enclosure, a railroad ran east and west about a half mile or more away.

"How do you know they didn't just jump a train?" asked MacKensie. "It sure looks convenient."

"The railroad people are pretty cautious coming past here," said Reynolds. "Besides, the trains along this run are infrequent, about two a day and one at night. A prisoner would have a long wait in full view of the camp and the town if he tried to jump that train. Also, the run is straight, so the trains only slow down at the station. Anyone trying to jump on a straightaway stands a good chance of losing an arm or a leg."

MacKensie frowned at the railroad bridge for a few seconds, then looked back over the camp. "No, I don't think they took that train," he said.

They were almost at the gate now. The place smelled of cooking with a faint trace of hot tar. In the enclosures, prisoners played soccer, tended gardens, sat, strolled, or simply milled about. Many of the men turned to look at the car, grateful for a diversion from the daily monotony.

"The Germans are in this part of the enclosure. We have 1531 internees at the moment, including the U-boat crew," said Reynolds, motioning towards the buildings. About 1,000 are Italian and German merchant seamen who were in Canadian or British ports when war was declared. The rest are civilian internees; mostly people of German, Japanese, or Italian ancestry who have been involved in questionable activities under the National Defense of Canada Act. You know, members of the German Bund, or the Japanese Black Dragon Society, or the Italian Sons of Italy. Some are actually refugees from Germany and Austria. The British thought they might be dangerous too close to London."

"What?" said Van Marter in an incredulous tone of voice. "Do you mean to say you can just throw Canadian citizens in a prison camp because of their ancestry and what clubs they belong to? Don't citizens have any rights?"

"Some of those people can be saboteurs, or even spies," said Reynolds, somewhat defensively. "A lot of them have ties to Italy and Germany. We have to think of the safety of the country. If Hitler wins this war, nobody will have any rights."

Van Marter shook his head in amazement. At least we'd never do that in the United States, he thought.

"The worst part," said Major Reynolds," is that this is the second escape in two months. I believe the first escape was to gain information."

MacKensie's eyebrows raised. "Really? We'll need to see a complete report of the first escape."

"Certainly. Well, where would you like to go first?" said Reynolds.

MacKensie looked at the towers along the surrounding road and the fences. Several German prisoners looked at them impassively and he felt his stomach tighten at the sight of them. In his time in the navy, he had never seen the face of the enemy before, but he had seen his handiwork too many times. Now he looked at the faces on the other side of the wire. Strange, he thought, change the uniforms, and no one could tell them from Canadians.

"Inspector?" Reynolds repeated. "Where would you like to go?"

"Oh,….er, does that road go all around the camp?"

"The Burma Road? Yes, clear around."

"Then let's take a drive around. Then we'll take a look at the point the escape was made; from the outside if you would."

The car turned and drove along the perimeter road outside the wire. After going around the camp, they stopped near a corner by a guard tower.

"Here's the spot," said Reynolds. "We've repaired the wire, but you can see how it was cut."

MacKensie and Van Marter squatted down by the wire and inspected the strand that had been cut then later repaired. MacKensie walked slowly around the site, then returned.

"They didn't leave this way," he announced.

"What?" said Reynolds. "But they cut the wire and…"

"There is a wide band of dry grass about twenty yards away. It's impossible to avoid. Not a single blade is broken or even bent."

"And look at this," said Van Marter. Near the end of the strand that was cut is a small piece of twine. "It broke, but only after it had been cut part way through."

MacKensie looked at the twine. "It looks like they cut this in advance, probably during the same diversion in which they obtained a billfold. They cut the wire, then replaced it, but put the twine on so they could pull the wire loose again, then they pull until the twine breaks and reel in the evidence. Very nice indeed."

Reynolds looked at the small piece of twine left on the wire. "But why?"

"I don't know yet," said MacKensie. "Probably a diversion to make us think they went some other way than they did."

"They certainly went to a lot of trouble," said Reynolds, shaking his head.

"That they did," replied MacKensie, "and so far it seems to be paying off for them.

-5-

As MacKensie, Major Reynolds, and Van Marter continued to work their way around the perimeter fence, a crowd of German prisoners gathered to watch the show. A line of their smug faces smiled back insolently through the wire.

"Hey Mr policeman," came a heavily accented voice from the other side of the wire. "Did you lose something?"

Van Marter glared at the smirking Germans, but MacKensie ignored them. He stared at the grass for a few more moments then turned to Reynolds. "I'd like to walk around the southern part of the wire before we go inside."

"So you noticed the point about the escape on the north side too?" asked Van Marter as they walked towards the south side of the enclosure.

"Of course," said MacKensie quietly. "They wanted us to think they jumped that nearby train, eh? It was so plain even the FBI could see it."

"Not to mention the RCMP," retorted Van Marter. "I think they went from the south side and headed the same way once they were out."

MacKensie nodded. "I'd say that's.....wait a minute. What's that?"

MacKensie crouched by the fence and carefully took something from one of the barbs. He examined it carefully.

"Fresh wood shaving," he said. "Someone used something made of wood to pry these strands apart."

"And look at the ground," said Van Marter. "It's freshly scuffed. This is the way they came; heading south just as we thought."

"But how…" said Reynolds.

"Oh, I expect they made a wooden box of some sort," said MacKensie. "You'll probably find it in that patch of woods just south of here. The box would be open at each end. They just shoved it between the strands, forcing them apart, then crawled through the box, eh? Simple and easy."

Henderson suddenly remembered the wooden "planters" the prisoners had made last week.

"All right," said MacKensie. "They left heading south. Now that that's cleared up, let's go and see the scene of the crime."

Two guards opened the barbed wire gates to the prisoner's compound and led MacKensie and Van Marter inside. In spite of the relative spaciousness, they felt strangely claustrophobic. The prisoners mostly went about their leisurely business, but watched the newcomers warily, wondering who the rumpled older man and the stiff younger man could be. Several smirked and made remarks in German as they passed.

The yard was pretty much what they had expected, although with some surprising domestic touches, such as flower beds and vegetable gardens. Even here, the neatness and methodical care the Germans took was obvious. Flowers and vegetables stood in neat rows, segregated by variety and color, as if on parade. Van Marter could see MacKensie was also noting the neatness and orderliness of the gardens.

"An organized, hard working, and methodical people, eh?" MacKensie observed. "Whatever the plans for the escape are, I'll bet they were carefully planned and well thought out."

"They do seem to have a talent for organization," said Van Marter.

"I'm going to have a look in the barracks," said MacKensie. "Maybe we should split up and cover more ground, eh?"

"Sure, I'll see what I can out here," said Van Marter.

Van Marter went with a guard and strolled around the yard and behind the buildings. Prisoners looked at them curiously, but otherwise made no attempt to interfere. Van Marter looked at the prisoners with interest. The U-boat men were easy to spot. They wore the battered caps and short jackets of the Kriegsmarine and walked with a combination of surliness and cockiness. So these were the German submarine men he'd heard so much about. They looked ordinary, but until a few months ago they had been killers. How long would it be, he wondered, until men very much like these were at war with the United States?

As Van Marter walked in the yard with two guards, he still felt uneasy and uncertain, but was determined to attack the problem the systematic FBI way. Of course, his job would be easier if he knew just what he was looking for. He poked around the fence and in a few barracks without finding anything remarkable.

Finally, behind one of the barracks, he glimpsed a garden with a pile of freshly turned earth in one corner. He couldn't take his eyes off of it for some reason. The area looked wrong, somehow, and it bothered him. His grandmother had been an avid gardener, and he tried to remember what her gardens looked like. Suddenly, he realized what was wrong; weeding was not usually confined to a small area such as this. If they were weeding, they would have done the entire plot, not just a corner. Why did they stop there? He decided to investigate and began walking towards the garden.

"Good morning," came a voice from behind him. Van Marter turned and saw a short thin German Officer with owlish looking glasses and a big smile. "Are you an American, sir?

Van Marter saw the man had his hand extended. He took it warily. "Why do you ask?"

"I thought so. I heard one of the guards say you were. Americans are a wonderful people. When this war is over, I want to visit your country. I have always wanted to see Texas. Oh, I'm sorry. Where are my manners? My name is Kolza; Hans Kolza. I always am grateful for a chance to practice my English."

"Well, your English is very good. Maybe you can tell me about Leutnant Meinhoff and his friends?"

"Meinhoff?" Kolza said, looking puzzled. "Oh, he just wandered off somewhere. I wouldn't be surprised if he didn't show up in time for supper. But tell me about the United States. Do they really have cowboys there?"

Van Marter looked at him suspiciously. Something in this German's manner was a little too friendly; a little too familiar. He saw Kolza glance briefly behind him and he spun around in time to see two men frantically digging something out of the small garden plot he had been on his way to investigate.

"Corporal, stop those men!" he shouted. The corporal raised his rifle and the men stopped. They looked angry and frustrated. Van Marter turned back to Kolza.

"Well, Herr Kolza, your attempt at distraction almost worked. Just what was it you didn't want me to see?"

"It is merely a garden," Kolza said, shrugging innocently. "There was no need to chase those men away. Did you think they were digging a tunnel to Berlin, perhaps?" He gave a forced laugh.

"Well, let's see what's growing in that particular garden," said Van Marter, rubbing his hands together. "I have a feeling a little pruning is in order."

Van Marter squatted in the fresh earth and dug with a shovel he took from one of the prisoners. The shovel hit something hard.

*   *   *

In the U-boat barracks, MacKensie was examining the bunks, especially Meinhoff's. There was nothing about it that seemed any different; just a thin mattress over a metal frame. MacKensie had hoped for some clue that might have been left, but the bunk seemed like the rest. He had been through Meinhoff's locker and found nothing unusual, but as he ran his hand over the sheets then the pillow, he noticed something.

"Was Meinhoff losing his hair?"

Henderson was surprised by the question, but thought about it carefully. "I don't think so. His hair seemed rather thick, if anything."

MacKensie picked up the pillow. "Where did all these hairs come from then?"

Henderson looked at the pillow and saw five thick hairs on it.

"Well, I'll be damned. I never noticed that."

"So we have a young man with thick hair who somehow leaves a good bit of it on his pillow," said MacKensie, holding up a hair to the light.

"I don't understand. Where could they have come from?" said Henderson.

"From this," came a voice from the doorway. They turned and saw Van Marter standing there holding a carved wooden head, complete with human hair.

"The Germans had buried this in a garden in the back and were trying to dig it up before we found it. They probably planned to break it up after dark, but we got here too soon. There are two more just like it."

The heads were crude but probably very effective in a darkened barracks. Someone had carved several blocks of wood to look like human heads, smoothed them with soap, and pasted real hair on them.

"Not a bad job," said MacKensie, holding the still dirty head up to the window. "This explains the hairs on the pillow. These guys went to a lot of trouble. Where did they make these?"

"There's a shop area where prisoners can make shelves, birdhouses and the like," said Major Reynolds. "The idea was to keep them out of trouble."

"You may have to rethink that idea," said MacKensie. "That's no doubt where they made the box they used to force the wire apart as well. Doesn't anyone watch what they're making?"

Reynolds reddened somewhat. "We do spot checks, of course, but we're especially careful to see the tools are all turned in afterwards."

"So all the tools are present and accounted for, eh?" said MacKensie. "It's too bad we can't say the same for the bloody prisoners who were using them."

Reynolds looked resentfully at Sergeant Henderson.

"Can we see the shop?" asked Van Marter.

"Sure, it's right on the side of the compound," said Reynolds, whose face was now the color of a tomato. "But I don't understand what the heads were for?"

"Isn't it obvious?" said MacKensie. "The heads, along with a few pillows can make it look like someone is in bed when they aren't."

"Yes," said Reynolds scratching his head slowly, "I understand that, but then why did the Germans remove them? The escapees' beds were empty this morning. Once the heads have allowed the prisoners to escape and the escape is discovered, why go to so much trouble to hide them? What would the Germans have to gain?"

MacKensie and Van Marter looked at each other.

"Andre do you think…."

"When was the last roll call?" MacKensie asked Reynolds.

"2300…11 PM. After that was lights out and we went to random bed checks."

"Eleven…." MacKensie muttered. "Oh, jeez. Do you know what that means, Tom?"

"You bet I do," he replied. "The heads were used to fool the bed checks during the night and the heads were removed by reveille so that we'd think the escape wasn't until after the last bed check at 4:30."

Reynolds nodded. "Yes, that makes sense. But what does it mean?"

MacKensie threw the head on the bed in disgust. It bounced off and rolled grotesquely on the floor until it came to rest against the wall. The wooden face seemed to be watching them.

"It means our escapees have been gone five hours longer than we thought."

"Five hours," said Reynolds, finally realizing the deception. "But that means the roadblocks have all been placed too close to camp. If they had that much head start, they could easily have been past the road-blocks by the time they were set up. I'm going back to the office and arrange to have them set up further away."

Van Marter looked at the wooden head, then at MacKensie. "Well, we're off to a great start. So far it's Prisoners 3- Cops 0."

The wood shop was a fairly large shed near the washroom. No one was inside as the guard pushed open the door. A work bench and a store of scrap lumber stood on one side and a trash barrel made from an old oil drum on the other. Although uncomfortably warm, the place smelled pleasantly of freshly cut wood, paint and varnish. MacKensie and Van Marter stood in the doorway looking around before either of them crossed the threshold. They both noted that the position of the shed made it easy for a lookout to alert a woodworker that a guard was approaching. Van Marter's eyes lingered for a moment on the old band saw in the corner. A nice piece of machinery, he thought, and wondered what horsepower the motor was. Then he noticed a large trash barrel nearby. No doubt that was where the heads were hidden when a guard approached. He walked over to the trash barrel and was surprised to find it almost full of wood shavings. Someone had done a tremendous amount of work to make this escape succeed.

"Dump out the shavings, would you, sergeant?" said Van Marter.

Sergeant Henderson looked uncertainly at MacKensie and MacKensie nodded. Henderson turned the barrel upside down releas-ing a small avalanche of wood shavings onto the floor. Van Marter got on his knees and started rummaging through the pile with his hands.

"What's he doing?" Henderson whispered to MacKensie.

"Well, with the FBI it's hard to say for sure, but I expect he's looking for evidence of forged documents."

Van Marter nodded and kept looking.

"Documents in a wood shop?" said Henderson.

"Of course," said MacKensie. "When you manufacture documents you have bits of scrap paper left over, and it's too warm to burn them without arousing suspicion. Where better to get rid of them than a barrel of wood shavings?"

"Not bad, Andre," said Van Marter over his shoulder. "You sound like an FBI agent."

"Actually, I was thinking that you're starting to act like an RCMP inspector," he retorted.

Van Marter stopped suddenly. "Hold on a minute," he said, and produced a pair of rubber gloves. He put them on with loud snapping noises.

"What the hell…" said MacKensie.

"They're surgical gloves," said Van Marter, as if that explained everything.

"You're figuring on taking out someone's appendix, maybe?" said MacKensie in amazement.

"I'm avoiding contaminating evidence. Here, look at this, but don't smudge it." He handed a strip of card stock paper to MacKensie.

MacKensie examined the paper carefully, holding it by the edges and turning it over in his hand. "Yes, this looks like the remnants of a poster from the notice board. This would do nicely for forged documents. Too bad nothing is written here."

Van Marter continued sifting through the pile of wood shavings. "Here's another one….wait a minute; look at this." He held up two pieces of torn paper about an inch square.

"This looks like an early attempt at a National ID card that didn't look good enough. They tore it up and threw it in with the chips." Van Marter took out a small folding magnifying glass with a lens about the size of a nickel.

MacKensie raised his eyebrows. "Can't Mr. Hoover afford to give you a full size glass?"

"This is the kind surveyors use to read the vernier on a transit; it's compact and has high magnification."

"Plus it doesn't wrinkle your regulation FBI suit," said MacKensie. "You've got a regular crime lab in there, eh?"

Van Marter ignored him. "Now let's see."

"You can see why they threw this away," said MacKensie looking over his shoulder. "Look at the corner. They smudged the word 'National' and made a mess trying to correct it. It's too bad they didn't write a name in first. We'd know what alias is being used."

"Wait a minute, maybe they did." Van Marter took the scrap of paper to the light of the window and peered at it intently through his magnifying glass.

"Andre, look at this; to make this card they first carefully laid it out in light pencil then inked in the final version. Right here they had very lightly drawn the name that was going to be on the card in pencil, but they destroyed the card before they inked it."

MacKensie squinted through the glass. "Yes, I can see something, but it's faint and I can't make it out. It looks like they erased it."

"I think the first name starts with an F or an E and the last starts with a W, but I can't tell the rest. We need a modern crime lab like the Bureau has in D.C."

"All right," said MacKensie. "We'll send it to the RCMP lab in Ottawa. Maybe they can make it out."

Using the code he had been given to assure top priority, MacKensie arranged for the local fighter wing to fly the card scraps to Ottawa on their fastest plane. MacKensie then asked if a call could be placed to Ottawa. Reynolds said the call might take several minutes and he'd let them know as soon as it had gone through.

"Now we've got to let Donna know the I.D. card scraps are on their way. Let's go in the conference room and look at the maps while the call is being placed."

When MacKensie and Van Marter were alone in Reynolds' small conference room, they sat in two hard backed wooden chairs. MacKensie, to Van Marter's surprise, produced one of his briar pipes and lit it, causing a dense cloud of smoke to almost fill the room.

"What is that tobacco?" said Van Marter, coughing, "Old newspapers?"

"I dunno," MacKensie replied. "I get it from a tobacco shop in Ottawa. They just call it Blend 22. Too strong?"

Not only strong, but sickeningly sweet at the same time," said Van Marter, opening a window. "But how come I never saw you smoke during the last two weeks?"

"I only smoke when I need to do some heavy thinking. This is the first time I've needed to."

Van Marter nodded. "Oh, like Sherlock Holmes?"

"No, like Andre MacKensie. Now let's look at the report of the first escape."

After they read the report, they examined a map of the area, carefully measuring how far the escapees might have gotten if they had left five hours earlier than originally thought.

"You never finished telling me about the prisoners and why they're so important," said Van Marter as he marked a spot on the map.

"Well," MacKensie began, still examining the map, "as I was saying, when the U-boat had been forced to the surface, the British destroyer HMS BULLDOG was bearing down to ram so all the Heinies jumped overboard without having time to scuttle, but the BULLDOG's captain decided the sub would be worth more in one piece. So he pulled away, took the U-boat's crew on board, and sent over a party to see what they could find."

"And I take it they found something important?"

"Oh yes. They found a fully intact Enigma machine."

"A what?"

"It's no secret that the war isn't going well for England and the Commonwealth. Britain needs a staggering amount of imported food and material just to keep alive, and more to pursue the war. The only way to move that much tonnage is by ship, but the U-boats have been sinking ships bound for England at a phenomenal rate; 800,000 tons a month. Think of it; 800,000 tons of vital shipping that never gets there. They are actually sinking ships faster than they can be replaced. In short, they are winning the war."

Van Marter nodded. That much he knew. He also felt it was only a matter of time before the United States was dragged in also.

"One reason the U-boats are so deadly," MacKensie continued, "is the wolf pack tactic where the subs radio each other and gather to attack when one of them finds a convoy. They also keep track of each other's position. The whole thing is coordinated in their U-boat headquarters in Lorient on the coast of occupied France."

"All German radio transmissions are in a code we have not been able to break. If we knew their code, of course we would know where the subs were patrolling and we could avoid them, eh?"

"The encoding device is a machine called Enigma. It is about the size of a large typewriter and produces coded letters when plain language is typed in. The Kraut on the other end simply types in the coded letters he receives and out comes the message. The encoding is based on settings of three metal wheels within Enigma. Each wheel has the 26 letters of the alphabet around its circumference. By simply rotating the wheels to different positions, entirely new codes can be sent. The codes used on any given day are based on the three letters of the three wheel settings for that day. So you can see such a machine would be a great help in outwitting the U-boats. It could possibly reverse the course of the war."

"What a great gadget," said Van Marter, who had always appreciated gadgets, especially complicated and clever ones. "Three rotors with constantly changing settings. Let's see, the possible combinations would be about, uh, 26 raised to the third power…, about 17,000. And each combination sets up another code. Wow. No wonder it's so hard to break."

"Uh…right. Anyway, they found not just the Enigma itself, but the charts of the North Atlantic showing the grid system they use for positioning, and wheel settings for the next six months. With this information, we can read their communications, find out where the U-boats are stationed, and guide convoys to avoid them. The implications are staggering. Well, the British took the U-110 in tow and started for Liverpool, but they soon realized what they had. The U-110 was badly damaged and soon sunk, so they reported it lost with all hands. The captured crew was told the sub sank right away, and they were sent in secret to this camp."

"You mean nobody knows they're here?"

"And nobody must know. If Berlin finds out we have the Enigma and the wheel settings, they'll change them and we'll have nothing. As it is, this break is what we need to keep our heads above water until the Americans get in."

"The Americans?" said Van Marter. "But Roosevelt…"

"Roosevelt realizes you'll soon be at war on the side of the Allies. He knows that any world in which the Nazis are the winners will be intolerable. He's doing everything he can to help, but he has to respect the congress and public opinion. But believe me, sooner or later, something will happen to push you over the edge, eh? Meanwhile, the convoys have to reach England."

Van Marter frowned. "So you think the prisoners have figured this out and are trying to get word back to Germany?"

"Maybe not all of them, but we believe a few have, and we believe this breakout is the result. Just look at the evidence. The first escape attempt was a spur of the moment thing and the men were quickly caught, eh? But now, only a few weeks later, we have an orchestrated attempt involving teamwork, forgery, deception, and precise timing. On top of that, we have the escape led by an officer and the chief Nazi in the camp."

"I see what you mean," said Van Marter. "It's looks like something happened between the first attempt and the second to make the Germans more determined."

"Exactly. My nose tells me the Huns figured out what happened and are going to spill the beans." MacKensie was pacing the room, the smoke from his pipe trailing behind him. "Well, we're going to stop them, eh? Those bastards are going to get nabbed and we're the ones who are going to do it; you and me. Then we'll talk about improving the security so they'll rot here until that son of a bitch Hitler becomes a paperhanger again."

"Whew! We've certainly got some good incentive to catch these guys. Does Donna know all of this?"

"She's more aware than you know," said MacKensie gravely. "Her kid brother Dennis is in the 1st Ottawa Fusiliers. He just finished basic training and is due to ship out for England in two weeks. His chances of ending up in London and not on the bottom of the Atlantic will depend to a large extent on how quickly we can nab these jokers....or if."

-6-

Van Marter's mouth hung open for a moment. He was shocked to hear about Donna's brother. He hadn't really grasped what being at war meant to people. There must be thousands of stories like that, and a lot of them end in tragedy. Catching these escapees wasn't just an intellectual exercise any more: it was a matter of life or death.

"One more question," said Van Marter finally. "Whatever made the RCMP brass decide to ask for me?"

MacKensie looked at him blankly.

"I did."

"What?" Van Marter leaped to his feet. "You asked for me? But why? We've been bickering since I came here. We don't see eye to eye on anything. I try to do things scientifically and you're always talking about your damn nose!"

MacKensie smiled. "And my nose told me you'd come in handy. Don't look so surprised. You may have an unfortunate tendency to do everything in a ridiculously precise and orderly fashion, but so do the Krauts, eh? Maybe you can help guess what they're up to. Two heads are better than one; even when one of the heads is as hard as yours."

"I guess I'd be flattered if I didn't suspect you did it for spite," muttered Van Marter.

"Now as soon as we talk to Ottawa we've got to get cracking," MacKensie continued. "Our quarry is getting further away by the minute and we're five hours further behind than we thought we were. Are you ready to go?"

"Sure, but where?"

"To visit the escape route from the first breakout."

"To do what?"

"Excuse me, gentlemen. We've got Ottawa on the line."

MacKensie looked up at the face of Major Reynolds in the doorway. "Thank you Major. Why don't you do the honors Tom?"

Van Marter anxiously picked up the receiver. "Hello. Van Marter here."

"Good afternoon, Tom," came the voice of Donna Hastings. Van Marter found himself smiling foolishly.

"Hello Donna. How are you doing?"

There was the faintest pause on the other end of the line, then Donna Hastings got down to business. "The question is; how are you and Andre doing?"

"We haven't caught them yet, if that's what you mean. But we have found a couple of scraps of a phoney I.D. card they made. They're on the way to Headquarters now via Hurricane fighter. They should be at Rockliffe in a little over an hour. The name the Germans intended to fill out is in very light pencil. We figure the lab boys might be able to read it."

"I've seen them do it before," she replied. "I'll put them on alert and let you know as soon as they have something."

"Great," said Van Marter. "If we knew what alias they're using it could make things a lot easier."

"Of course," she replied. "That is, assuming we can read the name, and assuming they didn't use a different name when they made the final card."

"I hope not; we need a break."

"Since you left I have gotten dossiers of the three men who escaped. Two are young seamen; apparently nonpolitical and inexperienced. They might not even know the reason for the escape. The third one is the one you've got to look out for. Gregor Johann Meinhoff, Leutnant. The information we've got is what has been pieced together; Meinhoff himself is extremely tight lipped and non cooperative. He appears to have been the third watch officer on the sub, behind the captain and Oberleutnant Strauss. From his age and rank, we estimate he joined the Navy around 1939. From an offhand remark overheard by one of the German speaking guards, the camp intelligence officer found that Meinhoff spent a year in the United States as an exchange student somewhere in Pennsylvania. The FBI checked Pennsylvania colleges that had exchange programs between 1935 and 1939 and found that Meinhoff attended The University of Pennsylvania; electrical engineering. He got good grades, but was arrested twice for brawls arising from political arguments. From this we infer that he's a probably a dedicated Nazi. His father died in 1918, probably in the Great War. That might account for Meinhoff's political leanings. Meinhoff speaks passable French and fluent, unaccented English, and is familiar with American slang and customs. He is also reputed to be an experienced woodsman. In short, he seems to be a dedicated and dangerous foe with skills that will make him hard to catch."

"Then he must be the brains behind it, or at least the leader."

"That's what I think. At any rate, I've asked for major crime reports for the surrounding towns, in case they stole a car or broke into a shop for food or provisions."

"Good. But I've been thinking; how about minor crimes as well? You know, anything that seems out of place or unusual. Maybe they stole wash off a clothesline for a disguise or something. Who knows?"

"I'll get on it. We are also monitoring any radio signals, in case they get hold of a short wave and try to send a message out. Jamming gear is in place."

"All right. Any reports yet?"

"Not yet. Anything else to report?"

"Only confirmation of what we suspected. The break was well planned and involved. They even fooled everyone into thinking they left five hours later than they actually did. They must have wanted it badly."

"Five hours? Then that means…."

"We know. The roadblocks are being relocated."

"Good. Maybe we can get a jump ahead. How was your flight?"

Van Marter was grateful for this more personal note. "Scary. Rags McLaughlin thinks he's still a barnstormer. I was half expecting a few barrel rolls."

She laughed, a warm and happy sound. "He's a good pilot all the same. Most of these instructors are somewhat reckless, I'm afraid. They try to show off enough to get sent to combat duty."

"Great."

"Well, I'd better be going; I have to arrange for a car to pick up the evidence from the airport. Good bye Tom."

"Donna?"

"Yes, Tom?"

"We're going to get them. I promise you."

There was a pause, then she replied in a softer voice. "I know. Good luck."

Van Marter stood looking at the receiver even after the line had gone dead. Finally, MacKensie called from the doorway to say a car was waiting to take them along the first escape route. Van Marter replaced the phone and headed out the door.

*   *   *

The Germans could hardly believe their luck and how everything had gone according to plan so far. The escape had been nearly discovered, but had gone smoothly. The first few hours had been a blur of confused action and tension, but now they were at cruising speed and felt an exhilaration that was intoxicating. After the months of idleness in the camp, they were in action as a team once again and striking a blow for the fatherland behind enemy lines. No one had stopped them and now they knew no one would.

The old Nash they had stolen had performed flawlessly as they headed towards the point they had picked. As the miles of Canadian countryside rolled by, the U-boat men were struck by the vastness and peacefulness of the place. Gently rolling countryside seemed almost empty except for occasional small towns and neat painted farmhouses briefly glanced through passing foliage.

Seaman Theimann was at the wheel, and he was as excited and fascinated by the passing countryside as by the escape itself. Before joining the Kriegsmarine, he had seldom been outside the small town in Bavaria where he had been born. The air was warm and clear and there were only a few wisps of clouds in the sky. After being confined in the bowels of the U-110, then in the prison camp, he felt suddenly free and unrestrained. It was a great day to be alive. The first escape had been clumsy, a mere scouting expedition. But this effort was different. The planning had been meticulous and it showed. They had not seen a soldier or policeman of any kind since leaving the camp. They had also managed to completely elude the roadblocks by the simple expedient of being ahead of them before they were set up.

"How is our petrol?" A voice broke through Theimann's daydreaming, and he looked at the gage; a little under a quarter tank.

"We will need some more before too long," Theimann replied.

"I haven't seen any unattended autos we could siphon from. We may have to stop when we see a petrol station. We have about a hundred Canadian dollars, so we can afford it."

"What if we see a roadblock or a check point?"

"They should all be behind us, but if not, our orders are to avoid it if they don't see us. If they do see us, we'll have to try to bluff our way through with our forged documents."

"And if that doesn't work?"

"We still have a shotgun."

*   *   *

"And he was standing right about here when I saw him," said Corporal Ogleby of the Ontario Provincial Police. MacKensie and Van Marter had tracked the apparent route of the escape about seven miles from the camp south to where the first escapee had been recaptured. They were near the town of Val Gagne along the Old Mill Road where Corporal Ogleby had captured Seaman Theimann. The road was narrow here, with birch trees overhanging on both sides. A small stream ran alongside of the road and the sound of water gurgling around the weathered rocks was soothing.

"Yeah, he was sneaking along trying to get around the town before anybody saw him, eh? I pulled the car into the bushes here and waited for him to come around that bend. When he got close, I jumped out and asked him for identification. He didn't have any, plus he talked in a German accent, so I knew I had my man. He came peacefully enough. Anything else you want to see?"

MacKensie examined the area and followed the road back towards the camp for a half mile or so.

"How about the other one? Where was he recaptured?"

"Oh, we got him over to Fergusen's farm. Well, I guess it would be more accurate to say old man Fergusen got him, eh? Saw him in the field as he was leaving the house to go hunting birds. He does a lot of shooting to supplement the so called meat ration, you see. Anyway, old man Fergusen is just stepping out his door when he sees that other prisoner fellow standing there. He got the drop on him with his shotgun and that was that. He called us and we picked him up. When we got here, Fergusen had the German sitting on his porch just as peaceful as can be, sipping a lemonade. Can you beat that? Of course Joe still kept the gun on him."

MacKensie looked around and seemed to be smelling the air. "Is Fergusen's farm far from here?"

"Just a few miles," Ogleby replied. "We can be there in 15 minutes or so. Come on. Follow me."

They started down the road behind Ogleby with MacKensie at the wheel. Van Marter sat sullenly, annoyed that they were wasting valuable time.

"Look, Andre," he said finally. "I realize I may not be fully up on the RCMP's uniquely Canadian methods of doing things, but it seems to me the object of this search is to find the ones who escaped THIS time. What do you think we're going to learn from seeing where the last escapees went? "

"I don't know; maybe nothing," MacKensie replied. "The old nose has been wrong before, but I don't think it's a coincidence that two of the escapees are the same ones who made the first break. I think those two are along to take advantage of what they learned last time. They may have even taken the same route. Anyway, it can't hurt to look. Maybe if we see what they saw, something will give us a hint of their plan."

Van Marter was not convinced. "Even if they did come the same way, they're long gone by now. We should be back coordinating the search. They've got five more hours jump on us than we first thought. We can't afford to be tramping around in the backwoods. We're being tourists while they're getting closer to breaking free. We've got to start the search."

MacKensie shrugged. "Maybe, but I just thought it would be better if we had some idea where to look, eh?"

"And this will give us that idea? Not likely. I can just see my report now: we spent an hour visiting old MacDonald's farm because that's where one of them went last time and the RCMP believes they always return to the scene of the crime. Holy cow."

"Now, now. Just give the nose a bit of leeway, will you now? Besides, it's Joe Fergusen's farm; MacDonald's is down the road some."

"But…."

"We'll discuss it later," MacKensie snapped. "We should be almost there."

A few minutes later, they were standing on a quiet stretch of road near Shillington. Trees waved softly in the afternoon breeze and the countryside was a place of tranquility.

"He came through the woods and came out at Joe Fergusen's place up the hill there," Corporal Ogleby said, indicating a white farmhouse set back from the road. "Joe lives alone since his wife died a few years ago, and he does a lot of hunting so he had his gun with him."

"Could we talk to Mr. Fergusen?" said MacKensie.

"No problem usually. Old Joe'll talk your ear off, but he's not at home now."

"How do you know?"

"His car's gone, eh? He has an old gray Nash he keeps parked right by the house there."

"That's all right," said Van Marter. "You told us everything he could have anyway. We've learned all we can here. You ready to go back Andre?"

But MacKensie was looking at the house and cocking his head curiously.

"I feel my nose twitching," he said quietly.

"Oh, for the love of Pete," Van Marter grumbled. "Not the damned nose again…."

Three sets of footsteps clumped on the wooden porch as MacKensie, Van Marter, and Corporal Ogleby approached. As MacKensie pressed the button, they could hear the doorbell sound faintly in the house, but there was no answer. They rang a second time with the same result.

"Look, old Joe'll probably be back soon," said Corporal Ogleby. "Why don't we just leave him a note?"

Van Marter checked the back door and found it was locked as well. "See, it's just like the corporal said; Fergusen's gone somewhere. If we had any sense, we'd do the same thing."

"Yep," said Corporal Ogleby. "Joe's off somewhere. He never locks his door when he's at home."

"I think I'd like to see for myself," said MacKensie, peering through a glass door panel.

"Well that's just great," said Van Marter, throwing up his arms in exasperation. In spite of a few flashes of competence, it seemed MacKensie was reverting to his previous hardheaded 19th century ways. "I knew this partnership was a mistake," Van Marter snapped. "So now we're going to wait around for some farmer to come back from the market? Or are we going to conduct a search somehow? And what is the procedure for getting a search warrant in Canada? Is there a local court handy with a judge wearing a white wig, or do we have to petition King George? I thought we were short on time?"

MacKensie nodded and looked around. "I'm sorry gentlemen, but my nose is twitching something fierce. Would you stand back please?"

With that, MacKensie calmly but firmly kicked in the front door. Pieces of splintered wood and broken glass sprayed across the foyer as the heavy wooden door crashed into the hallway, shattering the stillness.

"What the hell?" Corporal Ogleby and Van Marter were equally surprised.

"That's the first size twelve search warrant I've ever seen," Van Marter remarked as the dust settled.

MacKensie stepped into the house. "Now let's see if we can find out what's making my nose twitch."

Their footsteps crunched on shards of broken glass as the three men entered the front hallway. Dust motes from the broken front door hung and lazily swirled in the air. Corporal Ogleby called for Joe Fergusen but heard only echoes.

"Let's spread out," said MacKensie. "I'll take this level, Tom take upstairs and Corporal, you see what's in the basement."

The house was in perfect order except the gun cabinet was open and empty. Wherever Fergusen had gone, he had gone armed. Van Marter started up the stairs as MacKensie entered the kitchen and noticed an almost empty refrigerator and an equally empty pantry.

"Inspector?" came the voice of Corporal Ogleby. "The door to the basement's locked"

MacKensie hurried to the basement door and noticed the key hanging on a nail nearby.

"Here's the key. Let's take a look."

As the door opened, they saw the light was on and looked at each other silently. They called for Fergusen and there was still no reply. They crept down the rickety stairs; the air was cool and musty. As they reached the bottom, they saw a figure lying on an old sofa.

"Oh my God!" gasped Corporal Ogleby. "It's old Joe; they killed him!"

*   *   *

The grey Nash rolled easily through the lush Canadian countryside as if carrying its occupants on a picnic. The backwash of the car stirred up a small rolling cloud of dust from the dry dirt along the side of the road. Spirits were still high among the Germans inside as the sounds of Glenn Miller poured from the radio and they sang to themselves as the miles rolled by.

"Don't these Canadian radio stations play any German music?" one of them said.

"Of course," another laughed. "Don't you recognize Glenn Muller?"

"That looks like a petrol station up ahead," said one of the men in the car. "We'd better stop. How's your English?"

"Good enough," said Theimann, who was still driving. "We are only buying petrol, after all."

A fading overhead sign said "Sam's Speedy Esso Service". The station was a neat looking place, painted white with red trim and red garage doors. Hand-lettered cardboard signs announced prices for a lube and oil change. They pulled up at the lone pump, and ancient affair with a glass reservoir on top. Through a big window, the Germans could see a short, heavy set bald man sitting at a desk under a cheap portrait of King George and crossed British and Canadian flags.

"A patriot," one of them commented. "He would be quite surprised to know his gasoline will help the German war effort, wouldn't he?"

Sam Collier, owner and operator of Sam's Speedy Esso Service rose with a grunt and ambled in a decidedly unspeedy way out to meet them. He hadn't seen these men before, but that wasn't unusual on this road. As Collier got to the driver's window, he could see there were two men in the front and another bundled in a blanket sleeping on the back seat. Collier nodded to the driver.

"Afternoon; fill it up?" It was an optimistic question since few filled their tanks in these days of gasoline rationing. Still, it didn't hurt to ask. occasionally he got someone who had been carefully saving ration coupons and was ready to splurge a bit.

"Yes, please," the driver said. Sam thought he detected an accent, but couldn't quite place it.

"Yes sir," he said, reaching for the hose. "Don't get many fillups these days. Now if I could have your coupons…"

The man at the wheel jerked his head around. "What?"

"Coupons. You know, ration coupons," Sam said patiently. He was used to people pretending to "forget" the coupons to try to get a few more gallons, but he never let them get away with it. After all, he had to account for his sales and the coupons he took in. He wasn't getting into trouble on their account.

The man at the wheel seemed confused for a moment, then recovered. "Oh, ration coupons. Look in there will you?" he said to the man next to him. Again the accent. What was it, Sam thought? It sounded German, but what would three Germans be doing here? Besides, with so many European refugees from the war, strange accents were not unusual.

The other man in the front seat made a show of fumbling in the glove box but came up empty.

"I have forgot them," the driver said, smiling nervously.

Sam slowly put the hose back on the pump and pulled an oily rag out of his pocket to wipe his hands. "Well, I'm sorry, but I can't give you no gas without them coupons. The war you know."

The driver looked at the other man and for a moment, no one spoke.

*   *   *

Donna Hastings ran through the documents she had spread out on the conference room table in front of her. Only two years ago, she had been a secretary at RCMP headquarters, but now, with so many men fighting the war, she had been made a search coordinator. She liked the excitement and mental challenge of the work, most of which involved the paperwork and phone inquiries necessary in tracking down fugitives and escapees from the jails. She had looked on it almost as an abstract intellectual exercise up until now, but this was different, and considerably more important.

She looked again at the documents, then at the small picture she had placed on the file cabinet. Her brother Dennis, proud in his new uniform smiled down at her just as he had when they were children. She could still see make out the small scar on his chin, a scar he had gotten the day he fell of his bike at age eight. She regarded the picture for a moment, then returned to the job.

Finding a fugitive usually meant surveillance of the subject's friends, contacts, and family. Most fugitives were predictable and easy to find. A few were more wily, and fewer still eluded capture indefinitely. But this was much more complicated. Three determined German prisoners with no known contacts and with time limited. Ironically, the lack of contacts, friends or relatives would make escape more difficult for the Germans, but would also make tracking them much harder.

She scanned the police reports from the surrounding areas. There was the usual jumble of petty thievery and property crimes; a broken shop window here, a stolen bicycle there. Could any of those incidents be connected with the fugitives?

"Well, they'd hardly be traveling by bicycle," she said. "And here are four cases of gasoline being reported siphoned from vehicles." There had been a lot of that since rationing started.

"If the fugitives stole a car, they might be responsible, but there are no reports of stolen cars," she said out loud. Donna Hastings often said things out loud in private. She looked at the reports again. The five cases were spread almost in an arc in different directions from the prison camp.

"One of them could be the fugitives of course, but which one?"

"Any developments Miss Hastings?" The voice of the Commissioner interrupted her. He was carrying a cup of steaming tea in which a thin lemon slice floated.

"Aside from the torn I.D. card, you mean?"

"Yes, but we don't know anything about that yet."

"We have a lot of other data, but we don't know how much is relevant. Andre and Agent Van Marter have inspected the camp, interviewed a few other prisoners and are presently interviewing the OPP officer who apprehended the escapees the first time. This escape seems to have been remarkably well planned."

The commissioner grunted. "Yes; that damned German efficiency shows up at the least opportune times. The Prime Minister's office has been calling almost on the hour and we still have nothing to report. The only progress is that being made by the Germans as they travel towards the border. We've been monitoring radio traffic as well, in case the Germans get hold of a short wave and try to get their message out that way, we can jam it. Nothing there so far. What is your feeling about their chances?"

She frowned. "Well, I'm not really sure, but I think they have planned too well for the usual methods to work in time."

The Commissioner raised his eyebrows. "Not very optimistic, I must say, Miss Hastings. But then how will we catch them?"

Donna motioned to the maps spread out on the table. "They've a long way to go in a country that is unfamiliar to them."

"Meaning?"

"Meaning we'll have to hope that sooner or later, they make a mistake."

-7-

"The bastards!" shouted Corporal Ogleby. "Why would anyone want to kill old Joe Fergusen? And look, the sonsabitches tied him up first."

Van Marter appeared at the head of the basement stairs. "Oh hell," was all he could say when he looked at the body on the sofa.

MacKensie bent down by the sofa and examined the body.

"He's still warm, and there's not a mark on him. I wonder…Do you hear that?"

Van Marter listened carefully. "I hear it. It sounds like…."

"Snoring. He's not dead. He's asleep. Help me untie these ropes."

"Asleep? Why would he be sleeping in the basement? And why didn't he wake up with all the noise and commotion?"

"Here's why," said Van Marter, picking up something from a nearby table. "An empty bottle of sleeping pills. The Germans must have remembered the house from the first escape and come here for the vehicle. They tied him up and made him take sleeping pills to keep him quiet until they were safely away. They must not have counted on anyone finding him this soon. See if there's a cloth we can wet."

"Come on old timer; wake up." MacKensie was slapping the sleeping figure on both cheeks.

"Huh?" was the garbled reply.

"Get some water. We've got to wake him up."

"I…I'm awake," said Fergusen, slowly and unconvincingly.

"Mr Fergusen, I'm Inspector Andre MacKensie of the RCMP. Who did this?"

Joe Fergusen just blinked at MacKensie for a few seconds. MacKensie shook him again. "Come on; we need your help."

"The...the Germans," he finally replied. He was becoming more alert now, but was still groggy. He shook his head trying to clear the cobwebs. "They.....they came just about two o'clock this morning, eh? There were three of them."

"Did you recognize any of them?" asked MacKensie.

Joe Fergusen nodded. "One was the man I captured the other day. Another one I didn't know seemed to be in charge; he was ordering the others around, and he spoke perfect English. The leader knocked on my door and said his car had broken down and he needed to use my phone. As soon as I opened the door the other two appeared and grabbed me. They took my car keys, my guns, and they cleaned out my pantry."

The words "car" and "guns" made MacKensie and Van Marter look at each other.

"Did they take anything else?"

"Uh...oh yes. They asked me which key opened the lock on the pump. I keep a tank for petrol out by the barn."

"What else did they say?"

"Say? Uh, let's see. They was polite, eh, but pretty set on having their way. They tied me up and made me take three sleeping pills. They said they didn't want to hurt me, but they had to keep me quiet for a while; said they'd send me a thank you letter when they got back to Germany."

"Did they say anything that indicated what they were going to do next?"

Fergusen shook his head as if trying to stay awake. "Well, no, but they made me find them a road map of Ontario and Quebec, so I suppose they were going to be driving some, eh? Oh, and after they gave me the pills, I could hear them upstairs until I fell asleep. As near as I could tell, one of them was looking at the map and the other asked him how far it was to the Soo."

Van Marter was puzzled. "The what?"

"The Soo," said MacKensie. "It's what we call Sault Ste Marie, an industrial city about 350 miles southwest of here. The Soo's on the canal locks between Ontario and Michigan. Not a bad place to get out of the country."

"It sounds like a damned good place …for the Germans," said Van Marter. Then he turned to Joe Fergusen again.

"How much gas…petrol do you have in the tank and in the car?"

The old farmer scratched his head. "Oh, maybe two or three gallons in the car, and in the storage tank…Let's see, I dipped the tank just last week and it was about a quarter full. That'd be about 15 gallons I guess."

"And what kind of a car is it?"

"It's a Nash…1936. Only got 55,000 cliks on it."

"Clicks?"

"Kilometers," MacKensie translated.

"What engine? Flathead six?"

Fergusen nodded.

"Thanks, Mr Fergusen. Why don't you take it easy for a few minutes. Corporal, would you help Mr Fergusen upstairs?"

As Ogleby helped the old farmer to his feet, Van Marter took MacKensie aside. "That means the Germans have a car and as much as 18 gallons of fuel. And those are Imperial gallons, which means about 25 U.S. gallons. On these roads, a '36 Nash with a flathead six and three passengers should get close to 15 miles to the gallon, and that means they can get well over 300 miles if somebody doesn't stop them."

MacKensie nodded. "Maybe. We'll have to assume they have all the petrol they need, but have to hope they don't. Fergusen might be wrong in his estimate or the car might get lousy mileage, or they may not have been able to find a container for the extra gas, or the pump may not have been able to drain the entire storage tank. A lot of things can happen to foul up careful plans."

"Yeah," said Van Marter, "and too many of them already have. The trouble is, they've all happened to us."

"All right. We'll check the gas level in the storage tank and find out from Fergusen if he had any containers that the Krauts could have used to carry extra petrol. But most of all, we'll have check points set up along the road to the Soo. They may have enough fuel, but that doesn't mean they'll make it."

"Andre, if they left here about 2:30-3:00 A.M. in a car there's a good chance they've ALREADY made it."

MacKensie didn't reply, but turned and walked up the basement stairs and into the living room with Joe Fergusen and the corporal. "Thank you for your help, Mr Fergusen. We have a few more questions for you if you feel up to it, then Corporal Ogleby here will get you to the nearest doctor so you can be checked out."

But Joe Fergusen had other ideas. "Don't waste time with me. You get them Huns, eh? Just look what they did to my front door!"

*   *   *

"Sault Ste Marie?" said Donna Hastings as she put down the phone. "Well, that's the closest crossing. Maybe they've made that mistake I was hoping for."

Anxiously, she called the customs office at Sault Ste Marie and the RCMP patrol headquarters to tell them that the three fugitives were headed their way and had to be stopped. MacKensie and Van Marter had ordered roadblocks set up just outside of Sault Ste Marie. Donna Hastings called the dog training unit and arranged to have the RCMP's only three bloodhounds taken to Sault Ste Marie immediately. After that was done, she got out a reference book and started calling every police department from Cochrane to Sault Ste Marie. She gave them a detailed description of the vehicle the Germans had stolen and asked them for copies of every incident report of the last 24 hours, no matter how small or petty. Somewhere was the vital piece of information they needed. The net was closing, but they didn't have them yet.

"Donna?" came a voice from the doorway. "The lab has information on the card pieces you sent."

She looked up and saw Lisa Alexander, a dark haired woman about her own age standing there with a piece of paper in her hand. Lisa was one of the newer crime lab technicians and always seemed to have various chemical stains on her hands.

"Good. What did you find?" Donna said, reaching for the one page report.

Lisa proudly handed it to her. "This was a bit of a challenge. They used a number two pencil and the thing was smeared from erasing. With a microscope and some angled lighting, however, we reconstructed the name that was going to be on the card: Frank J. Wilson."

Donna nodded. "Nice anonymous sort of name; easy to remember; easy to spell, but easy to lose in a crowd. Just the sort of name they'd choose. Good job, Lisa. Anything else?"

"Yes, as a matter of fact. We found fingerprints that matched one of the prisoners at Camp Q, an officer named Hans Kolza. He was an architect before the war, so they must have used him for his drafting skills."

"Good. They can question him; not that he'll probably tell them anything. Well, thanks for the report."

Lisa shrugged nonchalantly. "Hey, we girls have to stick together. Besides, it was a nice change from analyzing hair follicles and blood samples."

Donna verified the information on the report then placed a call to Monteith.

✶   ✶   ✶

"I have to hand it to you, Andre, or to your nose. I wouldn't have bothered to even question Fergusen, let alone kick his door down." They were at the Cochrane airport waiting for Rags McLaughlin to finish his preflight check.

"It wasn't just that," MacKensie admitted. "I noticed tracks where Fergusen's car had been driven away and noticed that they missed the driveway by a wide margin at the road; as if the car had been driven by someone who wasn't familiar with the road. It looked suspicious."

"And that was what tipped you off?" said Van Marter.

"Well, no, I was suspicious when Corporal Ogleby first said Fergusen had gone out."

Van Marter looked confused. "Why would that be suspicious?"

MacKensie smiled mischievously. "Well, jeez, where would a widower have to go on a weekday in Northern Ontario, eh?"

Van Marter laughed. "I must have missed that point in the FBI Manual. So now we head for Sault Ste Marie to continue the search from there?"

"You got it. Now we know which way to go. Now the fun really begins and I want to be in on the kill. I want to see those bastards behind a barbed wire fence where they belong."

Van Marter looked at him curiously. "You seem to take this very personally. Is it Donna's brother?"

"It's a lot more than that," he replied. "I can't abide Nazis and most of all I hate U-boats and anyone associated with them as only someone who served on a corvette can."

"You were on a corvette?"

"For almost a year. Convoy duty, eh? It mostly consisted of fighting a losing battle with both the sea and the Krauts. I was on HMCS Oshawa. Some bright boy at the Admiralty decided to name British corvettes after flowers, of all things, but we had better sense in Canada, eh?."

Van Marter nodded. "I've read about corvettes. They're economical and fast to build, but I understand they're sort of small. Are they effective for convoy duty?"

MacKensie laughed mirthlessly. "Corvettes would be ideal for convoy duty….. if only they didn't need crews. They're cheaper to build than destroyers, simple, and highly maneuverable. The only trouble is the damned things'll roll on a mill pond. In a rough sea you spend as much effort to keep yourself standing and your breakfast in your stomach as you do fighting the Germans. We had more men injured by falling or being thrown against something or being struck by some falling object than we did from enemy action. That's how I hurt my leg. There was a wicked beam sea running and a rouge wave caught me on deck and slammed me into a bulkhead. The damned thing picked me up like a rag doll."

"Protecting the convoys must be a tough job."

"Almost impossible. It was like trying to protect Toronto with a toothpick. A convoy of 50 ships would have only five escorts. The U-boats would hit and run; they never stood and fought. One minute some poor merchant sailor is sitting in his rack writing a letter to the wife and kids and the next he was blown to bits or trying to swim in a sea of burning oil. There was no warning and no mercy. A lot of brave men died because of the damned U-boats."

"You mean they just stayed underwater and picked off the merchant ships?"

"Oh no. They would fire from the surface, usually after dark. On the surface they could run on diesel power at 18 knots. Submerged they'd have to run on their batteries at five or six knots. They would only submerge after firing to avoid the escorts. I suppose that's the part that galled me the most; the pure sneakiness of it all. What kind of a man fires at an unarmed ship, then runs and hides? We'd chase them and drop depth charges until the Atlantic boiled but only got one of the bastards. They almost always snuck away to kill again. So if you think I'm taking this all personally, you're damned right. And I'll tell you another thing; if you'd ever stood on the bridge of a corvette on a freezing winter's night and seen an oil tanker blow up with a fireball so hot you could feel it three miles away, or if you'd ever dragged a torpedoed merchant seaman out of the water and have his burned skin come off in your hands, then by God, you'd feel the same way."

Van Marter opened his mouth but no sound came out. Nothing seemed appropriate somehow. MacKensie unconsciously rubbed his hip and Van Marter felt a new sense of his mission.

"Inspector MacKensie?" came a voice from behind. "You have a phone call at the airport office."

Without a word, MacKensie rose and followed the man.

Van Marter stared at the waiting airplane as MacKensie's words haunted him. One thought kept coming back again and again: what happens if the fugitives get away? How many more ships would be sunk; how many men burned, frozen, drowned or blown to pieces? And would Donna's brother be one of them?

A minute later, MacKensie came running back to the runway.

"Lets move out. They've been spotted!"

"Spotted?" asked Van Marter as he hustled into the plane. "When? Where?"

"About an hour ago, in Sudbury, about a hundred miles east of the Soo. A gas station owner got suspicious when three men in a car spoke with an accent and tried to buy gas without ration coupons. They were heading west."

"The ration coupons," said Van Marter, nodding with satisfaction. "I didn't think they would know about them. It looks like they've slipped up after all. This might be the break we've been looking for."

"We haven't got them yet," growled MacKensie.

With a roar of the engines, Rags lifted the Annie off the runway and headed southwest. MacKensie and Van Marter scanned the countryside as they flew over as if the fugitives would be visible.

"That's Timmins," shouted MacKensie, indicating the built up area below. "The Soo's about 250 miles southwest. Once you get there, the States are just across a bridge over the canal between Lake Superior and Lake Huron. There are also trains going to the States and a lot of ship traffic headed towards the St. Lawrence. There are a lot of ways of slipping out. Let's just hope to God they haven't gotten there yet."

Van Marter looked at his watch. "Not too bad. It's only three o'clock; less than 16 hours since the breakout. I was getting worried. The area to be searched increases as the square of the distance the fugitive covers and the distance after 20 hours is huge. By all rights, we should have lost them hours ago."

"Yeah, well maybe we just live right, eh?"

"Maybe…" Van Marter's voice trailed off. He was frowning and looked troubled. "Andre, you know I'm as anxious to catch these guys as anyone, but something's been bothering me."

"Not enough FBI methods?" MacKensie smirked.

"No, it's the times. They don't add up."

"What? What doesn't add up?"

"Look, Fergusen said they came to his farm about two A.M. That's about how far I would have expected them to be after two hours on foot. So let's say it takes them about another hour to tie up Joe Fergusen, check his maps, steal his food, get the car ready, and get the gas from his tank. So they set off at three A.M. The next we hear of them, it's two P.M. and they're in a gas station 100 miles outside of Sault Ste Marie, a distance of about 300 miles."

"You and your damned calculations," MacKensie grumbled. "So what?"

"Andre, that's over 11 hours to go 300 miles. That's about, oh, twenty seven miles an hour. If you were running for your life in someone else's vehicle in a strange county in the middle of a war and carrying vital information, wouldn't you go a little faster than that?"

"That's the average speed. They may have stopped to siphon gas at some point," MacKensie said hesitantly. He sounded less sure now.

Van Marter shook his head. "Nix on that. If they had stopped to siphon gas, what were they doing at the gas station? And why did they even need gas? We already figured they probably had enough gas to get to Sault Ste Marie."

"We didn't know that for sure. We just thought it was possible."

"All right, all right, we weren't sure; I'll grant you that. They could very well have been running low, or afraid of running low later. So forget the gas. The real point is they should have gotten that far at least two hours earlier than they did."

"Maybe they got lost or took another route or something. How the hell would I know?" said MacKensie with annoyance. "All I know is however they got to Sudbury, they were there and now we're on them. We're tightening the noose and when we do, those Katzenjammer kids' Aryan necks will be smack in the middle of it."

In the tiny cockpit, Rags turned around and motioned for MacKensie. MacKensie undid his seat belt and made his way to the cockpit.

"I'm getting a message. They want to talk to you, inspector."

MacKensie put on the headphones, nodded, asked a few questions, then handed them back to Rags.

"What is it?" asked Van Marter when MacKensie was in his seat once more.

"Headquarters."

"And?"

"Well, if you're still curious about the times, just wait a while; you can ask the bastards yourself. We just found their car."

"What? Where?"

"About 30 miles west of Sudbury and 80 miles from the border. It was pushed into the woods; out of petrol."

"Then they must be on foot now. Is that a wooded area?"

"Wooded hardly describes it; the place is a wilderness. Even the Cree and the Chippewa can get lost in some parts of it. It's a good thing Donna had the bloodhounds flown in. The Sudbury detachment of the

RCMP are organizing a search at this very moment. We'll fly into the strip at Sudbury and meet them there. We could have them in custody in an hour's time. Game, set, and match, eh?"

Van Marter nodded. He hoped MacKensie was right, but there was still the matter of the travel times. The question kept nagging at him: why had it taken the Germans so long to get to where they abandoned the car? Rags gently pushed the stick forward and descended into the middle of a vast green wilderness that seemed to go on forever, rolling on until it was lost in the haze of the far horizons to the north and Lake Huron to the south. Off to the right, Van Marter noticed a large bird, probably a hawk or even an eagle, slowly circling in the sky over the trackless forest far below.

Rags steadily guided the plane lower and lower until it seemed he would crash into the thick green canopy of treetops just below the landing gear. Van Marter's knuckles were getting white as he gritted his teeth for the expected impact. But at the last minute, a clearing suddenly opened up below them and a tiny dirt airstrip appeared near a small town nestled in the woods, Rags swooped down and pulled off a perfect landing in a nasty cross wind and the yellow Annie came to a stop in front of a waiting Royal Canadian Mounted Police officer.

"What did I tell you?" said Rags proudly. "I greased that landing smooth as a baby's bottom. It just takes a little skill is all."

"Great, Rags," said Van Marter appreciatively. "The smoother the better as far as I'm concerned."

"Good morning Inspector," said a short stocky man with a well trimmed black moustache. MacKensie greeted him warmly.

"How are you doing Jack? How are the Muskie running this year?"

"They're mostly running away from my hook," the man laughed. "All the fish have lockjaw lately. But maybe if we can catch these runners fast enough, we'll have time to go for bucketmouth."

"You got a deal. Tom, this is Jack Davies, the RCMP officer in charge in this area. We were patrolmen together years ago. He's a native Sooite and part Chippewa, so he should be a good man to have on a local search."

Van Marter shook hands. "Tom Van Marter, FBI."

Davies laughed good naturedly. It was the easy laugh of a man who laughed often. "Ah, so the G-Men are helping out, eh? Splendid! The more the merrier. At least we'll outnumber the Germans. Well, I expect you'll want to see the car so hop in."

They piled into a dusty RCMP car and sped off down the road.

"Running out of gas was actually a bit of luck for the fugitives," said Davies over his shoulder. "We had a check point set up about a mile further along the road. If they hadn't run out of gas, they'd have run right into it."

"Their luck hasn't quite run out yet, it would seem. How long do you figure the car has been there?" asked Van Marter.

Davies looked at his watch. "About 53 minutes."

"What? How can you be so precise?" said MacKensie.

"A westbound truck driver saw the car being pushed into the brush and reported it to the OPP when he got to the Soo about 25 minutes later. When they found the empty car, the OPP checked the license number and found out it was the one we're after. By the time the OPP notified us and we'd gotten a search organized, the Germans had a pretty fair head start. Not to worry, though; the Jerries couldn't have gotten far, even though these woods can conceal an army. And I doubt that German boys off a submarine would be able to scare up a meal in the woods. They may surrender from hunger if we don't get them sooner."

"I wouldn't bet on that," said Van Marter. "These guys have surprised us before. We've consistently underestimated them. So far they've been as slippery as 30 weight motor oil."

"No doubt," said Davies, "but the bloodhounds have arrived and we're going to turn them loose on the scents we get from the car. In woods like this a human scent will be easy to follow."

"That must be the car," said MacKensie, seeing several RCMP patrol cars surrounding a gray Nash by the side of the road."

MacKensie flashed his badge at the police and ran to the Nash with Van Marter. The keys still dangled from the ignition and the trunk had been opened. In the front seat were several wrappers and cans that showed the prisoners had eaten along the way; all from the pantry of Joe Fergusen, no doubt. In the back seat were several heavy blankets and an old pair of boots, but no evidence of food. In the trunk were several boxes of crackers, five cans of stew, two cans of sardines, a bunch of carrots, three potatoes and two bottles of Molson's beer.

"Quite a selection of provisions," observed MacKensie. "Those boys could have lived in the car if they had a little more gas, eh? Did you find anything interesting in the boot or the glove box?"

"The what?" said Van Marter.

"The trunk or the glove compartment," said MacKensie. "I keep forgetting to translate from English into American."

Davies chuckled. "Well, there were more canned goods in the trunk. I guess they had too much to carry. The glove box just had some assorted papers of the longsuffering Mr Ferguson."

"I didn't think they'd leave anything really interesting, eh?" said MacKensie, finishing looking around the back seat. "Well, I've seen enough. We should join the search party."

"Wait a minute," said Van Marter. "I have to check something." He produced his rubber gloves and put them on as he walked to the front of the car.

"Don't mind him, Jack." said MacKensie to a puzzled Captain Davies. "He really wanted to be a Proctologist."

Van Marter lifted the hood and examined the engine carefully.

"I think we should dust for prints," he said, finally.

"Prints?" said MacKensie, his jaw dropping in amazement. "You want to dust for fingerprints? Why? Are you expecting someone else in the damned car?"

"It's standard procedure," insisted Van Marter. "You never know what you'll find. Besides, this car doesn't look right."

MacKensie looked at Davies, who simply shrugged his shoulders, then turned back to Van Marter. "Doesn't look right? Jeez Louise; now what's wrong?"

"This engine hasn't been touched in months. The grease hasn't been disturbed, even around the plugs, the battery, the air cleaner or the distributer cap. If they had had car trouble, they would at least have checked the engine."

"So they didn't have car trouble…So what?"

"Then there's the back seat," said Van Marter. "Why were the men in the front seat eating as they went, but the one in the back seat wasn't?"

"He was asleep! Don't you remember what the man at the Esso station said?"

"He wasn't asleep for 11 hours," shouted Van Marter, waving his arms in frustration. "Look, I can accept your nose; I can accept kicking in doors without a warrant; and I can even accept flying with a pilot who thinks he's an airborne cowboy; but let's at least do one thing by the book. Dust for fingerprints!"

MacKensie looked at Davies with a "see what I have to put up with?" expression on his face and sighed.

"You two boys ought to get married," said Davies, laughing.

"Jack, you're not helping," said MacKensie.

"Well, we have a crime lab in Sudbury," Davies said soothingly, "I could get someone here in an hour or so. I don't see as how it would do any harm, Andre."

"All right, all right," MacKensie replied. "Why not? In for a penny, in for a pound."

"What?" said Van Marter.

"Never mind. We'll get someone from the lab here. Maybe he'll find an autographed copy of 'Mein Kampf' hidden under the seat."

A radio crackled in one of the RCMP cars. Davies went over and returned the call. In a few moments he emerged smiling.

"What did I tell you? There was nothing to worry about. We have apprehended two of the prisoners and expect to get the third any time now."

"Two? Which two?" said MacKensie.

Davies shrugged. "We don't know yet. Does it really matter? We'll have them all in a few minutes anyway. Meanwhile, we can have a word with these boys if you'd like. They're being held just about two miles down the road."

"Great," said MacKensie. "I'll feel a lot better when we nab the last one, but meanwhile, we need to question the first two separately. Come on, Tom, you can personally ask Mr. Fritz to enlighten you on his messy ways."

-8-

At least twenty police were gathered at a small clearing by the side of Highway 17. The day was still reasonably warm, and a paddy wagon was parked alongside a dozen police cars, some with flashing lights as if a traffic accident had occurred. Police radios squawked and crackled in the background. Davies, Van Marter and MacKensie jumped out of their car and ran to the officer in charge.

"Good work, Jean," said Davies with a smile. "Where are they?"

Jean DuVall, an eager young Lieutenant, smiled proudly. "We're keeping them separate, sir; just as you said. One is in the wagon and the other is in that car over there."

"Did you get the prisoners' names?" asked Van Marter.

DuVall nodded and checked a small folding notebook. "The prisoners' names are Theimann and Fleisher."

"Damn it, I was afraid of that," grumbled MacKensie to Van Marter. "The one that's still on the loose is Meinhoff, the leader and most dangerous one. Well, we can question the other two while the hounds are tracking him down. Jack, how about bringing Theimann over to that area under the tree over there. Tom and I can have a little talk with him."

"You got it."

MacKensie watched Davies walk away.

"I assume the RCMP is up on the latest interrogation techniques?" said Van Marter. "Do you want to try the good cop/bad cop act? I have a feeling you'd make an excellent bad cop."

"I'm not in the mood to put on an act for these jerks," said MacKensie, "but if they don't cooperate, then they'll see just how bad a cop can be, eh?"

Werner Theimann looked surprisingly rested for a man who had been a fugitive until less than an hour earlier. He wore an old blue jacket taken from Joe Fergusen and sat stiffly beneath the tree awaiting his questioners. MacKensie and Van Marter regarded him silently for a few moments and were struck by how young he was.

"This guy looks like he should be chasing cheerleaders or going to the junior prom," whispered Van Marter. "It's hard to imagine him sinking shipping in the North Atlantic."

Theimann looked nervous but confident, as if proud of the chase he had led them on.

"Do you speak English?" asked MacKensie.

Theimann looked up at MacKensie warily and nodded. "Yes, but not, how do you say it, fluid."

"Fluent?"

"Yes, fluent. That is right." Theimann hissed when he pronounced words with s in them. MacKensie looked at him with distaste for a moment, then began the questioning.

"Well, Herr Theimann, you boys have had a nice little ride. Where were you going?"

Theimann shrugged. "Wherever we could get to."

"Oh, I think you planned it a little better than that. Where did you go when you got the car?"

"I came here, of course," he answered with little expression.

"Where else?" said Van Marter, who was anxious to confirm his theory.

Theimann looked at him curiously and frowned as if trying to recall. "North Bay, Sudbury, and several smaller places along the way. Their names I do not re....regard."

"You mean you don't remember their names?"

"Ja, yes...remember. That is the word." He pronounced word as vord.

"You took a long time to get this far. Where else did you go?"

"Only the places we passed through."

"We know you were delayed," said Van Marter reasonably. "We were just curious what happened."

Theimann looked uncertain, then spoke. "The... car became broken. We needed repairing. We have lose the time."

Van Marter looked at Theimann. MacKensie resumed the questioning.

"Who was sleeping in the back?"

"We all sleep there in turn. Because we escape, we have no sleep the last night."

"Where is Leutnant Meinhoff?"

"I do not know. When we have ran out of the petrol, we each went away...not together."

"You went away separately?"

"Yes, that is the word. We went away separately. We are to the United States going at the Sault Ste Marie border. Leutnant Meinhoff said we would be harder to find if we are...separately."

"Do you know where he planned to try to cross the border?"

"No. He said we would have to find our own way."

"Did you know we have captured Seaman Fleisher?"

Theimann did not reply.

"Did you know we have also captured Leutnant Meinhoff?"

Theimann looked startled for a moment, then recovered. He smiled and slowly shook his head. "You have not found him. You tell the lie."

MacKensie raised his eyebrows. "Why do you say that?"

"I know that him you will not find."

"Why will we not find?" said Van Marter.

There was a long pause. Finally, Theimann answered. "I think he will, how do you say it....fool you."

When Theimann had been led away, Van Marter turned to MacKensie.

"That is one confident escapee. How can he be so sure Meinhoff will elude us when they couldn't?"

MacKensie shrugged. "It could be Nazi arrogance. Or it could be that Meinhoff has something special up his sleeve."

"Do you believe the story about car trouble?"

"It's possible, I suppose," said MacKensie, scratching his head. "These submarine guys are pretty mechanical, and I could see them tinkering with the car, although you didn't see any signs of it on the engine. Of course, I'm sure you also noticed how clean Theimann's hands were."

"I did. I'm telling you those guys did not have car trouble."

"Well, let's see what Herr Fleisher has to say."

Seaman Fleisher's fingernails were also clean, and he spoke very little English, so he was questioned through an interpreter. The interview was slower for this reason, but was otherwise very similar. There were a few minor variations, but his story was almost the same as Theimann's. They had some problem with the car and it delayed them. He didn't know where Meinhoff went after they had split up. MacKensie tried the same ploy he had tried on Theimann.

"Tell him we just captured Leutnent Meinhoff."

The translator relayed this information and waited for a reply. Fleisher looked startled at first, then smiled knowingly and muttered something under his breath.

"What did he say?"

The translator looked puzzled. "He said you have not caught him and you will not catch him. He seems quite certain."

MacKensie took Van Marter aside and spoke in quiet tones the prisoner could not hear.

"They both are completely confident we not only haven't caught Meinhoff, but that we won't catch him."

"I know," Van Martter agreed. "But if they all started out on foot at the same time and place, and two of them have been nabbed already, how can they be so sure?"

An OPP officer appeared and told MacKensie he had a radio call patched through from Ottawa.

"You take it, Tom; it's probably Donna."

Van Marter needed no further urging. "Hello, Van Marter here."

"Hello, Tom," came the voice of Donna Hastings. "The boys at the lab were able to make out the name on the forged I.D. Card."

"Well, we might not need it now, but you never know."

"The name was Frank J. Wilson. They also found fingerprints that matched those of a prisoner named Hans Kolza who had been an architect before the war. Apparently he was the forger."

"Thanks, Donna. We've nabbed two of them, but Meinhoff is still on the loose. I'll keep you informed."

"That's wonderful, Tom," she said. The relief in her voice was obvious. "Now get the last one and call it a day." A half hour later, Van Marter and MacKensie were with a search party and a bloodhound combing the thick wooded areas near where Fleisher and Theimann had been captured. Several groups of searchers had fanned out across the area and the sound of bloodhounds barking echoed through the trees, muffled by the thick foliage. There was still plenty of light and the search parties had sealed the area off thoroughly, but there was no sign of Meinhoff. As they trudged through a thick carpet of fragrant brown pine needles, Van Marter looked around him at the heavy green canopy of tree branches above him and the dense undergrowth all around and shook his head.

"An elephant could hide out in these woods twenty yards away and we'd never find him unless he stepped on us," he said. "Meinhoff is an experienced woodsman; he could be anywhere by now. Why haven't the bloodhounds tracked him down yet?"

A bloodhound sniffed the ground rapidly and eagerly, but swung his head from side to side as if following several scents at once. He almost looked confused.

"They can't get a clean scent," said Davies, who seemed to be sniffing the air himself. "The first two weren't a problem, but the scent on Meinhoff is more elusive."

"But they started at the same time and place," said MacKensie. "How could they lose Meinhoff's scent?"

"The scents were all mixed together at first," said Davies, "Don't forget, the hounds don't have individual scents to go by since the men were all together in the car. So the scents they followed were all mixed together at first. Then the scents split in two."

"Two?"

Davies nodded. "Our theory is that two of them were together after they split, then the two split again, but they split in such a way as to cover the scent. They may have done it when crossing a stream. Meinhoff is the third scent. We haven't been able to separate it out yet, but we'll get him. He's got a long ways to go before he gets to the United States."

The hound continued to swing his head, looking for the scent.

The search continued, with search parties finding nothing but a startled moose who went crashing through the undergrowth like a freight train. The woods were a vast green realm, silent except for the hissing of wind through the gently swaying branches above. Footsteps were muffled by a soft carpet of leaves and pine needles. Under any other circumstances, the walk and the scenery would have been beautiful and relaxing.

MacKensie and Van Marter stopped to rest on a fallen tree trunk. The occasional cracking of a branch or the scratch of a radio exchange mingled with the soft rustle of the trees as the search continued without them. MacKensie grimaced and rubbed his hip.

"I thought I joined the FBI," said Van Marter, pushing a branch out of his face. "But it seems I'm in the Boy Scouts. I hope I at least get a merit badge out of all this clomping around in the woods."

MacKensie made his leg comfortable, sighed, and looked at the canopy of trees above them. Yellow shafts of light were streaming through the leaves at an angle, lighting scattered patches on the ground. He took a long deep breath. "I've always loved the woods. I used to bring my daughter Cindy here on holidays. Doris and I still hike when we get the chance, but Cindy's seventeen now and usually has other plans. There's something peaceful and almost holy about the woods."

Van Marter looked at MacKensie curiously. He wasn't used to seeing any display of sentiment, let alone philosophy from the crusty Canadian. "I'm a city boy myself, but now that you mention it, I guess it does look a little like a church."

MacKensie picked up a handful of brown pine needles and smelled them. "Yeah, it's like the old joke, eh? The preacher sees an Indian and says 'Why don't you ever come to church and hear me preach?' The Indian says 'I go to the woods; hear God preach.'"

Van Marter smiled. "I'll have to remember that story when this is over and I'm back on the pavement in D.C. or New York. But I still say I didn't bargain for this Daniel Boone stuff when I joined the bureau."

MacKensie smiled slightly and looked at Van Marter. "Well, if you didn't join the FBI to thrash about in the woods, why did you join, eh?"

Van Marter blushed slightly. "Well, I needed a job."

MacKensie looked at him in amazement. "You what?"

"When I got out of college, I had a degree in engineering in the middle of the depression when no one was hiring. Law enforcement seemed the only growth industry around. I applied to the FBI and here I am."

"You just needed a bloody job? Is that all being an FBI agent means to you?" MacKensie was still amazed.

Van Marter raised his hands as if defending himself from a punch. "At first, yes. I admit it. But pretty soon, I got to love the challenge of using science and logic to find someone who didn't want to be found. It was like a chess game with living pieces. On top of that, I started to notice that the people I was tracking down were pretty nasty characters; murderers, spies, and the like. Before too long, I got to feel proud of what I was doing and pretty satisfied as well. "

He looked at MacKensie, who was still regarding him skeptically. "All right, so maybe I wasn't filling a lifelong ambition, but I'm on the team now; just ask the people I've arrested. So what about you, Andre? I suppose you were born in the RCMP?"

"You might say that," he replied. "My great grandfather was with the Northwest Mounted Police on the Great March. That was when the police were first formed. Three hundred men were sent west to Alberta in the 1870s. It seems some bad elements from the United States had moved north and were selling arms and whiskey to the Indians. They were so confident, the whiskey traders even built a fort called 'Fort Whoop-up'. The police traveled over a thousand miles and drove every one of those traders back to the U.S. My grandfather was with the Northwest Mounted Police when they guarded the trails into the Yukon during the gold rush of 1898. My father chased liquor smugglers on the Great Lakes in the 20s. So when I was old enough, I joined as well. You see, I didn't need a job; I had a tradition."

Van Marter was impressed, but didn't want MacKensie to have the last word on this delicate subject. "Well, so you went into the family business. Now I know why you get so frustrated; all your ancestors succeeded in chasing Americans back across the border, but I'm still here."

"Don't remind me," MacKensie grumbled. "I'm liable to wind up with you here and Meinhoff in the states instead of the other way round."

"Save your well known grumpiness for Meinhoff," Van Marter said resentfully. "I'm not selling whiskey to the Indians, rushing to the gold fields, or bootlegging; I'm on your side."

MacKensie glared at him, then softened. "Yeah, you're right. I guess I'm beating up on you because I can't lay my hands on Meinhoff, eh?"

Just then, Davies suddenly appeared and sat heavily on the log beside them.

"Whew! I'm getting too old to be running around in the woods like this," he said, mopping his forehead with a big handkerchief. "If your prisoner friend would give himself up he would save everyone a lot of trouble."

"Yeah, maybe his boss Adolf should do the same thing," growled MacKensie.

Davies smiled and shook his head. "I would not have believed it how this man eludes us."

"He's a submariner," said Van Marter. "They're used to hiding and concealment."

Davies looked at Van Marter curiously. "Oh no; I'm afraid I can't agree with you, my young friend. A submarine sailor would be used to simply pulling the ocean over his head to hide. When he dives, he leaves no visible trace. But in the woods, everything you do can leave a sign that points to you long after you've gone."

MacKensie groaned. "Oh, jeez; not more Chippewa forest lore. This guy used to drive me batty with this stuff on our fishing trips."

"I'm quite serious," Davies insisted. "And it's not just a Chippewa tradition, although I'll admit we're pretty good at it. But I have seen white men who became very good in the woods and would have been hard to track, but only after they had lived in the woods long enough to know its ways. German boys fresh off a submarine would leave a trail a blind man could follow. Take the two we captured, for instance. They crashed about in the woods like wounded buffalo. Every few yards we found broken twigs, crushed grass, or a muddy footprint so clear you could tell the shoe size. Why, one of them even left a piece of his shirt stuck on a thorn bush. They might as well have walked to the station and surrendered."

Davies picked up a leaf and examined it for a moment, then frowned thoughtfully. "But this third boy is different. The Chippewa would say he's a 'man-who-casts-no-shadow'. Unlike his friends, he leaves no visible sign; not a blade of grass, a crushed leaf, a footprint, or even a stone overturned in a riverbed. He hasn't even left any clear scent the dogs can pick up. He's moving through the woods like a wisp of smoke. I've never seen anything like it."

"Maybe he's had experience the others didn't," said MacKensie.

Davies shook his head. "Andre, I've spent most of my life here. I spend most of my free time in the woods; hunting, fishing, and trapping. On my best day, I would have left more of a spoor than this boy does."

The three men sat silently a moment, then Van Marter suddenly stood up.

"Andre, do you suppose they've finished dusting the car for prints?".

"Not that again? What's with you and the damned fingerprints?"

"Andre, now MY nose is telling me something," Van Marter insisted. "Captain Davies, if you could point us palefaces in the right direction, maybe 'man-who-casts-big-shadow' here can find our way back." A half hour later a small fussy man from the RCMP crime lab was with MacKensie and Van Marter at the abandoned escape car. He had dusted, examined, photographed, frowned, then repeated the process. As he finished his investigation, Van Marter was impatiently pacing while MacKensie looked on skeptically.

"I still don't see what you expect to find," MacKensie said, shaking his head.

"I don't know either," said Van Marter, "but something's wrong and I've got to find out what it is."

The crime lab man wiped his forehead and finally got out of the car with a small notebook in his hand.

"I found four distinct sets of prints," he began, looking at his notes. "The first set probably was from the owner; they were everywhere, but most were covered with the other prints or with very old grime."

"Yes," said Van Marter. "But what about the others?"

"The other prints match those we have for Theimann and Fleisher, and the prints you brought with you from the prison camp from the man Meinhoff."

"Were there any prints around the hood?" asked Van Marter.

"Only some old ones from the owner.

Van Marter nodded. "So much for their mechanical trouble. There was some other reason for the time difference. I knew it."

The crime lab man consulted his notes again.

"Prints of Theimann and Fleisher were found in the front indicating that's where they were riding. The prints of Meinhoff were also found in the front, but were mostly covered by later prints of Fleisher."

MacKensie shrugged. "So Meinhoff and Fleisher changed places and Meinhoff wound up riding in the back."

"I'm afraid not. I found no prints from Meinhoff in the back."

MacKensie started. "None?"

"None."

"That proves it. Meinhoff was in the front and Fleisher was in the back," said Van Marter. "but at some point later, Fleisher went to the front but Meinhoff didn't go to the back; he left the vehicle."

"What?" said MacKensie. "But the man at the Esso station saw him."

"The man at the Esso station," said Van Marter, "saw a pile of blankets with those old boots at one end and assumed it was a third man, just as he was supposed to."

"Wait a minute. A pile of blankets wouldn't fool anyone."

"Listen, Andre. Do you remember when we saw the wood shop at the camp? I said I was surprised there were so many shavings for those three wooden heads the Germans used in the escape."

"I remember. So?"

"The reason there were so many shavings is there were actually FOUR heads made. It was all part of their plan. The fourth head was taken with the escapees and used to create the sleeping man in the back. They probably ditched the head in the woods after they ran out of gas.

I'm telling you Meinhoff split off from the others. Captain Davies and his men can track the woods until doomsday but they won't find Meinhoff for the simple reason that he isn't here. He wasn't with them!"

"But he was with them when they stole the car from Joe Fergusen. His prints were in the car too."

"Yes, but somewhere after that, he split off and went some other way."

MacKensie stood with his mouth open for a second, then snapped his fingers. "Of course. The bastards deked us. And that's why it took them so long to get here; they took Meinhoff somewhere and dropped him off! He's the one with the puck. The other two are just decoys."

Van Marter nodded. "It sure looks that way....but where did they drop him off?"

"More to the point," said MacKensie, "where is he now?"

-9-

Gregor Meinhoff dozed fitfully, his head lolling back and forth with the motion of the train. The rails made a soothing and monotonous metronome as he drifted in and out of sleep, and dreamed once more of the last moments of the U-110.

Once again, he was crouched in the dank gray metal tube of the U-110 bracing himself for the next round of depth charges. Like almost everyone else on the boat, he instinctively looked upward, even though they could see nothing but the water condensing and dripping off the overheads. All was quiet, then he heard the rhythmic churning sound of the escort destroyer's props growing louder until it passed overhead. Then he heard the dull splashing sounds of the depth charges plunging into the water above. He looked at his watch. At 50 meters, they had only a few seconds before…. The U-110 seemed to leap upward from the force of the explosions below. Men were thrown to the deck and the lights dimmed. Voices concealing barely controlled panic called out depth and damage reports. Fleisher was jammed in a corner trying to make himself as small as possible, and chewing his fist in sweaty claustrophobic terror.

The lights had returned now, and several crewmen were whispering nervously. Captain Lemp, squinting alertly in the gloom, motioned for silence.

"Here they come again," he said quietly.

Meinhoff felt sick when he heard the noise of the screws building again. Louder and louder they grew. He heard the splash of depth charges again and prayed he would live for the next few minutes.

"Rig for depth charges!" he blurted out loud, and was suddenly awake and sweating on the swaying railway car. He wiped his face with his hand and shook the last of the dream from his mind.

The pace of the clatter slowed as the train rounded a tight curve. Meinhoff looked out at the mountains and woods of the surrounding countryside. The sight settled him and let him turn his mind away from the last moments of the U-110.

"My God, what a beautiful country. It seems to go on forever. Mountains, rivers, and forests as grand as any in Germany. Canada will make a fine addition to the Third Reich when the time comes."

He smiled. When he got back to Germany, he would be a hero. The Fuhrer himself would decorate him with the *Rittercreuse*, the Knight's Cross. He, Gregor Meinhoff, would be the man who won the war for Germany. He, and he alone would alert the high command to the terrible danger of the loss of the Enigma encoding machine. Well, why not? He had been the one to deduce what had really happened from seeing a piece of Canadian newspaper article. He planned much of the escape, and he would escape in triumph to Germany while the stupid Canadians were still searching Sault Ste Marie.

He looked at his watch. By now, Theimann and Fleisher should have been apprehended trying to cross into the United States. As planned, they would abandon the car about a mile from the border and split up. When captured they would claim all three had been together and when the Canadians failed to find him, they would naturally assume he, Meinhoff, had made it across. Then the Americans and The Canadians would engage in a futile cross border search for the escapee. And the longer he remained at large, the further south into the United States they would assume he had gotten. Meanwhile, he would be pursuing a route where no one was looking.

Of course, there was a good chance Theimann and Fleischer hadn't gotten that far. The Canadians must have set up road blocks farther out by now, and Theimann and Fleisher might blunder into one. He had told them to abandon the car and set out on foot if they saw a roadblock ahead, but you could never be sure what they would actually do. One thing was for certain; the longer Theimann and Fleisher remained at large, or stuck to their story if caught, the more time they would buy him.

Meinhoff sat back and smiled, satisfied with himself and with the circumstances. In another day or two he would be out of Canada and in the United States. In another week he could be in the German Embassy in Washington, relaying his vital information. He felt so contented, he found himself softly singing the Horst Wessel marching song to himself with the clicking of the rails keeping time.

Meinhoff chuckled. He knew the real Horst Wessel had been a lowlife street thug who was killed in a brawl during the early days of the Nazi party, then was made a martyr. Still, he had always liked the song, and it had never seemed more rousing or more appropriate.

A dull thud suddenly snapped Meinhoff out of his daydreaming and he was instantly alert, reaching for his pistol. A shadow appeared and a second later a figure swung onto the car and rolled across the plank floor.

Meinhoff was on his feet and had his hand on the pistol he had taken from Joe Fergusen. The figure on the floor rolled to a stop and a very shabby looking bearded man looked up at him and smiled.

"Sorry, mate. I didn't know this car was occupied."

"Well, you know it now," said Meinhoff menacingly. "So get off."

The old man's eyes widened. "I'd be glad to, mate," he said. "The trouble is, the train's picked up speed and it's downright dangerous to be hopping around out there now. Besides, this is the only open car I saw. The boxcars are all packed to the gills and locked up tighter than a moneylender's heart. Tell you what; if you'll let me stay, I've got some smokes and a can of soup you can have."

Meinhoff looked at him and noticed a newspaper sticking out of his pocket. Well, the old man had seen him now, and there was no telling who he'd talk to if thrown off. Meinhoff considered killing the old man and dumping the body, but decided against it. If the old fool's body were discovered, it would draw a lot of police attention to the train and its destination. Better to simply deceive the old man while getting such information from him as he could. Meinhoff smiled and put the pistol back in his belt.

"All, right, old timer. You can stay until the next stop. Sorry about the gun, but you can't be too careful.""

The man smiled, revealing several missing teeth. "Why, that's mighty gracious of you, mate. I'm much obliged. The name's Atkins, Wilbur Atkins." He held out a grimy hand and Meinhoff took it hesitantly.

"I am…Wilson, Frank Wilson." he said. "Make yourself comfortable. You can keep your cigarettes and your soup, but lend me your newspaper. I have read no news in several days."

"Why certainly, Mr Wilson. Here you are. There's nothing but bad news these days, I'm afraid. You got the war and the shortages, and all the bombing in London and ships sinking in the Atlantic." He shook his head morosely while Meinhoff devoured the newspaper for information he could use.

"I have to admit you gave me quite a turn," said Atkins. "I'm not used to company anymore. Back before the war, lots of fellows were riding the rails from one town to the next looking for work. But the war ended the depression and now everyone's got a job and the cars are empty. I'm one of the few that are left. I guess I just sort of got used to riding."

Meinhoff did not respond, but Atkins was not the kind who was easily discouraged. "So, have you been riding the rails long, Mr. Wilson?"

Meinhoff still didn't answer. He was absorbed in the newspaper, its pages rapidly flapping in the wind as the train wheels clicked along the rails.

"I've been at it since '38 myself," Atkins continued. "I had a few odd jobs before that. I even worked for the Canadian Pacific for a while: did maintenance work on the roadbed and the snow sheds around Kicking Horse Pass in the Rockies. But every time a train went by, I wanted to be on it; always wanted to be somewhere else. I'm sure you know the feeling."

Meinhoff looked up from the newspaper. "Wanting to be somewhere else? I do indeed."

Atkins nodded, happy he was finally getting a response.

"That's what the others don't understand about people like us. We don't need luxury, or security, or even regular meals. We just want to see what's over the next horizon, or what's around the next bend." As if to emphasize the point, the train crossed a timber bridge with a loud vibrating rumble. A clear blue stream turned to foaming white as it tumbled rapidly over glistening gray rocks far below.

Meinhoff looked at the old man and decided he could be a valuable source of information.

"I've never ridden this line before, Mr Atkins," he said. "What's around the bend for us?"

Atkins looked out at the scenery rushing past, and the green hills in the distance.

"Oh, we've got maybe another hour or two before we get to the next stop. That's where they'll load more of the goods for shipment to Halifax to go over on the convoys to England. You've got to look out for the railroad police once we get in the yard; the bulls'll roust you out so fast you'll wonder where all the bars at the windows came from. That's if you're lucky."

"And what happens if we are unlucky?"

"They beat us into a bloody pulp with their clubs."

Meinhoff nodded. "I see. So how do we avoid these guards?"

"Well, there's a place the train'll have to slow down just before the main part of the station. If you jump off there, you can hide out until dark and jump another train, or simply walk through town and pick up the train again on the other side."

"Very neat. You must have done this many times." Meinhoff was beginning to be glad he hadn't thrown Atkins off the train.

Atkins pulled out a bent cigarette stub and carefully lit it. "Well, I learned the way I learn most things …the hard way. I got caught a few times and got the hell beat out of me. That sort of thing makes a man more cautious."

Meinhoff pulled out a piece of paper and a pencil.

"Well, Mr. Atkins, why don't you draw me a sketch of the railroad yard layout and the main line routes. I wouldn't want to get lost. You see it's very important I get where I'm going as soon as possible."

Atkins smiled. No one had ever asked for his advice before and he was flattered. "I'll do my best."

*   *   *

Donna Hastings rubbed her eyes. She was getting a slight headache from scanning so many records and local police reports. So far, she hadn't found anything of interest, but you could never be sure about these things, and whenever she got tired, she thought of her brother and the transport. Of course, the last escapee had probably been caught by now, but she pushed on regardless.

The reports had been arranged geographically on a series of tables around the conference room. She was beginning to regret she had asked for reports from the day of the previous escape attempt as well, but she thought it best to cover everything. After all, the escapees might have done something the first time that would shed light on their plans this time.

"Who would have guessed there would be so much crime in northern Ontario?" she mumbled, shaking her head. Of course the crime mostly consisted of petty vandalism, missing pets, and wash stolen from clotheslines, but she had to check them all. You never could tell.

On the wall was a map of Canada and a larger scale map of Ontario and Quebec. On the other wall was a map of northern Ontario, showing roads and small towns. On this map she methodically placed pins corresponding to each crime report and where it occurred. Red pins represented reports since midnight of yesterday and blue pins stood for reports during the time of the first escape attempt, Each pin had a small paper tag numbered to correspond to the report number.

Finally, the reports were finished and all the pins were in place. There was the red pin where Joe Fergusen's car had been stolen, and there were several more scattered within a few miles. She sighed. This wasn't too promising.

"A lot of tedious work for very little result," she said. Then she looked over at Shillington and saw two blue pins about a mile apart. One pin was very close to where Fleisher had been captured. She thumbed through the reports looking for number 17.

"Here it is. At 1923 hours, a Mrs. McGrain complained of her neighbor's dog barking. When the officer arrived, the dog was quiet and the owner was just arriving home from an errand.

"The dog might have been barking at Fleisher as he passed by," she said. "But that only tells us he was there and we already knew that. Let's see what the other one is."

She found report 18 and read aloud. "At 2034 hours, Mr. Ian Phillips reported someone apparently had rummaged through his automobile, which he kept parked in an overgrown area for shade. The front passenger side door was ajar and several items were missing from the glove box, including several road maps."

She looked up. "Road maps? Road maps. Maybe that's how they planned the break."

Just then the phone rang with a jarring sound that startled her. "Donna Hastings."

"Donna? This is Tom Van Marter. We're still between Sudbury and Sault Ste…The Soo, but Meinhoff is still on the loose."

"Still on the loose? But they were together," she said, the fatigue and frustration showing in her voice. She had a sinking feeling that Meinhoff was too elusive even for MacKensie and Van Marter.

"Not really," he replied. "Meinhoff wasn't with them. We're pretty sure he split off and went some other way, and he did it long before they ever got here. The guy's clever."

"Oh no. Do you have any idea where he could be?"

"Not yet. But we'll need to alert the RCMP from Cochrane south to Toronto."

"I'll do it. What about east to Ottawa or Montreal?"

"Yeah, better tell them too. Meinhoff could be anywhere by now."

Donna thought a moment, then had an idea. "Tom, did they drop him off along the way or did they take him in some other direction?"

"Judging by how long it took them to get to where we picked them up, I'd say they took him on some detour."

"How much time did they use dropping Meinhoff off? Can we back in the distance?"

"I plan to try as soon as I get a good road map, but there's a lot of ground to cover. Rags is ready to fly us anywhere, but we don't know where to tell him."

"I've been studying police reports from the area south of the camp," Donna said. "I think they probably had road maps from the previous escape."

"I'm not surprised," he replied. "Anyway, we questioned the other two but didn't get much. We're going to see if we can study the maps and compare times and distances to see where Meinhoff might have gone. It's a long shot, but it's all we have right now."

"All right, keep in touch," she said. "And be careful. Meinhoff is dangerous, especially when they have put so much time and effort into this escape. When you do find him, he might not be taken easily."

"Thanks, Donna."

"For what?"

"For saying 'WHEN you find him', not 'IF you find him'."

*   *   *

In a back room of the OPP station, Davies, Van Marter and MacKensie poured over several road maps of Ontario. Once again, MacKensie had lit up his briar pipe with the heavy and sweet odor of Mixture 22 tobacco from Duffy's Tobacco of Ottawa.

"The way I figure it," said MacKensie, as he exhaled a cloud of smoke, "they had to have dropped Meinhoff off along the way. The question is where? Come on, Tom; this is your specialty."

"Well, if they drove straight from where they got the car at about 3:00 A.M.," said Van Marter, "they had about 300 miles to travel to reach the Esso station at 2:00 P.M. How fast should they have been able to travel along the road from Cochrane to North Bay then west to Sudbury and where the car was ditched?"

Davies scratched his head. "I've traveled it many times myself. I'd say it should take about seven or eight hours, depending on traffic, weather, and how fast you can get through the small towns along the way."

"All right, let's say eight hours since they wouldn't be as familiar with the way and might be more cautious about being noticed."

"That means there's still over two hours to account for," said Davies. "But didn't they say they stopped for repairs? That could account for it."

"But they…" Van Marter began, but MacKensie interrupted.

"Jack," he said, addressing Davies. "It looks like we've done all we can here. We'll be heading back east in a few minutes, and we need to finish up a few things. Would you excuse us?"

Davies looked uncertain for a moment. "Oh…sure Andre. Let me know if you need anything else. Sorry we didn't get the other chap."

"Thanks, Jack. Your people did a hell of a job. Old Fritz never came up against a Chippewa before."

"I'll continue the search for 24 hours just in case," said Davies. "And if either of these two gentlemen spill anything more I'll let you know through Ottawa."

When Davies had left, Van Marter started to protest. "Why did you dismiss him like that? He could have been a big help."

"I know, but no one must know the background unless absolutely necessary. Besides, I suddenly figured out what Meinhoff is doing."

"Oh? And just what is Leutnant Meinhoff doing? Aside from making monkeys out of us that is."

MacKensie looked at him with excitement in his eyes. "I should have guessed it before, eh? I've seen it so many times. He's taking standard U-boat evasive action."

"Come again?"

"Look, a U-boat is too slow to outrun an escort vessel, especially submerged, so it has to evade. After they fire torpedoes, there is a minute or two before they hit, and before the escort vessels can try to figure out where the shots came from and react. During this time, the U-boat will travel as fast as it can to be away from the area the escorts expect to find them. With any luck, they can get the escort to dump depth charges in the wrong place while they're someplace else. That's just what these guys have been doing since they escaped; drawing us away from the place we should be for the kill."

"But we captured two of them…"

"Decoys, pawns, cannon fodder; call them what you like. They never really expected to escape. Their sole purpose was to draw us in the wrong direction so Meinhoff could travel unmolested. I'll bet part of the reason for the time difference is that they were purposely driving slowly to stretch out the time so Meinhoff could get that much farther away, eh? No, Meinhoff is the real danger, not those two. Remember how close their stories were, and how neither of them was specific about what kind of mechanical problem they had, and how sure they both were that Meinhoff had not been caught? And why do you think they talked of going to the Soo loud enough that Joe Fergusen could hear them? They wanted us to do just what we did and we fell for it. If they hadn't run out of gasoline, they would have abandoned the car so close to the border we'd never be sure that Meinhoff didn't make it across. We might have given up the search right then and there."

Van Marter could only nod. Everything MacKensie was saying made perfect sense. Finally, he spoke. "All right. What does a U-boat do after the escort goes to the wrong place?"

"It hides. It stays perfectly still and perfectly quiet while the escort churns up the ocean looking for it, just like we've been doing. More often than not, the escort gives up and goes on its way. When the heat is off, the U-boat comes to life again and quietly leaves the scene."

"Do you think that's what Meinhoff will do?"

"Maybe. If he gets to some good hiding place; someplace like a city where he can disappear, he could lie low for a few days. It would give him a chance to arrange his border crossing and help to convince us he was already gone. Then, when he does break for it, no one will be expecting it, making it all the easier for him."

"You mean he's still in Cochrane?" said Van Marter.

MacKensie shook his head. "I don't think so. Cochrane's too small for a stranger to hide in. He'd be more likely to go to a place he has heard of, a place he knows is both big enough and close enough to the border to do the trick. And a place within a day's travel of Cochrane to minimize the chances of his being spotted along the way."

"And where would that be?"

"Toronto, Ottawa, or Montreal."

"That doesn't narrow it down much."

"That's where you come in, cowboy. It's time to dazzle me with scientific FBI methods. Given what we know, which city would you say is most likely?"

"That's kind of a tall order, isn't it? Maybe you'd like me to figure out his mailing address while I'm at it."

MacKensie smiled. "If it wouldn't be too much trouble."

Van Marter ran his hand over his forehead and let out a low whistle. Then he smoothed out the road map in front of him.

"All right, the key has to be the missing 2-3 hours and where they took Meinhoff during that time. The whole purpose of whatever detour they took had to have been to get Meinhoff on his way to wherever he was going."

MacKensie nodded. "Agreed. They didn't have time to sightsee and I'm betting they didn't got lost."

"If they went off Rte 11, the main road south to North Bay, they probably went slower to find their way. Let's say their average speed for the three lost hours was 35 mph. That means they traveled 105 miles. But we're talking about a round trip, because they had to get back to the main road. So we can assume they detoured to a place that's about 50 miles off of Rte 11. That additional distance would also explain why they ran out of gas sooner than we figured. Let's look at the maps."

"Well, one thing's for sure," said MacKensie, "they didn't drive him directly to Toronto, Ottawa, or Montreal. They're all too far away."

Van Marter nodded. "That's true, but they must have taken him someplace that would allow him to get there himself. Maybe they cruised around until they found a car for him to steal."

MacKensie shook his head. "Not a chance. They couldn't count on a situation like Joe Fergusen again. Besides, a stolen car is a major crime in that area. It would be reported and he'd be stopped before he got where he was going. Then there's the petrol problem. Besides, at that time of the morning it wouldn't have taken that long to find an unlocked car."

"Well, let's see where 50 miles from Rte 11 turns up."

Carefully, Van Marter traced a line parallel to Rte 11 and 50 miles away. The results were not encouraging.

"There's nothing that seems to fit. Almost everything within 50 miles is forest or small towns. Where did they go?"

The door opened and Davies stuck his head in. "Excuse me, but I have a car waiting for you. Your pilot, Mr McLaughlin says he's ready anytime you say."

"Thanks, Jack. Well be along in a few minutes."

"The only thing I can figure," said Van Marter, "is that they took Meinhoff to some form of transportation. But that raises two questions; what transportation and how could they have known about it ahead of time? You can't get bus and boat schedules in a prison camp."

"Not to mention airplane or railroad," added MacKensie. "We can also rule out airplane, I think. There are too many clearances and checks involved, eh? Besides, for all they knew, we could have had police checking every flight. And if they could steal a plane, they'd all pile in and head for the border with no further need of deception."

"And busses and trains have the same problem," said Van Marter. "Any form of public transport is too risky under the circumstances. But if we've ruled out public and private transport, along with busses, airplanes, boats and trains, what's left?"

They both stared at the map as if to burn holes in it with their eyes. MacKensie continued to slowly puff on his pipe. Collectively they tried to force the answer out through sheer force of will.

"If your nose is all tuned up," said Van Marter, "this would be a good time to for it to start twitching."

Suddenly, MacKensie smiled. "That sneaky son of a bachelor. I know where he's going and how he's getting there. Come on, we've got to get to Rags and make a call to Ottawa."

*   *   *

"All this war news is depressing, eh?"

Wilbur Atkins, thought Meinhoff, was as irritating as he was good natured. An unusual combination, but one Atkins seemed to have mastered. Still, he had to admit Atkins was well versed in the finer points of riding trains without a ticket. As he talked, Atkins ate his can of soup, having heated it over a small fire he had made in a tin can using a rag soaked in grease from a wheel bearing as fuel.

"I swear them Germans is everywhere," he continued." Every time we ship something to England, why, it seems some German submarine sinks it."

Meinhoff stifled a smile but did not reply.

"But folks is rallying round King and country in spite of it all. I tell you, it makes a man proud. Oh, there's a few German sympathizers, but nobody pays them a bit of mind. They want hanging, I say. Of course, I was in the last war. We beat Jerry good in that one, you know, but what a time we had. That was the closest thing to Hell I'll ever see on this earth. I never saw such mud….and the damned artillery? Why it was enough to drive a man mad the way those guns kept pounding all night. A lot of good men died in that one. I sure hate to see it again. I remember one night when I was on wire detail, the star shells…."

"Did you say there were German sympathizers?"

"What? Sympathizers? Oh, yes, there's a few. People with business interests or family connections in Germany mostly. A man named Tysyn started up a 'love the Germans' sort of organization in Montreal a few years ago, but it's gone now of course. They said some good things about Hitler up until '39, but they've been quiet since war was declared and the government put a bunch of 'em in prison camps somewhere."

Meinhoff made a mental note, then noticed where they were. "We seem to be getting close to a town," he remarked. Meinhoff had already checked the map he was carrying and thought it was probably Senneterre, but didn't know if the train stopped there or not.

Atkins was on his feet and alert. "That'll be Senneterre. It's a pretty big place seeing as how it's in the middle of the wilderness and all."

"Does the train stop there?"

"It'll stop. They'll take on a few passengers and a few more cars with timber and such for the war effort. They'll search the cars when they stop and we don't want to be aboard when they do. We'll have to jump off ahead of time, stroll through town while the train is stopped, then jump back after it starts on its way again."

"And how do we do that?"

Atkins smiled, revealing his crooked teeth once again. "Well, Mr. Wilson, you just stick with me and you'll be fine. There's a tight curve about a mile ahead. When the train slows down we can step off as easy as you please. And if you want to catch another train, why you just let me know. Old Wilbur Atkins'll show you the way."

Meinhoff smiled. "Thank you Wilbur. You have been most helpful."

The squeal of brakes and the clank of couplings announced the slowing of the train a few minutes later. Meinhoff and Atkins crouched on the swaying steps to the flatcar waiting to jump. The wooden ties were a brown blur beneath their feet and the grey stone roadbed ballast rushing past did not look inviting.

"Jumping on and off trains is the same as anything else," said Atkins. "There's a right and a wrong way. If you do it wrong, you can get caught or maybe slip and wind up with a leg cut off. You got to make your move when a train slows down on a tight curve. There's always curves when going through hills or along a river, and usually the train'll slow down. That's the time to make your move to either get on or off. Otherwise the train'll be going too fast and you'll get your arm yanked out of its joint when you grab on."

"That is obvious," said Meinhoff. "Anything else?"

"Yes. Always jump on the outside of the curve, like we're doing now. If you're on the inside, you'll be in easy view of the engine and the caboose. On the outside, ain't nobody can see you. Besides, if you jump off on the outside, the motion'll carry you away from the wheels."

"All right. When do we jump? We're entering a switching yard already."

"Not yet," said Atkins, the voice of experience, at least as far as jumping trains was concerned. "Wait for it….wait…NOW!"

The jump was so perfectly timed, the two men seemed to merely step down as if alighting at a station. They scurried behind an old work shack as the rest of the train rolled by.

"What did I tell you?" said Atkins. "There's an art to getting on and off a train….especially if you don't have a ticket."

"Hold it right there," came a voice in French. They turned and saw a railroad guard, club in hand. He was tall and overweight, and had a stubble of beard darkening the lower part of his face. The guard took a step towards them.

"All right, you two come along with me. You're trespassing on railroad property. *Allez!*"

-10-

When he saw the railroad guard, Meinhoff felt a surge of panic. This buffoon could ruin everything. He felt for the bulk of his pistol and realized he couldn't use it. The guard would report it if still alive, and someone else would report it if the guard were killed. A dead railroad guard or a gunshot was sure to bring unwelcome attention and spoil the escape. Meinhoff stood frozen for a moment.

"*Je'ai dire allez*," the guard insisted, motioning with his club. "that is, unless you need a little encouragement." He smacked his palm with the club in a threatening manner. Meinhoff stepped toward the guard and was about to administer a swift kick to get the club away when he saw two more guards approaching out of the corner of his eye. They were only about 50 yards away, so he had to do something that would get him out without raising the alarm.

So he smiled.

"Tres bon, officer, Good work indeed!" he beamed. Then while the guard looked bewildered, said "I'm Wilson, from the head office security staff. This is my assistant Mr Atkins. I'm doing a little fact finding exercise to test rail yard security. We have to be extra alert these days for sabotage, you know. I salute you for your alertness. Your name will be in my report and I wouldn't be surprised if there weren't a promotion in this for you as well."

The guard lowered his club slightly. He was flattered, but still suspicious. "Wilson, you say? I've never heard of…"

"Of course not. I have to travel in secrecy to test security. If people knew who I was or when I was coming, they'd put on a show. The company doesn't want that. The whole point is to make inspections impromptu. And I have to say, you passed with flying colors. Now, what is your name?"

"Uh…" the guard hesitated. Meinhoff fingered his pistol. "Uh.. Chadreau; Henry D. Chadreau."

Meinhoff made a show of writing on the small notebook he had with him. "Very good M. Chadreau. Now, I must ask you one favor. In order to maintain security, those gentlemen approaching must not know who I am. They may not be as trustworthy as you are."

Chadreau looked at the approaching guards, then back to Meinhoff, then back to the guards. "Leave that to me sir. Ben! Grayson! Never mind. I've got these two under control."

The guards looked at Meinhoff and Atkins for a second, nodded, and went on their way.

"Excellent work, Mr. Chadreau," said Meinhoff. "Now, I will have my report in by the end of the month and I think you'll be hearing something soon after. Have you ever considered detective work?"

"Yes. I've dreamed of being a railroad inspector one day," Chadreau nodded eagerly.

"Well, you just remember that. You just may get there," said Meinhoff. "Meanwhile, may I depend on your continued secrecy until the end of the month?"

Chadreau snapped to attention. "Of course. You can count on me."

"Good man. Now I must ask one more small favor."

"Of course. Anything to help security."

"Wonderful. I think this yard is secure, but I have my doubts about some of the others."

"Oh, they're not as good as this one, you can bet on it," said Chadreau, shaking his head wisely. "Some of the other yards in Quebec…"

"I'm sure you're right, but I need to find out first hand. Now if someone wished to illegally reboard this train, where would be the best place? I may need to recommend extra security."

Chadreau hesitated, then smiled and winked conspiratorially. "I'll show you. Right this way."

*   *   *

"Yes… yes I thought so. Thanks, Donna, and call us as soon as you have those schedules." MacKensie hung up the phone at the airport and rubbed his hands together in satisfaction.

"I thought so. Donna was way ahead of us as usual, and I think she found a tidbit of information to confirm my theory."

"YOUR theory?" Van Marter raised an eyebrow.

"Oh, all right; OUR theory. Anyway, I think I know what our little U-boat *scweinehund* is up to."

"That's very reassuring," said Van Marter. "Care to let me in on it?"

"All right, look at the map again. This is a standard road map, the kind you get in service stations, eh? Camp Q is here at Monteith, near Timmins and south of Cochrane. Joe Fergusen's farm is here, about ten miles to the south of the camp. Now notice these lines with short cross lines on them."

"Railroad tracks."

"Right. We couldn't figure on a means of transport that was within 50 miles of the route to Sault Ste Marie, able to be used in secret, and which the prisoners could have known about in advance. Well here's the answer. The Canadian Pacific Railroad, along with several others run freight trains through Cochrane to Montreal, and all the way to Halifax. The route passes through Cochrane and goes through Northern Quebec all the way to Montreal. A man dropped off in Cochrane could jump on a freight train when it slows to round a curve and have a care-free, if somewhat uncomfortable ride all the way to Montreal."

Van Marter looked at the map and traced a rail line with his finger. "It could be. Even the fact that they didn't try to jump the train at Monteith helped to throw us off the scent. There's a rail line that goes south to …..North Bay. Holy Cow; only in Canada could you go south to get to a place called North Bay."

"Very funny. Let's keep our sticks on the ice, eh?" grumbled MacKensie. "After North Bay, the north-south route branches off to either Toronto or Ottawa." "So, assuming we're right and he jumped a train near Cochrane, how do we know which way he went?"

"We don't; not yet, anyway," said MacKensie with frustration in his voice. "But maybe we can narrow it down."

Van Marter nodded. "Maybe. What did you find out from Donna?"

"With her usual thoroughness, she traced all crime reports on not only the day of the escape but the day of the earlier escape. She found several road maps were stolen by the earlier escapees. That would have given them all the information they needed to plan it this way."

"But without a schedule, how did Meinhoff know how long he'd have to wait?"

"He didn't have to. He knew Cochrane was a direct rail hub and he knew Canada was shipping record amounts of minerals and forest products for the war effort. After all, he was spending a lot of time try-ing to sink some of it before he was captured, so he knew there had to be trains passing pretty frequently. Plus it was far enough from the camp that security would be lax."

Van Marter made some quick calculations. "O.K. If he arrived in Cochrane at between 5:00 and 6:00 A.M. what train did he catch?"

"I don't know yet. Donna's getting the schedules now."

The phone rang and they both jumped for it. Van Marter got there first. "Van Marter here."

The cool voice over the phone could only be Donna Hastings. "Hello, Tom. I have some information for you."

"Hello Donna. It's good to hear from you again. I'm getting a great tour of Canada."

"Well, maybe when this is over, I can show you around Ottawa," she said, and he thought she could see him flush over the phone.

"Yeah. That would be great. I'll take you up on it," said Van Marter, grinning foolishly.

"What about the damn train schedules?" sputtered MacKensie. grabbing the phone.

"Oh, yes, the trains. There were two trains through Cochrane between 4:30 and 6:00 A.M. A southbound to North Bay at 4:45 and an eastbound the locals call the Abitibi Express at 5:35."

"So which one did he take?"

"My guess would be the eastbound," Donna replied. "The southbound would take him back through the area we would be looking for him. Eastbound would take him well away from the camp and in the opposite direction from where we were looking."

"That makes sense. Where does the southbound go after North Bay?"

"There are east and west connections in North Bay, but that train turns around and heads north again. Even if Meinhoff didn't know that, I'd imagine he would have realized it was a possibility."

"So he had a choice of a train that would take him back the way he came and wouldn't take him near the border and a train that would head eastbound to Montreal. That's got to be the one he took," said MacKensie. "What's the timetable?"

"The eastbound Abitibi Express is actually a rather slow train. There are only a few scheduled stops, but it stops in a lot of small towns by passenger request. Its major scheduled stop along the way is at Senneterre in Northern Quebec at 5:30 tonight, and it's due in Montreal at 7:11 tomorrow morning."

MacKensie looked at his watch. It was already 6:02. "How long does the train stop in Sennenterre?"

"About an hour. It picks up passengers and additional freight."

MacKensie's eyes widened with excitement, and he pounded the table in delight. "That means it's there now! Donna, get on the phone to Senneterre. Tell them there is a fugitive on the train and not to leave until the local police can board it and do a thorough search. Give them a full description of Meinhoff, but don't give his real name. Tom and Rags and I will head up there right away."

"I'll get on it, Andre, but there's no RCMP post there, only the locals."

"Well, tell them this is their chance for glory. Tell them Meinhoff is wanted for auto theft and kidnaping. That's close enough. Let us know how you're doing. We've got to get going."

He put the phone back and grinned with excitement.

"Finally, we got a break. And with a little luck, we might just grab this guy."

✳   ✳   ✳

The massive gray form of the Abitibi Express sat idly at the rail station in Senneterre, so big it seemed to elbow the small buildings aside. Steam gently hissed in thin streams from various places on the locomotive, swirling, drifting, then dissolving in the cool, pine-scented air of northern Quebec. The string of cars, stretching off into the pine and birch woods, shuddered slightly as the bump and slam of couplings announced the addition of each freight car. About 25 new passengers were swarming into the single passenger car, joining the dozen already there and getting settled for the long slow trip to Montreal. The car was alive with bustling activity and rapid chattering French as servicemen returning from leave mingled with civilians sitting with parcels, thermos bottles, picnic baskets, and blankets. Mothers bounced babies on their knees and older children ran up and down the aisles. In the midst of wartime austerity, a trip to Montreal was an event, and the passengers were cheerful and excited.

"*Billets, Madames and Monsieurs; billets, s'il vous plait,*" called the conductor as he slowly made his way down the aisle checking tickets. As he punched each ticket, the conductor noted the usual crowd on the Abitibi run; mostly French speaking Quebecois with a few English from Ontario and sprinkling of Chippewa and Cree Indians as well.

"*Pardon,*" someone asked him. "*A quelle heure arrivons nous a Montreal?*"

"*A sept heurs et trente, Madame,*" he answered.

As he reached the end of the car, the conductor noted the two men he had seen in the yard earlier were not there. Strange, their disappearing like that, he thought. One of them was a bit ragged, it was true, but the other certainly looked like a passenger. Now neither of them was on board. He looked out the doorway at the end of the car and saw no sign of them. Where could they have gone?

In the weathered clapboard station building, meanwhile, the neatly uniformed station master looked at the brass framed clock on the wall, checked it against his own gold pocket watch, nodded, and decided it was time for his inspection. He prided himself on his attention to detail, especially with the importance of the cargos of war material that were flowing through Senneterre daily, so he made it a point to examine each train personally before it proceeded. Yes, he thought, he would check each coupling, make sure there were no "hot boxes" from dry wheel bearings. He had heard of tramps dipping grease from the bearing boxes to make fires, so he made a point of checking. He would then check with the guards and the conductor, and have a chat with the engineer and fireman. The whole process took over a half hour, but when the train was ready to move on, the station master would be confident all was in order. After all, there was a war on and you couldn't be too careful.

He stood up and brushed a few nonexistent specks of dust from his blue jacket, took his hat off its peg, placed it carefully on the exact center of his head, and strode out onto the platform. A few seconds later, he was at the engine greeting the engineer and beginning his inspection.

"*Bonjour, Louis,*" he said. "*Comme ca va?*"

"*Lentement, Pierre,*" the engineer grumbled. "*Trop lentement.*"

As the engineer complained of the slowness of the inspection, the station master continued his rounds at his deliberate pace. Meanwhile, in the station master's empty office, a phone started ringing with urgency and insistence. The unheard sound echoed off the wooden paneled walls of the empty room like an unanswered cry for help.

*   *   *   *

When they arrived back at the airstrip, Rags had seen them coming and started his preflight check,

"I'll be ready in a few minutes," he called to them. "This old girl is raring to go. There's birds up there that are starting to wonder where she got to. What's our next stop?"

"Senneterre, Quebec," said MacKensie.

"Nice place," Rags observed. "Mind you, they got a dirt airstrip up there that'll shake your fillings loose. I just hope one of you boys can parlez vous, if you know what I mean."

"*Mais certainment,*" MacKensie replied, then he looked at his watch and turned to Van Marter.

"It's 7:38. I'm going to call Donna before we leave and see if they bagged Meinhoff on that train."

Van Marter nodded as MacKensie ducked into the small control building to call Ottawa. Not knowing what else to do, he sat on a rickety wooden bench by the hanger to wait. He was still amazed by how fast the case was changing and how big an area they had to cover. Most of the manhunts he'd been involved with had only covered a single state, or a single city.

In spite of himself, his mind kept returning to Donna Hastings. He saw her back in Ottawa checking reports, making phone calls, and coordinating their support with single minded efficiency, pausing only to occasionally brush a few long strands of ash blond hair away from her face.

While Van Marter was thinking of Donna, Rags McLaughlin finished his pre flight check, ambled over to the bench and sat down with a heave of breath.

"That old girl's got a lot of hours on her, but she's not ready to cash in just yet. They don't call them Faithful Annies for nothing."

Van Marter started, not knowing just what Rags was talking about at first. Then he realized the old pilot was referring to the airplane. He nodded vacantly.

"Course all the newer planes been shipped to England by now. We get to keep the tired ones here." Rags reached in his jacket and pulled out a green pack of Lucky Strikes, lit one, and slowly let out a long stream of smoke that twisted and broke up in the breeze.

"When the war started," he said, looking back at the plane, "I joined up hoping for some action, but the RCAF figured I was a bit too old and kept me here to train new pilots and to fly officials around. Most of the training of Commonwealth pilots is done in the Can, you know."

"The what?"

"Canada. Anyway, all the training helps the war effort, but it wasn't really what I had in mind. I didn't always fly one of these trainers, you know. At the beginning, I had me a new Hawker Hurricane fighter. By god that was a sweet ride. That girl could fly rings around anything in the sky, and she looked like she was flying at top speed when she was just sitting on the tarmac. She had cannon, machine guns and bomb mounts. I always used to say she was like my first wife; beautiful and deadly.

I used to get up early in the morning and wash that Hurricane myself; kept her spotless and gleaming like the blade of a knife. I'd talk to her like she was a real person. Some quiet mornings, why I could swear she answered me."

Rags wasn't looking at Van Marter now. He was gazing sadly at the ground. His gravelly voice grew soft and wistful.

"And when we flew," he continued, with reverence and wonder in his voice, "it was like we were one person. She'd jump like a race horse every time I pushed the stick or worked the pedals. When we were up there, I used to feel sorry for all the poor souls on the ground who'd never know the pure gut bustin' joy of sailing through the clouds with the sun making your wings sparkle and the whole of God's creation spread out at your feet. I really loved that girl. We were going off together and bag us a few Messerschmidts, but the RCAF decided I was needed here."

Rags took another puff and exhaled slowly in what sounded very much like a sigh.

"What happened to the Hurricane?" Van Marter asked finally.

Rags didn't answer at first, and Van Marter was about to repeat the question when Rags finally spoke in a quiet voice. "They shipped her over on a transport to help the British about two months after the war started. I tell you, it damn near broke my heart to see her packed off like that. I was in Halifax at the time so I went down to the dock to see her off. They had her tied down to the deck like they was afraid she'd escape or something, and she looked like an eagle tied in a cage. I talked to her one last time; told her she'd get a new pilot who'd take good care of her and she'd finally get to do the job she was built for. By god, that was a sad day."

Van Marter felt strangely moved by the story, and looked at the pilot in a new light. "That's too bad, but at least she went where she was needed most," he said. "Do you have any idea what became of her?"

Rags ground out the cigarette, stood up and stretched. Then he turned to Van Marter with a look of sadness in his eyes. "Three days out of Halifax the ship was torpedoed by a U-boat. It sank with all hands."

"Damn it!" shouted MacKensie as he emerged from the control building raising his arms in frustration. "That Kraut has the devil's own luck."

Van Marter's attention was abruptly jerked away from Rags to see what MacKensie was cursing about.

"They couldn't raise the station at Senneterre. Nobody would answer the damned phone! Can you believe it? Where in the hell was the station master, eh? They tried to radio the train, but the engineer must have shut his set down while they were in the station. And the train has probably pulled out by now."

"So we missed him again. Now what?" said Van Marter.

"We can radio the train again and get them to stop or return to Senneterre, but if the train reverses, it will tip Meinhoff off and he'll jump off before we can get police in place."

"Where's the next town of any size between Senneterre and Montreal?"

"There isn't any," said MacKensie. "That's mostly vacation and hunting lodge country. It's like northern Maine, eh? The next town is Montreal."

MacKensie and Van Marter paced in silence for a moment, while Rags stood by the plane and looked on curiously. MacKensie stopped and snapped his fingers.

"We'll stop it at the outskirts of Montreal. The route swings out in an arc and enters Montreal at its eastern end. It's a slow train, so we've got 10 hours to round up RCMP and Surate police and get them to the site." He ran his finger over the map.

"Yes, here we are. Pointe Aux Trembles, at the eastern end of the island. It won't have much of a police force of its own, if any, but it's close enough to central Montreal to get a hundred badges out there by the time the train arrives in the morning. Meinhoff won't be expecting any police search, at least not so soon. The train will stop and Meinhoff will be surrounded before he can say seig heil."

Van Marter looked up from the map. "A hundred police stopping a train in an outlying urban area?" he said doubtfully. "Won't that attract a lot of attention?"

"Not as much attention as Meinhoff will get if he makes contact with any of his Nazi buddies, eh? Anyway, do you have an approved FBI method of grabbing him before he has a whole city to hide in?" demanded MacKensie.

"Well, not offhand, but still…" he began.

"But still what?" snapped MacKensie.

"Well, a hundred police boarding and searching a train on the outskirts of Montreal is liable to have tongues wagging from here to Ottawa. Didn't the Commissioner tell us to be quiet about this?"

MacKensie glared at Van Marter. "Look, god damn it. We've got a job to do: stop Meinhoff. This is our last chance before he loses himself in a major city. Once he's in Montreal, he might as well be in Berlin he'll be so hard to find. We've got to get him NOW. If you can put your FBI rulebook away long enough to help, then do it. If not, pack your damned toothbrush."

"I understand all that," Van Marter insisted, still trying to be reasonable. "Look, I know you're frustrated about this, but we can't jump off the deep end now. Why not just a few police and a few plainclothesmen. They can be discrete."

"And let Meinhoff slip away again? No thanks. That sneaky sonofabitch has made monkeys out of us for the last time. We're going to do it right this time. Nobody's going to care how damned discrete it was once I've got Meinhoff in handcuffs. Now let's go."

But Van Marter did not move. "Andre, you can't do it. A massive police raid on a passenger train will blow secrecy to smithereens. Everyone will know!"

"Correction; everyone will SUSPECT. They won't KNOW a damned thing."

"But…."

"Rags!"

"Yes sir!"

"Forget Senneterre. We're off to Montreal. How long will you take to get us there?"

"That depends. Do you want us to get there with the fabric on or off the wings?" Rags replied.

"I don't care. Just get us there as soon as possible. Oh, and raise Montreal then Ottawa on the horn as soon as we get airborne. It's not as secure or as clear as the telephone, but it'll save us time."

MacKensie turned back to Van Marter who was standing with his arms folded and an expression that was somewhere between resentment and anger.

"Come on G-man; stop your sulking. Your 'See Canada while chasing a Hun' tour is about to resume. Our next stop is Montreal. When we get there, we'll grab some shuteye, then we'll grab our man in the morning."

"We're also liable to grab a few headlines while we're at it," Van Marter muttered as he reluctantly climbed into the plane.

After a quick taxi and a roaring takeoff, they were in the air once more and turning towards the east. The lowering sun behind them cast long black shadows among the deep green of the trees below.

"We're all set," said MacKensie a few minutes later as he returned to his seat after talking on the cockpit radio. "Armand Templeton in the Montreal detachment of the RCMP says he can get the men we need from the Montreal Police and the Quebec Surete. They're always looking for training exercises anyway. He says he can get close to a hundred men out to Pointe Aux Trembles by the time we get there."

"But did you talk to Ottawa?" Van Marter asked. "They really should be aware of this."

"Oh yes. I just told Donna we were heading to Montreal to try to intercept Meinhoff when he arrives."

"You somehow failed to mention the hundred police?"

"Well, no sense getting her bogged down in details."

Van Marter shook his head and looked out the window at the glow of the engine exhaust in the deepening twilight.

"We'll be landing at Dorval in about ten minutes," shouted Rags over the drone of the engines two hours later. MacKensie and Van Marter looked down and saw a long panorama of black building silhouettes set on a river that sparkled with the reflected lights of the city.

"Wow," said Van Marter. "This place makes Ottawa look like a village."

"Ah, yes; Montreal," said MacKensie. "It's a little too cosmopolitan for my tastes, but you'll probably like it if you like Washington and New York, eh? Everyone else seems to. In fact, politicians and business people in Ottawa come here for a diversion. I once asked my cousin what he liked best about Ottawa; he said what he liked best was the train to Montreal."

Van Marter smiled. "Very impressive. I can see it looks like a place that's big enough to offer all kinds of attractions."

"Especially," said MacKensie, "to a man on the run. In addition to everything else, Montreal is one damned good hiding place."

"We're cleared to land at Dorval," shouted Rags over the engines. "Hang on. We'll hit the ground in five minutes."

"Couldn't he phrase that a little better?" said Van Marter, grabbing the armrests.

The Anson rolled to a stop on the tarmac at Dorval airport after making its way past neat rows of fighters, bombers and trainers painted dark green and sporting the insignia of the RCAF. Rags killed the engines, creating a sudden unnatural but welcome silence. A few scattered ground crew gave them a quick glance then went back to whatever they were doing.

"I'm always embarrassed to land here in a trainer," said Rags glumly. "They get to chase Jerries and I get to be trainer and chauffeur. They're probably all thinking 'Who's that dapster anyway?'" He sighed as he slid out of the pilot's seat.

An RCMP patrol car raced out to meet the plane just as MacKensie and Van Marter were climbing out.

"Good evening Inspector," came the voice of a huge man in an RCMP uniform who unfolded himself from the car. "Captain Armand Templeton of the Montreal detachment of the RCMP at your service. Hop in and I'll take you to the barracks for a few winks, then out to Point Aux Trembles for the fun."

"Good evening Captain. This is Agent Van Marter of the American FBI. He's along to help out."

"Call me Tom," said Van Marter.

"Well, well," said Templeton, shaking Van Marter's hand with a grip that could have cracked walnuts. "An international effort of the RCMP, the Surete de Quebec, the Montreal Police, and the FBI. This will be a first."

"It better be a last as far as our fugitive is concerned," said MacKensie as he climbed into the car. "Is everything set up at Point Aux Trembles?"

"It will be by morning," said Templeton as he pulled into the mostly empty streets. "The train engineer has been contacted and is coordinating his arrival time to 7:20 AM. The RCMP and the Surete are at the station and will seal off the train as soon as it stops. Each man has been given a description of the fugitive and will check all I.D. cards for anyone named Wilson. We've got 93 men. That way we can put at least four on each car with another 13 or so to guard the tracks and any escape route. Believe me, Inspector, if your man is there, we'll find him."

"What if all that manpower spooks him?" asked Van Marter.

"The way they'll be deployed, he won't see them until it's too late. But just in case, we've stationed a few men a hundred yards ahead."

"Good," said MacKensie. "This time our man'll be in a corner he can't get out of."

"So what do we do now?" asked Van Marter. "The train won't be here for another seven hours."

MacKensie yawned. "We get some beauty sleep, eh?"

They reached the RCMP station and MacKensie and Van Marter were given two folding cots in a storage room to grab a few hours sleep.

Van Marter tried to make one last appeal to MacKensie to scale back the police raid he had scheduled for the next morning, but MacKensie was more convinced than ever and eager with anticipation. Finally, Van Marter resigned himself to the inevitable and turned in with no further protest. They both fell asleep instantly.

*   *   *

Later that night, while MacKensie and Van Marter slept, the problem of U boats and codes was receiving attention elsewhere. Half a world away, in an office on the coast of German occupied France, an ornate gold Louis XV mantle clock showed the time to be almost nine o'clock in the morning. A German naval officer stood at the long window of this office and looked out at the street below at the French pedestrians. He stood with his arms crossed, the heavy gold admiral's braid on his sleeves shining in the morning light.

Grandadmiral Carl Donitz, commander of the submarine arm of the German navy was not a large man. When he stood in his Kreigesmarine bridge coat and his tall peaked hat, in fact, he looked like some file clerk at a masquerade, or perhaps a school teacher. Few people would guess that this insignificant looking man directed the entire German U-boat campaign from his office in Lorient. From here, he carefully tracked and coordinated the location of every boat and the tonnage of each ship sunk by means of radio signals carefully encrypted by the unbreakable Enigma machine. With this secure communication, he could manoeuver the wolf packs to pounce on any convoy that was spotted.

Outside the window were trees clad in summer leaves but the war was never far away. Reminders were everywhere; a sandbagged anti aircraft gun emplacement, a German troop truck passing by, or a crowd of raucous German sailors making their way up the street. But Donitz looked past the trees and the people to the dock area and the massive bomb proof concrete U-Boat pens. The U-179 was scheduled to leave on patrol this evening and he could just see it moving out of its berth beyond a line of cranes and cargo on the docks. The crew was on deck waving to a cheering crowd and a military brass band, as if it were a holiday cruise. The long black outline of the submarine gradually picked up speed and was soon out of sight. Heroic German sea warriors going forth to battle, he thought.

Donitz turned from the window and frowned. The reports and figures were still on his desk. Admiral Hermann Faust, his chief of communications stood warily a few feet away. Dontz walked over slowly, then picked up the papers again.

"I assume you are familiar with these tonnage figures, Hermann?" asked Donitz. waving the papers in the air.

Faust frowned. His heavy black eyebrows almost met in the middle.

"The figures have been dropping for several months, Herr Admiral," he replied.

"Do you have an explanation?"

"I have been studying the matter, sir. I think the drop in tonnage sunk by our U-boats is a direct result of some other figures on page five."

Donitz nodded. "The number of convoys engaged, you mean? Yes, I have noted that as well and you are quite correct. Our U-boats have sighted fewer convoys than any time this year."

"But there are just as many convoys out at sea," Faust replied. "We have spies and other sources to verify this. But the ships are eluding us."

"Exactly," said Donitz. his voice rising slightly. "The convoys are there, but are somehow evading. It is as if they know where we are. This can not be mere chance, or luck on the part of the English. Somehow, they must be getting information on where our patrols are. Could an Enigma machine have been captured?"

"We have had no such reports," said Faust. "When a U-boat is lost, it is usually destroyed without a trace. If any are forced to the surface, the captain is instructed to destroy the codes and scuttle the boat. We have no reports of any boat not doing this."

Donitz frowned. "What you say is true, and I have considered it. Still, we cannot avoid the conclusion that the convoys are successfully eluding us. We must find out how they are doing it. We must find the source of this information the English seem to be getting, and we must stop it at once. The blockade of England must succeed if the Reich is to succeed. Admiral Faust; if the U-boats fail to cut off the English from the supplies the convoys bring, the war will be lost."

"We will find the source of their information, Admiral. And when we have stopped it, our U-boats will sweep the seas of English shipping."

-11-

Thursday, August 14

Van Marter could have sworn he had just hit the pillow when a Mountie announced it was 5:00 AM.

"Come on Tom," said MacKensie, sitting on the edge of his cot and rubbing his eyes. "The game is afoot. This is the day we bag him."

Templeton picked them up at the door a few minutes later.

"Everything's in place," he said as they got in the car. "You can check the final deployment when we get there. The fly is heading for the parlor and the spider is waiting."

He turned on to the Rue Notre Dame and headed east as the yellow glare of the rising sun reflected off the hood and started to burn off the morning mist. They traveled parallel to the Saint Lawrence on their right, passing through Maisonneuve, Conquoce Point, and Montreal-Est. They were about ten miles east of Montreal proper now and as they approached the small railway station at Pointe Aux Trembles, they could see about a dozen police cars of the RCMP, the Quebec Surete, and the Montreal Police, along with several busses with police markings, all discretely parked so they couldn't be seen from the direction of a westbound train. At the tiny brick station house, marked by a wooden sign that said Gare Pointe-Aux-Trembles, the various police had lined both sides of the track, concealing themselves behind shrubbery, baggage carts, and idle rolling stock. Groups of two on each side were spaced so that each rail car would be simultaneously boarded by four men. About a hundred people lined the streets looking curiously towards the developing show at the rail line. MacKensie looked on with satisfaction, but Van Marter shook his head and muttered to himself at the big splash this operation was making.

Templeton pulled up to a stop by the station house and let out his passengers. A short, fussy looking man with a black moustache approached.

"*Bonjour*, Inspector MacKensie. I am Major Dollard of the Quebec Surete. I trust the men have been deployed to your satisfaction?"

"They look fine, Major," MacKensie answered, looking around. "Have they been instructed in what they have to do?"

"Yes, and you may rest assured they will be thorough."

"How many passengers are on this train?" asked MacKensie.

"About 50," Dollard answered. "but we cannot confine our attentions to the passenger cars alone. A fugitive would be just as likely to be riding among the freight cars. We will thoroughly search them as well."

MacKensie nodded, then frowned. "What is that big wooded area up the track? It looks like a park of some kind."

"That is the Hawthorne Dale Cemetery," Dollard replied. "Don't worry, the train will be well out of it when it stops. Our man will not be able to hide there."

"Now remember, Major," said MacKensie. "When you nab this bird, I want him taken to the RCMP station, and I don't want him talking to anybody or making any telephone calls, eh?"

"*D'accord*, Inspector," said Major Dollard with a slight bow. "Now we wait."

They did not have to wait long.

Fifteen minutes later, a faint rumble, accompanied by squeals and rattles announced the Abitibi train was approaching. The police on either side of the track shifted from foot to foot and readied their guns. MacKensie was actually licking his lips nervously. "Come on; don't be shy," he was saying out loud. "We've got a nice prison camp waiting for you."

About a quarter of a mile up the track, the engine appeared chugging slowly as it emerged from Hawthorne Dale. MacKensie rubbed his hands together in anticipation.

"It won't be long now. In a few minutes I'll get to see the look."

"Look? What look?" said Van Marter.

"One day when I was on escort duty in the Oshawa we chased a U-boat that disappeared," MacKensie said in a low voice as the train crept closer. "We depth charged her until we saw an oil slick and then we lost contact. The convoy moved on but the Captain figured the boat was just laying low. He said she had released the oil to snooker us. So we waited and listened all the rest of the night. Usually we wouldn't do that, but this sub had gotten three ships and we wanted her bad, eh? Finally, when we were ready to give up and catch up to the convoy, the ASDIC operator thought he heard air being pumped into buoyancy tanks. In a few minutes, he had a contact and a periscope poked up about 100 yards off our bow. It was beautiful. I could see the scope rotate as the sub commander scanned the horizon, then when it turned in our direction, the scope froze in place. I'd have given a month's pay to see that Kraut's face when he saw us. That's the same look Meinhoff will have when he finds out he's trapped and we're both going to see it."

The train was almost fully within the police cordon now and was slowing to a stop with a loud squealing of brakes and the sounds of metal against metal. Wide eyed passengers could be seen looking out the car windows and glimpsing the lines of police that were materializing. MacKensie and Van Marter intently scanned the faces for any that resembled Meinhoff.

"There," Van Marter said suddenly. "In that car just behind the red gondola. A bearded man who looks mighty surprised and nervous."

"I see him," said MacKensie with satisfaction. "And that's just the expression I was expecting. Let's get him."

They jogged alongside the train waiting for it to slow enough for them to swing aboard.

"So what happened to the sub?" said Van Marter as he reached for the train steps.

"The sub?"

"The one you surprised when it came up for air."

"Oh. We depth charged it."

"And?"

"This time the oil was for real. Let's go."

MacKensie was first into the car. Van Marter was surprised how fast and agile he was in spite of his somewhat flabby appearance and his limp. They were both running down the aisle of the car by the time the first uniformed officer entered. Near the middle sat the nervous bearded man looking sick and trapped.

"Get your hands up!" shouted MacKensie, and the man complied.

"Frisk him, Tom. All right, where's your I.D. card?"

"I…Inside coat pocket," the man stammered.

Van Marter completed his search. "He's clean, Andre. I've got his card."

"That won't be necessary," the man said quietly. "I'm the one you're looking for. I'll come quietly."

MacKensie smiled in triumph, but didn't move his gun an inch. "Off the train. Now."

The man rose. He was taller than he had looked sitting down. The man looked at MacKensie with cold, blue eyes, then walked down the aisle to the stares of the other passengers. MacKensie couldn't resist prodding him a few times with the gun barrel.

"I ..I really meant to report. I really did," the man was saying as he stepped off the train. "But I wanted to see my mother one more time before I went. I was going to report tomorrow. I know I'm late, but her health is bad and I…"

"What the hell are you babbling about?" MacKensie was getting annoyed.

"Andre…" came the voice of Van Marter, who was walking behind trying to read the I.D. card in the dim lighting. "You'd better take a look at this."

"Now what? The I.D. card? What about it?"

"See for yourself." Van Marter handed him the card.

MacKensie read the card and his jaw dropped. "What the….? 'Winslow Delbert'?"

"Yes?" said the man.

Police began to gather around them as they stood by the hissing bulk of the train.

"Quiet," said MacKensie impatiently. "We've got you. You're going back to the camp. It's far too late to be pretending you're someone else."

"But I'm not," the man protested. "I'm admitting I'm the Winslow Delbert you want."

"The Winslow…"

"Look, I know my conscription notice told me to report last Thursday. I tried to get an extension to see my mother in Montreal, but they wouldn't let me. I was going to report as soon as I'd seen her, I swear. I never dreamed I'd get in this much trouble, and have all these police looking for me. Here; I have plenty of other identification if you think I'm not telling the truth."

MacKensie looked at the man, then the card, then the man again. The documents left no doubt. The man's name was Winslow Delbert, and he wasn't an escaped German, merely a Canadian draftee with a guilty conscience who was overdue to report. MacKensie went pale, then red.

"Well what are you standing around for?" He shouted at the police gathered around. "Get back to searching the train!"

As Van Marter tried to reassure the terrified Mr. Delbert, the uniformed police were checking the I.D. cards of the other passengers, only a good bit more gently than MacKensie had done. MacKensie spurted off for the next car like a man possessed. He leaped onto the steps and bulled his way into the car.

"He's got to be here. He's got to be," MacKensie kept muttering through clenched teeth.

He went down every aisle, glaring at passengers and checking I.D. cards while Van Marter followed. When it became apparent Meinhoff was not among the passengers, MacKensie looked in every freight car along with the police. He pushed cargo aside in frustration, trying to find hiding places. He had the police check under the cars and on the roofs. But as each car was searched and researched, the truth slowly became clear; Meinhoff was not aboard the train. Finally, MacKensie stood beside the tracks looked drained and bewildered.

"Come on Andre," Van Marter said at last. "He's not here. That periscope will have to poke up somewhere else."

Major Dollard approached and asked if they wanted to search further. MacKensie started to answer, but Van Marter interrupted. "Thank you, Major. You've done a fine job, but I'm afraid there's no more you can do. Our quarry has given us the slip. You might want to assign a man or two to ride the train the rest of the way just in case our man reboards or is hiding somewhere we might have missed him."

Major Dollard looked uncertainly at the silent MacKensie, then nodded. "*D'accord.* I shall assign three of my best men."

Van Marter and MacKensie found Templeton and slowly made their way back to his car through the police that were standing around the train and preparing to leave. Mentally and physically exhausted, they got in the car to return to Montreal.

"He had to be on that train," MacKensie kept muttering in a disbelieving tone. "He had to be."

As the disappointed police were packing up the last of their gear and making their way back to Montreal, the crowd of people in Pointe Aux Trembles milled about hoping for something more to see, then reluctantly began to disperse. Low voices murmured and speculated about what it all meant.

"I have never seen so many police," one man said. "There must be big trouble on that train."

"Saboteurs perhaps?" said another.

"Spies?"

"Escaped criminals maybe?"

Among the milling crowd of excited and curious civilians on the streets of Pointe Aux Trembles was an athletic looking bearded man in his early 20s. He walked along the street towards the west, on a route that would take him parallel to the tracks. He noted the police and the trap they had laid and was grateful he had listened to Wilbur Atkins.

The old hobo had been annoying in many ways, thought Meinhoff, but he had some useful knowledge. Jumping off before a stop to avoid discovery was an excellent idea. When the train had slowed, Meinhoff thought they had arrived in Montreal and jumped off on a curve in a wooded area a few blocks before the station. When he saw what had been waiting at the station, he breathed a sigh of relief. He wasn't sure exactly where he was, but he could see the skyline of the city beyond, so he knew he was almost in Montreal. Meinhoff didn't know if any police remained on the train or if it would be searched again at a later stop, so he decided he would walk or perhaps take a bicycle the rest of the way. No point in pressing your luck too far.

*   *   *

After a long and almost silent ride back from Pointe Aux Trembles, MacKensie and Van Marter arrived back at the RCMP station in Montreal. The clock over the door showed it was close to 10 o'clock. At the main desk, a Mountie waited for them.

"Inspector MacKensie? I have a phone call for you from Ottawa."

MacKensie went into a side room like a condemned man, and slowly picked up the phone as if it were a poisonous snake.

"MacKensie," he said flatly.

"Andre, the Commissioner wants to speak to you," came Donna's voice. A few seconds later the Commissioner picked up the phone.

"Andre, just what is going on down there?" the Commissioner barked. "I just got off the phone with the Prime Minister; a very unhappy Prime Minister I might add. I wouldn't be surprised to hear from Churchill himself before the day is out."

"I'm sorry, Commissioner, I…"

"I thought we made it clear there was to be no public awareness for security reasons. Now everyone in….where's the damned place?…. Pointe Aux Trembles is buzzing about the mysterious police raid on a passenger train. The passengers are already telling everyone and I'm sure the railroad workers and the police won't be far behind. I'll be fending off reporters before long. What could have possessed you to arrange for a hundred police to gather and harass train passengers in full view of a town? This was supposed to be done quietly!"

"Commissioner," MacKensie stammered, "we had reason to believe we could nab him on that train. He's been very evasive. It was the only way…"

"Do you have any idea how many German agents are in Montreal?" the Commissioner continued, his voice rising. "We estimate at least 40. All it takes is one, just one to hear about this and have a chat with one of the police about who they were looking for and we could have a serious problem; very serious indeed."

"I understand, Commissioner," said MacKensie, growing red in the face. "But the police were never given Meinhoff's name. They were looking for Wilson…"

"Do you know what the Prime Minister is doing right now?" the Commissioner interrupted. "He's meeting with key cabinet ministers to set up a conference call to Churchill in Whitehall. They are to discuss a backup policy since it looks increasingly likely that this man will make good his escape and the public will know about it when he does."

From the open doorway, Van Marter had been looking on, shaking his head as the ashen-faced MacKensie took the rebukes. MacKensie drove him crazy, but he still hated to see him get grilled like this. After all, the man was only trying to get the job done. On an impulse, he grabbed the phone away from MacKensie.

"Commissioner? This is Agent Van Marter. We've had a setback, but I can promise you two things; Andre MacKensie is the best man you could have on this job, and he'll have Meinhoff back before anyone finds out anything."

The commissioner was surprised, but recovered quickly. His voice was both annoyed and coldly formal. "Agent Van Marter, I appreciate your interest, but this is not your concern. I can arrange for your return to Washington very easily."

"I'm sure you could, sir," Van Marter replied politely but firmly. "But until you do, this matter is very much my concern. You're talking about my partner. Now if you'll excuse me, we've got another lead we've got to check out and we don't have much time. We'll be in touch. Good bye."

MacKensie, who had been trying to recover the phone during this exchange only to be stiff armed by Van Marter looked at the cradled phone with his mouth hanging open.

"What the hell's the matter with you?" he snapped. MacKensie seemed to have snapped out of his funk.

Van Marter shrugged. "Well, I figured you couldn't get in any more trouble and I couldn't be fired; not by the RCMP Commissioner at any rate. Now are we going to catch this guy or what?"

⋆   ⋆   ⋆

After walking a safe distance from Pointe Aux Trembles, Gregor Meinhoff stole a bicycle and started to ride the ten miles into the heart of Montreal. As he peddled through the streets of an enemy city, he felt somewhat disoriented, as if he had fallen through the looking glass to a place where everything is backwards. Men in uniform were everywhere, as were Canadian and British flags, and pictures of King George. Handbills and billboards for war bonds or rationing were also frequent. He passed a street corner where children in their early teens were collecting scrap metal for the war effort. Piles of discarded household items such as old teapots, frying pans, hubcaps, and even a battered safe slowly grew bigger as passers by tossed in new items that loudly clattered to announce their arrival. As a backdrop to this spectacle was a handmade sign with a crude and extremely unflattering picture of the Fuhrer in the center of a target awaiting the airborne arrival of a very large artillery shell, presumably made from the scrap the people were contributing. Meinhoff looked on curiously, wondering how much of the metal in the growing piles would be used to make depth charges.

When he finally arrived in the center of the city, Meinhoff was tired. He had planned to rest on the train, but Wilbur Atkins's incessant jabbering had kept him awake. When they finally disembarked at a place a half mile before the train arrived at Pointe Aux Trembles, a place Atkins had recommended, but which Meinhoff would not have even noticed, he cordially said goodbye. In a low conspiratorial tone, Meinhoff gravely told Atkins he was a government agent and swore him to secrecy "in the interests of national security". Atkins agreed readily and actually saluted when Meinhoff walked away.

He stopped near the Place d'Armes by the old section, or Vieux Montreal, and left the bicycle in an alley near a hotel. He would walk from now on. After his experiences in America, Meinhoff thought Montreal had a strangely European air about it. There were cobblestone streets, ornate churches, gray stone buildings with mansard roofs, and horse drawn traffic mixing with pedestrians. From the open door of a bakery came the heady smell of fresh bread and from the middle distance came the sound of voices arguing in rapid French. The people looked a bit more cosmopolitan than he'd expected and he was suddenly aware of how the shabby, ill fitting farm clothes he had taken from Joe Fergusen made him stand out. He began to look for a shop where he could buy some better clothes; standing out in the crowd was the last thing he wanted.

Traffic was light, most of the men on the street were in uniform, and posters were everywhere. Meinhoff passed several posters exhorting the citizens to buy war bonds, telling them to save fuel, telling the men to join the army, warning of ration stamp misuse, and generally reminding Canadians there was a war going on. One poster in particular caught his eye. A cartoon citizen was making a phone call from a public booth and behind him eavesdropping was another man who looked a lot like Hitler. The slogan said "CARELESS TALK COSTS LIVES". Meinhoff smiled. There were as many likenesses of the Fuhrer here as in Berlin it seemed.

On one street corner a smiling young pigtailed girl of about 12, proudly wearing a bright red "Miss Canada" apron approached him and asked if he would buy some savings stamps to help the war effort.

"Remember," she said cheerfully, "twenty five cents buys a dozen bullets." Meinhoff wondered if this bright, fresh scrubbed young lady had any idea what a dozen bullets could do to human flesh. He politely declined, saying he was home on leave and hadn't received his pay yet. The girl looked suitably impressed and went on to accost another citizen.

As he walked down the street, he noticed few private vehicles, a surprising number of bicycles, and more than a few horse drawn carts. He realized this indicated gasoline was rationed and wondered how Fleisher and Theimann were faring. Well, it really didn't matter. The Canadians would never be able to find him now. As he crossed an intersection, another poster caught his eye. It said simply; "IS YOUR JOURNEY REALLY NECESSARY?"

"Extremely necessary," he said out loud, and laughed at his own joke.

*   *   *

MacKensie and Van Marter sat at the conference table surrounded by maps and incident reports. MacKensie was in his shirt sleeves, with his tie so loose it appeared to be a poorly fitting noose. Once again, he was smoking his pipe to help him concentrate. Van Marter had actually removed his jacket and hung it up carefully, though he had not yet felt it necessary to loosen his tie.

"All right Mr G Man," grumbled MacKensie. "Where the hell is he?"

"It's an interesting problem when you think about it," Van Marter remarked.

MacKensie did not reply.

"I mean usually, a fugitive can be traced through friends, relatives, or places he has a connection with," Van Marter continued. "But we have a man with no connections to anyone. The usual methods don't work with this guy."

MacKensie sighed, letting out a cloud of sweet smelling smoke. "Brilliant. Maybe you can write an article about it for Popular Mechanics when it's all over. But if we don't figure out something quick, you might have to write it in German."

Van Marter glanced at the clock on the whitewashed wall behind MacKensie. It showed a little past 11:00.

"We don't really know he was even on that train," said Van Marter. "What if we're wrong? What if he went some other way altogether? He could already have escaped through Detroit or Buffalo. Hell, he could be on a plane for Germany for all we know."

"No!" MacKensie almost shouted the word. "He's here. He was on that train and he slipped through. My nose knows it and I know it."

"But...."Van Marter stopped in mid sentence. He knew better than to argue with the nose. He sighed and tried to deduce where Meinhoff would go if he had gotten to Montreal.

"Logically, he should push on to the border."

MacKensie raised an eyebrow. "Why?"

"He's always stayed a step ahead of us so far. If he stops now, it could give us time to catch our breath. For all he knows, we may not have any additional border security in place yet. Montreal also has a large French speaking population, and I don't think Meinhoff's French is nearly as good as his English. Every minute he spends in Montreal he risks being spotted, tracked down, or picked up by a routine check. His best choice is to keep going."

Andre MacKensie sat quietly and idly tugged at his left earlobe while drumming his fingers on the table top and puffing slowly on his pipe. He didn't answer Van Marter or react in any way. He slowly looked at the map, then at Van Marter, then back at the map again.

"Wherever he is," MacKensie said in a voice almost too quiet to hear, "he is now within a few hours of the border. We have no more room for error. If we guess wrong, he's gone. And the Germans could well win the war."

The room was silent as each man contemplated the weight of the decision they both had to make.

"We can alert the police and border guards at both locations," Van Marter suggested.

"Donna's already taken care of that. But we both know the odds of them catching one determined man somewhere along several hundred miles of mostly unfenced border are pretty slim. Extra patrols are being put in place along the border and the Americans have been alerted as well. Officially they are being asked to apprehend a fugitive to face charges of breaking and entering, assault, and car theft."

"How about the trains?" said Van Marter, looking at the map and noticing the large Canadian National yards on the south side of the city at Pointe St Charles.

"That's been arranged. Each train is being stopped and searched as soon as it crosses the St Lawrence and again before it crosses the border. If he tries the train to the states we'll nab him, but I think he's too smart for that. I think he'll try a combination of automobile and walking. The problem is, we don't know when or where."

"What about bloodhounds? We could flood the area with them."

"The three bloodhounds we used near Sudbury constitute the entire number in the RCMP. Besides, they're good at following a scent from a starting point, not intercepting someone traversing a wide area. The only real chance is for us to find Meinhoff before he makes his run. And to do that, we have to know when he's going to make it."

"Well, pushing straight on to the border today seems most likely to me," Van Marter repeated. "Logically, it's the thing to do."

MacKensie nodded slowly. His eyes looked tired and sunken. "I agree with everything you've said. Running for Plattsburgh and Lake Champlain is the logical choice for Meinhoff to make." He paused for a few seconds as if uncertain what to say next. "And that is why I think he's still in Montreal."

"What? But you said…"

"Listen, maybe it's my nose or maybe it's just a bad taste in my mouth from chasing U-boats, but I think I'm starting to know this guy and how he thinks. He's a Nazi and he's arrogant, but he's also smart. When he hears about the train search at Pointe Aux Trembles, assuming he didn't watch it in person, he'll realize we're on to his scheme to get us chasing his stooges all over the Soo. Now he knows we're getting closer and he hasn't got as much breathing room as he had figured. He'll know the best hope he's got is to keep us off balance and chasing our tails. He's like a magician who's trying to make something disappear by making the audience look in the wrong place for a second. It's called misdirection and it works like a charm. I think he's going to stop in Montreal precisely because that's not where we'll expect him to be. Just look at the escape so far; everything was planned around creating deception, confusion, and misdirection. They rigged the escape to look like they left somewhere else; they had phony heads for bed check; they made Joe Fergusen think they were all heading for the Soo so we'd follow; they even had a phony head rigged to fool anyone who looked in the car. Why would Meinhoff start being predictable now? No, I think he's still in Montreal....and that's where we'll look for him."

MacKensie went to the door and called for Templeton who appeared in a few seconds.

"Armand, we think our man is at large in the city, but is probably laying low. I want you to brief every patrolman as he starts his shift to be on the alert for anyone answering the fugitive's description and to check ID cards for anyone named Frank Wilson. Tom and I will review incident reports, but we'll need help. Assign at least two dozen men to check hotel registration desks, flophouses, overnight boarding houses rooms for rent, and especially the whorehouses. Our boy might sweet talk some madam into putting him up for the night, eh? Oh, and roust anyone camping out in Park Mount Royal. Let us know about any incident, no matter how small. We figure we've got about 24 hours until this man makes his move."

Templeton nodded. "Anything else?"

"Yeah. Keep an eye on bus depots and train stations as well."

"I'll get on it," said Templeton, then disappeared.

Tom Van Marter slowly shook his head. "I hope to God you're right, Andre."

MacKensie ran his hand through his thinning hair. "So do I, Tom. So do I."

-12-

Meinhoff wandered deeper into the heart of old Montreal, basking in his anonymity, and feeling superior to the unsuspecting crowds that passed him. On a narrow twisting street named Rue Bayeux, Meinhoff stopped at a small shop that sold a variety of household goods. He purchased a safety razor and some shaving soap. At another shop, he purchased some second hand clothing; a white shirt, a hat, a nondescript brown jacket and somewhat darker cotton slacks. Two blocks later, he spied a public rest room and changed his clothes in one of the stalls. The water in the sink was hot enough, so he shaved off his beard, leaving the soap and stubble in a paper towel in the trash. Several men came and went as he was doing this, but no one gave him a second look.

Finally, Meinhoff was able to give himself a long appraising look in the steamy mirror over the sink. A clean shaven man with light brown hair and respectable but nondescript clothes looked back at him. He smiled; no one would notice him from the others in the city. He smoothed his hair, bundled up his old clothes and reemerged in the street outside. A block later, he pushed his bundle of discarded clothes into a trash can in an alley. Now he was indistinguishable from thousands of others, and all but invisible to those who were so desperately trying to find him.

After a few more streets, Meinhoff found a telegraph office. He watched it for a while from the other side of the street, then walked towards the door.

He knew he was taking a terrible chance. If the clerk recognized the address to which he was sending the telegram as the German Embassy in Washington, he would not only refuse to send the telegram, but would probably call the police as well. He also knew the message had to be something that the clerk would not think suspicious. For that matter, the message also would have to fool the FBI if they were intercepting telegrams to the embassy. Finally, the message would have to alert the embassy while seeming innocent to prying eyes. It was a tall order, but Meinhoff had been thinking about it while he rode the train and thought he had an answer.

Of course, he couldn't tell of the capture of the U-110 in the telegram. Even in the unlikely event such a message wasn't intercepted, the German government would think it was misinformation planted by the Canadians. No, he would have to see an embassy representative in person, and the best way to do that was to persuade them to travel to New York state to meet him. That way, even if he was subsequently recaptured, the vital message would get through.

When he had decided on his course of action, Meinhoff smoothed his hair back and strode confidently towards the shop. He paused and looked through the window before entering and was pleased to find no other customers inside. Behind a counter he saw a young dark haired woman in a most peculiar pose. She was bending at the waist with a mirror in one hand and an eyebrow pencil in the other. Meinhoff stared for a moment, then realized that she was drawing a black line up the back of each of her bare legs to make it appear she was wearing seamed nylon stockings. Because of wartime rationing, real stockings could not be found, so many women were making do this way, it appeared. Meinhoff smiled; a young lady concerned about her appearance. That was information he might be able to use to his advantage.

He waited until she was done, then went inside. A bell tinkled as he opened the door. The woman smoothed down her skirt, looked up and smiled; Meinhoff nodded and smiled back.

"Good day, Miss. Do you have a telegraph form?"

"Yes. Here you are." She handed him a thin piece of paper. Meinhoff thanked her and carefully wrote out the message he had composed in his head.

"Here you are," he said, handing her the form. She nodded and read the message while she counted the words.

"This is an unusual name," she said, pointing at a word. "Is that spelling correct?"

"It's correct. It's an old family name. How much is it?"

She told him and he paid her, but she still wasn't through.

"And this address; Embassy, 1305 Massachusetts Avenue; which embassy is it?"

Meinhoff was equal parts nervous and annoyed. Why was this damned woman so curious?

"Washington is not just politics and diplomacy," he replied. He had thought up a cover story in case anyone asked prying questions. "That's the Embassy Company, an old customer of our firm. The president of Embassy doesn't trust the mail since a letter went astray last month."

He had composed a telegram to the German embassy in Washington. The telegram simply said. "PACKAGE TO BE PICKED UP AT PLATTS-BURGH ON AUGUST 15(STOP) MUST RECEIVE IN PERSON OR OTHERS MIGHT(STOP) He had signed it 'Rawer, Ltd'.

The woman didn't reply, but continued to look at the message curiously. Meinhoff knew he had to do something fast.

"Do you know a nice place around here to eat?" he asked, flashing a smile he hoped was warm and sincere. She looked up and seemed surprised.

"Uh…Well, there are really plenty of them. But I like the Fleur de Lis on Rue Ducasse."

"Maybe you could show me where it is. When do you get off work? I'll buy you dinner."

The woman blushed. "But I don't even know you…"

"Oh. I'm sorry. Well, we can fix that. I'm Cheny. Lewis Cheny. Pleased to meet you Miss…."

"Uh..Phillips. Claudine Phillips, but…"

By now, Claudine Phillips had lost all interest in the telegram and was fencing clumsily with this handsome stranger.

"I really don't think…"

"Good," he replied," smiling even broader, "because there's nothing to think about. Why don't I come by at 7:00. Or better yet, if you're uncomfortable, I'll meet you there. What do you say?"

She hesitated. "Well…"

"Look," he pressed. "I'm tired of eating alone. All I do is work. I never get to meet anyone but a bunch of stuffy old businessmen. It'd be a real treat for me and I'll try to make it pleasant for you as well. Afterwards, you can walk away and I'll wish you the best. Come on, Claudine; what do you say? There's more to life than telegrams. With the war on, who can say where we'll all be tomorrow?"

Claudine smiled with hesitation. She had had the same thought herself. Day after day in the shop with most of the men gone to war had left her lonely and depressed. It almost seemed fate that this handsome stranger had walked in.

"Well, I suppose just this once…"

"Great," he said, patting her hand. "You won't regret it. I'll see you then. Good day, Claudine."

"Good day…Lewis."

"Oh, and Claudine?"

"Yes, Lewis?"

"Don't forget the telegram."

"Oh; of course. Consider it done." She was still smiling with excitement even after he was gone.

*　　　　*　　　　*

The telephone rang on the conference room in Ottawa. Donna Hastings picked it up and was surprised to hear the voice of her brother Dennis.

"Hey, Donna," he said. "Where have you been? I've been calling your place for two days."

"Hello Dennis. I've been sort of tied up on something."

"I'll bet. Something top secret, eh?"

"If it were, I couldn't tell you anyway, now could I? That's what secret means."

"Not even your own brother?"

"ESPECIALLY not my own brother," she replied. "You never could keep a secret."

"Aw, come on, Donna; just because I told Mom you broke her Ming vase when I was 10...."

"Dennis, I'm really busy here." There was exasperation in her voice.

"All right, all right. I just wanted to know if you can get down to Halifax to see me off next month."

Donna felt a chill remembering her brother's upcoming trip to England, a trip she was trying her best to see didn't end in tragedy.

"Dennis, I don't want to talk about it on the phone. Remember; loose lips sink ships, and I don't want yours to be one of them. I'll call you in a few days and we'll meet for lunch."

"But...."

"Dennis, I have to go. Good bye."

She hung up the phone and continued looking at the now dead receiver. Her eye drifted to the small picture of Dennis she kept on her desk. The picture was over a year old and Dennis smiled back at the camera. He was a skinny, freckle faced kid with an infectious grin. Her cheerful brother didn't know what she was doing, Donna thought, and had no idea the hellish danger he would be in when he boarded that troop ship in three weeks time if she didn't do it well enough. There were other things that could sink ships just as well as loose lips; things like an escaped prisoner.

The phone rang and she picked it up quickly, thinking it was Dennis with something he'd forgotten, but instead, she heard the voice of Tom Van Marter.

"Hi, Donna," he said. "I'm just checking in."

"Checking in?" she asked. "From what I heard of your last conversation I'd have thought you were checking out. You made quite an impression on the Commissioner. But at least he no longer refers to you as 'that bloody Yank'."

"So what does he call me now?"

"That bloody ARROGANT Yank," she replied. "You must have quite a way with words."

"I'm sorry about that. I was just trying to get Andre off the hook. I waited a while for things to calm down before calling."

"You'd have to wait a good deal longer if that's what you expect," she replied. "The Commissioner is still getting calls from everyone but Mother Brown."

"Who?"

"The lady in the song. You know; 'Knees Up Mother Brown'?"

"That's a song?"

"Never mind. I've been on the phone for an hour alerting police, border patrols, railroad police, and the Veteran Guards. Your friend Meinhoff will be chased by every Canadian in a uniform except the Girl Guides."

"How much have the police been told?"

"Only that there is a manhunt for a fugitive who is traveling under the name of Frank Wilson; that and a physical description. As each shift reports, they are briefed. Within the next four hours, we'll have everyone covered."

"Well, that should help, but we still need a lead."

"I'm afraid I haven't got one; not yet anyway. I think the police reports are the best place to look now."

"That's what we're doing. We have the local RCMP, and Montreal Police going through their records starting with this morning."

"What kind of records? Crime reports?"

"Yes, for a start. Anything that could point to our man getting supplies or transportation. You know, stolen bicycles; that sort of thing. But also any record of routine I.D. card checks or suspicious characters that resemble Meinhoff. We have to assume he made it to the heart of Montreal. Meinhoff's still being the 'man who casts no shadow' the Chippewa talk about, and now our problem is will he stop at Montreal or try to make it across to the U.S.?"

"I've alerted the Quebec RCMP and the Quebec Surate to be on the alert, both at the border and in the city."

"Good. Oh, one more thing," said Van Marter, reluctant to hang up. "I know the Commissioner is steamed, but is he sending me back to Washington?"

"Yes," she answered. "as soon as this is over. But in the meantime he has decided to keep you on the case on the unlikely chance you might actually make a contribution."

Van Marter grinned. "Great. Just as long as there's time for you to give me that tour you promised."

"Oh, I think there will be," she said.

"Great. How are things at headquarters, other than wanting my head, that is?"

"Anxious. The Prime Minister has called the Commissioner at least five times wanting to know what progress we're making. And aside from anxious citizens we had a reporter ask about the 'raid' on the passenger train in Pointe Aux Trembles. It seems one of the passengers has a spouse who works for the Montreal Star Times. To hear him tell it, swarms of armed police boarded and terrified innocent passengers for no reason."

"Actually," said Van Marter, "that's pretty close to the truth. But I guess we had to give it a shot. If we'd have bagged Meinhoff, MacKensie would have been a hero."

"If wishes were horses, beggars would ride. So what's your next move?" she asked.

"Nose around and try to scare up a lead somehow. It's pretty hard to find a specific person in a city; especially a clever person who doesn't want to be found."

"I've got a job as well:, somebody's got to run interference for you with the Commissioner."

"Run interference? Where did you learn that term? Do they have football in Canada?"

"Of course," she replied. "Only we call the Statue of Liberty play the Rule Britannia play."

"I don't know whether to believe you or not," he said cautiously.

"Well, you'd better believe this; you're closer to getting Meinhoff than you've ever been. But he's closer to escape than he's ever been. Don't let up. Get him and get him quickly. I've got to go. Good bye."

*   *   *

Meinhoff's original plan had been to stow away on a train crossing into the United States. When they had planned the escape, Kolza had correctly guessed that a large city such as Montreal would have regular service to New York. Security would no doubt be lax since the Canadians would be looking for him hundreds of miles to the west in Sault Ste Marie. It should be a simple matter to either stow away on a freight car or even to board as a passenger on forged or stolen documents. But the raid on the Abitibi express at Pointe Aux Trembles had changed everything. Meinhoff now knew the Canadians had discovered his ruse and knew he was headed for Montreal. The trains would no doubt be checked carefully. He decided to change his plans.

On the pretense of asking directions, Meinhoff had made a few discrete inquiries and learned where the industrial areas were. Apparently the poster about watching what you said had a limited effect on the helpful citizens. He then found a phone book and looked up the addresses of the largest trucking lines. His eye fell on one which seemed to fit his needs; the Panache Company on Dumount Street in the Verdun area, just southwest from where he was. He made his way casually along the streets, stopping only for a snack from a sidewalk vendor. Business was slow and the vendor, a veteran of the last war who wore his old army uniform jacket with a row of ribbons, felt talkative.

"There goes another lorry," the vendor said, as a tractor-trailer made its way through the intersection. "I'll bet it's going to the port. I've been on this corner for five years now and I can see the difference. We're moving more goods to England than we are to Nova Scotia. And the States? Why the traffic on Route 10's heavier than ever. Only now, as soon as we get the stuff from down south, we put it on a boat for Liverpool."

After hearing a little more about the truck traffic to and from the United States, Meinhoff excused himself and went on his way on foot. He didn't want to risk hailing a taxi in case the driver kept logs of passengers. The best way to avoid capture was to leave no tracks. So the best way was to go by "shank's mare" as these Canadians would say.

The crowds were thinning somewhat, probably rushing home to dinner, he thought. Well, no matter. Trucking companies worked all hours. He set off again and in another half hour had reached the outskirts of Verdun.

Near the trucking company, he turned down a grimy industrial street flanked by soot stained buildings. Only one other person was on the street, a tall man coming the opposite way. As the figure got closer, though, Meinhoff saw it was a policeman and softly cursed under his breath. It was too late to change directions; any avoidance would be sure to draw attention. The policeman came closer and Meinhoff could make out his red face and his small moustache. The man was wearing a blue military type tunic with a Sam Browne belt and a club. He seemed to be looking Meinhoff over, appraising him. Meinhoff looked as casual and friendly as he could.

"Good day," Meinhoff said, nodding as they passed. The policeman returned the greeting and Meinhoff breathed easier. He tried to walk on calmly.

"One moment, sir," came the policeman's voice and Meinhoff winced. He turned slowly and said in as unconcerned a voice as he could; "Yes officer?"

The policeman walked toward him, still looking at him suspiciously. "May I see your identification card please?"

Meinhoff stared at the policeman for a moment, not comprehending. Then he realized what was needed and reached into his pocket.

"Of course. Here you are, officer."

The policeman looked at the forged I.D. card that Kolza had made in the camp and frowned. He must see it's a fake, thought Meinhoff. He unconsciously felt the bulk of the pistol beneath his coat, looked around nonchalantly, and noted the street was otherwise deserted.

"You are Frank Wilson of Toronto?"

"Yes, that's me," Meinhoff answered. He loosely crossed his arms so his hand would be closer to his pistol.

"What are you doing in Montreal, Mr. Wilson?"

"I was visiting my cousin, and decided I'd see about a job as a lorry driver while I was here. I have asthma, you see and thought the warmer climate would be good for it."

"Asthma, eh? I suppose that's why you're not in the service?" the policeman said disapprovingly.

"That's right. I tried to join up last year, but they wouldn't have me. I thought driving a lorry, at least I could help move supplies."

The policeman nodded, then rubbed his fingers over the card. "What's the matter with this card? It seems limp."

Meinhoff laughed. "Oh, that's my fault I'm afraid. I accidentally sent it through the wash. I really should get it replaced." He started coughing for effect and slipped his hand into his jacket.

The policeman rubbed the card one more time, looked at Meinhoff, then handed it back. "Do you have any other identification, Mr. Wilson?"

Meinhoff cursed to himself and produced a phony driver's license, the only other document he had. The policeman looked at it, then handed it back.

"Thank you, Mr. Wilson. Good luck finding a job. There's such a shortage of manpower, you should do fine. All you need is permission from the National Selective Service Agency. If you've already been turned down for the army, that should be no problem."

"Permission?" Meinhoff asked.

"Of course. Nobody changes jobs without Selective Service permission. Otherwise, nobody'd stay on the farms or the dirty jobs; everybody'd be coming to the city for high paying war work. It'd be chaos. Not to mention how tough it would be to keep track of people subject to conscription. You didn't know that?"

"Know it? Oh, sure I knew about it," Meinhoff replied. "but frankly, I'd forgotten. I haven't switched jobs since before the war, you see, so it never came up."

The policeman looked at him curiously and Meinhoff tightened his grip on the pistol.

"Well," said the policeman finally, "there's so many new rules and regulations because of the war, I have trouble remembering them all myself. Good luck, Mr. Wilson."

"Thank you officer. Good bye," said Meinhoff as the policeman walked away. Meinhoff put the pistol back in the inside pocket of his coat.

-13-

The Panache Trucking Company was a medium sized operation with about a dozen trucks in the yard and several more coming and going. Meinhoff strolled into the busy yard and wasn't challenged. Meinhoff walked towards the office on the far side of the yard. Now that he knew he didn't have the documents to get hired as a driver, he planned to find a truck headed for the United States and stow away in the cargo. If he could get to the United States the next day, a representative from the German Embassy might be at Plattsburgh to meet him. Even if that meeting didn't work out, once in the United States, he could make his way to one of the German Consulates located in some of the major cities to get his message back to Germany. He was tempted to simply telephone one of them, but he didn't know if the lines to the Consulates were tapped. With Roosevelt in the White House, anything was possible. Of course, even if he did get through, there was no way to be sure the consulate would even believe him. They might well assume it was an allied attempt at deception and ignore it. No, he would have to deliver his message personally.

He continued across the yard nonchalantly, avoiding the water filled potholes. He smiled to himself. The diesel fumes reminded him of the U-110, one of many unpleasant odors that were constantly present on a submarine. One of the drivers waved and he waved back. The buildings were grime-streaked brick structures that looked like they were left over from the last war, if not the one before that. On a wall near the office he found what he was looking for, a large bulletin board with notices and schedules. The board hadn't been organized very well and had so many layers of notices and schedules on it he could hardly tell which was the most recent.

"Don't waste your time with that, pal," one of the passing drivers yelled to him out his cab window. "We're so busy now nobody bothers to put up any new schedules. That board hasn't been touched in a year. Just go to the office; they'll assign you a haul route. Don't worry; all the new drivers have the same trouble."

The driver laughed and went on his way with a grinding of gears and a roar of the engine. Meinhoff looked again at the chaos of the bulletin board. How would he find out which truck might be going to the United States? He thumbed through the layers of old notices.

"Decadent county," he grumbled to himself. "They can't even keep a notice board in order. No wonder they are losing the war."

As he looked through the notices, he could look sideways and see the loading area, trying to calculate how he could stow away on one of the trucks. The loading area was almost a block long and had rows of trucks arriving and being unloaded from suppliers to the west and south, or being loaded then departing for the trip to Halifax. A haze of diesel fumes hung in the air and men scurried about loading, unloading or directing traffic. Stacks of supplies were everywhere.

Meinhoff carefully noted the setup and the layout of the operation as he pretended to be preoccupied with the notices, mentally probing for a weakness that would allow him to slip on to a truck and get to the United States. After ten minutes, he was able to observe enough to convince him that stowing away on a southbound truck was going to be almost impossible. Even if he knew which trucks were going south, the area was too busy, too exposed, and too well lighted to give any opportunity of sneaking aboard a truck. He was especially disappointed to see that each truck's doors were closed and locked as soon as loading was completed. Reluctantly, he realized he could never stow away; he would have to find another plan.

Once again he considered continuing by train as originally planned, even though he now knew that the Canadians had figured out the ruse with Fleisher and Theimann, and were now closing in on him. But the Canadians searching for him were merely policemen or tired veterans of the last war, and he was a U-boat officer, the elite of the Kriegsmarine. He had been trained to be flexible and keep the enemy off balance. Surely he could elude them even on a train, he thought.

But reluctantly he realized his personal desire to humiliate the Canadians would have to come second to his duty to Germany. No, he had gotten far on trains, but had nearly been caught. The next time he could not count on being so fortunate. The net was tightening and he would have to be more clever and do the unexpected to elude it. He would find some other way; a way that would be so unexpected, the Canadians would be baffled and he would triumph.

As he had these thoughts, Meinhoff continued idly thumbing through the bulletin board in case anyone was observing him. Suddenly, amidst the piles of dog eared old notices, his eye fell on a name that seemed familiar; Tysyn. Where had he heard that name? He reached into the lower strata of papers and pulled out the one with the name. The notice was old and yellowed and had apparently been put there as a joke or for ridicule. It was an old handbill from 1939, the year war was declared. The faded letters were still legible;

A NEW ORDER OF WORLD PEACE AND PROSPERITY!
SUPPORT THE NEW GERMANY
IN A UNION OF ARYAN AND SAXON PEOPLES
TO STABILIZE EUROPE AND SAVE WESTERN CIVILISATION

Underneath the lettering was one of those "socialist realist" prints of happy Nordic looking men and women harvesting grain, running machinery, holding babies and standing nobly with rifles. Behind them was a portrait of the Fuhrer looking stern, but wise. Someone had crudely drawn devil's horns on Hitler with a crayon. Meinhoff smiled. A cheap piece of propaganda, but probably effective with some people. Then his eye returned to the bottom of the page where he had seen the name. In small print were the words "Canadian-German Bund, 411 Rue LeGrange, Verdun, Montreal, A. Tysyn, Chairman and Treasurer".

Meinhoff looked at the flyer intently and remembered that Atkins had mentioned Tysyn on the train; a German sympathizer and a man with some connections in Montreal. Meinhoff noted that the address was not far away.

Meinhoff scratched his chin. "Now this is interesting," he said softly. "A proven sympathizer who could possibly be duped into helping in the escape if he isn't already in custody. If nothing else he might provide shelter for a day or two away from the prying eyes of the police."

Meinhoff's mind raced, weighing the alternatives and the risks. He looked at his watch and saw it was after 6:00 PM; his time was getting short. The choice came down to a simple, but unanswerable question; which risk was greater, attempting to contact this Tysyn or attempting to get to the states alone now that so many doors had closed?

*　　　　　*　　　　　*

The house at 411 LeGrange was a small working class brick structure about eight blocks from the trucking company, its brick stained and cracked from too many Canadian winters. Many of the houses on the street were similar, though many had victory gardens growing vegetables in their yards. As the early evening shadows lengthened, lights glowed warmly in parlor windows and the smell of greasy cooking filled the air. His footsteps clumped on the worn wooden porch as Meinhoff walked up and rang the bell. As he waited for an answer, he noted the paint peeling on the door frame. The whole place had a run down, shabby air about it. After a few seconds Meinhoff heard stirring inside.

"Who is it?" came an unfriendly voice from the other side of the door. Meinhoff's heart leaped with hope. Maybe Tysyn was still around after all.

"Mr. Tysyn? My name is Anderson. I would like to speak with you."

"Tysyn doesn't live here anymore," said the voice.

"I'm sorry to hear that," said Meinhoff. "Do you have a forwarding address for Mr. Tysyn? I'd really like to speak to him."

"I told you. He doesn't live here anymore and I don't have any other address. Now go away."

Meinhoff paused. He was disappointed that Tysyn wasn't there, but maybe the man on the other side of the door was a sympathetic relative. "That's a shame. I'm from the Toronto News and I wanted to do a story on him. I think he's been misjudged and unfairly criticized. I was hoping to tell his side of the story."

There was no reply from behind the door. Meinhoff waited, then sighed loudly. "Well, sorry to have troubled you. Goodbye."

As he slowly walked off the porch, he heard the door being unlatched.

"Wait. Just a moment," the voice said. Meinhoff walked back and the door opened a crack. A stocky man with thinning brown hair plastered down in a vain effort to cover a balding head stood peering at Meinhoff from behind thick horn rimmed glasses. Meinhoff noted with disappointment that the man was almost certainly too young to be Tysyn.

"What newspaper did you say you are from?"

"The Toronto News."

"I've never heard of any paper called the Toronto News," the man said suspiciously.

"We're a new paper, and we're still very small."

Do you have any identification?"

"I'm afraid they haven't issued any. As I said, we're very small and just getting started."

"What is your name again?"

"Anderson; Charles Anderson. Are you Mr. Tysyn by any chance?"

The man regarded him suspiciously for a moment, then opened the door and motioned Meinhoff inside. The door opened onto a front parlor with a large yellow mohair sofa under the front window and an old fashioned small table holding a vase. Through a doorway, Meinhoff could see a kitchen with a sink still wet from cleaning. Meinhoff sat on the sofa and the man sat heavily in a hardbacked chair.

"I didn't want to talk on the porch," the man said. "The neighbors tend to be suspicious sometimes."

Meinhoff nodded sympathetically. "I understand. Then I assume you are Mr. Tysyn?"

"I'm his son; Walter Tysyn. He was taken to an internment camp a year ago."

Meinhoff tried not to show his disappointment. As he had feared, Tysyn had been taken away. His mind turned over possibilities. Would the younger Tysyn have sympathies that were similar to those of his father, or opposite? He decided to probe some more.

"I'm sorry to hear that. What was his crime?"

The younger Tysyn frowned. "Crime? Are you serious? He was drumming up support for the Nazis and we declared war. It's not hard to figure out."

Meinhoff nodded. "Of course. Well I suppose he was being idealistic in his own way…."

"I told him," Tysyn interrupted with frustration in his voice. "I told him over and over, but he always knew best. He'd never listen to me; he'd never listen to anybody. Now he's behind barbed wire. What a stupid waste."

"And just what is it you told him exactly, Mr. Tysyn?" Meinhoff was still trying to find out where Tysyn stood. If the father was in a camp, maybe the son would be sympathetic to the German cause, or maybe he'd be resentful towards the Canadian government.

"I told him to give it up of course. At first his interest in Naziism was unpleasant, but harmless. It was a way for him to be important, if only among others like him. At his job, he was always ordered about, but when the Bund meetings started, he and his pals were suddenly somebodies; they were noticed. They'd get together and wear uniforms, salute each other, and listen to records of Hitler's speeches. Sometimes they'd march and my father would even be in the newspaper occasionally. Most people just laughed at him, but at least he was noticed."

Meinhoff nodded sympathetically but said nothing.

"But as the Germans started overrunning their neighbors and talking nonsense about a master race," Tysyn continued, "why, anyone could see where it was going. Some of the others gave it up as a bad job when they saw what the Nazis were really like, but by that time my father was drunk with the power and recognition he got as the leader and wouldn't stop. When war was finally declared, he was a marked man. Then the Defense of Canada Act was passed providing for internment of aliens and subversives. The RCMP came by and asked my father a lot of questions. A few days later, they took him away. He's been in a camp ever since."

Meinhoff was disappointed by this answer. It was clear that Tysyn was no German sympathizer, and he seemed more angry at his father than at the government.

"If he knew he was in danger, why didn't he go to the United States?"

Tysyn shook his head. "Under wartime restrictions, it's not so easy. To travel to the United States, you need a letter from a solicitor; even then you can't carry out more than five dollars. That wouldn't have lasted long. One of the other members went to the states, but that was before war was declared."

"Could you have smuggled him over somehow?"

"I thought of it," Tysyn said, slowly wringing his hands in nervous frustration. "and if my father had been more reasonable, it might have worked. But I never got the chance; my father insisted he was in no danger and wouldn't hear of it."

"That is a shame, Mr Tysyn," Meinhoff said, his voice heavy with sympathy. "Your father may be misguided, but he is hardly a danger to the war effort, I would think."

"No, but he was caught up in the net. I have written to the Department of National Defense and to my M.P., but all they see is a dangerous Nazi."

Meinhoff looked appropriately gloomy, but his opportunistic mind was racing, trying to find a way of bending the situation to his advantage. "Very sad. A man like that torn from his family and kept in a prison. War is a terrible thing. If only…. No I suppose that is out of the question."

Tysyn looked up suddenly. "What is out of the question?"

"Oh, I was just thinking out loud. I do that sometimes I'm afraid. It can be embarrassing at the wrong time."

"But what did you mean?"

"It was just a thought and probably not even practical."

"What was it?" Tysyn's voice had an anxious edge to it.

Meinhoff paused as if reluctant, then spoke. "Well, as a reporter, I am exposed to a wide range of people as I'm sure you can appreciate. Only a month ago I met and interviewed a gentleman named Hans Kolza. Perhaps you have heard of him?"

Tysyn shook his head.

"Well, no matter. Anyway, Mr. Kolza is a very important official with the International Red Cross. He is traveling through Canada inspecting internment camps and questioning the government on its policies. He is especially concerned with civilian prisoners in the internment camps."

"Civilian…"

"Well, it is not public knowledge, but just a few weeks ago, Mr. Kolza was instrumental in gaining the release of a man in a camp in Alberta; a man whose situation was very similar to that of your father's."

Tysyn looked skeptical, but hopeful, as if he wanted to believe, but was afraid to. "I haven't read of any prisoner being released through Red Cross intervention."

Meinhoff chuckled knowingly. "Well, of course they hush up such things; national security they say. I suspect the real reason is they don't want to admit they might have made a mistake and they don't want a flood of inquiries from pesky relatives and friends of the thousands of remaining internees. Never the less, I can assure you it did happen. The government does not wish to appear unreasonable in the eyes of the Red Cross."

Tysyn eyes widened as he jumped to his feet. "Why this is marvelous. I have to contact this Mr. Kolza. Where is he now?"

Meinhoff waved his hand in a gesture of dismissal. "He would never speak to a citizen with an inquiry. If he did, he would be able to do nothing else. The other man released was accidentally brought to Mr Kolza's attention by the camp commandant, oddly enough."

"But you got to see Mr. Kolza."

Meinhoff nodded. "As a reporter, yes; not as a supplicant."

"So tell him you need to see him again to follow up on the interview, then tell him about my father. Please, Mr Anderson. You said yourself it was a sad case."

"Well yes, but…"

Tysyn was suddenly animated. "Mr. Anderson, you wanted an interview and I gave it to you. Now I am asking a favor of you. You cannot refuse. Besides, when he is released, you will have your story."

The bait had been taken, Meinhoff thought with satisfaction. Now to set the hook and reel him into the boat.

"I would gladly do it," he said, frowning with sympathetic concern. "but there is a serious problem."

"What?"

"Mr. Kolza has finished his tour. He is traveling to New York to board a ship to return to Europe next week. The only way I could possibly see him would be to travel to the United States, and as you have just pointed out, that is extremely difficult."

"But as a reporter…."

"As a reporter I might be able to travel on an exclusive story, but not on personal business. Oh, the release of your father would no doubt make a good story, but my editor prefers stories that have already occurred over those that might. Besides, I doubt that such a story would be allowed by the censors in any event."

"Then save it for after the war," said Tysyn anxiously. "it'll be welcomed then."

Meinhoff nodded slowly. "Well, that is a good point, but there are other difficulties; our travel budget is extremely frugal. As I said, we are a struggling newspaper. Besides, it would take weeks to obtain the proper clearances. No, I'm afraid I can't get to the United States to see Mr. Kolza."

Tysyn bit his lip as if thinking hard and trying to decide something. Meinhoff scratched his chin as if thinking rather than waiting. Finally, Tysyn spoke.

"What if I arrange for your trip and pay your expenses?"

Meinhoff's heart leaped, but he tried not to show it. "You could do that?"

"My father was also treasurer of the Bund. He kept the money in a place I know of. Everyone else left in the group was also arrested, so no one will miss it. If I can get you to Plattsburgh in the New York State part of Lake Champlain, there is a train that goes to New York City twice a week. You could be there and back in a few days."

Meinhoff nodded slowly, as if carefully considering the matter. "Well, I suppose, but how can I legally carry enough money out of the country?"

Tysyn chewed his lower lip in thought. "That's right. Travelers to the states can carry only five dollars. We've got to get both you and the money out somehow. I'll have to think about this some more."

"Yes, it's an interesting idea, Mr. Tysyn, I just don't know if it's practical. Well, we can discuss it further tomorrow."

Meinhoff stood as if to leave, then looked at the clock on the kitchen wall. "Well, it looks like I've missed my train back to Toronto anyway, so I'll have to stay in town tonight. Maybe I'll see you tomorrow. Can you recommend a hotel that would fit within my rather meager travel allowance?"

Tysyn looked confused. He was still trying to formulate a plan. "Hotel? Why don't you stay here?"

Meinhoff tried to look nonchalant. This was what he'd hoped for; a place to stay that was private and an unwitting accomplice to help him escape. By this time tomorrow, he thought, he could well be in the United States.

"All right, if it's not too much trouble. I've left what little luggage I carry at the train station. I can certainly do without it tonight. There's nothing in it but a few toilet articles and a change of clothes anyway."

"Good," said Tysyn anxiously. "Maybe we'll think of a plan after a good night's sleep."

"I wouldn't be at all surprised," said Meinhoff, smiling.

They climbed up narrow, creaky stairs made even more narrow by the dusty collection of old magazines, boxes, and bottles lining one side. Tysyn led Meinhoff to a drab and drafty back bedroom and, like a bellboy, turned down the bed and showed him the bathroom. He excused himself and left Meinhoff in the room. Meinhoff locked the door and looked around. A sagging bed and several items of mismatched furniture sat forlornly amid walls covered with faded green wallpaper. After he heard Tysyn's fading footsteps on the creaking stairs, Meinhoff began looking through drawers and the closet for anything he could use. On the bureau he found a picture of the elder Tysyn and his late wife. Tysyn was a dull looking man with thinning hair and a pencil thin moustache. Even in a uniform, he must not have cut a very impressive figure. Well, no matter, thought Meinhoff. If Tysyn's plight could lead to Meinhoff's escape, the man should get the Iron Cross.

Meinhoff then looked through several dog-eared old phone books he found in a drawer in the bureau. One of the books interested him greatly; a directory of Plattsburgh, N.Y. He thumbed through looking for a German consulate or German Bund, but found none. Too bad, he thought; if he had a contact in the states, it would make his task easier. Then he looked up the phone number of the train station and the bus terminal just in case and noted them in his notebook.

As he was putting the book back in the cabinet, he noticed a small brown loose leaf notebook at the back of the drawer and looked through it. His eyes widened as he realized it was a directory of Tysyn's old Canadian-German Bund members. There were only about 20 of them; not a very dangerous organization after all. He hoped they could be of some use, but realized they were all in internment camps by now. Suddenly, his eye fell upon one address that had been crossed out and updated.

Roger Tredegger, 812 Confederation, Montreal, Do-2653

The address had been crossed out and another scrawled underneath in pencil. Now it read:

Roger Tredegger, 1514 Ticonderoga, Plattsburgh, NY, La-9865

An American in the Canadian-German Bund? No. The more likely explanation was that this Tredegger had fled to the states when things had started to get hot, but had kept in touch, at least for a while. Tysyn had mentioned one of them doing just that. Meinhoff copied the information down and carefully put the book away. If he could contact this man, Tredegger could perhaps pick him up on the American side and take him to the rail station in Plattsburgh. If the German Embassy had sent someone to meet him, the information about the U-110 would get back to the Reich all the sooner. But how to get a message to

Tredegger? And could he be trusted? He would have to give this matter careful thought.

Satisfied there was nothing else for him in the room, Meinhoff turned out the light and fell into a contented sleep.

*   *   *

About 600 miles to the south, streetlights glowed in the mist of a rainy night in Washington, D.C. The tires of the traffic in the streets hissed and splashed as long lines of runny headlights made their way up and down Massachusetts Avenue past stately buildings standing aloof from the rushing humanity outside. Even in daylight the German legation on that street had a dark and sinister look about it. The dark rust colored stone parapets and twisted black iron railings of the 19th century building reflected the nature of the government represented within. The darkness of the rainy night enhanced, rather than hid the effect. On the second floor, a single window glowed faintly with a yellowish light. Behind that window, a tall, blond haired man stood with a telegram in his hand. Hans Thomsen had been German envoy in Washington, D.C. since late in 1938, when the German ambassador, Hans Dieckhoff, had been recalled by Hitler in the face of American protests to Nazi persecution of the Jews during Kristellnacht.

Thomsen read the curious telegram one more time. He knew that the FBI had probably already read it, but it interested him none the less. First of all, they seldom received telegraphs from Canada, a nation with which they were at war. He was somewhat surprised the FBI hadn't confiscated it altogether. But the most intriguing thing was the message. He had to assume it was written in some sort of indirect way so it would make it past any prying American eyes. Still, what could they mean about a package? And why couldn't it at least be delivered someplace closer than upstate New York?

The sender was someone named Rawer, a name with which Thomsen was not familiar. Thomsen looked through the rain streaked window to the dripping branches of the trees outside and rubbed his eyes. The telegram could be a ruse by the Canadians, of course, but to what purpose? He sighed. The German espionage efforts in the United States were getting more difficult all the time. Some of their best agents had recently been picked up by the FBI in the Yorkville section of New York City. Why should he waste his time with a mystery telegram when there was so much else to do? But with information getting harder to obtain, perhaps even a vague lead such as this one should be investigated. He read the telegram one more time, then reached for the phone.

"Get me Herman Brautsch in New York. I need to talk to him immediately."

-14-

Friday, August 15

Andre MacKensie woke up from a fitful sleep on a cot in the back room of the RCMP barracks in Montreal. The room was cool and smelled of musty files and stale coffee. A few feet away, Van Marter was already sitting on the edge of his cot and rubbing his eyes.

"What time is it?"

"Almost five in the morning," answered Van Marter. "Ready for another crack at the police reports?"

"I guess so," MacKensie replied. "God, did I need that sleep. I just hope Meinhoff didn't get to the U.S. during the night."

"He has to sleep sometimes too. Let's check in with headquarters and grab some breakfast."

A few minutes later, after finding there were no messages from Ottawa while they had been sleeping and no developments from the Montreal police, they sat at a sidewalk cafe in the Vieux Montreal section in front of steaming mugs of coffee. Van Marter took his loaded with cream and sugar, but had to settle for milk and very little sugar due to the rationing. MacKensie took his black. All around them the city was waking up, as shopkeepers cranked open awnings and swept dirt into the wet cobblestone streets glistening in the weak morning sun. A few pedestrians shuffled past the round metal tables clustered in front of a small cafe called Le Chat Noir.

"Montreal," said MacKensie to no one in particular. "You know, I met Doris here. I was at a police conference and she was a graduate student at McGill. I was taking a break in the park near Mt Royal and she was sitting on one of the benches feeding the ducks. I tried to talk to her, but got so tongue tied she must have felt sorry for me. We had dinner that night at a cafe just like this one. I've always remembered the smell of the place; coffee, croissants and red wine. Vin Ordinaire they call it."

Van Marter took a deep breath. "It still smells that way."

"Anyway, it turned out she was from Ottawa too. She was just going to McGill for her nursing degree. We used to joke that she was going to patch up the people I shot. She works at the hospital now and patches up people Fritz has shot. Her business is now healing the wounded, and business is good." MacKensie took a sip of his black coffee and looked up and down the street. "Well, Meinhoff is one Fritz that's not going to get anyone else shot. He's out there. Somewhere in this city is the man we've got to find. The man who could help us win the war…or lose it."

Van Marter nodded and took another long drink from his steaming coffee cup. "We'll get him, Andre. The RCMP and the FBI always get their man. They may not get him in the same way, but they always get him. Meinhoff hasn't got a chance."

MacKensie smiled, then became serious again. "Look, Tom, I…I appreciate the way you argued with the Commissioner on my behalf; especially since you were against the train raid from the first. I guess I should have listened to you."

"Forget it, Andre. You drive me nuts sometimes with your damned nose and your intuition, and I know my FBI methods get under your skin as well. But we're partners on this job, and partners stick together. It's the only way we'll get the job done. The Commissioner has his battles to fight and we've got ours."

MacKensie looked at him. "You know, we could have used you on the Oshawa. We might have gotten that sub the first time."

∗   ∗   ∗

A few miles away, the Verdun section of Montreal was also waking up. In a slightly shabby sitting room with muddy tan wallpaper and grey lace curtains that filtered the pale morning sunlight, Tysyn was looking through the newspaper as he cooked breakfast and awaited the man from the Toronto News. The paper was mostly the same old depressing war news. Everywhere the government seemed to be rounding up people who were the least bit suspicious. There was even a small article that reported the police, presumably the RCMP, had stopped a train yesterday on its way into Montreal from the north and conducted a search among the passengers! Outrageous. The time was certainly not favorable to getting an internee released by conventional means, but maybe the Red Cross man could work a miracle after all. God knew his father needed one.

"Good morning," said Gregor Meinhoff as he descended the stairs yawning. "That was an excellent night's sleep, I must say. All this traveling looking for a story does get tiring."

Tysyn smiled. "Not to mention making a man hungry. Have a seat. Breakfast is almost ready."

A few minutes later, they sat down to a breakfast that consisted mostly of bread and hot mush cereal along with some boiled onions.

"Sorry I can't offer you sausage or bacon and eggs," said Tysyn. "But between rationing and shortages, I'm lucky to get this much. I'm growing some beans, tomatoes and corn in my victory garden, but they won't be ready to pick for another month. I suppose that's one thing you can say for the Germans. They appreciate a good sausage."

"Not as much as I would right now," Meinhoff laughed. "Oh, well, there's a war on after all."

"I've been thinking about how to get you to the states," Tysyn said between mouthfuls of hot mush. "It's a tough proposition. The border guards and police are suspicious of anyone who's heading that way without a good reason. Then there's the problem of physically getting there. I have an automobile in the garage, but only enough coupons for maybe five gallons of gasoline."

"Can you buy them from someone you know?" Meinhoff asked cautiously.

"Not legally, although there is a black market. But if I got caught, there would be no chance of convincing the government of the good citizenship of the Tysyn family, and my father would rot in the camp forever."

Meinhoff nodded sympathetically. "That is true, but getting someone into the states without going through customs is also against the law."

"It doesn't matter," said Tysyn waving his hand. "I have a better idea anyway. It's the way I was going to get my father out, and I think it should still work. I'm employed by a company called Wellsley, Ltd. We sell and service pumps and farm machinery. I have a small van I use for service calls and several customers on farms that are near the U.S. border. Here, take a look." He spread out a road map on the table while Meinhoff looked on trying to conceal his anticipation.

"As you can see, Route 15 takes you straight to the border," Tysyn began. "Of course, there is a sizable border control station there, so we won't go that way. Now, here, just about a mile or so before you get to the border crossing is Route 202, running east and west parallel to the border. It passes through a town called Hemmingford here."

Meinhoff nodded. He had studied this road before, but didn't know how to exploit it.

"About a year ago, I had a service call to a farm just outside of the town. There are several farms along the south side of Route 202 that back up to the U.S. border. Anyway, the farms aren't very well marked; just a mailbox with faded letters that you can hardly read, and I went in the wrong drive. I wound up in a farm that was deserted. The place I wanted was the next one, and when I finally found it, the owner told me the farm I went to first was owned by a man and his two sons. The sons went in the army when the war broke out and the man had taken sick and gone to live with relatives in Montreal. So, assuming the place is still deserted..."

"You can drop me there and I can walk across the border," said Meinhoff. "Perfect. But what about patrols and security?"

"Patrols cover the area, but the fields are overgrown and you'll have plenty of cover. The best bet would be to hide out in the barn until it gets dark, then make your move. Once you get across, you're about 20 miles from Plattsburgh."

Meinhoff nodded. "What about patrols on the American side?"

"They cooperate with us, but they aren't as thorough. After all, they're not at war; not yet, anyway. If you are caught, you can say you are merely testing security for a newspaper article."

"Good. When do we go?"

"I have to get to the company to pick up my van at 8:30. Then I'll return here. I think we'll leave about 11:00. That should get us there around half past noon. It won't be dark until close to 9:00 tonight, so you'll have a bit of a wait."

"It'll be worth it," said Meinhoff. "This could be a great story; that is, if they'll print it."

Tysyn looked at him seriously. "Do you really think this Mr Kolza can get my father released?"

"If he can't," said Meinhoff smiling reassuringly, "my name isn't Charles Anderson."

*   *   *

At the headquarters of the Montreal Police, the Quebec Surete, and the Montreal detachment of the RCMP, officers and detectives sorted through piles of reports that were filtering in from patrolmen on the beat, hotel records, train schedules and records of railroad ticket sales, and telegraph messages. They were looking for any trace of Frank Wilson, the mysterious fugitive who had eluded them the day before. Aside from MacKensie and Van Marter, no one knew who the fugitive really was. Donna had offered to have photos made and distributed, but MacKensie was afraid some old acquaintance from Meinhoff's college days might be in Montreal, recognize his picture, and talk in front of the wrong person. So only a general description was given out, along with a sketch that was close enough to narrow down the hunt, but not close enough to allow identification by acquaintances.

So the police burrowed through piles of reports and documents as methodically and thoroughly as the tedious task would allow. At the Montreal RCMP detachment headquarters, MacKensie and Van Marter looked with dismay at the piles of white papers stacked on tables, chairs and filing cabinets.

"Well, let's get started," sighed MacKensie. "This is not the most glamorous part of police work, but it's often the most productive, eh?"

An hour later, they had sent patrolmen to investigate a bicycle theft near Pointe Aux Trembles, a food store robbery, and a clothing store burglary.

"The bicycle theft was close to the area we searched the train," said Van Marter. "Our man could have used it to get the rest of the way into town."

"Could be," said MacKensie. "Let's circulate a description of the bicycle to the patrols. If they find it we'll at least know the direction he's headed."

"I'll get on it," said Templeton.

"How are we doing on finding our man through I.D. card checks?" said MacKensie. "Any luck at all?"

Van Marter read a summary from his notes. "No less than three patrolmen of the Montreal Police and one of the Quebec Surete turned up men named Frank Wilson in routine I.D. card checks over the last 24 hours, but one was in his sixties, one was only about 5'4" tall and the other weighed at least 300 pounds."

"Damn that Kraut," grumbled MacKensie. "He picked that name on purpose. There must be dozens of Frank Wilsons in Montreal."

"And there'll be one less if don't get lucky soon," replied Van Marter.

They went through more papers until they had headaches from eye-strain, but no further trace of Meinhoff could be found.

"Damn it. I really had hoped the hotel records would show a Frank Wilson had checked in last night," said Van Marter.

"He's too smart for that," replied MacKensie. "The bastard probably slept under a bridge or something."

"But the police checked there too. There was no sign of him. Maybe he's gone already."

Van Marter looked at the clock on the wall; 9:15. Time was draining away with still no leads. Where was Meinhoff? Was he in the United States already?

"Inspector MacKensie?" came a voice. They turned around and saw Captain Templeton with a paper in his hand. "I just got a call from Major Blevins of the Montreal Police. They've turned up another Frank Wilson on a routine I.D. check one of their men did on his patrol yesterday. There's no description, but they're trying to contact the officer. It seems he went off duty at midnight."

Van Marter and MacKensie leapt to their feet. "Where did he see him?"

"On Rue DeGrasse, in the Verdun section."

"Why didn't he tell someone? Wasn't he briefed about looking for a Frank Wilson?"

Templeton cleared his throat awkwardly. "Well, actually…no. It seems he was busy booking a drunk while we were giving the briefing and missed being told about who we were looking for."

MacKensie turned purple. "God almighty; when in the hell are WE going to get half the breaks this Heinie is getting? Where is this patrol-man now?"

"They're recalling him. He should be back at their Berri Street station in a few minutes."

"No," said MacKensie. "Have them bring him here. And I want an unmarked patrol car waiting."

"You've got it, Inspector," said Templeton, hurrying off.

MacKensie grabbed a map. "Verdun. It's only a mile or so away. But why would Meinhoff go to Verdun? It's a working type area with a lot of older houses and long time residents. He'd have a hard time hiding there. There's also a lot of small industry; factories, repair garages, and the like."

"Well, when we talk to the patrolman, maybe we can find out."

"Tom, why don't you call Donna while we're waiting and let her know what's happening."

"Sure thing," said Van Marter.

"Inspector MacKensie?" said a sergeant a few minutes later. "Patrolman Bouchard is here."

A tall man in the uniform of the Montreal Police stood in the doorway.

"Good," said MacKensie, springing to his feet. "I want to go where you saw Mr Wilson last night. We can talk on the way."

They piled into an unmarked RCMP car and sped off towards Verdun.

"All right Officer Bouchard," said MacKensie when they had gotten settled. "Tell me about this Mr Wison you stopped last night."

"It was on Rue DeGrasse, at 1730 hours…5:30 PM." the officer began. "DeGrasse is a residential street without much activity usually, at least not on a weeknight. I was on routine patrol and saw a man I didn't recognize. I know many of the people on my route, you see, and strangers are usually seen only in the commercial areas."

"What did he look like?" asked Van Marter.

"He was about 20-25 years of age, perhaps a little over six foot tall and weighing maybe 190 pounds. He was clean shaven and had well trimmed light brown hair. He was dressed in a white shirt with brown trousers and a brown jacket."

MacKensie and Van Marter looked at each other. Except for the clean-shaven part, the description fit Meinhoff perfectly.

"Why did you decide to card him?" said MacKensie.

"I don't know, really. I suppose he just looked like he didn't belong there. He was walking briskly as if he was hurrying to get somewhere else; most people in that area are already where they want to be. If they walk at all, it's at a leisurely pace. And maybe it was my imagination, but when he first saw me, it seemed as if he hesitated a bit."

MacKensie turned to Van Marter and smiled proudly. "It seems I'm not the only one with a good nose, eh?" He turned back to Bouchard. "So, what happened?"

"I asked him for his card and he gave it to me. I noticed it felt thinner than I.D. cards usually are. He said it had gone through the wash. He also had a driver's license that agreed. Anyway, he said he was from Toronto and was visiting a relative, a brother, I think. He said he was looking for the Panache Trucking Company to ask for a job."

"Where's that?"

"It's about two blocks from where I saw him. Stop here."

The car came to a stop on a quiet residential street.

"This is where I saw him. He was proceeding that way."

"Toward the trucking company?"

"Yes."

"And coming from the direction of downtown?"

"Yes, I suppose he was."

"He sounds like he could be our man; let's go."

The Panache Trucking Company, Ltd was busy. Men and trucks swarmed around the yard barely avoiding colliding with each other in an intricate ballet of loading, unloading, and driving. The air was full of engine noise and diesel fumes. MacKensie, Van Marter and Patrolman

Bouchard made their way through the chaos to the small and cluttered office at one end of the yard.

"Sorry, guys," said the harried looking bald man from behind a desk piled high with papers and a telephone that seemed to be perpetually ringing. "Nobody came in here for a job last night. Everybody I saw wanted cargo hauled or wanted to change his route. I tell you, this place has been a madhouse for the last year. We're hauling stuff in from the states and out to Halifax 24 hours a day."

"How many trucks go to the states for cargo in any given day?" asked Van Marter.

"Oh, maybe ten or so," was the reply. "It's a shame but most of them are dead heading. You know, returning empty. It's not very efficient, but we're buying more than we're selling. Excuse me."

The man grabbed the ringing phone. "Yes? What? How much?" he grabbed a pencil stub and began writing furiously. "A hundred tons? How is it packed? Yes, yes. I won't be able to get it out today, but tomorrow still looks good. And I can't store it for more than 24 hours. All right. If you arrive before noon take it to dock three, otherwise dock one. Right."

He hung up and made a few more notes.

"If someone wanted to get to the states on one of those trucks, how hard would it be?" said MacKensie, bringing the man back to the business at hand.

The man laughed. It was a hoarse laugh that sounded almost like a cough. "Unless you're a bit of cargo, forget it. We double check all the cargo against the bill of lading then we lock the doors. The border police'll check it again most of the time. Oh, and we aren't allowed to carry passengers. If you want to get to the states in one of these trucks, you'd better be holding the steering wheel."

The phone rang again. MacKensie handed him his card.

"If anyone shows up in the next week looking for work, you let me know, all right?"

The man nodded and reached for the persistently ringing phone.

"Yes? No, I haven't received it yet. What? Be patient? Tell that to the convoy that's waiting for it! Didn't anyone tell you there's a war on?"

Out on the street in front of the Panache Trucking Company, Van Marter turned to MacKensie.

"Well, there's one more dead end. Meinhoff might be on his way to the border right now and we still don't know where to start looking. Now what?"

But MacKensie just frowned.

-15-

A few blocks away, Tysyn and Meinhoff were making last minute preparations.

"All right. I've got the van out back. How much money do you think you'll need?" said Tysyn. "I can cover up to $500."

"That won't be necessary," said Meinhoff. He didn't want to appear greedy and risk arousing Tysyn's suspicions. "I'll need train fare, some food, and a night or two at a New York hotel. "I'd say $150 or so would be plenty."

Tysyn nodded and left the room. In a few minutes he returned with a large brown envelope. "Here is $175 just to be on the safe side. We can settle up when you return."

"Thank you," said Meinhoff, taking the money. "Is this from the Bund's treasury?"

"I'm afraid so," Tysyn admitted. "But I'm sure they'd approve. It's certainly not much use to anyone else."

"I'll tell you what," said Meinhoff taking out his notebook and a pen. "I'll give you a receipt just so no one will accuse you of taking the money for something frivolous. Here we go: 'Received from Walter Tysyn: $175 for expenses to secure release of father. Signed Charles Anderson, Toronto News, August 15, 1941.'"

Tysyn took the receipt and put it in his pocket. "Thank you, Mr Anderson. We should be ready to go in about a half hour or so."

"Good. Say, did you mention there was a telegraph office nearby?"

"Yes; down at DeGrasse Street. Why?"

"It occurred to me that I could telegraph Mr Kolza and let him know I am coming. It would be a shame to miss him after all this trouble."

"Good idea," said Tysyn. "Can I send it for you?"

"Oh, no. If anyone you knew saw you sending a telegram…."

"Right. Well, I'll be ready when you get back."

Meinhoff walked down the street towards the telegraph office. In his pocket was the address and phone number of Roger Tredegger, the ex Bund member who had moved to Plattsburgh. Meinhoff had no intention of sending a telegram, having done that the day before. No, the telegram story was a ruse for Tysyn's benefit; Meinhoff's real intention was to find a phone that had no chance of being tapped. With Tysyn's father's situation, Meinhoff did not want to take a chance of using the phone at Tysyn's house. He would call Tredeggar in Plattsburgh and, with any luck, obtain another dupe to help with the escape.

As he waited for Meinhoff to return, Tysyn got ready to leave. He called his work and told them he would be on a job to the south and would check in that afternoon. He went to the kitchen to pack lunches and get his work log in order. Finally, he was ready and sat in the parlor to await Meinhoff's return. He was excited about the prospect of getting his father released, even though the method was as unusual as the man who had suggested it. Tysyn was grateful to Mr Anderson, but as he thought about it, he was a little confused by how things were moving so quickly. Another odd thing was the fact that Anderson asked questions about how to get to the states but not about how or when to return. And there was something about his face…….It was all a little strange, but he seemed an honest man, Tysyn thought. He even gave a receipt for the money.

Tysyn fished in his pocket and looked at the receipt. He looked at it a long time because something seemed wrong with it, but he wasn't sure what it was. The name was correct, as was the date and the amount:

$175. So what was it? He sighed and returned the paper to his pocket. His nerves were making him imagine things.

The old clock on the kitchen wall showed the time to be almost 11:00. Tysyn looked at it and hoped Mr. Anderson would return quickly so they could be on their way. It wouldn't do to have the company van parked outside too long. He was going to have trouble accounting for his time today as it was. Maybe if he dropped Mr. Anderson off soon enough, there would still be time for a few service calls.

He picked up the newspaper and idly paged through it again. Once more he saw the article on the police search of the Abitibi train and shook his head. What was the world coming to?

After a few minutes, he threw the newspaper down in a heap, went to the kitchen, and put a small kettle on for tea. He'd make two cups; one for himself and one for Anderson. They would drink to the success of the upcoming mission. He was lucky to have tea, he knew. Everything was rationed and it was a struggle to find the essentials. Sugar was almost nonexistent, even on the black market, and coffee was almost as bad. And how long had it been since he had been to a butcher shop?

As he waited for the pot to come to a boil, Tysyn sat back, closed his eyes and let the image of the butcher shop fill his daydreaming mind. Years ago, his father would take him there on Saturdays sometimes. He could see the butcher behind the counter once again. What was his name? Zenski, Zaleski; something like that? He was wrapping a prime cut in heavy brown paper, writing the price on it, and tying it with heavy string. Tysyn smiled at the memory. All that meat and you could buy whatever you wanted without ration coupons. Such a long time ago....

Tysyn's eyes flew open. He reached into his pocket and pulled out the receipt again. With his hands fumbling he unfolded the wrinkled paper and read it once more. Suddenly, he knew what was wrong; suddenly it all made sense. As the pieces fell into place, he felt faint for a moment. The terrible truth hit him like a freight train. He was being used; used for some dark purpose by a stranger who could be dangerous. How could he have been so blind? More to the point, what should he do now? He stood up from the chair and walked slowly into the parlor like a man sleepwalking. The room seemed to be spinning. What should he do?

Finally, Tysyn went to the window and looked up the street. Mr Anderson, or whoever he really was, was nowhere in sight. Tysyn stared at the telephone a long time, torn between what he hoped and what he knew. Finally, with a trembling hand, he picked up the clunky black receiver. His nervous fingers slipped out of the "O" hole on the dail twice before he was finally able to get his call through.

"Operator, this is an emergency; I….I wish to speak to the RCMP Headquarters in Ottawa."

-16-

Andre MacKensie paced the street in front of the Panache Trucking Company in frustration. "This is just like tracking a U-boat. He's out there; probably within a few miles, but we can't quite lay our hands on him. He's just out of reach. We see traces, unconfirmed sightings, or clues, but we're always a step behind. At least with a U-boat we could use depth charges to flush them out."

"We could start a house to house search," Van Marter suggested. "Maybe someone saw him after Bouchard did."

MacKensie frowned in thought. "Yeah, maybe. Bouchard, how about getting on the radio back to your station and see if they can get some men down here to go door to door and ask if anyone's seen a man answering the description of the one you saw yesterday. We know he was here at 6:00 or so last night. Maybe we can get another lead, or at least find out which way he went, eh?"

Bouchard nodded and got in the car to call in, still puzzled by MacKensie's references to U-boats.

"Maybe we can still get lucky," said MacKensie, looking around at the somber brick buildings. "But time's running out, He could be on his way south already. We've got to have a break. So far, Meinhoff's had all the luck. Everything he planned worked and everything we planned didn't. We're due."

"Could he have had any contacts around here?" Van Marter asked. "Maybe somebody to hide out with or even help?"

MacKensie shook his head. "As far as we know, he's never even been to Montreal. But I suppose anything's possible. All we know is that he didn't get a job driving a truck south and probably couldn't have stowed away."

Van Marter nodded. "Let's assume that was his intention. It would explain why he came to Verdun. But apparently he failed and went somewhere else. That means he's improvising."

"So we're back to the question we've been trying to answer for two days: where is he?"

"Inspector?" came the voice of Bouchard from the open window of the car. "We can get 25 men down here in 15 minutes. They'll go door to door and let us know what they find. But there's something else. You're being asked to call your contact in Ottawa right away."

MacKensie looked at Van Marter. "Donna? What could she want? Didn't you just talk to her an hour ago? What could have happened?"

Van Marter shrugged. "Maybe Meinhoff gave himself up."

"Sure," MacKensie snorted. "And maybe Hitler became a Rabbi."

A public phone booth was a block away and in a few minutes. MacKensie was through to Ottawa.

"Andre, is that you?" said Donna. "Where are you?"

"Still in the Verdun section of Montreal following a lead. What's going on?"

"Andre, I just got the strangest phone call from Montreal. Some man insisted on speaking to whoever was in charge of the hunt for the escaped prisoner."

"What?" MacKensie was astounded. "But how…"

"Of course the RCMP duty officer who answered the phone didn't know anything about it, but asked me to talk to the man since he remembered that I had worked on manhunts before. Anyway, the man on the line said 'I know who you're looking for in Montreal and I can deliver him to you.'"

"What? Did he mean Meinhoff?"

"I think so. I asked him to explain what he meant and he said his father was in an internment camp and he wanted to trade a German prisoner for a Canadian one. He was doing this as proof of his loyalty and his value to the war effort."

"What the…? Well who is this model citizen anyway? And more importantly, where's Meinhoff?"

"I don't know," she replied with exasperation in her voice. "I asked for more information and he said he knew we were looking for an escaped German prisoner when we raided the Abitibi Express yesterday at Pointe Aux Trembles. He said he had met the man we are looking for and will see him again in a few minutes. The man is claiming to be Charles Anderson of Toronto. He's trying to cross the border into the United States and the description fitted Meinhoff perfectly. He said he called to turn the man in to get his father released."

"Yeah, yeah; but what about Meinhoff? Where can we pick him up?"

"I don't know. The line went dead."

"Dead?….You mean he just decided to hang up after all that?"

"I don't think so. He was in the middle of a sentence when the line went dead. I think someone hung up for him."

"So you have no name or anything?"

"No, and there wasn't time to trace the call completely, but we can tell it came from Montreal."

"You don't think this guy was a crank?"

"It's hard to say, but his description was dead on. And he knew we were looking for a German POW."

"Did he mention Meinhoff by name?"

"No, but I'm sure Meinhoff's using an alias anyway."

"Why did he call the RCMP and not the Montreal Police?"

"He said the RCMP took his father away and they can help bring him back."

"Could you tell anything about him from his voice?"

"He was nervous and talked almost in a whisper, as if he was afraid someone would hear. He sounded to be middle aged, and an English speaker; no French accent. No other accent either. Beyond that nothing."

MacKensie thought for a minute. "Who runs the civilian side of the camps? Isn't it the Commissioner of Internment Operations? See if you can get a hold of them and get a list of civilian internees from Montreal."

"That might be a lot of names to go through. Maybe I can narrow it down by concentrating on the Verdun area."

"Good. And see if they have records of which ones have sons living in the city. Oh, and check to see if either the internment people or RCMP Headquarters have any letters on file asking for the release of one of those names. If our boy is this determined, he may have tried before, eh?"

"All right Andre. Maybe you can do the same at RCMP Montreal Detachment HQ. Keep in touch."

He hung up the receiver and looked at Van Marter who had been listening in.

"Well, what do you think, Tom?"

Van Marter let out a low whistle. "I think we'd better find out who this caller was, and we'd better find out fast."

A half hour later, police were going door to door in every block of Verdun asking residents if they had seen anyone answering Meinhoff's description or answering to the name of Wilson. They started from the trucking company and fanned out from there, walking up to the weather beaten brick houses and knocking on each door in turn. When residents asked why they wanted this Wilson, the police answered that it was just routine, though anyone could see it wasn't. Van Marter and MacKensie supervised the operation with Patrolman Bouchard, driving slowly up one street then down another.

"It's still a damn needle in a haystack," grumbled MacKensie. "But now we're looking for two needles."

At the next intersection, a policeman saw the car and hailed them. He was young and had a thin blond moustache.

"Inspector MacKensie?" he asked breathlessly.

"That's me. You got anything?"

"A man just told me he saw our suspect walking down the street just an hour ago."

Every eye in the car went wide. "Is he sure?"

"Yes, sir. He said the man was walking towards DeGrasse and he was carrying a package that looked like it had a gun in it."

They looked at each other. "A gun? That's all we need. And this guy was headed for DeGrasse?"

"That's what the man said," the officer said checking his notes.

"That checks out," said MacKensie excitedly. "That's just about where I'd expect him to be."

"Who was the witness?" asked Bouchard.

The officer squinted at his notes. "Norris, Mr Quentin Norris. Nice old guy."

Bouchard sighed heavily. "I wouldn't get my hopes up, Inspector. Mr Norris is on my beat. I know him quite well, I'm afraid. He's a bit, well…imaginative. Everything you ask him about he's seen and then some. Just last week he said German spies had pulled up all his petunias and were sending them to Berlin for Hitler's girl friend. Last month he said his neighbor was digging a secret tunnel to his basement and the month before he said….well, you get the idea. He's about half full, as they say. Sorry, Inspector."

"He seemed pretty sure," the officer said, reluctant to give up.

"He ALWAYS seems pretty sure," answered Bouchard. "And the crazier his story the more sure he sounds. Thanks officer. Keep trying."

"Great," said Van Marter. "Now what?"

"We keep looking. What else?"

✶   ✶   ✶

Shafts of sunlight slanted through the tall windows of RCMP Headquarters in Ottawa casting bright yellow squares of light on the green tile floor of the cluttered room on the third floor. Tiny specs of dust floated lazily into the sunlight, then out again. In the center of the room, oblivious to both the cheerful sunlight and the dust, Donna Hastings sat poring over RCMP's incoming correspondence files for the past year. Letter after letter paraded by with complaints, suggestions, and even an occasional thank you. So far she had found over fifty letters objecting to the RCMP carrying off a friend or relative to an internment camp. Their tone ranged from reasonable suggestions that perhaps a mistake had been made to outrage and vituperation at the "Canadian Storm Troopers" as one letter put it.

She leaned back and rubbed her eyes. Last night she had slept on a cot in the room and she had slept like the dead. It was slow and tedious work she was doing, but it had to be done. A list of "relative letters" she had found had so far revealed only two from non foreign English speakers in Montreal, and they were from north of Mt Royal Park, a long way from the Verdun section. Still, she sent the names to the Montreal detachment to investigate.

The black phone on the corner of the table rang with a jarring sound and she knocked it off the receiver and scrambled to pick it up.

"Miss Hastings?" said the voice over the phone. It was an efficient sounding voice; the voice, perhaps, of a technician. Donna brushed a hair out of her face and set the phone on her shoulder.

"Yes, that's right."

"This is James Carre over at the POW Service. We've checked our records of non foreign civilian internees from Montreal. Then we narrowed it down to the Verdun area, a bit of a challenge, I can tell you. The area is not well defined by street names."

"Yes," she interrupted. "What did you find?"

"We don't have separate records of which detainee have adult sons, so we then narrowed the search down to married males between the ages of 35 and 65."

"Good. How many do you have?"

"Well, let me see….31."

"Thirty one? How will we ever check out all of them? How about letters from sons asking for release?"

"None, I'm afraid. Of course, letters can go all kinds of places. I daresay most of the public don't know we even exist. If a civilian were writing to get a relative released, he'd probably write to the RCMP wouldn't he?"

"I suppose so. I've already found several, but none fill the bill. Well, thank you Mr. Carre. Call me if you turn up anything else."

She hung up the phone and tapped he pencil on the table nervously. She had already checked most of the RCMP headquarters files and found nothing from that area. This mysterious caller was proving as elusive as the man he had wanted to turn in. She looked at the clock. Over an hour had passed since she had received the call. Where was the caller now? And how could they find him with time slipping away?

"Any luck, Donna?" The Commissioner stuck his head in the doorway for the third time that morning.

"Yes," she replied, "and it's all bad. Only two letters from relatives in Montreal have turned up and they're from north of the park. Still, I'm having them checked out."

"Well, keep at it," the Commissioner said with disappointment in his voice. "The Prime Minister called me again a few minutes ago."

He came in the room and closed the door behind him.

"It seems Churchill has decided on a different strategy."

She looked at him curiously. "A different strategy sir? What do you mean?"

The Commissioner ran a hand through his thinning gray hair. The static electricity made several hairs stand up comically.

"They have decided we cannot keep the existence of the U-110 survivors secret forever. It's bound to leak out. Besides, it's a violation of the Geneva Convention."

Donna nodded. The same thought had occurred to her, but she hadn't said so.

"So we will probably be forced to inform the Germans of the capture of the U-110 crew. We'll claim we didn't inform them sooner because of an administrative mixup. There have been enough of them after all. None of the crew actually saw us board the sub; they were herded below by then. The sub had sunk by the time they were allowed up on deck again so none of them can be certain. When they write letters home, of course, they will be censored to make sure no one's suspicions reach Berlin. We will split up the crew and plant agents among each group who will claim they have come from another camp where another group told them they saw the U-110 sink immediately. With any luck, we can keep the secret indefinitely."

Donna nodded. "It could work, Commissioner. There's only one little fly in that particular ointment."

The Commissioner stood up to leave. "I know; if Meinhoff gets out and tells all he knows without a censor filtering the story, it'll be too late. Well, we'll just have to see that he doesn't, won't we?"

"Yes sir."

The Commissioner paused at the door and shook his head. "Sometimes I wonder who is more difficult to deal with; the Germans or the politicians."

As the door closed once again, Donna went back to the files. She laughed about the politician remark. Elected officials and career civil servants were both mutually dependent and mutually suspicious. She supposed the Germans had the same problem. As she thumbed through the last of the letters, the politician remark kept forcing its way back into her mind until she suddenly stopped and looked up.

"Politicians…of course," she said out loud. "Perhaps he wrote to his local Member of Parliament."

Eagerly she put the letters aside and grabbed her government phone directory. She dialed the number for Parliament and asked who was the MP for the southern Montreal area. After a moment the operator told her it was the Honorable James P. Quinn and offered to connect her to his office.

"Good Morning. This is the Honorable Mr Quinn's Office. How can I help you?" said a female voice.

"This is Donna Hastings at RCMP Headquarters. I need to find out if you've received any letters asking for the release of any internees in the last year."

"Who did you say you were, dear?"

"Donna Hastings at RCMP Headquarters in Ottawa. What about the letters?"

"Why yes, we've had a number of them," was the reply.

"I only need one. I don't have a name, but it would be a son asking for the release of his father. It would probably have come from the Verdun area."

There was a pause on the other end. "What's he done?"

"What has who done?"

"The man you're looking for; Walter Tysyn. I'm certain that's who you mean. We've received several letters from him. Of course there's nothing we can do, what with his father being a German sympathizer and Bund leader."

"What?"

"Oh, yes. Mr Tysyn's father was picked up early in the war, as were most of his fellow Bund members. The son seems a nice enough fellow, but he also seems to be a little naive. His mother is dead and he moved into his father's house when he was interned. I always thought he…"

"What's the address?" Donna interrupted.

"Well, young lady, you certainly seem to be impatient, That's the trouble with people nowadays. They just don't take the time."

"What's the address?" Donna shouted.

"I'll have to check and call you back. I have several calls waiting," the woman said coldly.

Donna gritted her teeth and tried to control what was left of her temper.

"Listen carefully. This is a matter of national security. I need that address and I need it now. If you can't locate it right away, I will send several very large men over to help you find it."

There was a pause accompanied by the rapid shuffling of papers.

"Here is his last letter; dated five months ago. Mr. Walter Tysyn, 411 LeGrange... Hello?...Hello?"

But Donna Hastings had already hung up so she could redial.

*   *   *

MacKensie and Van Marter stood near the corner of Tilbury and Clemenceau Streets looking at a street map and marking off areas that had already been covered. Blue uniformed police could be seen further down each street knocking on doors and talking to residents.

"Nothing," Van Marter said in disgust. He stood with his arms folded. In his dark vested suit, he almost resembled a men's clothing advertisement. MacKensie leaned over the car hood with his elbows on the spread out map and his stomach resting against the fender. "Don't worry, Agent Tom. That periscope has to come up sometime. You said so yourself. If he's here, these boys'll flush him out. That'll be one sweet moment, I can tell you. He'll surface somewhere thinking he's safe, and I'll be waiting."

"We've been saying that for two days," said Van Marter, his voice raising in frustration. "And all we've done is to tag behind him as he gets ever closer to the border."

He kicked a can in the gutter and sent it clattering down the street.

"This is no way to run a search. We need teams all over the city. We need multiple roadblocks and checkpoints. We need radio and newspaper announcements. We need to take the gloves off for God's sake!"

MacKensie looked at Bouchard, who looked bewildered.

"More FBI advice to your frozen cousins in the north?" said MacKensie sarcastically.

"Look, I'm on your side, Andre. But how long are we going to have one hand tied behind our backs?"

"Until that periscope comes up, that's how long!"

"At the rate we're going, the only place the damned periscope will come up is in Berlin! We'll never even get close enough to wave goodbye. We've got to flood Quebec with police; alert the citizens…"

"You were the one who didn't want 100 police searching the Abitibi Express! Make up your mind, eh?" MacKensie stood with his hands on his hips and his jaw jutting out belligerently.

"That was before he got within spitting distance of the border; we've got nothing to lose now." Van Marter was toe to toe with MacKensie as Bouchard looked on nervously.

"Nothing but the whole damned war. Or do you think you're smarter than the entire Canadian government?"

"Right now I don't think either one of us is as smart as one escaped prisoner!"

"Well, let me tell you…."

"Base to all cars in Verdun area," the radio crackled suddenly. "Proceed to 411 LeGrange to apprehend search suspect; suspect's name is Walter Tysyn. Acknowledge."

The three men looked at each other. MacKensie and Van Marter's argument was suddenly forgotten.

"Come on cowboy," said MacKensie, jumping into the car. "You wanted to wave goodbye? Well, you can wave goodbye as the sonofabitch goes back to camp."

LeGrange was only three blocks away and they were the first to arrive with a skidding and screeching of tires as MacKensie slammed on the brakes.

"Bouchard, you go around back and cover the back door," MacKensie ordered as he jumped out of the car. "Tom and I will see if Mr Tysyn has any house guests."

"Look," said Bouchard. "I know this guy. His father's a Nazi, but Walter seems harmless enough. Go easy on him will you?"

"He's not the one I'm concerned about," answered MacKensie drawing his Smith and Weston .38 service revolver and checking the ammunition. "I don't want anyone getting away; even if we have to shoot somebody. Come on Tom."

Windows of nearby houses silently overlooked the Tysyn house. Neighbors' at thosae windows peeked discretely from behind lace curtains at the sight of two men with guns drawn approaching the front door of the Tysyn house. Now they saw four more police cars pull up on the street. Had they come for the son now that they had the father?

Van Marter and MacKensie reached the front door of Tysyn's house. The door had a glass panel in the center, but a shade had been drawn behind it giving no view of the house beyond. Instinctively, MacKensie and Van Marter took positions on either side of the entrance in case shots were fired through the door. They each remembered the guns that had been taken from Joe Fergusen's farm. Without a word, MacKensie rapped on the door with the butt of his revolver. No answer. He rapped again.

"Ready to use your leather search warrant again?" Van Marter whispered.

"Sometimes the old ways are the best," MacKensie smiled. He shifted in front of the door and kicked it in. He and Van Marter were inside in an instant with guns at the ready.

"Police! Come out with your hands showing. Now!"

There was no answer. Van Marter looked at MacKensie and noticed a slight film of sweat above his lip. MacKensie motioned Van Marter upstairs while he crept towards the kitchen.

The house was small and run down. Sunlight filtered in through dirty windows and cast dull patches of light on brownish wallpaper. Stirred up by the falling door, a thin haze of dust hung in the air. The dark and heavy furniture added to the gloom, as did the threadbare scatter rugs. MacKensie crept into the empty kitchen and noticed two sets of newly washed dishes draining on the sink.

"Andre," came Van Marter's voice from upstairs.

"In the kitchen," he replied. "All clear downstairs."

Van Marter came down the steps and motioned the waiting police inside to do a more thorough search.

"He had company all right," said MacKensie, pointing to the sink.

"And look at this," said Van Marter. "Remember the abrupt end to the phone call Donna received? Look in the parlor."

MacKensie looked and saw the telephone and the wires that had been pulled from the wall. Chunks of plaster littered the floor.

"You shouldn't need a pipe to figure this one out," said Van Marter.

"No, either Tysyn was being duped, or he decided to double cross his pal for dear old dad's sake. Either way, it appears Meinhoff caught him and Mr Tysyn is now helping against his will."

"And where does this leave Meinhoff?"

"The same place he's always been; ten steps ahead of us," said MacKensie. "But now it's worse than ever. He's got help and we don't have any idea where they are."

MacKensie took a deep breath, then turned to Van Marter. "Tom, I never thought it would get this far, but we've got to get permission from your government to conduct a hot pursuit across the border if necessary."

Van Marter nodded. "I'll call my boss. He'll know who to ask."

"No," said MacKensie. "I think we'd better let Donna arrange a request through official channels. It'll be faster, and less likely to cause and international incident."

"All right, I'll give her a shout, but I hope to hell we won't need it."

Van Marter went to the radio and relayed the request to Donna Hastings who relayed it to the Commissioner who relayed it to the Prime Minister's Office. A "hot pursuit" meant that an officer from one jurisdiction was authorized to continue a pursuit and arrest in a neighboring jurisdiction. It wasn't usually done between countries, but then, the outcome of wars seldom depended on it.

-17-

A battered dark blue service van marked with yellow script letters that read "Wellsley, Ltd" crossed the Champlain Bridge on its way to Route 15. The summer sun was high in a blue cloudless sky and the St Lawrence sparkled silver as it flowed to the horizon. Below was the Ile-des-Souers, and on the horizon to the right, the Lachine rapids. The air was pleasantly warm, and seagulls wheeled lazily overhead. It would have been a perfect day for a picnic, but the occupants of the van were not on a pleasure trip.

Clutching the wheel nervously was a grim faced Walter Tysyn. His eyes looked straight ahead, but he occasionally glanced sideways at his traveling companion.

Gregor Meinhoff, wearing Wellsley, Ltd coveralls over his clothes sat easily on the other side of the seat with his brown jacket in his lap. Under the jacket was the pistol he kept pointed towards Tysyn. They rode in tense silence until they were almost over the bridge.

"So how did you know?" Meinhoff said finally.

Tysyn said nothing, but grimly stared ahead as he drove.

"Come now, Walter," Meinhoff said in a friendly tone. "I am curious. There is no harm in telling me. In a few hours I will be gone and will be of no further trouble to you. Besides, I admire the surprising deductive skills you exhibited. No one else has discovered me. So I repeat; how did you know?"

"It was the seven," Tysyn replied flatly.

Meinhoff raised his eyebrows. "The what?"

"The way you wrote the number seven on the receipt you gave me for the money. The number seven was written with a short horizontal line through the vertical leg. Some of the French speaking people around here write that way, but I couldn't figure why an English speaker from Toronto would. Then I remembered the butcher on the next block, an immigrant from Poland, had written sevens that way. It was the way it is done in Europe. And then I realized you didn't write that way because you're French Canadian, but because you're European."

Meinhoff nodded. "Crossing the seven. I should have known that. People used to notice it when I was at Penn. But that could have been a peculiarity, nothing more. It doesn't make me a German escapee."

"Maybe not by itself," Tysyn replied, "but I remembered the story in the newspaper about the search of the train in Pointe Aux Trembles just a few hours before you appeared on my doorstep with no luggage and no identification. Someone was on that train that the police wanted very badly. From my father's situation, I know there are several POW camps in northern Ontario, so an escaped prisoner seemed likely. When I got to thinking about it, I also realized that you had asked no questions about how or when to return from the states, made no arrangements to contact me again, and in fact, had asked for no information concerning the man you were supposedly going to plead for. You never even asked the location of his camp. Then there was your face."

Meinhoff started. "My face?"

"Your face is tanned, but is somewhat paler along the chin and above the lip; as if you had a beard, but shaved it off recently. It all fit together. You had no intention of doing what you said, you only wanted to get across the border secretly. There was only one conclusion I could draw; you are an escaped German POW. Furthermore, your capture is very important to the government, or they wouldn't be sending a hundred men to search a train for you. You were playing me for a fool to help you escape to America."

"So you called the RCMP," said Meinhoff. It was not so much a question as a statement of fact.

"I could see you were not going to get my father released," Tysyn continued, "so I decided I would call the RCMP and make a deal. That's when you appeared behind me with that gun in your hand."

Meinhoff was silent a moment, then laughed. "Very good, Walter. Very good indeed. I commend you on your powers of observation and deduction, I really do. We Germans respect such things. But you should not be so disappointed. I told you I would get a man released from a prison camp, and so I will. But it will not be your father, I'm afraid. In fact, once the police discover your role in this, and rest assured, they will, I wouldn't be surprised if they didn't arrange a family reunion."

Tysyn glared at him. "How do you know I won't simply run off the road or turn you in?"

"Walter, Walter," Meinhoff mocked. "I know what kind of man you are. You play it safe. You will take me where I want without interference because you are hoping something will happen. Perhaps I will have a heart attack, or perhaps a patrol will stop us and arrest me. As long as there is a chance, you will not risk your neck."

Tysyn gritted his teeth but did not reply. He knew Meinhoff was right.

"By the way, if we do get stopped, you will tell them we are both employees of Wellsley, Ltd. on our way to a service call. If you make the slightest move to betray me, I will kill you. Is that understood?"

"Y….yes. I understand. But the police may discover you with no help from me."

"You had better pray they don't my friend; you'd better pray hard."

Tysyn sat quietly, wondering what Meinhoff meant, but afraid to ask. Out of the corner of his eye, he saw Meinhoff reach back behind the seat to a bin where broken or discarded parts were kept. Meinhoff rummaged around with a loud clanking and rattling until he pulled out an old pump motor black with grease, and a rag. Meinhoff placed them on the floor in front of him and nodded in satisfaction.

"These will do quite nicely," he said. "Really, Walter, you are an excellent host. You have provided everything."

"Did you really go to send a telegram?" Tysyn asked finally.

"No, and certainly not to Herr Kolza, who does not exist, I'm afraid. Well, not as a Swiss official at any rate."

They were on the other side of the bridge now, entering the southern suburb of Brossard. In a few more minutes, the houses thinned out and Montreal was left behind. The motor droned and the wheels whined toward an expanse of flat open country opening up ahead of them. The border was only 30 miles away.

"That looks like a check point up ahead," said Meinhoff, squinting at a line of cars ahead. "Now you just go along and you will live to see the German victory. If not…" He left the thought unfinished.

A line of cars was being funneled through three sets of police and Tysyn steered the van to the shortest line on the right. As they crept closer, Tysyn became tense and started to sweat from nerves. He pulled out a handkerchief and wiped his forehead several times. He hoped Meinhoff would be discovered, but was afraid what would happen if he were. Ahead of them was a sedan with an argumentative French Canadian loudly complaining about the delay to an unreceptive audience. The policeman did not respond but looked annoyed as he checked documents, looking for a card that identified a Frank Wilson. Tysyn was on the verge of panic at the thought that the man ahead had gotten the policemen so mad he would make a more thorough search of the van and then who knows what would happen?

Finally, the car in front sped off and the policeman motioned the van forward. He was a tall man with a no nonsense air and a scowling expression. Tysyn watched as the man looked the van over, then came around to the driver's window and greeted Tysyn. The man looked at Tysyn, then at Meinhoff, then back to Tysyn again.

"Good afternoon. What is your destination?"

"A farm on route 102," Tysyn answered. "We have a service call there."

"Identification cards please."

Tysyn complied and the man examined it, saw it was not for Frank Wilson, and handed it back. Then he took Meinhoff's card and frowned.

"What's this?" he said indignantly.

Tysyn looked at Meinhoff, who was sitting with the old motor in his lap and black grease all over his hands.

"Oh. I'm sorry," Meinhoff said with an embarrassed grin. "I was working on this motor to save time on our next call. Did I get any grease on the card?"

"Did you get grease on the card?" said the officer incredulously. "Look at it." He held up the card showing a black grease mark in the center. "I can't even make out the name!"

"Oh. Sorry. It's Fred Walton. I guess I'll have to get a new card now. I keep forgetting to wipe my hands."

"Do you have a driver's license, Mr Walton?"

Meinhoff looked apologetic. "I'm sorry, officer. I don't drive. That ID card is the only identification I carry."

The policeman looked at Tysyn. "Is he your partner in this job?"

Tysyn hesitated. He could be a hero and turn this man in. He could tell the truth and damn the consequences.

"Yes," he replied faintly. "He works with me."

The policeman turned back to Meinhoff. "This is a government document. Defacing it is against the law, even through carelessness. If the name is not legible, the card is worthless."

Meinhoff looked uncomfortable. "I'm sorry. It was really stupid of me. What will we do at the other check points?"

"This is the last one unless you're crossing the border," the policeman answered. "So you're all right today, but get it replaced first thing tomorrow."

"Yes, officer," said Meinhoff. "I will be sure to."

The policeman looked at Meinhoff. "What are the last three letters of the alphabet?"

For the first time, Meinhoff looked rattled, but calmly replied. "X, Y, and Zed."

The policeman frowned again, looked at the line of cars waiting and finally said "All right; you can go."

The van pulled away from the roadblock and continued south towards the U.S. border.

*   *   *

At 411 LeGrange, the curious neighbors had finally summoned the courage to emerge for a closer look at the excitement at the Tysyn house. A crowd gathered to watch the police searching the house and to cluck among themselves.

"I knew there was no good coming from that place. I coulda told you," one grey haired woman said, shaking her head wisely and clutching a blue plaid shawl tightly about her ample frame..

"The old man was a nut, but Walter seemed a decent enough sort," said another, somewhat younger and paler woman.

"About time they locked him up," grumbled a huge bald headed man. "Like father, like son I always says."

"No," said another. "Walter seemed all right to me. he never got into that Nazi nonsense."

"Then why are the police looking for him?" asked the bald headed man in a told-you-so tone of voice. "The police don't look for you for no reason, you know."

Amid the chatter and craning necks, police circulated asking if anyone had any information about the whereabouts of Mr Tysyn. Everyone had speculation, but few facts. Mr Tysyn, it seemed, kept to himself and so did his neighbors.

"So it looks like Tysyn tried to rat on Meinhoff and Meinhoff found out and cut the phone line," Van Marter was saying as he and MacKensie stood on the front porch waiting for some clue to be turned up.

"And we didn't find Tysyn in the house, so they must have gone somewhere together," said MacKensie. "Well, police and the Border Guards are already on the alert for a man answering Meinhoff's description and calling himself Frank Wilson. If they're headed south they might get nabbed."

"Maybe," said Van Marter, "but somehow I don't think it'll be that easy. Meinhoff has shown us over and over that he's just too damn smart to fall into an obvious trap."

"Inspector?" said a young Patrolman coming up breathlessly. "We found a car in the old garage out back. It has a current license plate."

"What the...? If they didn't take the car, then how did they get away so fast?" MacKensie said.

"Well, the lady next door says she thinks Tysyn sometimes drives a van from the place he works," said the patrolman.

"Now we're getting somewhere," said MacKensie, rubbing his hands together in anticipation. "Where does he work?"

"She doesn't know."

"Well, what does it say on the side of the van?" MacKensie's tone was showing some exasperation. "Does she know that?"

"She doesn't remember."

"Great. Give her a badge," said MacKensie..

"She did say she thought it was sort of a bluish color," the patrolman said hopefully. "Oh, and she wants to know if she'll get a reward."

"Not in this life," muttered Van Marter.

MacKensie thought a moment. "Bouchard?"

"Yes sir."

"Get on the radio to the RCMP station and tell them I need any information they've got on the Tysyns, especially where Walter Tysyn is employed.

"Right," Bouchard answered. "But I've got an idea."

"What?"

"Well, there's an equipment service company about three blocks from here and they use blue vans. It might be worth a look."

"Well, let's go see."

"Right," said Bouchard, rushing off to fetch the car.

"We're closing in, but Meinhoff's getting a pretty good lead," said MacKensie.

Van Marter was looking off into space and scratching his earlobe in thought. Suddenly he spun around.

"Maybe not," he said. "Officer, ask the neighbor if we can use her phone."

✳   ✳   ✳

Rags McLaughlin sat on a barrel at the open door of a hanger at Dorval Airport surrounded by a circle of wide eyed young RCAF pilots. Waving his arms to indicate the various gravity defying stunts he was describing, Rags was coming to the conclusion of one of his air stories with which he had been enthralling and terrifying his audience.

"And so the ground was coming up at me so fast, I could hardly catch a breath. I could see people looking up in horror and running to get out of the way. The wind pressure was pushing my skin back like it was going to pull off my face. I was yanking on the stick like the devil himself was after me when the thing broke off in my hand!"

He paused for dramatic effect. The young pilots were staring at him open mouthed. Several were beginning to seriously reconsider their career choice. Just when the tension in the air peaked, a mechanic cleared his throat in the background.

"Excuse me, Flight Officer McLaughlin? There's an urgent phone call for you."

Rags reluctantly got up from the barrel. "Excuse me, gentlemen. It's probably Saint Peter wanting to know why I haven't gotten there yet," he remarked, and went to the small office in the corner of the hanger.

"Rags? This is Tom Van Marter. How soon can you get airborne?"

"Maybe five minutes," he replied. "I've just been doing a little hanger flying. The Annie's all gassed up and ready. Where are we off to now?"

"Not we, Rags; you. We think our man might be in a blue commercial van heading for the states. We're trying to confirm that now. But we think he's got almost an hour's head start. If we're right, we'll need someone with a cool head and a steady hand to fly low over the roads and track him down. And we need someone now. Can you do it?"

Rags eyes went wide. He drew himself up and stood at attention. "I can fly so goddamn low the worms'll take cover."

"Good man," said Van Marter. "And Rags, you remember your Hurricane and how you wanted to bag a German? Well here's your chance."

Rags hung up the phone and rubbed his hands together with glee. "Hot damn!"

With a flourish, he wrapped his flying scarf around his neck and started for the hanger door.

"Sorry boys," he said to the pilots who had been waiting for him to finish his story, "It's time to punch holes in some clouds. I'm gonna get me a Jerry!"

"Wait a minute!" one of the pilots yelled indignantly. "You were plunging to the ground out of control and the stick broke off in your hand. What happened?"

"What do you think happened?" Rags roared over his shoulder as he reached the door. "I got killed!"

★   ★   ★

Wellsley Limited was a drab red brick building with blackish streaks of age running like crooked fingers down its walls. The windows were wired glass and badly needed washing. MacKensie and Van Marter were ushered into a small office with knotty pine paneled walls where an oily looking man with black hair and a moustache looked up at them.

"Yes, I'm the president of Wellsley Limited. Claude Wellsley's the name."

"Good afternoon, Mr Wellsley. Can you tell us if you have a man named Walter Tysyn working at your firm?"

Wellsley nodded. "Walter? Oh yes. He's worked here for three years. Has he done something wrong?"

"What does he do for you, Mr Wellsley?"

"Mostly engine and pump sales and service. He goes to customers and replaces or repairs what the customer needs."

"Do you know where we could find him?" asked MacKensie.

"He should be out on some calls right now," Wellsley answered. "Does this have anything to do with that Nazi father of his? I knew something like this would happen."

"Something like what?" said Van Marter.

"Trouble, that's what. Walter seems a decent enough guy. He's quiet and keeps to himself, but his father is a damned Nazi and that's got to mean trouble sooner or later. That's what it is, isn't it? Something to do with his old man?"

"Do you have his itinerary for today?"

Wellsley sighed and rummaged through a pile of papers on his desk.

"He had three calls today, but he called and put them off until this afternoon. He said he had an emergency callback from an old customer…called him at his home."

Van Marter and MacKensie looked at each other.

"Do customers usually call at home?"

Wellsley shrugged. "Not usually. Walter said the man had his home number from the first service call. So he promised to go in the morning."

"Did he say where this call was?"

"Not an exact address, but I think he said somewhere to the south....towards the U.S. border."

MacKensie and Van Marter hurried out without saying goodbye.

"All right," said MacKensie. "Tysyn and Meinhoff are heading for the border in a blue van with 'Wellsley Ltd' in yellow lettering on the side. We've got to get word to the border police and to Rags."

"If we're right, we've still got hundreds of miles of roads they could be on," said Van Marter.

"Yes, but that van has to stick out a mile away. How many vans like that are tooling around south of the city, eh?"

"Six at the most," said Van Marter, unfolding a map.

"How do you know that?"

"On the side of the building were parking spaces reserved for service vans. I counted them."

MacKensie frowned at Van Marter. "Well, sure if you want to do it that way...."

"Oh, maybe we should have gone through vehicle registration records instead?" Van Marter challenged. "Admit it; you overlooked it. As Sherlock Holmes said, 'You see but you don't observe.'"

"Actually," said MacKensie calmly, "if you had noticed the board mounted on the back wall of the office, as I did, you could have saved the trouble. The keys for company trucks are kept on several rows of hooks on a board over by the file cabinet. The bottom row is labeled 'service vans'. There were eight hooks and six were empty. As Sherlock Holmes also used to say, 'It was elementary.'"

"I guess I must be picking up some French already, Andre." Van Marter said sheepishly. "The word 'touche' comes to mind."

"Right now the only French words I want to hear are 'cherchez le Hun'. But I can think of some American words that are even more appropriate."

"Like what?"

"Let's head the no-good varmint off at the pass."

-18-

The yellow Annie roared off the tarmac at Dorval and seemed to leap into the air. Rags climbed to 2,000 feet as he crossed the St Lawrence and saw the ribbon of roadway winding south to the horizon. He looked around and checked his instruments.

"All right," he said out loud. "Here's where I start to earn my pay. Tally ho!"

With that, he pushed the stick forward and plunged into a stomach wrenching dive before leveling out at 100 feet. From that height, even the startled expressions of the drivers on route 132 were visible.

"All right, Fritz. You'd better say your prayers, 'cause Flight Officer Rags McLaughlin of the Royal Canadian Air Force is on your six."

He ran parallel to Route 132 at a ground speed of 100 miles an hour; slow enough to make out any blue vans but fast enough to cover distances in a hurry. With the muscular roar of the twin Jacobs engines in his ears, Rags soared along as if on a strafing run, flying at 100 feet, dropping down to treetop level, then up again. The farmland of southern Quebec passed below him, green and almost ready for harvest. Periodically, he would roar over some painted wooden clapboard farmhouse, sending chickens, dogs, livestock, and the occasional farmer scrambling for cover. He grinned broadly. This was what he was born for; what he lived for; the exhilaration of flight; the mind numbing speed; the freedom; the great soaring euphoria, and the godlike power over the earth. He thought of his old Hurricane fighter, now at the bottom of the Atlantic. He could see her once again, a machine, but a graceful work of art, sleekly gleaming in the early morning sun, straining at the chocks to get into the sky once again.

"This one is for you, old girl," he said quietly. "We're gonna get us a German."

*　　　　*　　　　*

"Why did the police ask me the last three letters of the alphabet?" asked Meinhoff as the van headed south on Route 15. He had cleaned his hands and was alertly scanning the passing country for signs of search or pursuit. He still held the pistol in his lap.

"I'm not sure," Tysyn replied. "I think they do that more at the border crossings to see if a person is American or Canadian. Canadians sometimes try to cross the border to the U.S. by saying they're Americans, because of the restrictions. The question is a trick; Americans say X,Y,Zee, but Canadians say X,Y,Zed. Unfortunately, Germans say the same thing."

Meinhoff smiled. "Ah yes. A word to trap unwary foreigners into revealing themselves. A 'shibboleth' is what it's called. I believe it's a Hebrew word."

"If you say so," Tysyn said flatly, his eyes straight ahead.

"Really, Walter, you should be more well read. Then maybe you wouldn't waste your time with a lost cause."

"A lost cause? You mean…"

"Your father; he's a lost cause. I salute him for being a National Socialist of course, but be realistic. He's considered a traitor to his country and he's lucky to be in a prison camp. In Germany, he would have been shot."

"This isn't Germany," grumbled Tysyn.

"Not yet," was the reply.

*　　　　*　　　　*

"This is Bloodhound to wing one. Do you read me, Rags?"

Rags picked up the mike. "I read you. Is that you, Andre?"

"That's right. Where are you?"

"I'm over Route 132, coming up on Pike River. I flew down Route 132 through Ste Jean. I just saw two blue vans, but I don't know which one we're looking for."

"Well, we've just found out the blue van you're looking for has the words 'Wellsley Ltd' on the side in yellow letters."

"In that case, I'm coming up dry. One van was from Eton's and the other said Duffy's Plumbing. I'll turn west and fly along 202 then up 15. If I don't flush him out there, I'll come down 209 and east along 202 again."

"Good," MacKensie answered. "Are you flying low?"

Rags laughed. "Low? Hell, I got grass stains under the fuselage and bird shit on top. If I got any lower, I'd be taxiing."

"Good. Keep on it. Van Marter and I are still at Verdun, but we're getting a vehicle and heading down 15 to be near the border when you spot the van. We'll be at the 202 intersection in less than an hour. Good hunting, Rags."

"Roger, out."

As he clicked off the mike, Rags saw the intersection of 202 pass under him. He continued for a few more miles until he was in sight of the border crossing at Rouse's Point at the northern end of Lake Champlain. The lake sparkled like a blanket of diamonds as it wound between hazy black-green hills until it was lost on the southern horizon. He pulled the Anson up to 1,000 feet, made a graceful 180 degree turn and headed back to cover Route 202 westbound. He had not seen the van, but if it was on the road, he would.

*   *   *

With a grinding of gears and a squeal of tires, an unmarked RCMP car roared out of Verdun and headed for the Champlain Bridge. At the wheel was Andre MacKensie, and on the seat next to him was Tom Van Marter calling Ottawa on a radio-telephone patch. In a few minutes, he had been put through.

"Donna?" he said, raising his voice to be heard over the noise of MacKensie's heavy footed driving, "we've got a name and a description of the vehicle he's using. It looks like he's making his run. Rags is combing the roads from the air and Andre and I are heading for the border in a car. We think he has over an hour's head start. Do we have clearance to pursue across the border yet?"

"Not yet, Tom" she answered. "The Prime Minister has contacted the FBI but they assure us they can take care of it. If I didn't know better, I'd suspect them of trying to take the credit."

"Perish the thought," said Van Marter. "How about calling my boss Ted Winters at the Bureau. He'll understand. Maybe he can run interference."

"All right, I'll see what I can do. I've alerted the American police and U.S. Customs. Keep in touch. Good hunting."

"Thanks, Donna. Out."

"No hot pursuit authorized?" said MacKensie.

"Not yet," Van Marter replied. "But the U.S. Border Police have been alerted. If they catch our man entering the U.S. illegally, they would return him to the Canadian Border Police."

"Good. But what if they don't find him until he's already in the U.S.?"

"That gets a little stickier I'm afraid," he replied. "They'll still return him, but once he's in the U.S. he would be taken to the nearest police station to confirm his identity and get clearance for returning him to Canada. There's a good chance his capture by American police would cause articles to appear in the local papers as well. Our reporters are always anxious for a story and there's no wartime censorship to stop them. If any reporter gets near him, Meinhoff could tell them his name and origin. If the wrong people read the article, they could easily figure out the rest."

"Damn it," MacKensie groaned. "Then even if we got him back in the bag, the damage would be done. Well, maybe Donna can bend the right ears to get this guy sent back immediately, or at least isolated from the press. See if you can arrange a patch through to Rags. If he sees something, I don't want to have to go looking for a public phone to find out about it."

"You got it."

As Van Marter set up communication links, MacKensie drove the car towards Route 15. It was the fastest and most direct route to the border. Of course, there was no guarantee Meinhoff would be using the fastest and most direct route. He could be heading down 132 or 209; he could even be heading east to Magog before turning south. The truth was, there were hundreds of possible combinations of roads and even Rags couldn't hope to cover them all. The only real hope was that Meinhoff would be picked up at the customs station. But what was to say he would even try to enter at a customs station? Especially when there were miles of almost open border?

*   *   *

On a run down side street in Plattsburgh, New York, small, weather-beaten brick bungalows crowded together behind mostly treeless yards marked off by gray board fences in various states of disrepair. In a house that looked like every other house on the street, a slight, nervous man sat smoking in his living room trying to make up his mind. When Roger Tredegger had received the phone call from Canada a few hours ago, he had been flabbergasted. How was it possible? Yet he was sure of what the man said; his name was Kenneth Martin and he was a member of the Canadian Bund in Toronto. Martin had been in hiding until he had run into Tysyn's son Walter. Now Walter was helping Martin to escape to the

United States as well, and what's more, Martin was bringing over $20,000 from the Toronto Bund's treasury with him. Tredegger had been promised half the money if he would wait along New York Route 11, pick Martin up and drop him off at the railroad station in Plattsburgh. He could help a fellow persecuted Bund member and make a handsome profit besides.

Still, he couldn't help wondering about the whole thing. He hadn't heard from anyone connected with the Bund since Tysyn had been arrested in 1939, and he knew the younger Tysyn had never approved of his father's political activities. So why would he do something so risky for a Bund member? For that matter, why hadn't Walter Tysyn called him himself? Martin said he was calling in case Tysyn's phone was tapped or his house was watched, and that certainly seemed reasonable, but still…

He lit another cigarette and looked out the window at his old black Ford sedan parked by the curb. It would be so easy to just drive up past Moers to the place on Route 11 Martin had specified. What was the harm? It was only about 20 miles or so. He could be there in a half hour and back in another. Ten thousand dollars for an hour's work was hard to beat; and worth taking a risk for. But what if it was some sort of trap? He sighed. Being a national socialist could be trying sometimes. Not like the old days in Montreal. Then he had been somebody; he had stood in his uniform waving the banner of the new Germany. People noticed him. They turned their heads as they passed by. He sat back and let a long leisurely stream of smoke out, savoring the memory.

"Roger!" came a voice like nails on a blackboard. He turned abruptly to see his formidable wife, Claudia, or "the Colonel" as he referred to her behind her back, filling up the doorway to the kitchen. She was slightly taller and considerably wider than the diminutive Roger and she missed few opportunities to remind him of how far he fell short of being the master race.

"Why are you still sitting there?" she demanded, in a voice that made it clear that there was no acceptable answer. "I need you to pick up the ham I ordered at the butcher's. I told Mr. Benson, you'd be right by to pick it up. He's not going to hold it forever."

He looked at her and slowly rose from his chair. "I was just about to, Claudia."

She folded her arms and looked at him with a mixture of disapproval and suspicion. "I'll just bet you were. You were probably waiting for a personal invitation. If it weren't for me you'd starve to death. It's bad enough you can't get a job, but you could at least help out around here."

Roger Tredegger was already out the door and putting on his hat. "Yes, Colonel," he muttered to himself.

"And make sure you check the weight on that scale," she called out after him. "I'm not paying for Mr. Benson's thumb!"

He got in the old Ford, closed the door and sighed. If he had that money, she'd have to treat him with the respect he deserved; everyone would. He looked at his watch, There was still plenty of time to pick up Martin and get the ham as well. He looked back towards the house and made up his mind; he would do it.

*   *   *

Trees lining highway 202 cast dappled shadows on the road as they passed by under the yellow wings of the Anson. Rags kept one eye on the road below and another on the tree tops that were only yards below him. Traffic was lighter here than on the north-south roads, but that made each vehicle stand out all the more. Off to his left, Rags could see the hills of upstate New York and the Adirondacks, just a few miles away. Farms and cultivated fields made a green patchwork below him, and once again, he felt sorry for those stuck on the ground. He checked his air speed; 120 knots. Better slow it down a little.

"Whoa, what was that?" he exclaimed. As he turned his head from the instrument panel, he thought he saw a blur of blue go by beneath him. He twisted around in his seat, but couldn't see it again because of the trees. Could that have been a blue van? Well, best make another pass to be sure. He pushed the stick to the right and made a slow lazy 180 degree turn, circling back to a point near where he thought he saw the van. He straightened out along the road again, lowered the flaps, and dropped his airspeed to 80 knots. This time he kept his eyes firmly on the road below, but there was no blue van.

"Damn it, I know I saw something, but where is it?" he said. The trees were obscuring the road and he wasn't certain that he hadn't missed it the second time he passed over. He banked the plane again and repeated the search. Once more the road passed beneath him in patches seen through the treetops. Once more he saw no blue van. He picked up the mike and pressed the call switch.

"This is Wing one to Bloodhound. Wing One to Bloodhound."

After a pause of a few seconds, the radio crackled a reply.

"This is Bloodhound. Where are you, Wing One?"

Rags recognized MacKensie's voice over the static. "I'm over route 202, about a mile or so west of 15. I think I saw a blue van for a second, heading west, but by the time I circled back, it was gone."

"Could you have been mistaken?"

"Maybe; it was only for a second. But I'm thinking it might have turned off on one of these farms."

There was a pause. "All right, Rags. Do a pattern search from the point of sighting. We're on our way. We'll be there in about 45 minutes."

"Right oh. Wing one out."

A pattern search meant starting from the last known sighting and flying increasingly greater circles covering increasingly greater area. Sometimes a square or triangular pattern was flown, but the idea was the same. In theory, you would intersect your target regardless of which direction it went. In reality, though, the bigger the circle, the more area a target had in which to hide.

Rags dropped to a hundred feet and banked into a graceful turn that took him over the farms and buildings lining route 202. By this time, several people were standing on porches squinting up at the circling yellow airplane wondering what was going on. With the banking angle, Rags had a clear view of the ground, but could see no blue van. Ten minutes later, he was close to crossing the American border on his outward leg and had still seen nothing. The van had vanished.

He repeated the search from a slightly higher elevation, believing the van was big enough to be seen from a greater height. That way, he could cover more area visually. Once more the green fields and trees passed beneath him.

But there was no blue van to be seen anywhere.

*   *   *

Roger Tredegger pulled to a stop by the side of the road on the American side of the border. Canada was about two miles to the north across lightly wooded fields. This seemed to be where Martin had told him to wait, but he had been a little vague about the time. No wonder; the man was traveling on foot. Well, he could wait here peacefully until Martin arrived. At least he was far from the disapproving eye of the Colonel. It was a fine summer day and the cloudless sky was a deep blue. An airplane droned off in the distance somewhere on the Canadian side, but otherwise there was only the sound of birds and the occasional passing car. He sat back and relaxed for a moment, then remembered; Martin had left instructions to raise the hood as if there were engine trouble. This would enable Martin to recognize him and provide a reason for waiting by the side of the road if anyone should notice. A clever man this Martin.

Tredegger got out of his seat, raised the hood after some fumbling with the latch, and stood in front of the car for a few minutes; then, seeing no one coming from the north, he sat down again. Tredegger thought of the money and was pleased at the prospect of getting it, but he was more excited by the prospect of action in the national socialist cause. Someday Germany would triumph and he will have played a part. This action was simple enough; merely pick up Martin and take him to the train station in Plattsburgh. Well, no matter. He was making a contribution, and that excited him. He might even get to wear a uniform again one day. He felt so much more important when he wore his uniform, so much more in control. He looked up and down the empty road again and lit a cigarette. The stream of smoke he exhaled was carried away by a soft summer breeze. It might be a long wait, but for $10,000.....

✶   ✶   ✶

"If Rags really did spot a van where he thinks he did, it would be a good location for them to try a crossing," MacKensie said as he sped down Route 15. He was weaving in and out of traffic in an alarming way, with squealing tires and startled looks from other motorists, but Van Marter didn't feel it was a good idea to protest.

"Yeah. Crossing the border in that area would be a lot safer from prying eyes," said Van Marter. "But if the van is really there, what happened to it?"

"I'm guessing they pulled in somewhere. Maybe into a garage or barn or something," said MacKensie as he blew his horn at another hapless motorist.

"Oh, great. Just what we need to make our job harder. Holy cow, will you watch where you're driving? You almost hit that truck."

MacKensie grinned. "Well maybe this isn't standard FBI type driving, but in case you haven't noticed, we're trying to catch someone who doesn't want to be caught. I don't want to get there just in time to see him disappear over the border."

"Just as long as we get there in one piece."

MacKensie passed another truck, this time on the narrow shoulder of the road, throwing up dust and stones. The truck driver blew on his air horn furiously.

"Out of my way; I've got a Kraut to catch," MacKensie grumbled.

"I see a crossroads up ahead. Is that the 202 intersection?"

"That's it all right. If Rags is right, our boy is about a mile east of there."

As if for emphasis, Rags roared by a few hundred yards ahead. MacKensie picked up the radio. "This is Bloodhound to Wing One. Come in."

The radio crackled to life. "This is Wing One. Go ahead."

"Rags, we're going to be turning on to westbound 202 in about a minute. We're in a black, unmarked Ford sedan. I'll put the headlights on so you can tell it's us. How about keeping us in view and telling us when we get to the point where you saw the van?"

"Right-oh. I'll circle the area."

The car took the right turn onto Route 202 on two wheels as Van Marter held on. They shot down the straight road and were glad to see traffic was light. There were just enough large trees along the road to obscure the view from above. Farms and small houses were scattered along both sides of the road and a few people were still on their porches looking up at the sky. Rags had made a lasting impression.

Van Marter grabbed the microphone. "Wing One, do you read me?"

"Wing One. I read you."

"Rags, have you found the van again?"

"I've flown three more searches and haven't found a thing. I'm just drilling holes in the sky."

"We're on 202 now. Can you see us?"

"Not yet, but....ah, there we go. I see you now."

The plane roared overhead at that moment and Van Marter swore he could see the leaves on the trees shake.

"Are we where you saw the van?"

"Almost. It's about another quarter mile or so. Keep going…keep going…Better slow down, you're almost there….almost…..There; right there by that oak tree on your right."

The car skidded to a stop as the plane flew farther away, and suddenly everything seemed unnaturally quiet. There were four driveways in view, and each of them led off to a different farm complex in the distance.

"Now what?" said Van Marter.

"Pick one, Mr. G Man," MacKensie replied.

Van Marter looked at the driveways carefully. They all looked the same.

"Maybe we can figure this out rationally, Andre. If the van was here when Rags flew over, and Meinhoff pulled into the first driveway to hide before the plane returned, he'd have turned maybe 50-100 yards down the road. And if that was to be his jumping off point to the states, he'd have turned into a farm on the left side of the road, since they'd back up to the border."

MacKensie raised an eyebrow. "All right, but how would he hide? I think one of these farmers might have noticed a strange blue van in his cornfield."

"Yes, that's certainly true," said Van Marter, a little less sure of his theory. "Well, let's try the one with the green mail box on the left. It's about the right distance."

"Now you're talking." MacKensie fishtailed the car into a gravel driveway and sped towards the farmhouse kicking up a torrent of dust and gravel behind. As they pulled up to a grey clapboard farmhouse, the elderly farmer and his wife were already on the porch where they had been watching Rags swooping over the fields. They stared blankly at the dust covered car as it skidded and crunched to a stop and two men leaped out.

"You folks seen a blue van come by here?" MacKensie blurted.

"Well, good afternoon to you too, young fella," the unperturbed farmer replied. "Care for some lemonade?"

"Lemona….Look, we're with the RCMP. We're looking for a blue repair van. It came by here maybe 45 minutes ago."

"Wellll," the farmer replied with unhurried deliberateness. "We had a fellow come by here two weeks ago….or was it three? No, it was two. I remember because it was the day the dog got into the chicken house and …"

"Look," Van Marter interrupted, "We need to find the van and we think it may have turned off near here. Is there any other place it could go?"

The farmer looked at him with no change in his expression. Then, just as MacKensie was about to erupt, said "Wellll…there's farms all along the road here. There's George and Barbara Belle's place across the road. George's a Lutheran. Then there's Fred Weddle's over to the west. Fred has six children. And of course there's Marty Porter's over to the east, only Marty usually keeps a chain across the driveway. What color did you say the van was?"

"Blue," MacKensie said through gritted teeth.

The farmer considered this a moment, then resumed. "The widow Quimbey lives next to Fred Weddle's place. Elmer Quimbey died in the last war. Then there's Dave Hammond's place……"

"Come on, Andre," said Van Marter. "We're wasting time. Let's try another driveway." They turned to go.

"Of course Dave ain't there no more; not since his sons went in the army….or was it the navy?"

MacKensie had the door halfway opened and stopped. "What did you say?"

The farmer started. "What?"

"Did you say there was a place near here that was deserted?"

"Wellll…not deserted. It's just that nobody lives there. You see, old Dave…."

"Where is this place?"

"Dave Hammond's? Oh it's right on the other side of the Fred Weddle's place. The name's on the mailbox. You can't miss it. I remember when Dave painted that mailbox. Summer of '35 it was…no; '34. Anyway,…"

But MacKensie and Van Marter were already roaring back down the drive. The farmer watched the cloud of dust move down the driveway.

"They was nice fellas," he said. "But they never had any lemonade."

His wife harumphed. "Folks are always in such a hurry these days."

-19-

Donna Hastings paced the room restlessly. She knew Meinhoff was breaking for the border with MacKensie and Van Marter in blind pursuit. She felt frustrated and helpless to be in Ottawa. She had done all she could, but the hardest part was waiting. She looked at the black telephone as if she could will it to ring, but it was silent. At that moment, the Commissioner stuck his head in the door.

"Any word?" she asked.

"Not yet. The P.M. is contacting Roosevelt directly for hot pursuit permission. Apparently Mr. Hoover prefers not to have any RCMP stealing his thunder in his own back yard. He claims there is plenty of time to catch Meinhoff if he gets to the states. The FBI will take care of it. Of all the obstacles we have to overcome, I'm afraid Mr. Hoover's ego might prove to be the biggest. Have you heard any more from our lads?"

"Not yet. The only calls have been from reporters asking about the train search at Pointe Aux Trembles."

"Too right you are, Miss Hastings. I've gotten those calls as well, but they've been from assorted Members of Parliament. If you want my opinion, MP's shouldn't be allowed to have phones."

She smiled, and the door closed again. With a heavy sigh, she sat down at the long table and started going through messages that had come in from various intelligence sources; phone taps, embassies, prisoner interrogations, mail censorship, newspaper articles, and police reports. The information was in several piles according to date received. She started with the most recent, but even many of these were several days old by the time she received them. Finding useful information in these sources was almost as hard as finding Meinhoff himself, she thought. If there was anything good, it was no doubt buried in trivia.

The first sheet she picked up was a police report concerning a stolen car in Pointe Aux Trembles. But when she checked the time she saw it was reported three hours before the Abitibi Express had arrived. The next paper was a report of a prisoner interrogation at the Monteith camp from which Meinhoff had escaped. The prisoner spokesman, a U-110 man named Oberleutnant Strauss knew about the escape of Meinhoff, but had provided no information about his plans, saying Meinhoff had decided to simply improvise as he went along. It was a lot of nonsense, of course, but you could hardly blame him for declining to make the RCMP's job easier. The next sheet was a summary of interrogations of other prisoners, with pretty much the same results; apparently they knew less than the Canadians.

Donna shook her head and picked up the next piece of paper; an intelligence report from the American FBI.

"The following telegram was sent from the Devon Street Telegraph office in Montreal to the German Embassy in Washington at 1621 hours on 10 July, 1941:"

Donna frowned. She realized the FBI was fighting a running battle with Nazi agents in spite of America's supposed neutrality, but was surprised they were reading telegrams. She wondered how they did it, then returned to the report.

"Telegram addressed to A. Smith, 1607 Massachusetts Avenue NW, Washington, D.C.

PACKAGE YOU NEED AT PLATTSBURGH AUGUST 15-(STOP)-MUST RECEIVE IN PERSON-(STOP)-IF NOT OTHERS MIGHT-(STOP)—"

The telegram was signed simply "Rawer, Ltd".

She read it again. It didn't seem to make much sense. What package would have to be picked up at Plattsburgh for delivery to Washington? And what was the Rawer, Ltd? She reached for a Montreal telephone directory and turned the pages. There was no company or person named Rawer in the Montreal directory. She called the operator and asked her to see if there was a Rawer Company in Canada anywhere. A few minutes later, the operator called back and said there wasn't.

Now she was reasonably sure the telegram was a coded message to the German Embassy, but was it some small change espionage or did it have something to do with Meinhoff's escape? Meinhoff could be the package they were talking about, or it could be a case of beer. She read again.

"MUST RECEIVE IN PERSON-(STOP)-IF NOT OTHERS MIGHT-(STOP)—"

"Funny," she said out loud. "If you include the word 'stop', the sentence has an entirely different meaning. It would read 'If not, others might stop.' Others might stop. Might stop what?"

It still didn't prove anything. The RCMP was aware there were German agents in Montreal. But surely an agent would have used a code of some kind. And who or what was Rawer, Ltd?

It might have been the dust from all the paper in the room, but at that moment, Donna Hastings sneezed. By reflex, she said Gesundheit to herself. The word gave her an idea, and she reached for the German English dictionary on the shelf. There was no English word Rawer, of course, but she could check the German.

"Let's see," she said, flipping the pages rapidly. "Rawer is not a German word......Oh, my God."

She dropped the dictionary to the floor with a loud crash and dashed for the Commissioner's office.

"Commissioner, Meinhoff has contacted the German Embassy."

"What? How?"

"Look at this telegram," she said, spreading it on his desk. "and look how it's signed."

"Rawer?" said the Commissioner. "Who is Rawer?"

"Rawer is a word Meinhoff used to inform the embassy that the message came from an escaped German prisoner in Canada trying to get to the United States."

"All that from one word? What makes you think that?"

"Reverse the syllables and you get Werra, the Luftwaffe prisoner who escaped last year and made it all the way back to Germany."

The Commissioner looked at her, then read the message again. "By heavens, Miss Hastings, I believe you're right. And that means…"

"It means that there could be a German agent waiting for Meinhoff on the other side of the border," she said.

"And that means Meinhoff won't have to make it back to Germany to reveal his secret; all he has to do is make contact with the right person in Plattsburgh."

Donna Hastings had a sudden vision of her brother on a troopship as several torpedoes sped towards it through the darkness. She felt sick and almost mad with frustration.

"Let's pray Andre and Tom can stop him in time," she said quietly. "If he crosses the border and meets up with an agent, it's all over."

*   *   *

"There's the mailbox," Van Marter shouted.

"I see it. Hang on, Tom."

The car skidded sideways as MacKensie turned into the driveway without slowing down. A group of run down farm buildings could be seen almost a half mile away.

"This is a perfect set up for Meinhoff," said Van Marter. "How did he find it?"

"Through Tysyn, no doubt. How Tysyn found it is anyone's guess. He probably had a service call here once and remembered it."

"I don't see any van yet."

"Me neither, but I can see why Rags missed it. The whole driveway is overgrown with trees and honeysuckle. You could hide a tank in here."

"But where's the van?"

They pulled into a yard area with an old gothic farmhouse on one side and barns on two other. The house was a mass of peeling white paint and exposed grey wood. The car skidded to a stop and the men looked at each other in the stillness.

"Let's get him," MacKensie said.

Cautiously, they got out of the car with guns drawn. There was no sound but the faint rustle of a breeze in the trees, the occasional buzzing of insects, and the drone of the Anson making another circle somewhere to the west. The air was heavy with the smell of the honeysuckle that covered everything in twisting green tangles. A pear tree stood between the barns, its ripe, unpicked fruit buzzing softly with the bees it had attracted. MacKensie motioned to Van Marter to check the barn on the left while he crept towards the one on the right. Although both barns had open doors, the heavy blankets of vines and creepers cut off so much light it was difficult to see inside. A good place for an ambush.

Van Marter slowly looked around the splintered wood of the doorpost of the first barn. Several pigeons flew out in a flutter of feathers and he ducked to avoid them. As his eyes adjusted to the dim light inside the barn, he saw a broken down old wagon, but no blue van. He looked over to MacKensie, who was motioning frantically. Van Marter ran up to the second barn where MacKensie signaled for him to be quiet. He looked inside.

There was the blue van.

MacKensie and Van Marter looked at each other with satisfaction, but at that moment, a sound came from the van. Someone or something was banging against the inside panel with a dull metallic clang. The sound stopped.

"Could he still be here?" whispered Van Marter.

MacKensie shook his head. "I don't see how, not with the head start he had. Let's have a look."

The van was facing away from them, just as it had been left. They each walked softly with guns drawn. As they came even with the rear of the van, the banging came again, and they both flinched. There was a small window in the rear panel door facing the barn door opening. They were tempted to look in, but were afraid the back lighting would make them easy targets. So they carefully made their way to the front doors. MacKensie yanked it open.

"Don't move!" they both yelled at once as they held their guns on whatever was inside.

On the floor of the van, just behind the driver's seat was the bound and gagged form of a heavy-set, middle aged man, his eyes wide with terror. MacKensie reached in and pulled off the gag.

"Walter Tysyn, I presume?"

"Yes. That's me," the figure replied weakly.

"Where's Wilson?"

"Wilson?"

"The man you helped escape," said Van Marter.

"No, he tricked me," Tysyn protested. "Then when I found out, he threatened to kill me. I didn't help him to escape on purpose."

"How did you get him through the roadblock? Did he force you to do that too?"

Tysyn blurted out the story of his ride with Meinhoff, including Meinhoff's ploy with the greasy hands, and the fact that Meinhoff was now calling himself Charles Anderson. Tysyn wailed about his innocence.

MacKensie was becoming impatient. He grabbed Tysyn by the shirt front. "Shut up! I don't care about you. I want Anderson! What is his plan?"

"He's going to cross the border and go to New York City. At least, that's what he said he was going to do."

"How is he getting to New York? Did you arrange for someone to pick him up?"

"No, I swear. He was going to walk to Plattsburgh and go from there by train."

"Walk?" said Van Marter. "That's about 40 miles. Are you sure he didn't make some other arrangements?"

"I…I don't know," said Tysyn, looking miserable and defeated. "That's what he told me."

"Give us a description."

"Uh…about six feet tall, clean shaven with light brown hair. He's in his 20s I think, and is wearing brown slacks and a white shirt."

"All right," said MacKensie. "We're wasting time. It's about two miles to the U.S. border and another three miles to a highway. He's had over an hour's head start. He's probably in the states already. Tom, how about waiting outside, I want to have a word with Mr Tysyn here."

He untied Tysyn and looked him in the eye severely. "Now look. Here's what you're going to do," MacKensie said. "You get in that truck and head back to Montreal. When people ask you what happened, you tell them you were helping out the RCMP in an important investigation and can't talk about it. Got that?"

Tysyn looked bewildered, then his face lit up with relief. "Oh yes. Of course," he sputtered. "Thank you inspector. Thank you very much. You won't be sorry. I won't tell a soul. You can count on me. Thank you."

"Go on; get going."

MacKensie walked back outside. He stood with Van Marter and looked over the rolling fields that stretched to the border and beyond.

"You're letting him go?" Van Marter asked.

"Of course. Remember he tried to turn Meinhoff in. Besides, Tysyn's just a dupe. If he wasn't, he'd have gotten the word out himself, eh?"

"Good point," Van Marter nodded."Do you think Rags can find Meinhoff?"

"Not a chance. Look at all the trees and brush, eh? There's too many places to hide. Even Rags can't fly UNDER the trees."

"I think you're right. The only chance we have left is to pick him up on the U.S. side. I'll let them know about Tysyn and find out about the hot pursuit permission."

Van Marter went back to the car and keyed the mike. "This is Bloodhound to base. I need to be patched through to Ottawa."

A few seconds later, Donna was on the speaker.

"Tom, is that you? What's going on?"

"We've got Tysyn, but our man's broken for the border. He's probably in the U.S. already. Do we have permission to pursue yet?"

"The Commissioner's still working on it, but we have some new information. We think our man got a coded telegram to the German legation in Washington asking them to send someone to meet him in Plattsburg at the train station. If they do, and he finds them before we find him, well, you figure it out."

"Jeez Louise. What next?"

"Well, you still have no permission to pursue into the U.S. yet. What are you going to do now?"

Van Marter thought for a moment. "I'll tell you after we've done it. So long, Donna. We'll have that Ottawa tour yet."

"All right, Tom. Where do we stand?" MacKensie had appeared by the side of the car.

"Hop in. I'll tell you on the way."

"We can pursue?" MacKensie asked anxiously.

"No, but I don't see how they could complain if you were to give me a lift to the Plattsburgh station."

MacKensie looked at him slyly. "I got you. Let's go, partner."

*　　　*　　　*

Roger Tredegger was getting sleepy sitting in the warm car waiting for the mysterious Mr. Martin, and he was almost dozing off when the sight of a New York State Police patrol car in his rear view mirror made him instantly alert. His stomach knotted up as he realized the car was pulling up behind him.

"Oh, my God. What if they know?" he whispered to himself. "What if they came to arrest me?"

With all his self control, Tredegger willed himself to be calm, but was sweating just the same. With agonizing slowness, the patrolman got out of his car and walked up to the driver's window. He was a short man in a dark grey uniform and a black hat, and he bent down until his face was only inches from Tredegger's.

"Good afternoon," he said evenly. "Got car trouble?"

Tredegger smiled at the patrolman in a way he hoped was innocent. "I'm afraid it's been overheating a little. I'm waiting for it to cool down, then I'll be on my way."

The trooper glanced at the engine. "That's too bad. Do you want me to call a tow?"

"Oh, no thanks, officer. This has happened before. It'll be fine when it's cooled down."

The patrolman made no reply, but went to the front of the car and reached down to feel the engine.

"It doesn't feel too hot now."

"Sometimes it fools you, officer. The surface is cool, but it's still hot inside. I'm getting a new radiator next week, so I'm taking no chances until then. I think I'll wait another twenty minutes or so, just to be on the safe side."

The trooper looked at Tredegger curiously, then shrugged. "Suit yourself. Could I see your license and registration card please?"

Tredegger fumbled for the documents and handed them over. The policeman examined them slowly and deliberately, then handed them back.

"All right, Mr Tredegger. Oh, and by the way; don't pick up any hitch-hikers, O.K.?"

"Hitchhikers? Oh, no. Of course."

Tredegger exhaled with relief as he watched the patrolman drive off. But why had he mentioned hitchhikers? Did he know something, or was it just a casual caution? Treddeger nervously tapped his fingers against the steering wheel. The raised hood ploy had worked perfectly, but how long could he wait? Where was Martin?

*　　　　　*　　　　　*

At the same time, Hermann Brautsh of the German Legation in Washington was yawning as he got off the overnight train from New York in the Plattsburgh station. He had been visiting some of the Reich's New York agents when he had gotten a call from Hans Thomsen. Since Hitler and Roosevelt had withdrawn their ambassadors a few years before, the German Embassy had been downgraded to a legation, and Thomsen was the Reich's Emissary, not the Ambassador. Still, it gave the Fatherland a golden opportunity to coordinate spying activities for Admiral Canaris and the SA. The Yorkville section of New York City had been particularly active, although the FBI seemed to be increasingly suspicious. They had even made several arrests recently.

Even so, the flow of information and the potential for sabotage were great in the United States and every help to the war effort was welcome. Perhaps that was why Thomsen has sent him off to upstate New York based on a telegram he received from Montreal. The instructions were maddeningly vague; meet someone whose code name may or may not be 'Rawer' and who had some sort of package or information to hand over. Then bring back this package or information to the legation in Washington. Thomsen believed Rawer could be an agent, a sympa-thizer, or possibly an escaped German POW. Thomsen deduced that Rawer was someone who had information, but was not free to travel.

Possibly he was a fugitive, or in hiding. Of course the whole thing could well be a hoax, but Hans Thomsen usually had a pretty good sense about these things.

Brautsh looked up and down the platform. A few groups of holiday travelers awaited the next train, and a group of schoolchildren chased each other around one of the columns, their squeals echoing hollowly in the station. On the other side of the tracks, a conductor checked his watch while a bored looking porter slowly pushed a luggage cart. There was no sign of anyone or anything that could possibly be of interest, but the telegram had only said the day, not the time. He could be here for hours. He slowly walked into the main waiting room and found a reasonably comfortable place on a bench. He realized there was a chance the FBI had seen the telegram, and might even have agents at the station, but if so, they'd probably be as much in the dark as he was. At any rate, even if they found him here, they could do nothing about it. He was still a representative of a sovereign nation and was doing nothing illegal.

Brautsh yawned again. The overnight train had been full of families on holiday and teenagers returning to Montreal from summer camps in New York. He had gotten little sleep. Whoever this "Rawer" was, he had better have something worthwhile to justify all this trouble.

-20-

MacKensie and Van Marter turned south on Route 15 and were soon in sight of the customs station. An American flag lazily flapped in the breeze just beyond the barriers. Several cars were already stopped and being scrutinized for anyone fitting Meinhoff's description.

"Why won't they give us permission to pursue in the U.S.?" grumbled MacKensie. "Are you guys on our side or not?"

"Well, politics isn't my specialty," Van Marter answered, "but I imagine Mr Hoover would be embarrassed if a Canadian caught a spy on American soil. That's the FBI's job."

"Holy…you mean he'd risk letting this guy escape just to keep from looking bad?"

"Maybe it's not as big a risk as you think," Van Marter said, somewhat defensively. "The FBI isn't exactly helpless, you know."

"Jeez, Tom. Where have you been? We've both been helpless when dealing with this guy. He's smart, resourceful and dangerous. Besides, there's a good chance somebody from the German legation will be there to meet him, eh? If that happens, we may as well buy Meinhoff a first class ticket to Berlin."

They were at the customs booth now. Van Marter showed his FBI credentials and the rest of the formalities magically evaporated. In one minute they were heading south into New York state.

"All right," said MacKensie, looking over his shoulder as the customs station receded behind them, "We're in your neighborhood now. I suppose you want to head for Plattsburgh."

"Plattsburgh? No. Once Meinhoff gets to Plattsburgh, he's won; game, set, and match. He'll tell everything to the man from the German legation and then it won't matter if Meinhoff is arrested; Hitler will know the Enigma machine has been compromised and take steps accordingly. No, we've got to stop Meinhoff before he gets there. The question is: how?"

MacKensie nodded approvingly. "I'm on side with that. It's good to know the southern air hasn't clouded your thinking, eh? But stopping him has been what we've been trying to do all along. So far we haven't been very successful at it, and this is the last chance we're ever going to get. I say we head to the spot on the American side where he's likely to emerge."

"But with the head start he had, he could have passed that point already. And if he's managed to steal a car, he could be halfway to Plattsburgh already."

"Well, maybe we should just stake out the railway station and grab him then. Assuming he hasn't altered his appearance so that we don't recognize him. Can you find out if the locals have seen anything?"

Van Marter nodded grimly and switched the radio to the local highway patrol frequency.

"Unit 42 eastbound on Rte 111, 5 miles west of 15. Departing routine traffic stop for stalled motorist with overheated engine."

"That's only about eight miles from here," Van Marter said, frowning in thought. "And it's right where Meinhoff would be appearing if he crossed on a straight line. Kind of a strange coincidence somebody should stall out right at that spot."

"You think he could be waiting for Meinhoff?" said MacKensie.

"I don't know, but I've never been a great believer in coincidences. If this guy is waiting for Meinhoff it means he hasn't gotten there yet. That means we might be able to intercept him there."

"But how could Meinhoff have arranged that? He doesn't have any contacts here."

Van Marter shrugged. "Who knows? Maybe somebody he knew from school, or one of Tysyn's father's old pals. It's worth taking a look. If he is waiting for Meinhoff, maybe we could chase him off and take his place. Then…"

"Then Meinhoff walks right into our waiting arms!" shouted MacKensie, thumping the dashboard with his fist. "Well, what are we waiting for?"

"But if we're wrong, Meinhoff could be on his way to Plattsburgh while we're off harassing an innocent bystander."

"Not a chance. My nose just started twitching again. Let's go."

✶   ✶   ✶

Under any other circumstances, Meinhoff thought, the last few hours would have been delightful. A motor tour through the Canadian countryside on a clear summer day, and a brisk hike through the woods and meadows of Quebec and New York state would usually be invigorating and relaxing. The wind sighed through the trees, birds sang, and insects hummed in the soft summer air as he pushed along. The hike had been easy and he had made good time, covering the five miles from the farm in a little over an hour and a half. He was perspiring from the heat and exertion and was splattered with mud and various burrs and stickers, but otherwise was going strong.

Meinhoff was happy he had gotten this far. The Canadians who were looking for him were proving as inept as he had hoped. Various citizens had either ignored him or actively assisted him in his quest to escape. About forty minutes earlier, he had crossed the border. Now he was in the United States, a country that, officially at least, was neutral in the great struggle for Germany's destiny. That meant that security and restrictions were much looser here. Unless caught actually crossing the border, he knew he stood a good chance of delaying being sent back to the camp at least long enough to get his story out to the Reich. If his message to the Embassy got through, in fact, he might get the message out in the next hour or two.

Of course, there was the matter of Roger Tredegger to consider. The Canadian exile had seemed willing but hesitant on the phone. Meinhoff knew the type; a big talker who balked when it came time for action. One of Meinhoff's classmates at the University of Pennsylvania had been from Texas and had a term for such men; big hat, no cattle. He smiled at the memory. Still, the lure of the money and the ease of the task should be enough to get him where he was needed. All the man has to do is pick him up and take him to the train station. Even an unreliable like Tredegger should have little problem doing that. Once at the station, Meinhoff would have Tredegger find the German Embassy man and bring him out in case the FBI was watching the platforms. And if Tredegger didn't show up, Meinhoff would simply have to either steal a car or hitchhike to Plattsburgh. That should be no trouble; the Americans were even more trusting and helpful than the Canadians.

A pheasant suddenly rose from some bushes ahead and flapped off into the sky. Meinhoff smiled, If only he had a proper rifle with him. This was good place for stalking game.

*   *   *

"No; my car overheated. I swear!" protested Roger Tredegger to the two men who had pulled up behind him and flashed badges. He waved his arms in pleading frustration and periodically wiped his brow with a large white handkerchief.

"Come on, we know you were waiting for someone," Van Marter insisted. "Who is it?"

"No, I'm just waiting for my car to cool down. You must believe me."

"Come on, Tredegger," Van Marter sneered. "Do we look like we just escaped from the Home for the Incurably Stupid? The engine isn't even warm, you've been here so long. Were you waiting for winter?"

MacKensie examined Tredegger's license and noted the number. "We'd better get him out of here before our friend arrives," he said quietly to Van Marter. "We wouldn't want to scare him off."

Van Marter glared at the trembling Tredegger, who seemed to shrink before him. "All right, get going. But stay close to home for the next week; we may want to talk to you later."

Tredegger jumped in his car without another word and sped off in a swirl of dust and loose gravel as if he were being chased. As he disappeared from sight, the road became quiet once again.

"He was waiting for Meinhoff, all right. In a few more minutes I'd have gotten him to admit it."

"Forget him, eh?" said MacKensie. "He's not the one we want."

"No, I guess he isn't," sighed Van Marter. "Now all we can do is wait."

✳   ✳   ✳

Meinhoff walked with enthusiasm in his step as he got ever closer to his goal. He was tired, but happy. He had beaten them every step of the way and soon would be back in Germany.

He paused to rest a moment and peered through the trees ahead. His eye caught movement in the distance; a truck traveling on a still unseen road. That must be the American road that travels parallel to the border. He was almost there. If Tredegger was there, he had won. He started off again with a new lightness in his step.

As he got ever closer to the road, he could make out features and see more of it. As he got within a few hundred yards, he could see most of the road from the east to the western horizon. His excitement rose as he wondered if Tredegger was waiting for him. He peered intently at the road again, and there it was.

Almost directly in his line of march was a black sedan parked by the side of the road with the hood up.

"Well, Herr Tredegger," Meinhoff said with satisfaction. "You have come through for the fatherland. My congratulations. It is a pity you will not be receiving the money, but we can save that bit of sad news until we arrive at the railway station in Plattsburgh."

As he got closer, he could see a man standing by the raised hood pretending to look at the engine, but obviously looking north just as much. Meinhoff looked up and down the road. There were no other cars in sight. The man in front of the car suddenly spotted him and waved. Meinhoff grinned and waved back.

Meinhoff was within a hundred yards now and could see the man waiting for him through the trees. Tredegger was pretty much as Meinhoff had imagined him; a somewhat sloppy, balding, middle aged man with a comfortable looking stomach. A typical middle class clerk with dreams of glory, Meinhoff thought. The man stood watching him impassively.

Meinhoff was only about 50 yards away now, and could see the man and the car more clearly. The man looked as he expected, but the car was covered with a thick coating of reddish brown dust, and there were mud splashes around the wheel wells. Tredegger, he knew, lived in Plattsburgh; where did the dirt and mud come from? He stopped. The man by the car raised his arm and waved again and Meinhoff thought he could make out a brown leather strap under the man's coat; a shoulder holster? He ducked behind a tree and got out his pistol.

"Come on," the man standing by the car muttered to himself. "Don't stop now. Come to papa. What the…? Where the hell did he go? He disappeared. Maybe he smelled a rat. Now what?"

"Get behind the car," said Van Marter, who was crouched down behind the opposite fender, out of sight. "Remember, he's armed. I'll radio for backup."

"Hurry up, Mr Anderson," MacKensie bluffed. "We have to get going before the police get here."

No sooner had these words left MacKensie's mouth than a fusillade of gunfire erupted from the woods. MacKensie dived behind the car as six shots slammed into the driver's side door, leaving silver rimmed holes in the black paint.

"He must have changed his alias again," MacKensie gasped. "Sorry I tipped him off. At least he's a bad shot."

"On the contrary," Van Marter replied. "He's a pretty good shot. He wasn't trying to get you; he's just trying to get us to dive for cover so he can break free."

The firing suddenly stopped as the sound of the last shot echoed through the trees. Van Marter cautiously opened the passenger side door and grabbed the radio microphone. He pressed the key but got no response.

"Oh, great. It looks like a slug smashed the radio. Now we can't call for reinforcements."

"But where is Meinhoff now?"

"Probably took off while we were pinned down."

"There!" MacKensie pointed down the road. Van Marter turned in time to see Meinhoff dash across the road and plunge into the woods on the south side.

"Look, Andre. Our radio's dead, so you drive to get the State Police while I go after Meinhoff."

"Are you crazy?" retorted MacKensie. "Going after him alone in the woods would be like going after a wounded lion in tall grass. I'll go with you. We can run a coordinated sector search on him and close in together, each covering the other so he doesn't get the drop on us."

"We need backup," Van Marter insisted. "And we haven't got a radio to call for it."

"Then let's park the car across the road, eh? The next car that comes by will know something's wrong and notify the police. They have our license number and will put two and two together."

Van Marter though a moment, weighing options.

"All right, let's go."

After the warmth of the road, the woods were cool and damp as MacKensie and Van Marter cautiously entered with guns drawn. They stopped to listen, but only heard a bird call somewhere out of sight. Using hand signals, they took turns advancing a few steps at a time as each one covered the other. Deeper into the woods they went, the only sound the occasional crack of a twig beneath their feet and the gentle hum of locusts. The air was thick with the smell of wet leaf mulch.

They halted about 100 yards into the woods. There was still no sign of Meinhoff. Was he running ahead of them, or was he lying in ambush behind the next tree? Van Marter wiped a bead of perspiration from his upper lip as he looked around cautiously. About 50 yards away, MacKensie started moving forward as they slowly converged on where Meinhoff should be.

A few steps later, Van Marter saw a thin branch freshly broken and hanging about waist high; he was on the right track. He signaled MacKensie to come closer and they adjusted their search pattern to put the broken branch in the center.

They stopped again. MacKensie thought he saw movement in the brush ahead, or was it the wind? Van Marter stepped on a twig that snapped with a loud crack. He cursed his clumsiness and started more cautiously.

From somewhere close ahead a several shots rang out. Van Marter ducked instinctively as several pieces of foliage clipped by the bullets drifted down on him like green snowflakes.

"Holy cow," he gasped. "That guy is liable to kill somebody."

He looked up and was surprised to see MacKensie next to him.

"Come on partner," he said. "Let's get him. We've got to hurry."

"Are you nuts? He just ambushed us. He could be waiting a few yards ahead. We've got to circle around and flank him."

"No," said MacKensie excitedly. "Don't you see? He knows he's got to get to Plattsburgh and relay his information. The longer he's delayed the more likely he'll be intercepted, eh? He counted on Tredegger giving him a lift so he's way behind schedule. He doesn't have time to play cowboys and Indians in the woods with us; he's got to cover distance."

"Well he sure found the time to almost blow my head off."

"Put yourself in his place," said MacKensie. "You're trying to get away through the woods from a couple of pursuers who are probably no faster than you are. What do you do?"

Van Marter started to understand. "You slow them down."

"Exactly. You wait in hiding and fire a few shots at them to pin them down and make them proceed slowly while you get away. He knows if he gets a good head start we'll never catch him, eh?"

"All right, let's stay about 20 yards apart and go get him."

Onward they went through the woods, faster now. They could see only about 40 to 50 yards ahead, but pushed on steadily, bulling their way past undergrowth and climbing over fallen tree trunks, half expecting to be fired on any second. But after ten minutes, there was still no sign of Meinhoff.

"Whew," said Van Marter. "Maybe he got that head start he needed after all. He's disappeared. Do you suppose he holed up somewhere and let us go past?"

"I don't think so. That would place us in between him and his objective. No, I still think he's up ahead."

Van Marter squinted, as if forcing his vision through the trees. "It looks lighter up ahead. I think there's a clearing….maybe a farm."

*　　　*　　　*

John Alscoe looked at the blue sky over his cornfield and wished it would rain. His corn crop still looked pretty good, but was beginning to get a bit dry. Farming in upstate New York was a chancy proposition, what with the short growing season, and a stretch of dry weather could be trouble. While he was still looking at the sky, he heard the screen door slam as his wife Clare came out on the wooden porch.

"John," she said, drying her hands on her apron, "I thought I saw someone out in the field just now."

He shaded his eyes and squinted where she was pointing. Sure enough, the tasseled tops of corn stalks were moving slightly, as if someone was pushing his way past them.

*   *   *

MacKensie and Van Marter kept moving. In a few minutes they were at the other side of the woods and looking at a field of corn with a farm beyond. The corn was over five feet tall, high enough for a crouching man to be hard to spot traveling between the rows. MacKensie and Van Marter stood at the edge of the woods surveying the scene.

"Now what?" said MacKensie. "He could be anywhere in that corn field and traveling in any direction."

Van Marter nodded. "He could be, but he's only going in one direction; to that farm. Because it has the one thing he needs right now...."

"A car!" MacKensie finished the thought for him. "Let's get to that farm."

"Wait a minute," said Van Marter, frowning. "If we show up at the farm on his heels and before he has a chance to get the car, he might take someone on the farm hostage."

"Too right," said MacKensie frowning. "We have to take him after he leaves."

"Andre, look over there. See how the driveway curves around to the right? It runs along the edge of the cornfield. He has to go that way to get out of here. We could get over there and cut him off as he's leaving in the car. It's cleaner that way and safer for the people who live there."

"You got it. Let's go."

They plunged into the cornfield and navigated their way to a point halfway along the driveway and stopped to catch their breath.

"I hope to God we guessed right," said MacKensie.

"We guessed right," said Van Marter. "I just hope there isn't another driveway out of this place."

MacKensie scowled. "Now there's a cheerful thought. And the way our luck has been running…."

"All right. Now we have to be careful. We don't want to shoot Meinhoff if we can possibly help it, but we do have to stop him."

"No we can't shoot him," said MacKensie, "There'd be an investigation, newspaper stories, and then the secret would be out, eh?"

"We could shoot out his tires as he drives away," suggested Van Marter.

MacKensie shook his head. "This isn't a Gene Autry movie. Maybe you're that good a shot, but I'm certainly not. If we miss, he's gone. And even if we do manage to hit the tires, he can still get far enough to duck back into the corn again. "

"You're right, we can't risk it," said Van Marter.

"Then how do we stop him?" said Mackensie.

"I'm thinking."

*   *   *

The farmer and his wife, thought Meinhoff, almost looked like a somewhat younger version of the couple in the Grant Wood "American Gothic" painting, except that they were standing terrified with their hands over their heads at the moment. Meinhoff, gun in hand, stood a few feet away near a battered old 1934 Ford.

"I am very sorry to be borrowing your car this way," said Meinhoff motioning with his pistol, "but I can assure you it is for a good cause. Now there is one other matter we must discuss. Do you have a telephone?"

John Alscoe, an elderly man with rimless glasses and bald head indicated he had no phone. Meinhoff looked at the wire coming to the house, saw electric only and decided the man was telling the truth.

"In that case, I must bid you good day. The keys please?"

"They… they're in the ignition," stammered the farmer.

"Ah, so they are. It is good to see that trust is still alive. *Auf wiedersehn.*"

With a grinding of the gears and a glance over his shoulder, Gregor Meinhoff set off down the driveway that led to the main road and to Plattsburgh. Those idiotic policemen had almost ruined everything, he thought, but they were still cautiously creeping through the woods fearful of another ambush. In spite of the change in plans, he had only lost less than an hour from his schedule. Very good.

The car gained speed as it passed the thick rows of corn crowding the curving driveway. Meinhoff placed his gun back in his jacket pocket. He wouldn't need it now. He was on his way to Plattsburgh and to immortality.

Suddenly a stocky man emerged from the cornfield and stood in the middle of the driveway pointing a gun at him; the same man who had been standing beside the car pretending to be Tredegger.

"*Was ist los?*" Meinhoff gasped. In a quick reflex reaction, he slowed for a second, then he accelerated straight at MacKensie, who scrambled back into the corn.

"*Dumbkopf!*" Meinhoff snorted. "I knew he wouldn't have time to shoot."

"But I do," came a voice. "Stop the car."

Meinhoff snapped his head around to the source of the voice. The first thing he saw was a Smith and Wesson .38 service revolver pointing at him through the open passenger side window. The second thing he saw was FBI agent Tom Van Marter standing on the car's running board holding that revolver.

-21-

It worked like a charm," said MacKensie, after returning from explaining to the farmer and his wife why they would be borrowing the Ford. "When he saw me he slowed down and was distracted enough for you to emerge from the corn and jump on his running board. And now, Herr Meinhoff, it's back in the bag for you."

Van Marter snapped a pair of handcuffs on Meinhoff. Who protested loudly.

"Take these off. I am not a criminal!" he sputtered.

"No, but you are a bit slippery," Van Marter replied. "We'll take them off when we get you into a real police car."

Meinhoff reluctantly folded himself into the back seat, still wondering what had happened. MacKensie turned to Van Marter. MacKensie's face was tired, red, and glistening with sweat, but had an expression of satisfaction and relief Van Marter had never seen before. MacKensie shifted into gear and they headed off to return to their damaged car.

"Thanks, Tom. You can take him in now. It was worth it just to see the expression on his face. The periscope finally came up and I was there."

Van Marter smiled. "Hey, what are partners for?"

"Well," said MacKensie, "I guess we've got to turn him over to the American authorities."

Meinhoff overheard this remark, and perked up. "You are quite right," he said confidently from the back seat. "The United States government did not apprehend me illegally crossing the border, and the United States is officially neutral. You must turn me over to the American police and they must keep me while authorizations are obtained. You may rest assured I will tell everyone my identity and that I am from the U-110. Even if the story is kept out of the newspapers, at least some of the police will tell their friends. Soon Germany will know the real fate of the U-110....and its contents."

MacKensie turned and glared at Meinhoff. "Why, you arrogant son of a...."

"Gentlemen, gentlemen," Meinhoff interrupted in a soothing voice, "You have my sincere congratulations for your dogged pursuit. You have done a fine job. I am certain no one else could have apprehended me. But you must realize the game was over the moment I crossed the border. I have won. I must be taken into custody and it is only a matter of time before someone unknowingly tells Berlin of my existence and the curious circumstances surrounding the sinking of the U-110. Your efforts have gone for naught, I'm afraid, but cheer up; such are the fortunes of war."

"Maybe I'll just keep on driving across the border," MacKensie grumbled.

"I'm afraid the American Customs agents would ask some awkward questions," said Meinhoff. "A policeman kidnaping a foreign national in another country would be a great embarrassment to both the United States and Canada. After all, international law must be observed, must it not? Admit it, gentlemen: you have no choice but to take me to the local police at Plattsburgh."

"Just shut the hell up," snapped MacKensie.

Van Marter sighed. "I'm afraid he's right. Well, we've done all we could. The higher ups decided against hot pursuit, and there's nothing more to say. There's our car, and there's a New York State Highway patrol car next to it."

"I guess they'll be taking Fritz here off our hands," said MacKensie glumly.

"Yes, gentlemen," gloated Meinhoff. "This is where we must part. Better luck next time. I will have an informative chat with this policeman once you've gone."

They pulled near the patrol car to the surprised look of the patrolman.

"How are you doing?" said Van Marter, stepping out of the car. "I'm inspector Van Marter, FBI. This is…"

"Inspector MacKensie?" the trooper finished the sentence. "I'm Sergeant A.K. Ketter of the New York State Highway Patrol. We've been looking for you guys. And apparently we're not the only ones. They've been calling you from Ottawa."

"Probably wondering where we went," said Van Marter. "Our radio is on the blink. Could I call them on your radio, Sergeant? And we have a prisoner for you to take into custody."

"Sure thing. Always glad to help the FBI. "

Van Marter sighed, slipped into the front seat of the cruiser, and closed the door behind him while MacKensie kept watch on Meinhoff in the farmer's car.

"I'd better tell them we got him," he said, "at least for the moment."

The radio instantly sprang to life with the voice of the Montreal station.

"….reading me? Come in Bloodhound. I repeat; are you reading me? This is Montreal base."

"Bloodhound here," said Van Marter.

"Is everything all right, Bloodhound? We've been trying to raise you for the last forty five minutes."

"We're fine. We just had the radio shut down, then it got, uh, disabled. What's the message?"

"Hold for a patch from Ottawa."

A few seconds passed and the radio spoke again. "Tom, Andre? Are you there?"

"Donna? Yes; we're here. And just listen to this…"

"You've got permission for hot pursuit," she interrupted breathlessly. "I repeat; permission for hot pursuit has been granted! You can chase him into the states, and you can bring him directly back to Montreal. No local clearances are necessary."

"When was the permission granted?"

"About a half hour ago, but we couldn't raise you…"

Van Marter looked back towards the farmer's car. Apparently Meinhoff hadn't heard.

"Tom, Andre; what's going on?"

"We got him Donna. We got our man!"

"Wonderful," she cried. "I never doubted it for a minute. Where are you now?"

"About five miles from the border. We're going to get him back before anybody changes his mind. We'll call you back from Montreal."

Van Marter got out of the New York State Police patrol car, quietly thanked Sergeant Ketter, and told him there had been a change of plans, and he was to go to the farm down the next road and bring the farmer back to pick up his car. The trooper drove away. As the car left, Meinhoff's head snapped around in surprise.

"Come on Andre," Van Marter said, walking over to the MacKensie and Meinhoff. Let's get Herr Meinhoff in our old car and take him back to Montreal. We got permission for hot pursuit."

"I protest!" shouted Meinhoff. "This is an outrage; a clear violation of international law!"

"Well, you can protest to your embassy," said MacKensie, "after the war! Now get into the car; the one with the bullet holes in the door."

MacKensie and Van Marter were still laughing when they crossed back into Canada.

The RCMP Detachment in Montreal had contacted the Prisoner of War Service which had in turn arranged for a detail of Veteran's Guards to be waiting to pick up the prisoner when he arrived. MacKensie pulled the car up to the front of the building to the stares of patrolmen gaping at the bullet holes in the driver's door, and proudly marched Meinhoff inside and to a back room. A no nonsense-looking Veteran's Guard Captain stepped forward.

"Captain LeCon Shear, VGOC, here to take the prisoner in charge."

MacKensie looked at the guard, then at Meinhoff, then back to the guard. "Here you are, Captain Shear. What arrangements have you made?"

"I have six men with me. We're leaving on a special train tonight. He'll be guarded every minute and back at Monteith in 48 hours. This time, he'll stay there."

Meinhoff, who had been looking off in the distance since they arrived at Montreal turned to MacKensie and Van Marter. "You can't win, you know," he said. "The secret will get out. Too many people know about it and the Reich has operatives everywhere. It is only a matter of time until someone talks. Then all your efforts will have been for nothing. Believe me, gentlemen, sooner or later, someone will tell the Reichsministry what really happened to the U-110."

"Maybe," said Van Marter, staring directly into Meinhoff's eyes, "but it won't be you."

"Get your prisoner out of here, Captain Shear," said MacKensie, who was starting to turn red again.

Meinhoff was laughing as he was taken out the back door to a waiting car. MacKensie and Van Marter sat down heavily in two battered chairs. They sat for a long time without speaking. Finally MacKensie grumbled.

"Arrogant bastard. We run him down and he acts like he beat us."

Van Marter smiled. "So what did you expect him to say? You caught me fair and square; good work? A man who sinks merchant shipping from a U-boat might not necessarily have a highly developed sense of sportsmanship."

Van Marter stretched and stood up again. "Besides, if you had just blown a chance to help your side win the war you might be experiencing a few sour grapes yourself. He's just compensating, as the psychologists would say. So what do you say we head back to Ottawa?"

"Just as long as we can catch some sleep when we get there," said MacKensie. "I'm ready to drop."

A sergeant appeared in the doorway. "Inspector MacKensie? Phone call from Headquarters in Ottawa."

MacKensie turned to Van Marter. "You want to take that, Tom? I can talk to Donna any time."

Van Marter anxiously picked up the receiver. "Hello. It's great to hear your voice again. I can't wait to see you when we get back."

There was a pause on the other end of the line. Finally, Van Marter heard the voice of the Commissioner. "Well, Agent Van Marter. You certainly were not this cordial the last time we spoke."

"Uh…Commissioner," Van Marter stammered. "I …uh thought you were someone else. I'm sorry."

The Commissioner laughed. "Forget it my boy. You and Inspector MacKensie have performed a great service. You have my congratulations. The Prime Minister sends his 'well done' also."

"Thank you, Commissioner. I'll tell Andre."

"I'd prefer to tell him myself. Put him on, will you?"

"Sure Commissioner."

A few minutes later, MacKensie and Van Marter found themselves in front of the RCMP building waiting for a car to be brought around to take them to Dorval Field for the trip back to Ottawa. The excitement had died down and the two men were suddenly alone on the quiet street as the streetlights were coming on. With the tension of the pursuit suddenly gone, everything seemed strangely empty. After a few seconds of silence, Van Marter spoke.

"Well, I guess I'll be heading back to Washington in another day or two," he said. "You can go back to working alone, Andre. Give your nose a clear field."

MacKensie nodded. "Yeah, well you can go back to helping J. Edgar chase bootleggers."

There was a long silence. Then MacKensie spoke again.

"Look, Tom. You did a hell of a job. There's no way that guy would have been caught if you hadn't been there, eh? I don't usually work with a partner, but you did good. Thanks."

"Forget it, Andre. You're one old dog who taught me a lot of new tricks. I just hope if I stick around long enough, my nose will develop too."

MacKensie blushed. "Well, Tom, I….."

"And don't go getting sentimental on me," said Van Marter sternly. "I wouldn't recognize you."

"Well," said MacKensie thoughtfully, "Maybe you can come over for that dinner after all. You can finally meet Doris. She'll be surprised to see you don't have horns."

"Andre, I'd be honored. And I also have a date with Donna Hastings."

MacKensie shook his head and laughed. "Always pursuing a fugitive, eh? Well, I'm inviting her too."

Their car pulled up to the curb and took them off. A little after midnight, MacKensie and Van Marter arrived at Dorval Field. Rags was waiting for them with his familiar oily rag in his hand.

"Great job, Rags," MacKensie said. "This has to be the first time a U-boat man was flushed out by an Annie."

"Nothing to it," said Rags. "Just a little grass clipping is all. I just hope the RCAF doesn't get the bill for all the curdled milk I must have caused when I buzzed those cows."

"There's probably a few automobiles with tire tracks on their roofs as well," said Van Marter. "What do you think of your Anson now?"

"Well, she's no Hurricane," he said, wiping an engine cowling tenderly, "but I'll tell you one thing; this old girl is pretty good in a tight corner. Chasing that guy was almost as good as shooting down a Messerschmidt."

"Rags, that guy was more important than a squadron of Messerschmidts," said MacKensie.

Rags smiled and looked up at the vast blackness of the night sky, speckled with thousands of glistening white pinpoints of stars. "Well, it looks like we got us some serious clear up there. Are you ready for a night flight back to Ottawa?"

"More than you know, Rags. Let's go."

*　　　*　　　*

About the time MacKensie and Van Marter were leaving for Ottawa after turning their prisoner over to the Veteran's Guard, Roger Tredegger's wife, also known as the colonel, had finally wound down after her tirade at her husband for being two hours late with the meat from the butchers. Roger Tredegger, still shaken by how close he had come to being arrested, decided he had had enough of national socialism.

At the same time, Hermann Brautsch of the German Embassy was still sitting in the railroad station in Plattsburgh looking at his watch for the hundredth time. He saw it was after midnight, and snorted in disgust. There was no Rawer and no package to receive. It had obviously been a stupid hoax, Brautsch fumed to himself. When the United States someday became part of the Reich they would be sorry they played these pranks. He stood up and stretched, then walked to the ticket window and purchased a return ticket on the next train to Washington. This time Thomsen had guessed wrong, and no wonder. How could he have expected to learn anything useful in Plattsburgh, New York?

-22-

After the congratulations had been passed around RCMP Headquarters, Van Marter heard from Ted Winters, his FBI boss.

"Helluva job, Tom," he said in a voice that sounded like a verbal back-slap, "you did the agency proud."

"Thanks, Ted. Make sure you spell my name right in your glowing report to the Director. Have you got another assignment for me?"

"Just take a few days to bask in the glory, Tom," he replied. "You know; international cooperation and all that. I'll call you the end of the week. Congratulations again."

Tom Van Marter smiled to himself. The extra time would be handy. He wanted time to have dinner at Andre's house, and most of all, to have Donna Hastings finally show him Ottawa.

              ⋆   ⋆   ⋆

"I must admit, Tom, you're not what I expected," said Doris MacKensie.

Tom Van Marter, Andre MacKensie, Donna Hastings, Rags McLaughlin, and Doris MacKensie sat around a long table in Andre MacKensie's house on Kingston Road. They were just starting a dinner of roast beef that must have absorbed the MacKensies' meat ration for a month. Andre had insisted Van Marter should not leave Canada without sampling what he called "northern gracious living".

Doris was a short woman with comfortable middle age proportions and a ready smile. She had taken the day off from her work at the hospital and had obviously spent most of it cooking.

"From Andre's description these last weeks," She continued, "I really thought you were, well…different."

"Different is as good a term as any, Mrs MacKensie," Van Marter replied. "Let's just say Andre may not have had a chance to appreciate my better attributes until now."

"Yeah," said Andre, "like modesty. I'm glad to see you decided to dress casually for this dinner, Tom; a suit without a waistcoat."

"Vest!" said Van Marter, with mock annoyance.

Rags shook his head. "As far as I'm concerned, nobody around here speaks the King's English properly. Why, in Newfoundland, you'd both need a translator."

"This beef is excellent, Doris," said Donna, who thought a change of subject was in order. "With the rationing, it almost feels decadent to eat this well."

"Absolutely," said Van Marter. "It's easily the best meal I've had since I've been in Canada. With this kind of cooking, I'm surprised Andre doesn't weigh 400 pounds by now."

"Why thank you Mr Van Marter," Doris replied, then turned to her husband. "You know, Andre, I like this young man. Why didn't you bring him over for dinner before?"

"I was afraid he'd ask for grits and collard greens," said Andre. "I'm surprised he hasn't starved to death by now."

"Come to think of it, Andre," Doris said, turning her attention to her husband, "you never have mentioned where you've been the last few days, although the presence of Mr. McLaughlin makes me think a good deal of travel was involved."

"Well…"

She held up her hand. "But as a good RCMP wife, I know better than to ask for all the details, at least for now. All I got was a phone call from

Donna saying you'd be away for a few days. And judging from the condition of your clothes, I'd say that wherever you were, you must have been dragged there."

"Now, Doris…"

"I do know one thing, though," she continued. "It involved a great service to your country."

"And why do you think that?" Andre asked, a little suspiciously.

"Because that's what it said on this letter of commendation that arrived this morning." She produced the document in question and handed it to him.

"No kidding?" Andre beamed, taking the letter. "That's great, but I've gotten them before."

Doris looked at him and grinned broadly. "Not signed by the Prime Minister you haven't."

*   *   *

In northern Ontario, another group of people was also finishing dinner. Hans Kolza sighed contentedly as he ate the last piece of sausage and wiped his mouth with his napkin. Strauss looked at him with admiration, wondering where such a small man managed to put all the food. Slowly the two men made their way out to the parade ground and toward the barracks, their hands in their pockets like burghers out for an evening stroll around Dusseldorf.

"It's not such a bad place, this camp," said Kolza thoughtfully.

"No," said Strauss. "It is comfortable and peaceful. There are diversions and chances to work in town for a change of scene now and again."

"A man could do worse," Kolza suggested.

Strauss nodded. "A man could indeed do worse."

"I hope you will not think me impertinent, Herr Oberleutnant," said Kolza, with mock formality, "but I am forced to conclude that the camp has improved considerably since the departure of Leutnant Meinhoff."

Strauss stifled a smile. "What a troublemaker you are, Kolza. Saying rude things about a superior officer. Remind me to have you court marshaled when we return to Germany."

Kolza saluted. "Jawohl, Herr Oberleutnant!"

They walked a little further and Strauss spoke in a lower and more serious tone of voice. "He should be in the United States by now."

Kolza nodded. "Yesterday, by my calculations. Berlin might have been informed already. Between the careful planning and Gregor's determination, I believe we have accomplished what we set out to do."

Strauss nodded with satisfaction, and noticed a small truck being let in through the main gate.

"More company," said Kolza. "I wonder where they picked up this bunch?"

The truck rolled to a stop in front of the camp office. Out jumped four guards and only one prisoner, who stood with his back to the parade ground.

Strauss casually lit a pipe as he watched. "Only one man? Well, things must be getting tight for our Canadian friends if they are taking captives one at a time. If they are not careful, their prisoners will be escaping faster than the Canadians can replace them."

Kolza snickered, until the prisoner turned around. Strauss's pipe fell out of his mouth.

"Oh my God," he whispered. "It's Gregor!"

∗   ∗   ∗

The Rideau Canal glides through the heart of Ottawa like a highway of silver, slowly passing by shaggy green trees and immaculate flower beds in front of parks and stately homes. Canal boats glide past strolling couples and children along the walkways as soft summer breezes rustle the leaves, and any thoughts of war seem far away. Beside the canal, about two blocks upstream from the locks and the Laurier Hotel, Tom

Van Marter and Donna Hastings sat on a wooden bench in the shade. The sun sparkled on the water and only a few streaks of white broke up an otherwise blue sky.

"This is beautiful. I can see you saved the best for last," he said, throwing a piece of bread to a squirrel.

"Well, I caught you yawning as we toured the Parliament buildings, so I thought you'd like some fresh air. Besides, I've always loved the Rideau. Did you know it was built a hundred years ago to move supplies in case the Americans blockaded the St Lawrence?"

"That's crazy," he protested. "We'd never do anything like that."

"During your war of Independence you attacked both Montreal and Quebec City. The expedition was led by Benedict Arnold, in fact."

"Oh. Well, we're friends now, at least," he said, a little embarrassed. "And you've got a beautiful canal to show for it."

She laughed and threw a piece of bread to a squirrel who grabbed it greedily and bolted for the nearest tree. "In the winter the canal freezes over and becomes one long skating rink. There's even a winter canal skating festival we call the Lude. My brother Dennis and I used to come here and play hockey when we were children."

"Hockey?" he laughed. "Somehow I can't picture you playing hockey."

"Oh? And why not?"

"Well, for one thing, you have all your teeth."

Donna laughed with a sound that made Tom Van Marter glad he had come to Canada.

"Well, Dennis and I played here all the same. And thanks to you and Andre, he may get to bring his children here one day. His troopship will be a far more elusive target thanks to what you did."

"Donna, we couldn't have done it without you," he said. "You helped keep it all together and fill in the many holes in what we knew. We're a pretty good team, the three of us."

She raised her eyebrows. "Oh, really? I thought you and Andre were like chalk and cheese."

"Like what?"

"I thought you didn't get along."

"Oh. Well, I guess we each have traits that are irritating to the other, but I'll tell you a secret; Andre's the best. He's tough, smart, and persistent. Most of all, he taught me that I don't have all the answers. I'd love to have him as a permanent partner."

She nodded and threw another piece of bread to another squirrel. The squirrel feigned disinterest, but then suddenly pounced on it. "Now I'll tell you a secret. Andre said the same thing about you."

"Thanks for telling me," he said. "But don't tell Andre you told me; it'd kill him."

"Oh, I think Andre can take it."

They laughed quietly and looked at each other.

"Donna, it's really been great being here and being with you. But I guess I'll have to head back to Washington in a day of two."

"Why do you say that?" she asked.

"Well, the purpose I had in being here is over. Besides, the Commissioner is just itching to send me back."

"Oh, I don't know, Tom. You may have misjudged the Commissioner. In fact, you may even find he wouldn't be opposed to having you stay on a while longer."

He looked at her curiously. "What do you mean?"

"Simply that the Commissioner may well be considering asking the FBI to loan you to the RCMP to consult on security and coordinate on border control. After all, with what you and Andre learned, we could make changes to prevent escapes in the future. The Commissioner knows how valuable you are, so he'll ask Mr Hoover for your services a while longer."

"How do you figure that?" Van Marter asked.

She looked at the specks of light dancing on the water and smiled. "He told me he would."

"He told you? And just how did that subject happen to come up? Donna, did you put the bug in his ear?"

"Really, Tom," she said, shaking her head with mock disapproval. "You've been chasing those devious fugitives too long; you're way too suspicious."

He laughed and placed his hand casually on her shoulder while moving closer to her. "Well, I can't say I'm disappointed. It'd serve Andre right. Anyway, you were pretty good at helping guess what our quarry would do next; can you guess what I'm going to do next?"

She raised an eyebrow. "Well, I…"

Before she could finish the sentence, he leaned over and kissed her. They embraced for a few seconds, then parted.

"Who said Canada was cold?" he said quietly. "Did I surprise you?"

"Well, let's just say it would not be a good idea for you to become a professional poker player."

He backed away slightly and looked at the sky. "It's getting late. I keep forgetting how much later it gets dark in the summer up here."

"We make up for it in the winter," she remarked.

"I'll bet. Anyway, I've taken the liberty of booking us a table at the Chateau Laurier on the canal over by the Parliament buildings. What do you say, Donna; how about a dinner for two?"

"I'd love to," she said, rising.

So as the shadows began to lengthen, Tom Van Marter and Donna Hastings made their way along the Rideau canal towards the pale green copper roofs of the Chateau Laurier rising above the trees in the distance, leaving the squirrels to nibble at the last of the bread they had dropped.

THE END

Postscript

In spite of Meinhoff's prediction, the secret of the U-110 was kept through the end of the war. No one escaped and no one talked. The story of the fate of the U-110 and the capture of the Enigma machine and the codes and charts was not made public until 1956, eleven years after the end of the war.

Breinigsville, PA USA
07 December 2010
250851BV00002B/29/A